BEST *of* LSU FICTION

Olympia Vernon

James Wilcox

Matt Clark

Michael Griffith

Laurie Lynn Drummond

Vance Bourjaily

Andrei Codrescu

Moira Crone

Tim Parrish

John Ed Bradley

James Gordon Bennett

Walker Percy

Allen Wier

Rebecca Wells

Valerie Martin

Charles East

David Madden

Jean Stafford

Peter Taylor

Robert PennWarren

BEST *of* LSU FICTION

EDITED BY

NOLDE ALEXIUS AND JUDY KAHN

[signature: Nolde Alexius]   *[signature: Judy Kahn]*

the Southern Review

LOUISIANA STATE UNIVERSITY • BATON ROUGE

Copyright © 2010 by Nolde Alexius and Judy Kahn
All rights reserved
Printed in Canada
First Edition
ISBN 978-0-615-35174-2

Book Design by Barbara Neely Bourgoyne
Typefaces used are Minion Pro and Zapfino.

Cover image is from the Allen Hall murals painted in the 1930s by students in professor Conrad Albrizio's art history class.

Since this page cannot legibly accommodate all the copyright notices, Permissions constitutes an extension of the copyright page.

Permission to reprint "Blackberry Winter," "The Gift of the Prodigal," "The Interior Castle," "Sky Watch," "Things About to Disappear," "E-Z Boy War" from *Little Altars Everywhere*, "Young Nuclear Physicist," "Famous Days" from *Tupelo Nights*, "After the River," "Gauguin," "Katherine's Elegy," and "The West Texas Sprouting of Loman Happenstance" reverts to the publisher upon publication.

Permission to reprint "Camping Out," "Flood Festival" from *Bibliophilia*, "A Part in Pirandello," "Spats," "The Perfect Mousse Ducktail," "The Amish Farmer," "In Praise of Goth Beauticians," "Young Werther at Decadence 2006," "Dead People in England," and *The Effigy* reverts to the author upon publication.

Contents

vii ACKNOWLEDGMENTS

ix JUDY KAHN Preface

1 JAMES WILCOX Introduction

3 ROBERT PENN WARREN Blackberry Winter

21 PETER TAYLOR The Gift of the Prodigal

37 JEAN STAFFORD The Interior Castle

49 CHARLES EAST Sky Watch

61 DAVID MADDEN A Part in Pirandello

79 ALLEN WIER Things About to Disappear

87 REBECCA WELLS E-Z Boy War from *Little Altars Everywhere*

101 VALERIE MARTIN Spats

109 WALKER PERCY Young Nuclear Physicist

127 JAMES GORDON BENNETT The Perfect Mousse Ducktail

139 JOHN ED BRADLEY Famous Days from *Tupelo Nights*

151 TIM PARRISH After the River

161 MOIRA CRONE Gauguin

175 ANDREI CODRESCU In Praise of Goth Beauticians; Young Werther at Decadence 2006; Dead People in England

181 VANCE BOURJAILY The Amish Farmer

195 LAURIE LYNN DRUMMOND Katherine's Elegy

215 MICHAEL GRIFFITH Flood Festival from *Bibliophilia*

CONTENTS

227   MATT CLARK   The West Texas Sprouting of Loman Happenstance

237   OLYMPIA VERNON   from *The Effigy*

245   JAMES WILCOX   Camping Out

257   Bibliography

259   Permissions

Acknowledgments

We would like to thank, together and individually, the following friends and family for their creativity, professional advice, eye for detail, and thoughtful suggestions: John Whittaker, Fred, Mira and Fritz Alexius, Charlotte Ryland, Jeanne Leiby, Leslie Green, Barbara Bourgoyne, Beverly Jarrett, David Madden, Charles East Jr., Nicholas Persac, Stephen Goodwin, The Methvins, Aza and Tim Bowlin, Elizabeth Robbins, Katherine Monceaux, Conway, Robert and Bobby Pettit, Eileen Arsenault, Cordell and Ava Haymon, Moira Crone, Anna Nardo, Ronlyn Domingue, Sam Oliver, Alison Barker, Jeremiah Ariaz, and Ross Taylor.

We thank the following students from Nolde Alexius' English 1002 course in the spring 2006 semester for their research and interviews: David Albus, Chase Bowers, Brittany Caillouet, Jamie Chaisson, Jekeitha Cook, Jordan Haddad, Chad Holmes, Karen Holmes, Brandon LaFell, April Morales, Vohn Mosing, Kathleen Meyers, Qwanisha Richardson, Bryan Rogers, Garrett Schram, Jye Turk, Wes Watkins, and Jenna White.

Preface

The idea for this book took hold some years ago as I sat down to write my syllabus for Introduction to Fiction, a course I had taught many times for the LSU English department. As a student at LSU, then as an instructor, I deeply appreciated the great writers who, long before my time, had stamped their literary mark on our department, our university, our national psyche. And, as coordinator of the creative writing program, I had formed friendships with our department's creative writers, many of whom often visited my class to read a story or to guest lecture. Who better to have my students read and study, I thought, than those talented authors—Moira Crone, David Madden, and Jim Bennett, along with past masters Robert Penn Warren, Jean Stafford, and Peter Taylor? And, for that matter, why not include some writers beginning their careers, for example, Nolde Alexius, a new instructor with an MFA degree from George Mason University?

As a start, I invited Nolde to read her story, "Hush in This Heat," recently published in *The Southern Review*. The students were spellbound. They never imagined that a young woman who looked about their age had written a story as rich, complex, and entertaining as this one. I was reminded of Robert Penn Warren's remark on meeting Fugitive poet John Crowe Ransom at Vanderbilt: "Ransom was the only live poet I'd ever seen. It was like looking at a camel or something." As soon as Nolde stopped reading, hands flew up and questions were fired: Was she the person in the story? Was the green moth symbolic? Why was the house called "Hush"? The atmosphere in the room sizzled. I was on to something.

As it turned out, my students loved to read stories set in Louisiana, especially in Baton Rouge. They felt, as Walker Percy would have put it, "certified" by seeing their own personal landscapes in published fiction. And studying their university's literary history connected my students to the writers we read. After all, some of those writers, such as Rebecca Wells, acted in the theater department; or served on the campus police force, as had Laurie Lynn Drummond; or played on the football team, like John Ed Bradley. My students' reactions were the kind every teacher hopes for as they began to understand that the literary heritage of their university still inhabited the very classrooms where they read, listened to, and discussed fiction.

When Nolde began teaching the LSU Fiction course, she and I bemoaned the fact that no book was in print which anthologized the work of LSU fiction writers; instead we taught using an electronic version on the university website. But we wanted a book that students could hold in their hands, take notes in, dog ear. To begin the research for such a project, Nolde created an assignment that required her students to conduct personal interviews with contemporary LSU writers such as Allen Wier, Olympia Vernon, Moira Crone, Andrei Codrescu, and James Wilcox. The results of these interviews further revealed to us the potential for an LSU fiction anthology; the stories of the writers in our course unveiled the layered and transcendant connections among writers, students, teachers, editors and staff. Like the oaks on our campus, strong and eternal, our well-known company of published fiction writers was obviously a fixed part of the university landscape.

And so we set about to compile our book of twenty LSU writers to take note of and record these connections, beginning with Robert Penn Warren. In creating *The Southern Review*, Warren linked his name forever with LSU and planted a literary tradition that will never die as long as the South continues to attract and produce young writers to nurture it. This collection, we believe, assures us continuation and growth of that legacy.

JUDY KAHN
Baton Rouge 2010

BEST *of* LSU FICTION

JAMES WILCOX

Introduction

When I was working at Random House in the 1970s, LSU seemed far away, so remote from Manhattan. Yet this distance was an illusion. Without LSU I wouldn't have been there on East 50th Street at that particular time. No, I hadn't gone to LSU myself—not officially, that is. Throughout high school, though, I would motor over to Baton Rouge from my hometown, Hammond, to take weekly cello lessons from Thaddeus Brys, a professor in the LSU School of Music. With my disappointing SAT scores, I never would have been accepted at Yale if my application hadn't been rounded out by that cello—such an awkward instrument for a self-conscious teenager to haul around. Imagine my mortification when a strapping letterman called out as I tried to hurry past, unnoticed, "What you got in there, boy, your grandma?"

Once I was settled in at Yale, I studied creative writing with Robert Penn Warren, who later, when I graduated, recommended me for a job at Random House with his editor, Albert Erskine. Warren and Erskine, of course, had their own connection with LSU. Little did I realize how much their past, the Depression years in Baton Rouge, would inform my future in the twenty-first century.

To refresh my memory about what it was like to study creative writing with Warren, I delved into Joseph Blotner's biography of my teacher. There on page 381 I found, "To James Wilcox he seemed 'a god from Olympus' with 'such an aura of mastery about him, true wisdom, that I couldn't help feel that just being there, in the same room with him, would somehow be beneficial. . . . His mind, razor-sharp, was always engaged with his heart, so that when he spoke, I had a sense of a whole person, not an abstracted intelligence. His sense of humor, his scorn for the spurious, helped sweep many of the Thomas Wolfe-like cobwebs from my writing."

I must disagree with myself about one thing: it's unfair to blame Thomas Wolfe for my cobwebs. A more likely source was the relentless fantasy I spun of instant fame, that Warren, my tutor for a novel I was typing as fast as I could my senior year, would give the manuscript to his agent at William Morris, who would sell it to Random House in a blaze of glory. Instead, I found myself on the other side of the editorial desk at Random House, learning from the man who had been Faulkner's editor how to help our authors bring out the best in their own manuscripts.

Today the twenty-first century is not quite as unimaginable as it seemed in my Random House days. There is no mono-rail to Allen Hall, whose physical condition retains much of its original charm, especially with the striking murals that adorn the ground floor. The very office I work in as head of LSU's creative writing program could have been one that Warren, as co-editor with Cleanth Brooks of *The Southern Review,* dropped in on from time to time. But there is one big difference: whereas Warren was a younger man vigorously making a name for himself in American letters, I am now nearing the age when he was my mentor.

When Warren was hired as assistant professor at LSU, he and Brooks encouraged Erskine, my future boss, to apply for a graduate assistantship, which he did. Eventually, Erskine became the business manager of *The Southern Review.* So powerful was Warren's reputation that, as a manuscript history of the department points out, a graduate student, John Palmer, transferred from Columbia University to study with Warren and Brooks at LSU. Palmer, in turn, became dean of my college at Yale, and my first creative-writing course instructor.

Although Warren's influence can be felt by many of the contributors in *Best of LSU Fiction*, the ideas he was developing while teaching at LSU would be an inspiration for an even wider range of writers. Brooks and Warren's *Understanding Fiction* was the text Flannery O'Connor used when she studied in Iowa as a graduate student. She kept this volume in her personal library and when consulting it later in life concluded that she herself was a literary descendant of Nathaniel Hawthorne.

Best of LSU Fiction is noteworthy not only for the literary tradition it reflects, but also for the innovative work that has emerged from Allen Hall. Authors David Madden, Andrei Codrescu, Moira Crone, and James Gordon Bennett continue to forge cutting-edge ideas in their fiction. And prize-winning MFA graduates Olympia Vernon, Laurie Lynn Drummond, and Michael Griffith have made names for themselves in today's literary world with their inimitable fiction.

From the outside, Allen Hall's early twentieth-century version of fourteenth-century Italian architecture is often misread as Spanish or Mexican. Inside, the classrooms brim with another creative enterprise engaged with the paradox of time. We live in a present that eludes any single definition, that is itself a fiction, in the best sense of the word, woven from a past that bears the kernel of our future. Ever since David Madden began the creative writing program in 1968, undergraduates have been learning skills that have blossomed into bestselling novels and stunning poetry. And since acclaimed poet and nonfiction author Rodger Kamenetz inaugurated the MFA Program in 1985, it has been steadily enhanced by a stellar faculty including award-winning poets Laura Mullen and Lara Glenum, Poet Laureate of Louisiana Brenda Marie Osbey, playwright and director Femi Euba, *The Southern Review* editor Jeanne Leiby, and screenwriters Mari Kornhauser, Rick Blackwood, and Louisiana Filmmaker of the Year Zachary Godshall. We're all indebted to Judy Kahn and Nolde Alexius for reminding us of this seamless legacy of creative endeavor as the MFA Program celebrates its 25th anniversary, *The Southern Review* its 75th, and LSU its 150th anniversary.

ROBERT PENN WARREN

On the second floor of Allen Hall, home to Louisiana State University's English department, students of all majors may take a class in the stately Robert Penn Warren Conference Room, a tribute to the one literary mind most often associated with the university. Founder of *The Southern Review* and three-time Pulitzer Prize winner, Warren transformed LSU's role in American letters. With co-editor and co-founder of the *The Southern Review*, Cleanth Brooks, Warren wrote two textbooks, *Understanding Fiction* and *Understanding Poetry*, which established a new approach to interpreting literature—close reading—that took hold and remained the primary critical theory for decades.

Warren's LSU legacy includes his classic novel, *All the King's Men*; it, along with the Academy Award-winning film version starring Broderick Crawford, lodged the state of Louisiana and its culture into the American consciousness, taking the charismatic and deeply flawed Governor Huey P. Long as inspiration for Willie Stark, the novel's tragic figure. While the setting of *All the King's Men* reflects the Louisiana landscape—the 2006 film version starring Sean Penn was shot entirely in-state—Willie's significance, according to former editor of *The Southern Review*, James Olney, "goes well beyond whatever Long was in life."

Warren joined the faculty of Yale University after teaching at LSU. There, he taught novelist James Wilcox, who remembers the individual attention Warren gave him: "His response to my stories made me aware that every word has to count." Of *Understanding Fiction*, Wilcox says, "This textbook . . . clearly shows how fiction is structured and what mistakes to avoid. I've referred to this book over the years. It wasn't just something I used in college." Warren's generosity marked him throughout his career. Many writers he published in *The Southern Review* such as Eudora Welty, Katherine Anne Porter, and Peter Taylor were unknown but became some of the greatest literary voices of the century.

"Blackberry Winter," Warren's most anthologized short story, presents a young boy's initiation into the harsh realities of the world during a flood in rural Tennessee. Set 100 years ago, this story, like all great literature, maintains relevance in any age.

Blackberry Winter

It was getting into June and past eight o'clock in the morning, but there was a fire—even if it wasn't a big fire, just a fire of chunks—on the hearth of the big stone fireplace in the living room. I was standing on the hearth, almost into the chimney, hunched over the fire, working my bare toes slowly on the warm stone. I relished the heat which made the skin of my bare legs warp and creep and tingle, even as I called to my mother, who was somewhere back in the dining room or kitchen, and said: "But it's June, I don't have to put them on!"

"You put them on if you are going out," she called.

I tried to assess the degree of authority and conviction in the tone, but at that distance it was hard to decide. I tried to analyze the tone, and then I thought what a fool I had been to start out the back door and let her see that I was barefoot. If I had gone out the front door or the side door she would never have known, not till dinner time anyway, and by then the day would have been half gone and I would have been all over the farm to see what the storm had done and down to the creek to see the flood. But it had never crossed my mind that they would try to stop you from going barefoot in June, no matter if there had been a gully-washer and a cold spell.

Nobody had ever tried to stop me in June as long as I could remember, and when you are nine years old, what you remember seems forever; for you remember everything and everything is important and stands big and full and fills up Time and is so solid that you can walk around and around it like a tree and look at it. You are aware that time passes, that there is a movement in time, but that is not what Time is. Time is not a movement, a flowing, a wind then, but is, rather, a kind of climate in which things are, and when a thing happens it begins to live and keeps on living and stands solid in Time like the tree that you can walk around. And if there is a movement, the movement is not Time itself, any more than a breeze is climate, and all the breeze does is to shake a little the leaves on the tree which is alive and solid. When you are nine, you know that there are things that you don't know, but you know that when you know something you know it. You know how a thing has been and you know that you can go barefoot in June. You do not understand that voice from back in the kitchen which says that you cannot go barefoot outdoors and run to see what has happened and rub your feet over the wet shivery grass and make the perfect mark of your foot in the smooth, creamy, red mud and then muse upon it as though you had suddenly come upon that single mark on the glistening auroral beach of the world. You have never seen a beach, but you have read the book and how the footprint was there.

The voice had said what it had said, and I looked savagely at the black stockings and the strong, scuffed brown shoes which I had brought from my closet as far as the hearth rug. I called once more, "But it's June," and waited.

"It's June," the voice replied from far away, "but it's blackberry winter."

I had lifted my head to reply to that, to make one more test of what was in that tone, when I happened to see the man.

The fireplace in the living room was at the end; for the stone chimney was built, as in so many of the farmhouses in Tennessee, at the end of a gable, and there was a window on each side of the chimney. Out of the window on the north side of the fireplace I could see the man. When I saw the man I did not call out what I had intended, but, engrossed by the strangeness of the sight, watched him, still far off, come along the path by the edge of the woods.

What was strange was that there should be a man there at all. That path went along the yard fence, between the fence and the woods which came right down to the yard, and then on back past the chicken runs and on by the woods until it was lost to sight where the woods bulged out and cut off the back field. There the path disappeared into the woods. It led on back, I knew, through the woods and to the swamp, skirted the swamp where the big trees gave way to sycamores and water oaks and willows and tangled cane, and then led on to the river. Nobody ever went back there except people who wanted to gig frogs in the swamp or to fish in the river or to hunt in the woods, and those people, if they didn't have a standing permission from my father, always stopped to ask permission to cross the farm. But the man whom I now saw wasn't, I could tell even at that distance, a sportsman. And what would a sportsman have been doing down there after a storm? Besides, he was coming from the river, and nobody had gone down there that morning. I knew that for a fact, because if anybody had passed, certainly if a stranger had passed, the dogs would have made a racket and would have been out on him. But this man was coming up from the river and had come up through the woods. I suddenly had a vision of him moving up the grassy path in the woods, in the green twilight under the big trees, not making any sound on the path, while now and then, like drops off the eaves, a big drop of water would fall from a leaf or bough and strike a stiff oak leaf lower down with a small, hollow sound like a drop of water hitting tin. That sound, in the silence of the woods, would be very significant.

When you are a boy and stand in the stillness of woods, which can be so still that your heart almost stops beating and makes you want to stand there in the green twilight until you feel your very feet sinking into and clutching the earth like roots and your body breathing slow through its pores like the leaves—when you stand there and wait for the next drop to drop with its small, flat sound to a lower leaf, that sound seems to measure out something, to put an end to something, to begin something, and you cannot wait for it to happen and are afraid it will not happen, and then when it has happened, you are waiting again, almost afraid.

But the man whom I saw coming through the woods in my mind's eye did not pause and wait, growing into the ground and breathing with the enormous, soundless breathing of the leaves. Instead, I saw him moving in the green twilight inside my head as he was moving at that very moment along the path by the edge of the woods, coming toward the house. He was moving steadily, but not fast, with his shoulders hunched a little and his head thrust forward, like a man who has come a long way and has a long way to go. I shut my eyes for a couple of seconds, thinking that when I opened them he would not be there at all. There was no place for him to have come from, and there was no reason for him to come where he was coming, toward our house. But I opened my eyes, and there he was, and he was coming steadily along the side of the woods. He was not yet even with the back chicken yard.

"Mama," I called.

"You put them on," the voice said.

"There's a man coming," I called, "out back."

She did not reply to that, and I guessed that she had gone to the kitchen window to look. She would be looking at the man and wondering who he was and what he wanted, the way you always do in the country, and if I went back there now she would not notice right off whether or not I was barefoot. So I went back to the kitchen.

She was standing by the window. "I don't recognize him," she said, not looking around at me.

"Where could he be coming from?" I asked.

"I don't know," she said.

"What would he be doing down at the river? At night? In the storm?"

She studied the figure out the window, then said, "Oh, I reckon maybe he cut across from the Dunbar place."

That was, I realized, a perfectly rational explanation. He had not been down at the river in the storm, at night. He had come over this morning. You could cut across from the Dunbar place if you didn't mind breaking through a lot of elder and sassafras and blackberry bushes which had about taken over the old cross path, which nobody ever used any more. That satisfied me for a moment, but only for a moment. "Mama," I asked, "what would he be doing over at the Dunbar place last night?"

Then she looked at me, and I knew I had made a mistake for she was looking at my bare feet. "You haven't got your shoes on," she said.

But I was saved by the dogs. That instant there was a bark which I recognized as Sam, the collie, and then a heavier, churning kind of bark which was Bully, and I saw a streak of white as Bully tore round the corner of the back porch and headed out for the man. Bully was a big, bone-white bull dog, the kind of dog that they used to call a farm bull dog but that you don't see any more, heavy chested and heavy headed, but with pretty long legs. He could take a fence as light as a hound. He had just cleared the white paling fence toward the woods when my mother ran out to the back porch and began calling, "Here you, Bully! Here you!"

Bully stopped in the path, waiting for the man, but he gave a few more of those deep, gargling, savage barks that reminded you of something down a stone-lined well. The red clay mud, I saw, was splashed up over his white chest and looked exciting, like blood.

The man, however, had not stopped walking even when Bully took the fence and started at him. He had kept right on coming. All he had done was to switch a little paper parcel which he carried from the right hand to the left, and then reach into his pants pocket to get something. Then I saw the glitter and knew that he had a knife in his hand, probably the kind of mean knife just made for devilment and nothing else, with a blade as long as the blade of a frog-sticker, which will snap out ready when you press a button in the handle. That knife must have had a button in the handle, or else how could he have had the blade out glittering so quick and with just one hand?

Pulling his knife against the dogs was a funny thing to do, for Bully was a big, powerful brute and fast, and Sam was all right. If those dogs had meant business, they might have knocked him down and ripped him before he got a stroke in. He ought to have picked up a heavy stick, something to take a swipe at them with and something which they could see and respect when they came at him. But he apparently did not know much about dogs. He just held the knife blade, close against the right leg, low down, and kept on moving down the path.

Then my mother had called, and Bully had stopped. So the man let the blade of the knife snap back into the handle, and dropped it into his pocket, and kept on coming. Many women would have been afraid with the strange man who they knew had that knife in his pocket. That is, if they were alone in the house with nobody but a nine-year-old boy. And my mother was alone, for my father had gone off, and Dellie, the cook, was down at her cabin because she wasn't feeling well. But my mother wasn't afraid. She wasn't a big woman, but she was clear and brisk about everything she did and looked everybody and everything right in the eye from her own blue eyes in her tanned face. She had been the first woman in the county to ride a horse astride (that was back when she was a girl and long before I was born), and I have seen her snatch up a pump gun and go out and knock a chicken hawk out of the air like a busted skeet when he came over her chicken yard. She was a steady and self-reliant woman, and when I think of her now after all the years she has been dead, I think of her brown hands, not big, but somewhat square for a woman's hands, with square-cut nails. They looked, as a matter of fact, more like a young boy's hands than a grown woman's. But back then it never crossed my mind that she would ever be dead.

She stood on the back porch and watched the man enter the back gate, where the dogs (Bully had leaped back into the yard) were dancing and muttering and giving sidelong glances back to my mother to see if she meant what she had said. The man walked right by the dogs, almost brushing them, and didn't pay them any attention. I could see now that he wore old khaki pants, and a dark wool coat with stripes in it, and a gray felt hat. He had on a gray shirt with blue stripes in it, and no tie. But I could see a tie, blue and reddish, sticking in his side coat-pocket. Everything was wrong about what he wore. He ought to have been wearing blue jeans or overalls, and a straw hat or an old black felt hat, and the coat, granting that he might have been wearing a wool coat and not a jumper, ought not to have had those stripes. Those clothes, despite the fact that they were old enough and dirty enough for any tramp, didn't belong there in our back yard, coming down the path, in Middle Tennessee, miles away from any big town, and even a mile off the pike.

When he got almost to the steps, without having said anything, my mother, very matter-of-factly, said, "Good morning."

"Good morning," he said, and stopped and looked her over. He did not take off his hat, and under the brim you could see the perfectly unmemorable face, which wasn't old and wasn't young, or thick or thin. It was grayish and covered with about three days of stubble. The eyes were a kind of nondescript, muddy hazel, or something like that, rather bloodshot. His teeth, when he opened his mouth, showed yellow and uneven. A couple of them had been knocked out. You knew that they had been knocked out, because there was a scar, not very old, there on the lower lip just beneath the gap.

"Are you hunting work?" my mother asked him.

"Yes," he said—not "yes, mam"—and still did not take off his hat.

"I don't know about my husband, for he isn't here," she said, and didn't mind a bit telling the tramp, or whoever he was, with the mean knife in his pocket, that no man was around, "but I can give you a few things to do. The storm has drowned a lot of my chicks. Three coops of them. You can gather them up and bury them. Bury them deep so the dogs won't get at them. In the woods. And fix the coops the wind blew over. And down yonder beyond that pen by the edge of the woods are some drowned poults. They got out and I couldn't get them in. Even after it started to rain hard. Poults haven't got any sense."

"What are them things—poults?" he demanded, and spat on the brick walk. He rubbed his foot over the spot, and I saw that he wore a black, pointed-toe low shoe, all cracked and broken. It was a crazy kind of shoe to be wearing in the country.

"Oh, they're young turkeys," my mother was saying. "And they haven't got any sense. I oughtn't to try to raise them around here with so many chickens, anyway. They don't thrive near chickens, even in separate pens. And I won't give up my chickens."

Then she stopped herself and resumed briskly on the note of business. "When you finish that, you can fix my flower beds. A lot of trash and mud and gravel has washed down. Maybe you can save some of my flowers if you are careful."

"Flowers," the man said, in a low, impersonal voice which seemed to have a wealth of meaning, but a meaning which I could not fathom. As I think back on it, it probably was not pure contempt. Rather, it was a kind of impersonal and distant marveling that he should be on the verge of grubbing in a flower bed. He said the word, and then looked off across the yard.

"Yes, flowers," my mother replied with some asperity, as though she would have nothing said or implied against flowers. "And they were very fine this year." Then she stopped and looked at the man. "Are you hungry?" she demanded.

"Yeah," he said.

"I'll fix you something," she said, "before you get started." She turned to me. "Show him where he can wash up," she commanded, and went into the house.

I took the man to the end of the porch where a pump was and where a couple of wash pans sat on a low shelf for people to use before they went into the house. I stood there while he laid down his little parcel wrapped in newspaper and took off his hat and looked around for a nail to hang it on. He poured the water and plunged his hands into it. They were big hands, and strong looking, but they did not have the creases and the earth-color of the hands of men who work outdoors. But they were dirty, with black dirt ground into the skin and under the nails. After he had washed his hands, he poured another basin of water and washed his face. He dried his face, and with the towel still dangling in his grasp, stepped over to the mirror on the house wall. He rubbed one hand over the stubble on his face. Then he carefully inspected his face, turning first one side and then the other, and stepped back and settled his striped coat down on his shoulders. He had the movements of a man who has just dressed up to go to church or a party—the way he settled his coat and smoothed it and scanned himself in the mirror.

Then he caught my glance on him. He glared at me for an instant out of the bloodshot eyes, then demanded in a low, harsh voice, "What you looking at?"

"Nothing," I managed to say, and stepped back a step from him.

He flung the towel down, crumpled, on the shelf, and went toward the kitchen door and entered without knocking.

My mother said something to him which I could not catch. I started to go in again, then thought about my bare feet and decided to go back of the chicken yard, where the man would have to come to pick up the dead chicks. I hung around behind the chicken house until he came out.

He moved across the chicken yard with a fastidious, not quite finicking motion, looking down at the curdled mud flecked with bits of chicken-droppings. The mud curled up over the soles of his black shoes. I stood back from him some six feet and watched him pick up the first of the drowned chicks. He held it up by one foot and inspected it.

There is nothing deader looking than a drowned chick. The feet curl in that feeble, empty way which back when I was a boy, even if I was a country boy who did not mind hog-killing or frog-gigging, made me feel hollow in the stomach. Instead of looking plump and fluffy, the body is stringy and limp with the fluff plastered to it, and the neck is long and loose like a little string of rag. And the eyes have that bluish membrane over them which makes you think of a very old man who is sick about to die.

The man stood there and inspected the chick. Then he looked all around as though he didn't know what to do with it.

"There's a great big old basket in the shed," I said, and pointed to the shed attached to the chicken house.

He inspected me as though he had just discovered my presence, and moved toward the shed.

"There's a spade there, too," I added.

He got the basket and began to pick up the other chicks, picking each one up slowly by a foot and then flinging it into the basket with a nasty, snapping motion. Now and then he would look at me out of the blood-shot eyes. Every time he seemed on the verge of saying something, but he did not. Perhaps he was building up to say something to me, but I did not wait that long. His way of looking at me made me so uncomfortable that I left the chicken yard.

Besides, I had just remembered that the creek was in flood, over the bridge, and that people were down there watching it. So I cut across the farm toward the creek. When I got to the big tobacco field, I saw that it had not suffered much. The land lay right and not many tobacco plants had washed out of the ground. But I knew that a lot of tobacco round the country had been washed right out. My father had said so at breakfast.

My father was down at the bridge. When I came out of the gap in the osage hedge into the road, I saw him sitting on his mare over the heads of the other men who were standing around, admiring the flood. The creek was big here, even in low water; for only a couple of miles away it ran into the river, and when a real flood came, the red water got over the pike where it dipped down to the bridge, which was an iron bridge, and high over the floor and even the side railings of the bridge. Only the upper iron work would show, with the water boiling and frothing red and white around it. That creek rose so fast and so heavy because a few miles back it came down out of the hills, where the gorges filled up with water in no time when a rain came. The creek ran in a deep bed with limestone bluffs along both sides until it got within three quarters of a mile of the bridge, and when it came out from between those bluffs in flood it was boiling and hissing and steaming like water from a fire hose.

Whenever there was a flood, people from half the county would come down to see the sight. After a gully-washer there would not be any work to do anyway. If it didn't ruin your crop, you couldn't plow and you felt like taking a holiday to celebrate. If it did ruin your crop, there wasn't anything to do except to try to take your mind off the mortgage, if you were rich enough to have a mortgage, and if you couldn't afford a mortgage you needed something to take your mind off how hungry you would be by Christmas. So people would come down to the bridge and look at the flood. It made something different from the run of days.

There would not be much talking after the first few minutes of trying to guess how high the water was this time. The men and kids just stood around, or sat their horses or mules, as the case might be, or stood up in the wagon beds. They looked at the strangeness of the flood for an hour or two, and then somebody would say that he had better be getting on home to dinner and would start walking down the gray, puddled limestone pike, or would touch heel to his mount and start off. Everybody always knew what it would be like when he got down to the bridge, but people always came. It was like church or a funeral. They always came, that is, if it was summer and the flood unexpected. Nobody ever came down in winter to see high water.

When I came out of the gap in the bodock hedge, I saw the crowd, perhaps fifteen or twenty men and a lot of kids, and saw my father sitting his mare, Nellie Gray. He was a tall, limber man and carried himself well. I was always proud to see him sit a horse, he was so quiet and straight, and when I stepped through the gap of the hedge that morning, the first thing that happened was, I remember, the warm feeling I always had when I saw him up on a horse, just sitting. I did not go toward him, but skirted the crowd on the far side, to get a look at the creek. For one thing, I was not sure what he would say about the fact that I was barefoot. But the first thing I knew, I heard his voice calling, "Seth!"

I went toward him, moving apologetically past the men, who bent their large, red or thin, sallow faces above me. I knew some of the men, and knew their names, but because those I knew were there in a crowd, mixed with the strange faces, they seemed foreign to me, and not friendly. I did not look up at my father until I was almost within touching distance of his heel. Then I looked up and tried to read his face, to see if he was angry about my being barefoot. Before I could decide anything from that impassive, high-boned face, he had leaned over and reached a hand to me. "Grab on," he commanded.

I grabbed on and gave a little jump, and he said, "Up-see-daisy!" and whisked me, light as a feather, up to the pommel of his McClellan saddle.

"You can see better up here," he said, slid back on the cantle a little to make me more comfortable, and then, looking over my head at the swollen, tumbling water, seemed to forget all about me. But his right hand was laid on my side, just above my thigh, to steady me.

I was sitting there as quiet as I could, feeling the faint stir of my father's chest against my shoulders as it rose and fell with his breath, when I saw the cow. At first, looking up the creek, I thought it was just another big piece of driftwood steaming down the creek in the ruck of water, but all at once a pretty good-size boy who had climbed part way up a telephone pole by the pike so that he could see better yelled out, "Golly-damn, look at that-air cow!"

Everybody looked. It was a cow all right, but it might just as well have been drift-wood; for it was dead as a chunk, rolling and roiling down the creek, appearing and disappearing, feet up or head up, it didn't matter which.

The cow started up the talk again. Somebody wondered whether it would hit one of the clear places under the top girder of the bridge and get through or whether it would get tangled in the drift and trash that had piled against the upright girders and braces. Somebody remembered how about ten years before so much driftwood had piled up on the bridge that it was knocked off its foundations. Then the cow hit. It hit the edge of the drift against one of the girders, and hung there. For a few seconds it seemed as though it might tear loose, but then we saw that it was really caught. It bobbed and heaved on its side there in a slow, grinding, uneasy fashion. It had a yoke around its neck, the kind made out of a forked limb to keep a jumper behind a fence.

"She shore jumped one fence," one of the men said.

And another: "Well, she done jumped her last one, fer a fack."

Then they began to wonder about whose cow it might be. They decided it must belong to Milt Alley. They said that he had a cow that was a jumper, and kept her in a fenced-in piece of ground up the creek. I had never seen Milt Alley, but I knew who he was. He was a squatter and lived up the hills a way, on a shirt-tail patch of a set-on-edge land, in a cabin. He was pore white trash. He had lots of children. I had seen the children at school, when they came. They were thin-faced with straight, sticky-looking, dough-colored hair, and they smelled something like old sour butter-milk, not because they drank so much buttermilk but because that is the sort of smell which children out of those cabins tend to have. The big Alley boy drew dirty pictures and showed them to the little boys at school.

That was Milt Alley's cow. It looked like the kind of cow he would have, a scrawny, old, sway-backed cow, with a yoke around her neck. I wondered if Milt Alley had another cow.

"Poppa," I said, "do you think Milt Alley has got another cow?"

"You say 'Mr. Alley,'" my father said quietly.

"Do you think he has?"

"No telling," my father said.

Then a big gangly boy, about fifteen, who was sitting on a scraggly little old mule with a piece of croker sack thrown across the saw-tooth spine, and who had been staring at the cow, suddenly said to nobody in particular, "Reckin anybody ever et drownt cow?"

He was the kind of boy who might just as well as not have been the son of Milt Alley, with his faded and patched overalls ragged at the bottom of the pants and the mud-stiff brogans hanging off his skinny, bare ankles at the level of the mule's belly. He had said what he did, and then looked embarrassed and sullen when all the eyes swung at him. He hadn't meant to say it, I am pretty sure now. He would have been too proud to say it, just as Milt Alley would have been too proud. He had just been thinking out loud, and the words had popped out.

There was an old man standing there on the pike, an old man with a white beard. "Son," he said to the embarrassed and sullen boy on the mule, "you live long enough and you'll find a man will eat anything when the time comes."

"Time gonna come fer some folks this year," another man said.

"Son," the old man said, "in my time I et things a man don't like to think on. I was a sojer and I rode with Gin'l Forrest, and them things we et when the time come. I tell you. I et meat what got up and run when you taken out yore knife to cut a slice to put on the fire. You had to knock it down with a carbeen butt, it was so active. That-air meat would jump like a bullfrog, it was so full of skippers."

But nobody was listening to the old man. The boy on the mule turned his sullen sharp face from him, dug a heel into the side of the mule and went off up the pike with a motion which made you think that any second you would hear mule bones clashing inside that lank and scrofulous hide.

"Cy Dundee's boy," a man said, and nodded toward the figure going up the pike on the mule.

"Reckin Cy Dundee's young-uns seen times they'd settle fer drownt cow," another man said.

The old man with the beard peered at them both from his weak, slow eyes, first at one and then at the other. "Live long enough," he said, "and a man will settle fer what he kin git."

Then there was silence again, with the people looking at the red, foam-flecked water.

My father lifted the bridle rein in his left hand, and the mare turned and walked around the group and up the pike. We rode on up to our big gate, where my father dismounted to open it and let me myself ride Nellie Gray through. When he got to the lane that led off from the drive about two hundred yards from our house, my father said, "Grab on." I grabbed on, and he let me down to the ground. "I'm going to ride down and look at my corn," he said. "You go on." He took the lane, and I stood there on the drive and watched him ride off. He was wearing cowhide boots and an old hunting coat, and I thought that that made him look very military, like a picture. That and the way he rode.

I did not go to the house. Instead, I went by the vegetable garden and crossed behind the stables, and headed down for Dellie's cabin. I wanted to go down and play with Jebb, who was Dellie's little boy about two years older than I was. Besides, I was cold. I shivered as I walked, and I had gooseflesh. The mud which crawled up between my toes with every step I took was like ice. Dellie would have a fire, but she wouldn't make me put on shoes and stockings.

Dellie's cabin was of logs, with one side, because it was on a slope, set on limestone chunks, with a little porch attached to it, and had a little whitewashed fence around it and a gate with plow-points on a wire to clink when somebody came in, and had two big white oaks in the yard and some flowers and a nice privy in the back with some honeysuckle growing over it. Dellie and Old Jebb, who was Jebb's father and who lived with Dellie and had lived with her for twenty-five years even if they never had got married, were careful to keep everything nice around their cabin. They had the name all over the community for being clean and clever Negroes. Dellie and Jebb were what they used to call "white-folks' niggers." There was a big difference between their cabin and the other two cabins farther down where the other tenants lived. My father kept the other cabins weatherproof, but he couldn't undertake to go down and pick up after the litter they strewed. They didn't take the trouble to have a vegetable patch like Dellie and Jebb or to make preserves from wild plum, and jelly from crab apple the way Dellie did. They were shiftless, and my father was always threatening to get shed of them. But he never did. When they finally left, they just up and left on their own, for no reason, to go and be shiftless somewhere else. Then some more came. But meanwhile they lived down there, Matt Rawson and his family, and Sid Turner and his, and I played with their children all over the farm when they weren't working. But when I wasn't around they were mean sometimes to Little Jebb. That was because the other tenants down there were jealous of Dellie and Jebb.

I was so cold that I ran the last fifty yards to Dellie's gate. As soon as I had entered the yard, I saw that the storm had been hard on Dellie's flowers. The yard was, as I have said, on a slight slope, and the water running across had gutted the flower beds and washed out all the good black woods-earth which Dellie had brought in. What little grass there was in the yard was plastered sparsely down on the ground, the way the drainage water had left it. It reminded me of the way the fluff was plastered down on the skin of the drowned chicks that the strange man had been picking up, up in my mother's chicken yard.

I took a few steps up the path to the cabin, and then I saw that the drainage water had washed a lot of trash and filth out from under Dellie's house. Up toward the porch, the ground was not clean any more. Old pieces of rag, two or three rusted cans, pieces of rotten rope, some hunks of old dog dung, broken glass, old paper, and all sorts of things like that had washed out from under Dellie's house to foul her clean yard. It looked just as bad as the yards of the other cabins, or worse. It was worse, as a matter of fact, because it was a surprise. I had never thought of all that filth being under Dellie's house. It was not anything against Dellie that the stuff had been under the cabin. Trash will get under any house. But I did not think of that when I saw the foulness which had washed out on the ground which Dellie sometimes used to sweep with a twig broom to make nice and clean.

I picked my way past the filth, being careful not to get my bare feet on it, and mounted to Dellie's door. When I knocked, I heard her voice telling me to come in.

It was dark inside the cabin, after the daylight, but I could make out Dellie piled up in bed under a quilt, and Little Jebb crouched by the hearth, where a low fire simmered. "Howdy," I said to Dellie, "how you feeling?"

Her big eyes, the whites surprising and glaring in the black face, fixed on me as I stood there, but she did not reply. It did not look like Dellie, or act like Dellie, who would grumble and bustle around our kitchen, talking to herself, scolding me or Little Jebb, clanking pans, making all sorts of unnecessary noises and mutterings like an old-fashioned black steam thrasher engine when it has got up an extra head of steam and keeps popping the governor and rumbling and shaking on its wheels. But now Dellie just lay up there on the bed, under the patch-work quilt, and turned the black face, which I scarcely recognized, and the glaring white eyes to me.

"How you feeling?" I repeated.

"I'se sick," the voice said croakingly out of the strange black face which was not attached to Dellie's big, squat body, but stuck out from under a pile of tangled bedclothes. Then the voice added: "Mighty sick."

"I'm sorry," I managed to say.

The eyes remained fixed on me for a moment, then they left me and the head rolled back on the pillow. "Sorry," the voice said, in a flat way which wasn't question or statement of anything. It was just the empty word put into the air with no meaning or expression, to float off like a feather or a puff of smoke, while the big eyes, with the whites like the peeled white of hard-boiled eggs, stared at the ceiling.

"Dellie," I said after a minute, "there's a tramp up at the house. He's got a knife."

She was not listening. She closed her eyes.

I tiptoed over to the hearth where Jebb was and crouched beside him. We began to talk in low voices. I was asking him to get out his train and play train. Old Jebb had put spool wheels on three cigar boxes and put wire links between the boxes to make a train for Jebb. The box that was the locomotive had the top closed and a length of broom stick for a smoke stack. Jebb didn't want to get the train out, but I told him I would go home if he didn't. So he got out the train, and the colored rocks, and fossils of crinoid stems, and other junk he used for the load, and we began to push it around, talking the way we thought trainmen talked, making a chuck-chucking sound under the breath for the noise of the locomotive and now and then uttering low, cautious toots for the whistle. We got so interested in playing train that the toots got louder. Then, before he thought, Jebb gave a good, loud *toot-toot*, blowing for a crossing.

"Come here," the voice said from the bed.

Jebb got up slow from his hands and knees, giving me a sudden, naked, inimical look.

"Come here!" the voice said.

Jebb went to the bed. Dellie propped herself weakly up on one arm, muttering, "Come closer."

Jebb stood closer.

"Last thing I do, I'm gonna do it," Dellie said. "Done tole you to be quiet."

Then she slapped him. It was an awful slap, more awful for the kind of weakness which it came from and brought to focus. I had seen her slap Jebb before, but the slapping had always been the kind of easy slap you would expect from a good-natured, grumbling Negro woman like Dellie. But this was different. It was awful. It was so awful that Jebb didn't make a sound. The tears just popped out and ran down his face, and his breath came sharp, like gasps.

Dellie fell back. "Cain't even be sick," she said to the ceiling. "Git sick and they won't even let you lay. They tromp all over you. Cain't even be sick." Then she closed her eyes.

I went out of the room. I almost ran getting to the door, and I did run across the porch and down the steps and across the yard, not caring whether or not I stepped on the filth which had washed out from under the cabin. I ran almost all the way home. Then I thought about my mother catching me with the bare feet. So I went down to the stables.

I heard a noise in the crib, and opened the door. There was Big Jebb, sitting on an old nail keg, shelling corn into a bushel basket. I went in, pulling the door shut behind me, and crouched on the floor near him. I crouched there for a couple of minutes before either of us spoke, and watched him shelling the corn.

He had very big hands, knotted and grayish at the joints, with calloused palms which seemed to be streaked with the rust coming up between the fingers to show from the back. His hands were so strong and tough that he could take a big ear of corn and rip the grains right off the cob with the palm of his hand, all in one motion, like a machine. "Work long as me," he would say, "and the good Lawd'll give you a hand lak cass-ion won't nuthin' hurt." And his hands did look like cast iron, old cast iron streaked with rust.

He was an old man, up in his seventies, thirty years or more older than Dellie, but he was strong as a bull. He was a squat sort of man, heavy in the shoulders, with remarkably long arms, the kind of build they say the river natives have on the Congo from paddling so much in their boats. He had a round bullet-head, set on powerful shoulders. His skin was very black, and the thin hair on his head was now grizzled like tufts of old cotton batting. He had small eyes and a flat nose, not big, and the kindest and wisest old face in the world, the blunt, sad, wise face of an old animal peering tolerantly out on the goings-on of the merely human creatures before him. He was a good man, and I loved him next to my mother and father. I crouched there on the floor of the crib and watched him shell corn with the rusty cast-iron hands, while he looked down at me out of the little eyes set in the blunt face.

"Dellie says she's might sick," I said.

"Yeah," he said.

"What's she sick from?"

"Woman-mizry," he said.

"What's woman-mizry?"

"Hit comes on 'em," he said. "Hit just comes on 'em when the time comes."

"What is it?"

"Hit is the change," he said. "Hit is the change of life and time."

"What changes?"

"You too young to know."

"Tell me."

"Time come and you find out everthing."

I knew that there was no use in asking him any more. When I asked him things and he said that, I always knew that he would not tell me. So I continued to crouch there and watch him. Now that I had sat there a little while, I was cold again.

"What you shiver fer?" he asked me.

"I'm cold. I'm cold because it's blackberry winter," I said.

"Maybe 'tis and maybe 'tain't," he said.

"My mother says it is."

"Ain't sayen Miss Sallie doan know and ain't sayen she do. But folks doan know everthing."

"Why isn't it blackberry winter?"

"Too late fer blackberry winter. Blackberries done bloomed."

"She said it was."

"Blackberry winter just a leetle cold spell. Hit come and then hit go away, and hit is growed summer of a sudden lak a gunshot. Ain't no tellen hit will go way this time."

"It's June," I said.

"June," he replied with great contempt. "That what folks say. What June mean? Maybe hit is come cold to stay."

"Why?"

"Cause this-here old yearth is tahrd. Hit is tahrd and ain't gonna perduce. Lawd let hit come rain one time forty days and forty nights, 'cause He wus tahrd of sinful folks. Maybe this-here old yearth say to the Lawd, Lawd, I done plum tahrd, Lawd, lemme rest. And Lawd say, Yearth, you done yore best, you give 'em cawn and you give 'em taters, and all they think on is they gut, and, Yearth, you kin take a rest."

"What will happen?"

"Folks will eat up everthing. The yearth won't perduce no more. Folks cut down all the trees and burn 'em cause they cold, and the yearth won't grow no more. I been tellen 'em. I been tellen folks. Sayen, maybe this year, hit is the time. But they doan listen to me, how the yearth is tahrd. Maybe this year they find out."

"Will everything die?"

"Everthing and everbody, hit will be so."

"This year?"

"Ain't no tellen. Maybe this year."

"My mother said it is blackberry winter," I said confidently, and got up.

"Ain't sayen nuthin' agin Miss Sallie," he said.

I went to the door of the crib. I was really cold now. Running, I had got up a sweat and now I was worse.

I hung on the door, looking at Jebb, who was shelling corn again.

"There's a tramp came to the house," I said. I had almost forgotten the tramp.

"Yeah."

"He came by the back way. What was he doing down there in the storm?"

"They comes and they goes," he said, "and ain't no tellen."

"He had a mean knife."

"The good ones and the bad ones, they comes and they goes. Storm or sun, light or dark. They is folks and they comes and they goes lak folks."

I hung on the door, shivering.

He studied me a moment, then said, "You git on to the house. You ketch yore death. Then what yore mammy say?"

I hesitated.

"You git," he said.

When I came to the back yard, I saw that my father was standing by the back porch and the tramp was walking toward him. They began talking before I reached them, but I got there just as my father was saying, "I'm sorry, but I haven't got any work. I got all the hands on the place I need now. I won't need any extra until wheat thrashing."

The stranger made no reply, just looked at my father.

My father took out his leather coin purse, and got out a half-dollar. He held it toward the man. "This is for half a day," he said.

The man looked at the coin, and then at my father, making no motion to take the money. But that was the right amount. A dollar a day was what you paid them back in 1910. And the man hadn't even worked half a day.

Then the man reached out and took the coin. He dropped it into the right side pocket of his coat. Then he said, very slowly and without feeling: "I didn't want to work on your —— farm."

He used the word which they would have frailed me to death for using.

I looked at my father's face and it was streaked white under the sunburn. Then he said, "Get off this place. Get off this place or I won't be responsible."

The man dropped his right hand into his pants pocket. It was the pocket where he kept the knife. I was just about to yell to my father about the knife when the hand came back out with nothing in it. The man gave a kind of twisted grin, showing where the teeth had been knocked out above the new scar. I thought that instant how maybe he had tried before to pull a knife on somebody else and had got his teeth knocked out.

So now he just gave that twisted, sickish grin out of the unmemorable, grayish face, and then spat on the brick path. The glob landed just about six inches from the toe of my father's right boot. My father looked down at it, and so did I. I thought that if the glob had hit my father's boot something would have happened. I looked down and saw the bright glob, and on one side of it my father's strong cowhide boots, with the brass eyelets and the leather thongs, heavy boots splashed with good red mud and set solid on the bricks, and on the other side the pointed-toe, broken, black shoes, on which the mud looked so sad and out of place. Then I saw one of the black shoes move a little, just a twitch first, then a real step backward.

The man moved in a quarter circle to the end of the porch, with my father's steady gaze upon him all the while. At the end of the porch, the man reached up to the shelf where the wash pans were to get his little newspaper-wrapped parcel. Then he disappeared around the corner of the house and my father mounted the porch and went into the kitchen without a word.

I followed around the house to see what the man would do. I wasn't afraid of him now, no matter if he did have the knife. When I got around in front, I saw him going out the yard gate and starting up the drive toward the pike. So I ran to catch up with him. He was sixty yards or so up the drive before I caught up.

I did not walk right up even with him at first, but trailed him, the way a kid will, about seven or eight feet behind, now and then running two or three steps in order to hold my place against his longer stride. When I first came up behind him, he turned to give me a look, just a meaningless look, and then fixed his eyes up the drive and kept on walking.

When we had got around the bend in the drive which cut the house from sight, and were going along by the edge of the woods, I decided to come up even with him. I ran a few steps, and was by his side, or almost, but some feet off to the right. I walked along in this position for a while, and he never noticed me. I walked along until we got within sight of the big gate that let on the pike.

Then I said: "Where did you come from?"

He looked at me then with a look which seemed almost surprised that I was there. Then he said, "It ain't none of yore business."

We went on another fifty feet.

Then I said, "Where are you going?"

He stopped, studied me dispassionately for a moment, then suddenly took a step toward me and leaned his face down at me. The lips jerked back, but not in any grin, to show where the teeth were knocked out and to make the scar on the lower lip come white with the tension.

He said: "Stop following me. You don't stop following me and I cut yore throat, you little son-of-a-bitch."

Then he went on to the gate, and up the pike.

That was thirty-five years ago. Since that time my father and mother have died. I was still a boy, but a big boy, when my father got cut on the blade of a mowing machine and died of lockjaw. My mother sold the place and went to town to live with her sister. But she never took hold after my father's death, and she died within three years, right in middle life. My aunt always said, "Sallie just died of a broken heart, she was so devoted." Dellie is dead, too, but she died, I heard, quite a long time after we sold the farm.

As for Little Jebb, he grew up to be a mean and ficey Negro. He killed another Negro in a fight and got sent to the penitentiary, where he is yet, the last I heard tell. He probably grew up to be mean and ficey from just being picked on so much by the children of the other tenants, who were jealous of Jebb and Dellie for being thrifty and clever and being white-folks' niggers.

Old Jebb lived forever. I saw him ten years ago and he was about a hundred then, and not looking much different. He was living in town then, on relief—that was back in the Depression—when I went to see him. He said to me: "Too strong to die. When I was a young feller just comen on and seen how things wuz, I prayed the Lawd. I said, Oh, Lawd, gimme strength and meke me strong fer to do and to indure. The Lawd hearkened to my prayer. He give me strength. I was in-duren proud fer being strong and me much man. The Lawd give me my prayer and my strength. But now He done gone off and forgot me and left me alone with my strength. A man doan know what to pray fer, and him mortal."

Jebb is probably living yet, as far as I know.

That is what has happened since the morning when the tramp leaned his face down at me and showed his teeth and said: "Stop following me. You don't stop following me and I cut yore throat, you little son-of-a-bitch." That was what he said, for me not to follow him. But I did follow him, all the years.

PETER TAYLOR

In 1940, Peter Taylor enrolled at LSU to take graduate-level English classes with Robert Penn Warren. Taylor and Warren had something in common—their studies at Vanderbilt University with the Fugitive poet, John Crowe Ransom. So under Warren's direction Taylor maintained a tie to the Southern literary traditions that Ransom had imparted. Taylor's period at LSU was brief—he left after one year to join the Army. Better known are his years as a growing boy in his native Tennessee, his undergraduate student days at Kenyon College, and his professorships at both Kenyon and the University of Virginia, where he helped establish the MFA program. However, Warren's influence, Taylor said, came "just at the right psychological moment" for understanding the possibilities of fiction-writing in and about the South. Additionally, Warren was the first editor to pay Taylor for his fiction—the story, "A Spinster's Tale," which appeared in *The Southern Review's* Autumn 1940 issue, *Literature and the Professors: a Symposium*, a collection of mostly essays and poetry. In 1941, Warren's last year as editor and the magazine's last year of publication until 1965, Warren published two more stories by Taylor—"The Fancy Woman" and "Sky Line." Warren's belief in Taylor's talent, as well as that of Katherine Anne Porter and Eudora Welty, proved prophetic. All three of these determined new writers went on to win Pulitzer Prizes in fiction. Taylor's prize in 1987 honored his first novel, *A Summons to Memphis*.

Both Taylor's short stories and his novels portray intimate relationships among multi-generational members of genteel Southern society, in particular their struggles with loneliness, regional separateness, and racial divides. As the parable goes, in "The Gift of the Prodigal," son Ricky turns to his father, the story's introspective narrator, after one of many dreadful "scrapes." *The New Yorker* magazine, where Taylor's work appeared regularly throughout his career, first published the story. Later, it was included in *The Old Forest and Other Stories*, which won the PEN/Faulkner Award. In "The Gift of the Prodigal," as in many of his other stories, Taylor relates the longings of both youth and old age, one for the other.

PETER TAYLOR

The Gift of the Prodigal

There's Ricky down in the washed river gravel of my driveway. I had my yardman out raking it before 7 A.M.—the driveway. It looks nearly perfect. Ricky also looks nearly perfect down there. He looks extremely got up and cleaned up, as though he had been carefully raked over and smoothed out. He is wearing a three-piece linen suit, which my other son, you may be sure, wouldn't be seen wearing on any occasion. And he has on an expensive striped shirt, open at the collar. No tie, of course. His thick head of hair, parted and slicked down, is just the same tan color as the gravel. Hair and gravel seem equally clean and in order. The fact is, Ricky looks this morning as though he belongs nowhere else in the world but out there in that smooth spread of washed river gravel (which will be mussed up again before noon, of course—I'm resigned to it), looks as though he feels perfectly at home in that driveway of mine that was so expensive to install and that requires so much upkeep.

Since one can't see his freckles from where I stand at this second-story window, his skin looks very fair—almost transparent. (Ricky just misses being a real red-head, and so never lets himself get suntanned. Bright sunlight tends to give him skin cancers.) From the window directly above him, I am able to get the full effect of his outfit. He looks very masculine standing down there, which is no doubt the impression his formfitting clothes are meant to give. And Ricky *is* very masculine, no matter what else he is or isn't. Peering down from up here, I mark particularly that where his collar stands open, and with several shirt buttons left carelessly or carefully undone, you can see a triangle of darker hair glistening on his chest. It isn't hard to imagine just how recently he has stepped out of the shower. In a word, he is looking what he considers his very best. And this says to me that Ricky is coming to me *for* something, or *because of* something.

His little sports car is parked in the turnaround behind this house, which I've built since he and the other children grew up and since their mother died. I know of course that, for them, coming here to see me can never really be like coming home. For Rick it must be like going to see any other old fellow who might happen to be his boss and who is ailing and is staying away from the office for a few days. As soon as I saw him down there, though, I knew something was really seriously wrong. From here I could easily recognize the expression on his face. He has a way, when he is concerned about something, of knitting his eyebrows and at the same time opening his eyes very wide, as though his eyes are about to pop out of his head and his eyebrows are trying to hold them in. It's a look that used to give him away even as a child when he was in trouble at school. If his mother and I saw that expression on his face, we would know that we were apt to be rung up by one of his teachers in a day or so or maybe have a house call from one of them.

Momentarily Ricky massages his face with his big right hand, as if to wipe away the expression. And clearly now he is headed for the side door that opens on the driveway. But before actually coming over to the door he has stopped in one spot and keeps shuffling his suede shoes about, roughing up the smooth gravel, like a young bull in a pen. I almost call out to him not to *do* that, not to muss up my gravel, which even his car wheels haven't disturbed—or not so much as he is doing with his suede shoes. I *almost* call out to him. But of course I don't really. For Ricky is a man twenty-nine years old, with two divorces already and no doubt another coming up soon. He's been through all that, besides a series of live-ins between marriages that I don't generally speak of, even.

For some time before coming on into the house, Ricky remains there in that spot in the driveway. While he stands there, it occurs to me that he may actually be looking the place over, as though he'd never noticed what this house is like until now. The old place on Wertland Street, where he and the other children grew up, didn't have half the style and convenience of this one. It had more room, but the room was mostly in pantries and hallways, with front stairs and back stairs and third-floor servants' quarters in an age when no servant would be caught dead living up there in the attic—or staying anywhere else on the place, for that matter. I am not unaware, of course, how much better that old house on Wertland was than this one. You couldn't have replaced it for twice what I've poured into this compact and well-appointed habitation out here in Farmington. But its neighborhood had gone bad. Nearly all of Charlottesville proper has, as a matter of fact, either gone commercial or been absorbed by the university. You can no longer live within the shadow of Mr. Jefferson's Academical Village. And our old Wertland Street house is now a funeral parlor. Which is what it ought to have been five years before I left it. From the day my wife, Cary, died, the place seemed like a tomb. I wandered up and down the stairs and all around, from room to room, sometimes greeting myself in one of Cary's looking glasses, doing so out of loneliness or out of thinking *that* couldn't be *me* still in my dressing gown and slippers at midday, or fully dressed—necktie and all—at 3 A.M. I knew well enough it was time to sell. And, besides, I wanted to have the experience at last of making something new. You see, we never built a house of our own, Cary and I. We always bought instead of building, wishing to be in an established neighborhood, you know, where there were good day schools for the girls (it was before St. Anne's moved to the suburbs), where there were streetcars and buses for the servants, or, better still, an easy walk for them to Ridge Street.

My scheme for building a new house after Cary died seemed a harebrained idea to my three older children. They tried to talk me out of it. They said I was only doing it out of idleness. They'd laugh and say I'd chosen a rather expensive form of entertainment for myself in my old age. That's what they *said*. That wasn't all they *thought*, however. But I never held against them what they thought. All motherless children—regardless of age—have such thoughts. They had in mind that I'd got notions of marrying again. Me! Why, I've never looked at another woman since the day I married. Not to this very hour. At any rate, one night when we were having dinner and they were telling me how they worried about me, and making it plainer than usual what they thought my plans for the future were or might be, Ricky spoke up—Ricky who never gave a thought in his life to what happened to anybody except himself—and he came out with just what was on the others' minds. "What if you should take a notion to marry again?" he asked. And I began shaking my head before the words were out of his mouth, as did all the others. It was an unthinkable thought for them as well as for me. "Why not?" Ricky persisted, happy of course that he was making everybody uncomfortable. "Worse things have happened, you know. And I nominate the handsome Mrs. Capers as a likely candidate for bride."

I *think* he was referring to a certain low sort of woman who had recently moved into the old neighborhood. You could depend upon Rick to know about her and know her name. As he spoke he winked at me. Presently he crammed his wide mouth full of food, and as he chewed he made a point of drawing back his lips and showing his somewhat overlarge and overly white front teeth. He continued to look straight at me as he chewed, but looking with only one eye, keeping the eye he'd winked at me squinched up tight. He looked for all the world like some old tomcat who's found a nasty morsel he likes the taste of and is not going to let go of. I willingly would have knocked him out of his chair for what he'd said, even more for that common look he was giving me. I knew he knew as well as the others that I'd never looked at any woman besides his mother.

Yet I laughed with the others as soon as I realized they were laughing. You don't let a fellow like Ricky know he's got your goat—especially when he's your own son, and has been in one bad scrape after another ever since he's been grown, and seems always just waiting for a chance to get back at you for something censorious you may have said to him while trying to help him out of one of his escapades. Since Cary died, I've tried mostly just to keep lines of communication open with him. I think that's the thing she would have wanted of me—that is, not to shut Rick out, to keep him talking. Cary used to say to me, "You may be the only person he can talk to about the women he gets involved with. He can't talk to me about such things." Cary always thought it was the women he had most on his mind and who got him into scrapes. I never used to think so. Anyway, I believe that Cary would have wished above all else for me to keep lines open with Rick, would have wanted it even more than she would have wanted me to go ahead in whatever way I chose with schemes for a new house for my old age.

The house was *our* plan originally, you see, hers and mine. It was something we never told the children about. There seemed no reason why we should. Not talking about it except between ourselves was part of the pleasure of it, somehow. And that night when Ricky came out with the speculation about my possibly marrying again, I didn't tell him or the others that actually I had already sold the Wertland Street house and already had blueprints for the new house here in Farmington locked away in my desk drawer, and even a contractor all set to break ground.

Well, my new house was finished the following spring. By that time all the children, excepting Rick, had developed a real enthusiasm for it. (Rick didn't give a damn one way or the other, of course.) They helped me dispose of all the superfluous furniture in the old house. The girls even saw to the details of moving and saw to it that I got comfortably settled in. They wanted me to be happy out here. And soon enough they saw I was. There was no more they could do for me now than there had been in recent years. They had their good marriages to look after (that's what Cary would have wished for them), and they saw to it that I wasn't left out of whatever of their activities I wanted to be in on. In a word, they went on with their busy lives, and my own life seemed busy enough for any man my age.

What has vexed the other children, though, during the five years since I built my house, is their brother Ricky's continuing to come to me at almost regular intervals with new ordeals of one kind or another that he's been going through. They have thought he ought not to burden me with his outrageous and sometimes sordid affairs. I think they have especially resented his troubling me here at home. I still go to the office, you see, two or three days a week—just whenever I feel like it or when I'm not playing golf or bridge or am not off on a little trip to Sarasota (I stay at the same inn Cary and I used to go to). And so I've always seen Ricky quite regularly at the office. He's had every chance to talk to me there. But the fact is Rick was never one for bringing his personal problems to the office. He has always brought them home.

Even since I've moved, he has always come *here*, to the house, when he's really wanted to talk to me about something. I don't know whether it's the two servants I still keep or some of the young neighbors hereabouts who tell them, but somehow the other children always know when Ricky has been here. And they of course can put two and two together. It will come out over Sunday dinner at one of their houses or at the Club—in one of those little private dining rooms. It is all right if we eat in the big dining room, where everybody else is. I know I'm safe there. But as soon as

I see they've reserved a private room I know they want to talk about Ricky's latest escapade. They will begin by making veiled references to it among themselves. But at last it is I who am certain to let the cat out of the bag. For I can't resist joining in when they get onto Rick, as they all know very well I won't be able to. You see, often they will have the details wrong—maybe they get them wrong on purpose—and I feel obliged to straighten them out. Then one of them will turn to me, pretending shocked surprise: "How ever did you know about it? Has *he* been bringing his troubles to *you* again? At his age, you'd think he'd be ashamed to! Someone ought to remind him he's a grown man now!" At that point one of the girls is apt to rest her hand on mine. As they go on, I can hear the love for me in their voices and see it in their eyes. I know then what a lucky man I am. I want to say to them that their affection makes up for all the unhappiness Ricky causes me. But I have never been one to make speeches like that. Whenever I have managed to say such things, I have somehow always felt like a hypocrite afterward. Anyway, the talk will go on for a while till I remember a bridge game I have an appointment for in the Club lounge, at two o'clock. Or I recall that my golf foursome is waiting for me in the locker room.

I've never tried to defend Rick from the others. The things he does are really quite indefensible. Sometimes I've even found myself giving details about some escapade of his that the others didn't already know and are genuinely shocked to hear—especially coming from me. He was in a shooting once that everybody in Farmington and in the whole county set knew about—or knew about, that is, in a general way, though without knowing the very thing that would finally make it a public scandal. It's an ugly story, I warn you, as, indeed, nearly all of Ricky's stories are.

He had caught another fellow in bed with a young married woman with whom he himself was running around. Of course it was a scandalous business, all of it. But the girl, as Rick described her to me afterward, was a real beauty of a certain type and, according to Rick, as smart as a whip. Rick even showed me her picture, though I hadn't asked to see it, naturally. She had a tight little mouth, and eyes that—even in that wallet-sized picture—burned themselves into your memory. She was the sort of intense and reckless-looking girl that Ricky has always gone for. I've sometimes looked at pictures of his other girls, too, when he wanted to show them to me. And of course I know what his wives have looked like. All three of his wives have been from good families. For, bad as he is, Ricky is not the sort of fellow who would embarrass the rest of us by *marrying* some slut. Yet even his wives have tended to dress themselves in a way that my own daughters wouldn't. They have dressed, that is to say, in clothes that seemed designed to call attention to their female forms and not, as with my daughters, to call attention to the station and the affluence of their husbands. Being the timid sort of man I am, I used to find myself whenever I talked with his wife—whichever one—carefully looking out the window or looking across the room, away from her, at some inanimate object or other over there or out there. My wife, Cary, used to say that Ricky had bad luck in his wives, that each of them turned out to have just as roving an eye as Ricky himself. I can't say for certain whether this was true for each of them in the beginning or whether it was something Ricky managed to teach them all.

Anyway, the case of the young married woman in whose bed—or apartment— Ricky found that other fellow came near to causing Ricky more trouble than any of his other escapades. The fellow ran out of the apartment, with Rick chasing him into the corridor and down the corridor to a door of an outside stairway. It was not here in Farmington, you see, but out on Barracks Road, where so many of Rick's friends are—in a development that's been put up on the very edge of where the horse farms begin. The fellow scurried down the outside stairs and across a parking lot toward some pastureland beyond. And Rick, as he said, couldn't resist taking a shot at him from that upstairs stoop where he had abandoned the chase. He took aim just when the fellow reached the first pasture fence and was about to climb over. Afterward, Rick said that it was simply too good to miss. But Rick rarely misses a target when he takes aim. He hit the fellow with a load of rat shot right in the seat of the pants.

I'll never know how Rick happened to have the gun with him. He told me that he was deeply in love with the young woman and would have married her if her husband had been willing to give her a divorce. The other children maintain to this day that it was the husband Rick meant to threaten with the gun, but the husband was out of town and Rick lost his head when he found that other fellow there in his place. Anyhow, the story got all over town. I suppose Ricky himself helped to spread it. He thought it all awfully funny at first. But before it was over, the matter came near to getting into the courts and into the paper. And that was because there was something else involved, which the other children and the people in the Barracks Road set didn't know about and I did. In fact, it was something that I worried about from the beginning. You see, Rick naturally took that fellow he'd blasted with the rat shot to a doctor—a young doctor friend of theirs—who removed the shot. But, being a friend, the doctor didn't report the incident. A certain member of our judiciary heard the details and thought perhaps the matter needed looking into. We were months getting it straightened out. Ricky went out of town for a while, and the young doctor ended by having to move away permanently—to Richmond or Norfolk, I think. I only give this incident in such detail in order to show the sort of low company Ricky has always kept, even when he seemed to be among our own sort.

His troubles haven't all involved women, though. Or not primarily. And that's what I used to tell Cary. Like so many people in Charlottesville, Rick has always had a weakness for horses. For a while he fancied himself a polo player. He bought a polo pony and got cheated on it. He bought it at a stable where he kept another horse he owned—bought it from the man who ran the stable. After a day or so, he found that the animal was a worthless, worn-out nag. It couldn't even last through the first chukker, which was humiliating of course for Ricky. He daren't try to take it onto the field again. It had been all doped up when he bought it. Ricky was outraged. Instead of simply trying to get his money back, he wanted to have his revenge upon the man and make an even bigger fool of *him*. He persuaded a friend to dress himself up in a turtleneck sweater and a pair of yellow jodhpurs and pretend just to be passing by the stall in the same stable where the polo pony was still kept. His friend played the role, you see, of someone only just taking up the game and who thought he *had* to have that particular pony. He asked the man whose animal it was, and before he could get an answer he offered more than twice the price that Rick had paid. He even put the offer into writing—using an assumed name, of course. He said he was from up in Maryland and would return in two days' time. Naturally, the stableman telephoned Ricky as soon as the stranger in jodhpurs had left the stable. He said he had discovered, to his chagrin, that the pony was not in as good condition as he had thought it was. And he said that in order that there be no bad feeling between them he was willing to buy it back for the price Ricky had paid.

Ricky went over that night and collected his money. But when the stranger didn't reappear and couldn't be traced, the stableman of course knew what had happened. Rick didn't return to the stable during the following several days. I suppose, being Ricky, he was busy spreading the story all over town. His brother and sisters got wind of it. And I did soon enough. On Sunday night, two thugs and some woman Ricky knew but would never identify—not even to me—came to his house and persuaded him to go out and sit in their car with them in front of his house. And there they beat him brutally. He had to be in the hospital for five or six days. They broke his right arm, and one of them—maybe it was the woman—was trying to bite off the lobe of his left ear when Ricky's current wife, who had been out to some party without the favor of his company, pulled into the driveway beside the house. The assailants shoved poor Ricky, bruised and bleeding and with his arm broken, out onto the sidewalk. And then of course they sped away down the street in their rented car. Ricky's wife and the male friend who was with her got the license number, but the car had been rented under an assumed name—the same name, actually, as some kind of joke, I suppose, that Ricky's friend in jodhpurs had used with the stablekeeper.

Since Ricky insisted that he could not possibly recognize his two male assailants in a lineup, and since he refused to identify the woman, there was little that could be done about his actual beating. I don't know that he ever confessed to anyone but me that he knew the woman. It was easy enough for me to imagine what *she* looked like. Though I would not have admitted it to Ricky or to anyone else, I would now and then during the following weeks see a woman of a certain type on the streets downtown—with one of those tight little mouths and with burning eyes—and imagine that she might be the very one. All we were ever able to do about the miserable fracas was to see to it finally that that stable was put out of business and that the man himself had to go elsewhere (he went down into North Carolina) to ply his trade.

There is one other scrape of Ricky's that I must mention, because it remains particularly vivid for me. The nature and the paraphernalia of this one will seem even more old-fashioned than those of the other incidents. Maybe that's why it sticks in my mind so. It's something that might have happened to any number of rough fellows I knew when I was coming along.

Ricky, not surprising to say, likes to gamble. From the time he was a young boy he would often try to inveigle one of the other children into making wagers with him on how overdone his steak was at dinner. He always liked it very rare and when his serving came he would hold up a bite on his fork and, for a decision on the bet, would ask everyone what shade of brown the meat was. He made all the suggestions of color himself. And one night his suggestions got so coarse and vile his mother had to send him from the dining room and not let him have a bite of supper. Sometimes he would try to get the other children to bet with him on the exact number of minutes the parson's sermon would last on Sunday or how many times the preacher would use the word "Hell" or "damnation" or "adultery." Since he has got grown, it's the races, of course, he likes—horse races, it goes without saying, but also such low-life affairs as dog races and auto races. What catches his fancy above all else, though, are the chicken fights we have always had in our part of the country. And a few years ago he bought himself a little farm a dozen miles or so south of town where he could raise his own game chickens. I saw nothing wrong with that at the time. Then he built an octagonal barn down there, with a pit in it where he could hold the fights. I worried a little when he did that. But we've always had cockfights hereabouts. The birds are beautiful creatures, really, though they have no brains, of course. The fight itself is a real spectacle and no worse than some other things people enjoy. At Ricky's urging, I even went down to two or three fights at his place. I didn't bet, because I knew the stakes were very high. (Besides, it's the betting that's illegal.) And I didn't tell the other children about my going. But this was after Cary was dead, you see, and I thought maybe she would have liked my going for Ricky's sake, though she would never have acknowledged it. Pretty soon, sizable crowds began attending the fights on weekend nights. Cars would be parked all over Ricky's front pasture and all around the yard of the tenant house. He might as well have put up a sign down at the gate where his farm road came off the highway.

The point is, everyone knew that the cockfights went on. And one of his most regular customers and biggest bettors was one of the county sheriff's right-hand men. I'm afraid Rick must have bragged about that in advertising his fights to friends—friends who would otherwise have been a little timid about coming. And during the fights he would move about among the crowd, winking at people and saying to them under his breath, "The deputy's here tonight." I suppose it was his way of reassuring them that everything was all right. I don't know whether or not his spreading the word so widely had anything to do with the raid, but nevertheless the deputy was present the night the federal officers came stealing up the farm road, with their car lights off and with search warrants in their pockets. And it was the deputy who first got wind of the federal officers' approach. He had one of his sidekicks posted outside the barn. Maybe he had somebody watching out there every night that he came. Maybe all along he had had a plan for his escape in such an emergency. Rick thought so afterward. Anyhow, the deputy's man outside knew at once what those cars moving up the lane with their lights off meant. The deputy got the word before anyone else, but, depend upon Ricky, he saw the first move the deputy made to leave. And he was not going to have it. He took out after him.

The deputy's watchman was prepared to stay on and take his chances. (He wasn't even a patrolman. He probably only worked in the office.) I imagine he was prepared to spend a night in jail if necessary, and pay whatever fine there might be, because his presence could explain one of the sheriff's cars' being parked in the pasture. But the deputy himself took off through the backwoods on Ricky's property and toward a county road on the back of the place. Ricky, as I've said, was not going to have that. Since the cockfight was on his farm, he knew there was no way out of trouble for himself. But he thought it couldn't, at least, do him any harm to have the deputy caught along with everybody else. Moreover, the deputy had lost considerable amounts of money there at the pit in recent weeks and had insinuated to Ricky that he suspected some of the cocks had been tampered with. (I, personally, don't believe Ricky would stand for that.) Ricky couldn't be sure there wasn't some collusion between the deputy and the feds. He saw the deputy's man catch the deputy's eye from the barn doorway and observed the deputy's departure. He was right after him. He overtook him just before he reached the woods. Fortunately, the deputy wasn't armed. (Ricky allowed no one to bring a gun inside the barn.) And fortunately Ricky wasn't armed, either, that night. They scuffled a little near the gate to the woods lot. The deputy, being a man twice Rick's age, was no match for him and was soon overpowered. Ricky dragged him back to the barn, himself resisting—as he later testified—all efforts at bribery on the deputy's part, and turned in both himself and his captive to the federal officers.

Extricating Ricky from that affair and setting matters aright was a long and complicated undertaking. The worst of it really began for Ricky after the court proceedings were finished and all fines were paid (there were no jail terms for anyone), because from his last appearance in the federal courthouse Ricky could drive his car scarcely one block through that suburb where he lives without receiving a traffic ticket of some kind. There may not have been anything crooked about it, for Ricky is a wild sort of driver at best. But, anyhow, within a short time his driving license was revoked for the period of a year. Giving up driving was a great inconvenience for him and a humiliation. All we could do about the deputy, who, Ricky felt sure, had connived with the federal officers, was to get him out of his job after the next election.

The outcome of the court proceedings was that Rick's fines were very heavy. Moreover, efforts were made to confiscate all the livestock on his farm, as well as the farm machinery. But he was saved from the confiscation by a special circumstance, which, however, turned out to produce for him only a sort of Pyrrhic victory. It turned out, you see, that the farm was not in Ricky's name but in that of his young tenant farmer's wife. I never saw her, or didn't know it if I did. Afterward, I used to try to recall if I hadn't seen some such young woman when I was down watching the cockfights—one who would have fitted the picture in my mind. My imagination played tricks on me, though. I would think I remembered the face or figure of some young girl I'd seen there who could conceivably be the one. But then suddenly I'd recall another and think possibly it might be she who had the title to Ricky's farm. I never could be sure.

When Ricky appeared outside my window just now, I'd already had a very bad morning. The bursitis in my right shoulder had waked me before dawn. At last I got up and dressed, which was an ordeal in itself. (My right hip was hurting somewhat, too.) When finally the cook came in, she wanted to give me a massage before she began fixing breakfast even. Cary would never have allowed her to make that mistake. A massage, you see, is the worst thing you can do for my sort of bursitis. What I wanted was some breakfast. And I knew it would take Meg three quarters of an hour to put breakfast on the table. And so I managed to get out of my clothes again and ease myself into a hot bath, groaning so loud all the while that Meg came up to the door twice and asked if I was all right. I told her just to go and get my breakfast ready. After breakfast, I waited till a decent hour and then telephoned one of my golf foursome to tell him I couldn't play today. It's this damp fall weather that does us in worst. All you can do is sit and think how you've got the whole winter before you and wonder if you'll be able to get yourself off to someplace like Sarasota.

While I sat at a front window, waiting for the postman (he never brings anything but circulars and catalogs on Saturday; besides, all my serious mail goes to the office and is opened by someone else), I found myself thinking of all the things I couldn't do and all the people who are dead and that I mustn't think about. I tried to do a little better—that is, to think of something cheerful. There was lots I *could* be cheerful about, wasn't there? At least three of my children were certain to telephone today—all but Ricky, and it was sure to be bad news if he did! And a couple of the grandchildren would likely call, too. Then tomorrow I'd be going to lunch with some of them if I felt up to it. Suddenly I thought of the pills I was supposed to have taken before breakfast and had forgotten to: the Inderal and the potassium and the hydrochlorothiazide. I began to get up from my chair and then I settled down again. It didn't really matter. There was no ailment I had that could really be counted on to be fatal if I missed one day's dosage. And then I wholeheartedly embraced the old subject, the old speculation: How many days like this one, how many years like this one lay ahead for me? And finally, irresistibly, I descended to lower depths still, thinking of past times not with any relish but remembering how in past times I had always *told* myself I'd someday look back with pleasure on what would seem good old days, which was an indication itself that they hadn't somehow been good enough—not good enough, that is, to stand on their own as an end in themselves. If the old days were so damned good, why had I had to think always how good they would someday seem in retrospect? I had just reached the part where I think there was nothing *wrong* with them and that I ought to be satisfied, had just reached that point at which I recall that I loved and was loved by my wife, that I love and am loved by my children, that it's not them or my life but *me* there's something wrong with! —had just reached that inevitable syllogism that I always come to, when I was distracted by the arrival of Saturday morning's late mail delivery. It was brought in, it was handed to me by a pair of black hands, and of course it had nothing in it. But I took it upstairs to my sitting room. (So that even the servant wouldn't see there was nothing worth having in it.) I had just closed my door and got out my pills when I heard Ricky's car turn into the gravel driveway.

He was driving so slowly that his car wheels hardly disturbed the gravel. That in itself was an ominous phenomenon. He was approaching slowly and quietly. He didn't want me to know ahead of time what there was in store for me. My first impulse was to lock my door and refuse to admit him. I simply did not feel up to Rick this morning! But I said to myself, "That's something I've never done, though maybe ought to have done years ago no matter what Cary said. He's sure to send my blood pressure soaring." I thought of picking up the telephone and phoning one of the other children to come and protect me from this monster of a son and from whatever sort of trouble he was now in.

But it was just then that I caught my first glimpse of him down in the driveway. I had the illusion that he was admiring the place. And then of course I was at once disillusioned. He was only hesitating down there because he dreaded seeing me. But he was telling himself he *had* to see me. There would be no other solution to his problem but to see his old man. I knew what he was thinking by the gesture he was making with his left hand. It's strange how you get the notion that your children are like you just because they have the same facial features and the same gestures when talking to themselves. None of it means a thing! It's only an illusion. Even now I find myself making gestures with my hands when I'm talking to myself that I used to notice my own father making sometimes when we were out walking together and neither of us had spoken a word for half an hour or so. It used to get on my nerves when I saw Father do it, throwing out his hand almost imperceptibly, with his long fingers spread apart. I don't know why it got on my nerves so. But, anyhow, I never dreamed that I could inherit such a gesture—or much less that one of my sons would. And yet there Ricky is, down in the driveway, making the same gesture precisely. And there never were three men with more different characters than my father and me and my youngest child. I watch Ricky make the gesture several times while standing in the driveway. And now suddenly he turns as if to go back to his car. I step away from the window, hoping he hasn't seen me and will go on off. But, having once seen him down there, I can't, of course, do that. I have to receive him and hear him out. I open the sash and call down to him, "Come on up, Ricky."

He looks up at me, smiles guiltily, and shrugs. Then he comes on in the side entrance. As he moves through the house and up the stairs, I try to calm myself. I gaze down at the roughed-up gravel where his suede shoes did their damage and tell myself it isn't so bad and even manage to smile at my own old-maidishness. Presently, he comes into the sitting room. We greet each other with the usual handshake. I can smell his shaving lotion. Or maybe it is something he puts on his hair. We go over and sit down by the fireplace, where there is a fire laid but not lit in this season, of course. He begins by talking about everything under the sun except what is on his mind. This is standard procedure in our talks at such times. Finally, he begins, looking into the fireplace as though the fire were lit and as though he were watching low-burning flames. I barely keep myself from smiling when he says, "I've got a little problem—not so damned little, in fact. It's a matter that's got out of hand."

And then I say, "I supposed as much."

You can't give Ricky an inch at these times, you see. Else he'll take advantage of you. Pretty soon he'll have shifted the whole burden of how he's to be extricated onto your shoulders. I wait for him to continue, and he is about to, I think. But before he can get started he turns his eyes away from the dry logs and the unlit kindling and begins looking about the room, just as he looked about the premises outside. It occurs to me again that he seems to be observing my place for the very first time. But I don't suppose he really is. His mind is, as usual, on himself. Then all at once his eyes do obviously come to focus on something over my shoulder. He runs his tongue up under his upper lip and then under his lower lip, as though he were cleaning his teeth. I, involuntarily almost, look over my shoulder. There on the library table behind me, on what I call my desk, are my cut-glass tumbler and three bottles of pills—my hydrochlorothiazide, my Inderal, and my potassium. Somehow I failed to put them back in my desk drawer earlier. I was so distracted by my morbid thoughts when I came upstairs that I forgot to stick them away in the place where I keep them out of sight from everybody. (I don't even like for the servants to see what and how much medicine I take.) Without a word passing between us, and despite the pains in my shoulder and hip, I push myself up out of my chair and sweep the bottles, and the tumbler, too, into the desk drawer. I keep my back to Ricky for a minute or so till I can overcome the grimacing I never can repress when these pains strike. Suddenly, though, I do turn back to him and find he has come to his feet. I pay no special attention to that. I ease myself back into my chair saying, "Yes, Ricky." Making my voice rather hard, I say, "You've got a problem?" He looks at me coldly, without a trace of the sympathy any one of the other children would have shown—knowing, that is, as he surely does, that I am having pains of some description. And he speaks to me as though I were a total stranger toward whom he feels nothing but is just barely human enough to wish not to torture. "Man," he says—the idea of his addressing *me* that way!—"Man, you've got problems enough of your own. Even the world's greatest snotface can see that. One thing sure, you don't need to hear *my* crap."

I am on my feet so quick you wouldn't think I have a pain in my body. "Don't you use that gutter language with me, Ricky!" I say. "You weren't brought up in some slum over beyond Vinegar Hill!" He only turns and looks into the fireplace again. If there were a fire going I reckon he would have spat in it at this point. Then he looks back at me, running his tongue over his teeth again. And then, without any apology or so much as a by-your-leave, he heads for the door. "Come back here, Ricky!" I command. "Don't you dare leave the room!" Still moving toward the closed door, he glances back over his shoulder at me, with a wide, hard grin on his face, showing his mouthful of white teeth, as though my command were the funniest thing he has ever heard. At the door, he puts his big right hand on the glass knob, covering it entirely. Then he twists his upper body, his torso, around—seemingly just from the hips—to face me. And simultaneously he brings up his left hand and scratches that triangle of dark hair where his shirt is open. It is like some kind of dirty gesture he is making. I say to myself, "He really is like something not quite human. For all the jams and scrapes he's been in, he's never suffered any second thoughts or known the meaning of remorse. I ought to have let him hang," I say to myself, "by his own beautiful locks."

But almost simultaneously what I hear myself saying aloud is, "Please don't go, Rick. Don't go yet, son." Yes, I am pleading with him, and I mean what I say with my whole heart. He still has his right hand on the doorknob and has given it a full turn. Our eyes meet across the room, directly, as they never have before in the whole of Ricky's life or mine. I think neither of us could tell anyone what it is he sees in the other's eyes, unless it is a need beyond any description either of us is capable of.

Presently Rick says, "You don't need to hear my crap."

And I hear my bewildered voice saying, "I do . . . I do." And "Don't go, Rick, my boy." My eyes have even misted over. But I still meet his eyes across the now too silent room. He looks at me in the most compassionate way imaginable. I don't think any child of mine has ever looked at me so before. Or perhaps it isn't really with compassion he is viewing me but with the sudden, gratifying knowledge that it is not, after all, such a one-sided business, the business between us. He keeps his right hand on the doorknob a few seconds longer. Then I hear the latch click and know he has let go. Meanwhile, I observe his left hand making that familiar gesture, his fingers splayed, his hand tilting back and forth. I am out of my chair by now. I go to the desk and bring out two Danlys cigars from another desk drawer, which I keep locked. He is there ready to receive my offering when I turn around. He accepts the cigar without smiling, and I give it without smiling, too. Seated opposite each other again, each of us lights his own.

And then Ricky begins. What will it be this time, I think. I am wild with anticipation. Whatever it will be, I know it is all anyone in the world can give me now—perhaps the most anyone has ever been able to give a man like me. As Ricky begins, I try to think of all the good things the other children have done for me through the years and of their affection, and of my wife's. But it seems this was all there ever was. I forget my pains and my pills, and the canceled golf game, and the meaningless mail that morning. I find I can scarcely sit still in my chair for wanting Ricky to get on with it. Has he been brandishing his pistol again? Or dragging the sheriff's deputy across a field at midnight? And does he have in his wallet perhaps a picture of some other girl with a tight little mouth, and eyes that burn? Will his outrageous story include her? And perhaps explain it, leaving her a blessed mystery? As Ricky begins, I find myself listening not merely with fixed attention but with my whole being. . . . I hear him beginning. I am listening. I am listening gratefully to all he will tell me about himself, about any life that is not my own.

JEAN STAFFORD

Pulitzer Prize-winning author Jean Stafford began writing "The Interior Castle" around 1940, the year that she lived on Chimes Street above Kean's Laundry in Baton Rouge with her husband, the poet Robert Lowell. While Lowell explored his craft in classes with Professor Robert Penn Warren, Stafford worked as Warren's secretary at *The Southern Review*, which was then publishing new writers such as Eudora Welty and Katherine Anne Porter. At night, Stafford ventured downtown to attend shorthand classes. During off times, the couple, along with Peter Taylor, who was then a student of Warren's, drove into the wilds of plantation country. Stafford and Taylor would become lifelong friends. His story, "1939," is a true-to-life depiction of the years during which they and Lowell began to discover themselves as artists, and captures Stafford's brief bohemian period in particular. "During that year in Baton Rouge," Stafford scholar, Mary Ann Wilson, wrote, "Jean Stafford was unwittingly living out the text of her own portrait of the artist."

Stafford drew on her own experience to write "The Interior Castle." Before marrying Lowell and moving to Baton Rouge, she had had reconstructive surgery due to a car accident in which Lowell was driving. The protagonist of "The Interior Castle" is characterized by the terrifying pain she feels under the surgeon's knife, and is one of several Stafford characters for whom an external force creates an internal change. The piece is included in *The Collected Stories of Jean Stafford*, which won the Pulitzer Prize in 1970. Another story, "In the Zoo," published originally in *The New Yorker*, won the O. Henry Prize. Later in life, Stafford married A.J. Liebling, and the two returned to Louisiana to further his work on *The Earl of Louisiana*, an evocative account of Governor Earl K. Long's last year in state politics. Stafford's personal story regularly intersects with those of other literary lights. During her year in Baton Rouge, she absorbed indirectly the education that shaped her later successes.

JEAN STAFFORD

The Interior Castle

Pansy Vanneman, injured in an automobile accident, often woke up before dawn when the night noises of the hospital still came, in hushed hurry, through her half-open door. By day, when the nurses talked audibly with the internes, laughed without inhibition, and took no pains to soften their footsteps on the resounding composition floors, the routine of the hospital seemed as bland and commonplace as that of a bank or a factory. But in the dark hours, the whispering and the quickly stilled clatter of glasses and basins, the moans of patients whose morphine was wearing off, the soft squeak of a stretcher as it rolled past on its way from the emergency ward—these suggested agony and death. Thus, on the first morning, Pansy had faltered to consciousness long before daylight and had found herself in a ward from every bed of which, it seemed to her, came the bewildered protest of someone about to die. A caged light burned on the floor beside the bed next to hers. Her neighbor was dying and a priest was administering Extreme Unction. He was stout and elderly and he suffered from asthma so that the struggle of his breathing, so close to her, was the basic pattern and all the other sounds were superimposed upon it. Two middle-aged men in overcoats knelt on the floor beside the high bed. In a foreign tongue, the half-gone woman babbled against the hissing and sighing of the Latin prayers. She played with her rosary as if it were a toy: she tried, and failed, to put it into her mouth.

Pansy felt horror, but she felt no pity. An hour or so later, when the white ceiling lights were turned on and everything—faces, counterpanes, and the hands that groped upon them—was transformed into a uniform gray sordor, the woman was wheeled away in her bed to die somewhere else, in privacy. Pansy did not quite take this in, although she stared for a long time at the new, empty bed that had replaced the other.

The next morning, when she again woke up before the light, this time in a private room, she recalled the woman with such sorrow that she might have been a friend. Simultaneously, she mourned the driver of the taxicab in which she had been injured, for he had died at about noon the day before. She had been told this as she lay on a stretcher in the corridor, waiting to be taken to the X-ray room; an interne, passing by, had paused and smiled down at her and had said, "Your cab driver is dead. You were lucky."

Six weeks after the accident, she woke one morning just as daylight was showing on the windows as a murky smear. It was a minute or two before she realized why she was so reluctant to be awake, why her uneasiness amounted almost to alarm. Then she remembered that her nose was to be operated on today. She lay straight and motionless under the seersucker counterpane. Her blood-red eyes in her darned face stared through the window and saw a frozen river and leafless elm trees and a grizzled esplanade where dogs danced on the ends of leashes, their bundled-up owners stumbling after them, half blind with sleepiness and cold. Warm as the hospital room was, it did not prevent Pansy from knowing, as keenly as though she were one of the walkers, how very cold it was outside. Each twig of a nearby tree was stark. Cold red brick buildings nudged the low-lying sky which was pale and inert like a punctured sac.

In six weeks, the scene had varied little: there was promise in the skies neither of sun nor of snow; no red sunsets marked these days. The trees could neither die nor leaf out again. Pansy could not remember another season in her life so constant, when the very minutes themselves were suffused with the winter pallor as they dropped from the moon-faced clock in the corridor. In the same way, her room accomplished no alterations from day to day. On the glass-topped bureau stood two potted plants telegraphed by faraway well-wishers. They did not fade, and if a leaf turned brown and fell, it soon was replaced; so did the blossoms renew themselves. The roots, like the skies and like the bare trees, seemed zealously determined to maintain a status quo. The bedside table, covered every day with a clean white towel, though the one removed was always immaculate, was furnished sparsely with a water glass, a bent drinking tube, a sweating pitcher, and a stack of paper handkerchiefs. There were a few letters in the drawer, a hairbrush, a pencil, and some postal cards on which, from time to time, she wrote brief messages to relatives and friends: "Dr. Nash says that my reflexes are shipshape (*sic*) and Dr. Rivers says the frontal fracture has all but healed and that the occipital is coming along nicely. Dr. Nicholas, the nose doctor, promises to operate as soon as Dr. Rivers gives him the go-ahead sign (*sic*)."

The bed itself was never rumpled. Once fretful and now convalescent, Miss Vanneman might have been expected to toss or to turn the pillows or to unmoor the counterpane; but hour after hour and day after day she lay at full length and would not even suffer the nurses to raise the headpiece of the adjustable bed. So perfect and stubborn was her body's immobility that it was as if the room and the landscape, mortified by the ice, were extensions of herself. Her resolute quiescence and her disinclination to talk, the one seeming somehow to proceed from the other, resembled, so the nurses said, a final coma. And they observed, in pitying indignation, that she might as *well* be dead for all the interest she took in life. Among themselves they scolded her for what they thought a moral weakness: an automobile accident, no matter how serious, was not reason enough for anyone to give up the will to live or to be happy. She had not—to come down bluntly to the facts—had the decency to be grateful that it was the driver of the cab and not she who had died. (And how dreadfully the man had died!) She was twenty-five years old and she came from a distant city. These were really the only facts known about her. Evidently she had not been here long, for she had no visitors, a lack which was at first sadly moving to the nurses but which became to them a source of unreasonable annoyance: had anyone the right to live so one-dimensionally? It was impossible to laugh at her, for she said nothing absurd; her demands could not be complained of because they did not exist; she could not be hated for a sharp tongue nor for a supercilious one; she could not be admired for bravery or for wit or for interest in her fellow creatures. She was believed to be a frightful snob.

Pansy, for her part, took a secret and mischievous pleasure in the bewilderment of her attendants and the more they courted her with offers of magazines, crossword puzzles, and a radio that she could rent from the hospital, the farther she retired from them into herself and into the world which she had created in her long hours here and which no one could ever penetrate nor imagine. Sometimes she did not even answer the nurses' questions; as they rubbed her back with alcohol and steadily discoursed, she was as remote from them as if she were miles away. She did not think that she lived on a higher plane than that of the nurses and the doctors but that she lived on a different one and that at this particular time—this time of exploration and habituation—she had no extra strength to spend on making herself known to them. All she had been before and all the memories she might have brought out to disturb the monotony of, say, the morning bath, and all that the past meant to the future when she would leave the hospital, were of no present consequence to her. Not even in her thoughts did she employ more than a minimum of memory. And when she did remember, it was in flat pictures, rigorously independent of one another: she saw her thin, poetic mother who grew thinner and more poetic in her canvas deck chair at Saranac reading *Lalla Rookh*. She saw herself in an inappropriate pink hat drinking iced tea in a garden so oppressive with the smell of phlox that the tea itself tasted of it. She recalled an afternoon in autumn in Vermont when she had heard three dogs' voices in the north woods and she could tell, by the characteristic minor key struck three times at intervals, like bells from several churches, that they had treed something: the eastern sky was pink and the trees on the horizon looked like some eccentric vascular system meticulously drawn on colored paper.

What Pansy thought of all the time was her own brain. Not only the brain as the seat of consciousness, but the physical organ itself which she envisaged, romantically, now as a jewel, now as a flower, now as a light in a glass, now as an envelope of rosy vellum containing other envelopes, one within the other, diminishing infinitely. It was always pink and always fragile, always deeply interior and invaluable. She believed that she had reached the innermost chamber of knowledge and that perhaps her knowledge was the same as the saint's achievement of pure love. It was only convention, she thought, that made one say "sacred heart" and not "sacred brain."

Often, but never articulately, the color pink troubled her and the picture of herself in the wrong hat hung steadfastly before her mind's eye. None of the other girls had worn hats, and since autumn had come early that year, they were dressed in green and rusty brown and dark yellow. Poor Pansy wore a white eyelet frock with a lacing of black ribbon around the square neck. When she came through the arch, overhung with bittersweet, and saw that they had not yet heard her, she almost turned back, but Mr. Oliver was there and she was in love with him. She was in love with him though he was ten years older than she and had never shown any interest in her beyond asking her once, quite fatuously but in an intimate voice, if the yodeling of the little boy who peddled clams did not make her wish to visit Switzerland. Actually, there was more to this question than met the eye, for some days later Pansy learned that Mr. Oliver, who was immensely rich, kept an apartment in Geneva. In the garden that day, he spoke to her only once. He said, "My dear, you look exactly like something out of Katherine Mansfield," and immediately turned and within her hearing asked Beatrice Sherburne to dine with him that night at the Country Club. Afterward, Pansy went down to the sea and threw the beautiful hat onto the full tide and saw it vanish in the wake of a trawler. Thereafter, when she heard the clam boy coming down the road, she locked the door and when the knocking had stopped and her mother called down from her chaise longue, "Who was it, dearie?" she replied, "A salesman."

It was only the fact that the hat had been pink that worried her. The rest of the memory was trivial, for she knew that she could never again love anything as ecstatically as she loved the spirit of Pansy Vanneman, enclosed within her head.

But her study was not without distraction, and she fought two adversaries: pain and Dr. Nicholas. Against Dr. Nicholas, she defended herself valorously and in fear; but pain, the pain, that is, that was independent of his instruments, she sometimes forced upon herself adventurously like a child scaring himself in a graveyard.

Dr. Nicholas greatly admired her crushed and splintered nose which he daily probed and peered at, exclaiming that he had never seen anything like it. His shapely hands ached for their knives; he was impatient with the skull-fracture man's cautious delay. He spoke of "our" nose and said "we" would be a new person when we could breathe again. His own nose was magnificent. Not even his own brilliant surgery could have improved upon it nor could a first-rate sculptor have duplicated its direct downward line which permitted only the least curvature inward toward the end; or the delicately rounded lateral declivities; or the thin-walled, perfectly matched nostrils.

Miss Vanneman did not doubt his humaneness or his talent—he was a celebrated man—but she questioned whether he had imagination. Immediately beyond the prongs of his speculum lay her treasure whose price he, no more than the nurses, could estimate. She believed he could not destroy it, but she feared that he might maim it: might leave a scratch on one of the brilliant facets of the jewel, bruise a petal of the flower, smudge the glass where the light burned, blot the envelopes, and that then she would die or would go mad. While she did not question that in either eventuality her brain would after a time redeem its original impeccability, she did not quite yet wish to enter upon either kind of eternity, for she was not certain that she could carry with her her knowledge as well as its receptacle.

Blunderer that he was, Dr. Nicholas was an honorable enemy, not like the demon, pain, which skulked in a thousand guises within her head, and which often she recklessly willed to attack her and then drove back in terror. After the route, sweat streamed from her face and soaked the neck of the coarse hospital shirt. To be sure, it came usually of its own accord, running like a wild fire through all the convolutions to fill with flame the small sockets and ravines and then, at last, to withdraw, leaving behind a throbbing and an echo. On these occasions, she was as helpless as a tree in a wind. But at the other times when, by closing her eyes and rolling up the eyeballs in such a way that she fancied she looked directly on the place where her brain was, the pain woke sluggishly and came toward her at a snail's pace. Then, bit by bit, it gained speed. Sometimes it faltered back, subsided altogether, and then it rushed like a tidal wave driven by a hurricane, lashing and roaring until she lifted her hands from the counterpane, crushed her broken teeth into her swollen lip, stared in panic at the soothing walls with her ruby eyes, stretched out her legs until she felt their bones must snap. Each cove, each narrow inlet, every living bay was flooded and the frail brain, a little hat-shaped boat, was washed from its mooring and set adrift. The skull was as vast as the world and the brain was as small as a seashell.

Then came calm weather and the safe journey home. She kept vigil for a while, though, and did not close her eyes, but gazing serenely at the trees, conceived of the pain as the guardian of her treasure who would not let her see it; that was why she was handled so savagely whenever she turned her eyes inward. Once this watch was interrupted: by chance she looked into the corridor and saw a shaggy mop slink past the door, followed by a senile porter. A pair of ancient eyes, as rheumy as an old dog's, stared uncritically in at her and a toothless mouth formed a brutish word. She was so surprised that she immediately closed her eyes to shut out the shape of the word and the pain dug up the unmapped regions of her head with mattocks, ludicrously huge. It was the familiar pain, but this time, even as she endured it, she observed with detachment that its effect upon her was less than that of its contents, the by-products, for example, of temporal confusion and the bizarre misapplication of the style of one sensation to another. At the moment, for example, although her brain reiterated to her that *it* was being assailed, she was stroking her right wrist with her left hand as though to assuage the ache, long since dispelled, of the sprain in the joint. Some minutes after she had opened her eyes and left off soothing her wrist, she lay rigid experiencing the sequel to the pain, an ideal terror. For, as before on several occasions, she was overwhelmed with the knowledge that the pain had been consummated in the vessel of her mind and for the moment the vessel was unbeautiful: she thought, quailing, of those plastic folds as palpable as the fingers of locked hands containing in their very cells, their fissures, their repulsive hemispheres, the mind, the soul, the inscrutable intelligence.

The porter, then, like the pink hat, and like her mother and the hounds' voices, loitered with her.

Dr. Nicholas came at nine o'clock to prepare her for the operation. With him came an entourage of white-frocked acolytes, and one of them wheeled in a wagon on which lay knives and scissors and pincers, cans of swabs and gauze. In the midst of these was a bowl of liquid whose rich purple color made it seem strange like the brew of an alchemist.

"All set?" the surgeon asked her, smiling. "A little nervous, what? I don't blame you. I've often said I'd rather break a leg than have a submucous resection." Pansy thought for a moment he was going to touch his nose. His approach to her was roundabout. He moved through the yellow light shed by the globe in the ceiling which gave his forehead a liquid gloss; he paused by the bureau and touched a blossom of the cyclamen; he looked out the window and said, to no one and to all, "I couldn't start my car this morning. Came in a cab." Then he came forward. As he came, he removed a speculum from the pocket of his short-sleeved coat and like a cat, inquiring of the nature of a surface with its paws, he put out his hand toward her and drew it back, gently murmuring, "You must not be afraid, my dear. There is no danger, you know. Do you think for a minute I would operate if there were?"

Dr. Nicholas, young, brilliant, and handsome, was an aristocrat, a husband, a father, a clubman, a Christian, a kind counselor, and a trustee of his preparatory school. Like many of the medical profession, even those whose specialty was centered on the organ of the basest sense, he interested himself in the psychology of his patients: in several instances, for example, he had found that severe attacks of sinusitis were coincident with emotional crises. Miss Vanneman more than ordinarily captured his fancy since her skull had been fractured and her behavior throughout had been so extraordinary that he felt he was observing at first hand some of the results of shock, that incommensurable element, which frequently were too subtle to see. There was, for example, the matter of her complete passivity during a lumbar puncture, reports of which were written down in her history and were enlarged upon for him by Dr. Rivers' interne who had been in charge. Except for a tremor in her throat and a deepening of pallor, there were no signs at all that she was aware of what was happening to her. She made no sound, did not close her eyes nor clench her fists. She had had several punctures; her only reaction had been to the very first one, the morning after she had been brought in. When the interne explained to her that he was going to drain off cerebrospinal fluid which was pressing against her brain, she exclaimed, "My God!" but it was not an exclamation of fear. The young man had been unable to name what it was he had heard in her voice; he could only say that it had not been fear as he had observed it in other patients.

Dr. Nicholas wondered about her. There was no way of guessing whether she had always had a nature of so tolerant and undemanding a complexion. It gave him a melancholy pleasure to think that before her accident she had been high-spirited and loquacious; he was moved to think that perhaps she had been a beauty and that when she had first seen her face in the looking glass she had lost all joy in herself. It was very difficult to tell what the face had been, for it was so bruised and swollen, so hacked-up and lopsided. The black stitches the length of the nose, across the saddle, across the cheekbone, showed that there would be unsightly scars. He had ventured once to give her the name of a plastic surgeon but she had only replied with a vague, refusing smile. He had hoisted a manly shoulder and said, "You're the doctor."

Much as he pondered, coming to no conclusions, about what went on inside that pitiable skull, he was, of course, far more interested in the nose, deranged so badly that it would require his topmost skill to restore its functions to it. He would be obliged not only to make a submucous resection, a simple run-of-the-mill operation, but to remove the vomer, always a delicate task but further complicated in this case by the proximity of the bone to the frontal fracture line which conceivably was not entirely closed. If it were not and he operated too soon and if a cold germ then found its way into the opening, his patient would be carried off by meningitis in the twinkling of an eye. He wondered if she knew in what potential danger she lay; he desired to assure her that he had brought his craft to its nearest perfection and that she had nothing to fear of him, but feeling that she was perhaps both ignorant and unimaginative and that such consolation would create a fear rather than dispel one, he held his tongue and came nearer to the bed.

Watching him, Pansy could already feel the prongs of his pliers opening her nostrils from the insertion of his fine probers. The pain he caused her with his instruments was of a different kind from that she felt unaided: it was a naked, clean, and vivid pain that made her faint and ill and made her wish to die. Once she had fainted as he ruthlessly explored and after she was brought around, he continued until he had finished his investigation. The memory of this outrage had afterwards several times made her cry.

This morning she looked at him and listened to him with hatred. Fixing her eyes upon the middle of his high, protuberant brows, she imagined the clutter behind it and she despised its obtuse imperfection. In his bland unawareness, this nobody, this nose-bigot, was about to play with fire and she wished him ill.

He said, "I can't blame you. No, I expect you're not looking forward to our little party. But you'll be glad to be able to breathe again."

He stationed his lieutenants. The interne stood opposite him on the left side of the bed. The surgical nurse wheeled the wagon within easy reach of his hands and stood beside it. Another nurse stood at the foot of the bed. A third drew the shades at the windows and attached a blinding light that shone down on the patient hotly, and then she left the room, softly closing the door. Pansy stared at the silver ribbon tied in a great bow round the green crepe paper of one of the flowerpots. It made her realize for the first time that one of the days she had lain here had been Christmas, but she had no time to consider this strange and thrilling fact, for Dr. Nicholas was genially explaining his anesthetic. He would soak packs of gauze in the purple fluid, a cocaine solution, and he would place them then in her nostrils, leaving them there for an hour. He warned her that the packing would be disagreeable (he did not say "painful") but that it would be well worth a few minutes of discomfort not to be in the least sick after the operation. He asked her if she were ready and when she nodded her head, he adjusted the mirror on his forehead and began.

At the first touch of his speculum, Pansy's fingers mechanically bent to the palms of her hands and she stiffened. He said, "A pack, Miss Kennedy," and Pansy closed her eyes. There was a rush of plunging pain as he drove the sodden gobbet of gauze high up into her nose and something bitter burned in her throat so that she retched. The doctor paused a moment and the surgical nurse wiped Pansy's mouth. He returned to her with another pack, pushing it with his bodkin doggedly until it lodged against the first. Stop! Stop! cried all her nerves, wailing along the surface of her skin. The coats that covered them were torn off and they shuddered like naked people screaming, Stop! Stop! But Dr. Nicholas did not hear. Time and again he came back with a fresh pack and did not pause at all until one nostril was finished. She opened her eyes and saw him wipe the sweat off his forehead and saw the dark interne bending over her, fascinated. Miss Kennedy bathed her temples in ice water and Dr. Nicholas said, "There. It won't be much longer. I'll tell them to send you some coffee, though I'm afraid you won't be able to taste it. Ever drink coffee with chicory in it? I have no use for it."

She snatched at his irrelevancy and, though she had never tasted chicory, she said severely, "I love it."

Dr. Nicholas chuckled. "De gustibus. Ready? A pack, Miss Kennedy."

The second nostril was harder to pack since the other side was now distended and this passage was anyhow much narrower, as narrow, he had once remarked, as that in the nose of an infant. In such pain as passed all language and even the farthest fetched analogies, she turned her eyes inward thinking that under the obscuring cloak of the surgeon's pain, she could see her brain without the knowledge of its keeper. But Dr. Nicholas and his aides would give her no peace. They surrounded her with their murmuring and their foot-shuffling and the rustling of their starched uniforms, and her eyelids continually flew back in embarrassment and mistrust. She was claimed entirely by this present, meaningless pain and suddenly and sharply, she forgot what she had meant to do. She was aware of nothing but her ascent to the summit of something; what it was she did not know, whether it was a tower or a peak or Jacob's ladder. Now she was an abstract word, now she was a theorem of geometry, now she was a kite flying, a top spinning, a prism flashing, a kaleidoscope turning.

But none of the others in the room could see inside and when the surgeon was finished, the nurse at the foot of the bed said, "Now you must take a look in the mirror. It's simply too comical." And they all laughed intimately like old, fast friends. She smiled politely and looked at her reflection: over the gruesomely fattened snout, her scarlet eyes stared in fixed reproach upon her upturned lips, gray with bruises. But even in its smile of betrayal, the mouth itself was puzzled: it reminded her that something had been left behind, but she could not recall what it was. She was hollowed out and was as dry as a white bone.

They strapped her ankles to the operating table and put leather nooses round her wrists. Over her head was a mirror with a thousand facets in which she saw a thousand travesties of her face. At her right side was the table, shrouded in white, where lay the glittering blades of the many knives, thrusting out fitful rays of light. All the cloth was frosty; everything was white or silver and as cold as snow. Dr. Nicholas, a tall snowman with silver eyes and silver fingernails, came into the room soundlessly for he walked on layers and layers of snow that deadened his footsteps; behind him came the interne, a smaller snowman, less impressively proportioned. At the foot of the table, a snow figure put her frozen hands upon Pansy's helpless feet. The doctor plucked the packs from the cold, numb nose. His laugh was like a cry on a bitter, still night: "I will show you now," he called across the expanse of snow, "that you can feel nothing." The pincers bit at nothing, snapped at the air and cracked a nerveless icicle. Pansy called back and heard her own voice echo: "I feel nothing."

Here the walls were gray, not tan. Suddenly the face of the nurse at the foot of the table broke apart and Pansy first thought it was in grief. But it was a smile and she said, "Did you enjoy your coffee?" Down the gray corridors of the maze, the words rippled, ran like mice, birds, broken beads: Did you enjoy your coffee? your coffee? your coffee? Similarly once in another room that also had gray walls, the same voice had said, "Shall I give her some whisky?" She was overcome with gratitude that this young woman (how pretty she was with her white hair and her white face and her china-blue eyes!) had been with her that first night and was with her now.

In the great stillness of the winter, the operation began. The knives carved snow. Pansy was happy. She had been given a hypnotic just before they came to fetch her and she would have gone to sleep had she not enjoyed so much this trickery of Dr. Nicholas' whom now she tenderly loved.

There was a clock in the operating room and from time to time she looked at it. An hour passed. The snowman's face was melting; drops of water hung from his fine nose, but his silver eyes were as bright as ever. Her love was returned, she knew; he loved her nose exactly as she loved his knives. She looked at her face in the domed mirror and saw how the blood had streaked her lily-white cheeks and had stained her shroud. She returned to the private song: Did you enjoy your coffee? your coffee?

At the half-hour, a murmur, anguine and slumbrous, came to her and only when she had repeated the words twice did they engrave their meaning upon her. Dr. Nicholas said, "Stand back now, nurse. I'm at this girl's brain and I don't want my elbow jogged." Instantly Pansy was alive. Her strapped ankles arched angrily; her wrists strained against their bracelets. She jerked her head and she felt the pain flare; she had made the knife slip.

"Be still!" cried the surgeon. "Be quiet, please!"

He had made her remember what it was she had lost when he had rammed his gauze into her nose; she bustled like a housewife to shut the door. She thought, I must hurry before the robbers come. It would be like the time Mother left the cellar door open and the robber came and took, of all things, the terrarium.

Dr. Nicholas was whispering to her. He said, in the voice of a lover, "If you can stand it five minutes more, I can perform the second operation now and you won't have to go through this again. What do you say?"

She did not reply. It took her several seconds to remember why it was her mother had set such store by the terrarium and then it came to her that the bishop's widow had brought her an herb from Palestine to put in it.

The interne said, "You don't want to have your nose packed again, do you?"

The surgical nurse said, "She's a good patient, isn't she, sir?"

"Never had a better," replied Dr. Nicholas. "But don't call me 'sir.' You must be a Canadian to call me 'sir.'"

The nurse at the foot of the bed said, "I'll order some more coffee for you."

"How about it, Miss Vanneman?" said the doctor. "Shall I go ahead?"

She debated. Once she had finally fled the hospital and fled Dr. Nicholas, nothing could compel her to come back. Still, she knew that the time would come when she could no longer live in seclusion, she must go into the world again and must be equipped to live in it; she banally acknowledged that she must be able to breathe. And finally, though the world to which she would return remained unreal, she gave the surgeon her permission.

He had now to penetrate regions that were not anesthetized and this he told her frankly, but he said that there was no danger at all. He apologized for the slip of the tongue he had made: in point of fact, he had not been near her brain, it was only a figure of speech. He began. The knives ground and carved and curried and scoured the wounds they made; the scissors clipped hard gristle and the scalpels chipped off bone. It was as if a tangle of tiny nerves were being cut dexterously, one by one; the pain writhed spirally and came to her who was a pink bird and sat on the top of a cone. The pain was a pyramid made of a diamond; it was an intense light; it was the hottest fire, the coldest chill, the highest peak, the fastest force, the furthest reach, the newest time. It possessed nothing of her but its one infinitesimal scene: beyond the screen as thin as gossamer, the brain trembled for its life, hearing the knives hunting like wolves outside, sniffing and snapping. Mercy! Mercy! cried the scalped nerves.

At last, miraculously, she turned her eyes inward tranquilly. Dr. Nicholas had said, "The worst is over. I am going to work on the floor of your nose," and at his signal she closed her eyes and this time and this time alone, she saw her brain lying in a shell-pink satin case. It was a pink pearl, no bigger than a needle's eye, but it was so beautiful and so pure that its smallness made no difference. Anyhow, as she watched, it grew. It grew larger and larger until it was an enormous bubble that contained the surgeon and the whole room within its rosy luster. In a long-ago summer, she had often been absorbed by the spectacle of flocks of yellow birds that visited a cedar tree and she remembered that everything that summer had been some shade of yellow. One year of childhood, her mother had frequently taken her to have tea with an aged schoolmistress upon whose mantelpiece there was a herd of ivory elephants; that had been the white year. There was a green spring when early in April she had seen a grass snake on a boulder, but the very summer that followed was violet, for vetch took her mother's garden. She saw a swatch of blue tulle lying in a raffia basket on the front porch of Uncle Marion's brown house. Never before had the world been pink, whatever else it had been. Or had it been, one other time? She could not be sure and she did not care. Of one thing she was certain: never had the world enclosed her before and never had the quiet been so smooth.

For only a moment the busybodies left her to her ecstasy and then, impatient and gossiping, they forced their way inside, slashed at her resisting trance with questions and congratulations, with statements of fact and jokes. "Later," she said to them dumbly. "Later on, perhaps. I am busy now." But their voices would not go away. They touched her, too, washing her face with cloths so cold they stung, stroking her wrists with firm, antiseptic fingers. The surgeon, squeezing her arm with avuncular pride, said, "Good girl," as if she were a bright dog that had retrieved a bone. Her silent mind abused him: "You are a thief," it said, "you are heartless and you should be put to death." But he was leaving, adjusting his coat with an air of vainglory, and the interne, abject with admiration, followed him from the operation room smiling like a silly boy.

Shortly after they took her back to her room, the weather changed, not for the better. Momentarily the sun emerged from its concealing murk, but in a few minutes the snow came with a wind that promised a blizzard. There was great pain, but since it could not serve her, she rejected it and she lay as if in a hammock in a pause of bitterness. She closed her eyes, shutting herself up within her treasureless head.

CHARLES EAST

For his 1996 short story, "Sky Watch," Charles East chose perhaps the only physical setting left unexplored in New Orleans literature. Instead of occupying the famed French Quarter, Gentilly, or the Irish Channel, the story's protagonist, Officer Scott McLaurin, takes to the sky in his Cessna, reporting the Interstate-10 morning traffic snarls for a local clear-channel radio station, where disc jockey Danny at Daybreak accepts calls from grounded New Orleanians. With its unusual setting, the story marked a change in the late-20th century South itself. McLaurin's bird's-eye view of the city shows it to be a close relation of the rest of the country rather than a strange, distant cousin. As a result, separateness—the condition so firmly established by Southern literature—gives way to homogenization.

Recalling his early influences, East described seeing the first Broadway production of Tennessee Williams' play, *The Glass Menagerie*. The experience for him was unparalleled, and, he said, "I left the theater in a daze." Later, as a student at LSU, he followed through on his early attraction to literature by founding the *Delta*, the English department's undergraduate literary journal that exists today. Classes with Professor John Hazard Wildman broadened his understanding of the short story by requiring that he read Eudora Welty, then a new voice on the literary scene, whose primary interests included regional separateness.

"Sky Watch" appeared in *Distant Friends and Intimate Strangers,* which was published thirty years after his debut collection, *Where the Music Was*, winner of the Henry H. Bellamann Award. As founder of The University of Georgia Press' prestigious Flannery O'Connor Award for Short Fiction, East, editor of the Press, energized the genre of the short story, encouraging writers of collections to vie for publication by the Press.

From 1970 to 1975 he was director of LSU Press, and in 1984 he was inducted into the LSU School of Journalism Hall of Fame. Well known locally as a successful literary figure, East lived in Baton Rouge with his wife, Sarah, until his death in 2009.

Sky Watch

Officer Scott McLaurin can't sleep. At a quarter to two he gets up and takes a leak, drinks a glass of water. Still he can't sleep and he knows he has to be up by six, a few minutes to six, ready to fly the Cessna, unless there's fog or a line of squalls, and this particular morning there isn't. At a little after two he turns on the light and punches in Gloria's number. He wakes her up, of course. "Hi, it's me," he says.

"Mmmm," she says. She's half asleep.

"What about," he says, "what about I come over?"

"Scotty," she says, "do you know what time it is?"

"Yeah," he says, "but I'm all tensed up. Can't get back to sleep."

"Well," she says. She doesn't sound too sure. "Yeah, I guess so."

Her apartment is in the next building. She's at the door in her robe to let him in, locks it behind him. "You know," she says, "this is crazy."

"I know," he says. "But I thought if I could just lie there by you. It's not like I'm trying to start nothing." He strips down to his shorts and gets in bed with her.

"You better set the alarm," she says. "Here . . . what time?"

He tells her six. "I'll skip the shower. Got to be flying by seven—ten to." He kisses her on the arm and tells her what a bitch of a life this is, up at that time of the morning to fly the Cessna. Off-duty job. He can't make out with what he gets from the department. "What you want to do tonight?"

She doesn't answer him.

"They got the Jayne Mansfield death car out on the parking lot at Lakeside. I thought we might go see it, then go to a movie. You awake?" he says. He moves over closer to her.

She can tell he's getting ideas. She pulls away. "Scotty . . . "

"How about," he says, "how about we make it a short one?"

But the words are scarcely out of his mouth when she can tell by his breathing that he's sleeping. She turns out the light. "Sleep tight, Scotty," she says, but he doesn't hear her.

He's on in the mornings from seven to nine and some afternoons from four to six, 950 on the dial, a clear-channel station. At that time of the day the drivers are on their way to their jobs in Metairie or Chalmette or the downtown business district, or headed home from their jobs, annoyed with the traffic ahead, glancing into the sky for a glimpse of the plane. They've never seen him, but they know his voice, and when he turns the Cessna down over the interstate and says there's an accident in the eastbound center lane of I-10 or a slowdown on the High Rise, there's something about it that makes them listen.

"Now," says Danny at Daybreak back at the station, "we're going to Sky Watch and Officer Scott McLaurin."

That's his cue. Officer Scott McLaurin always begins by saying, "All right." His voice tells you he's young, probably in his twenties. But he doesn't fool around the way some of the others before him have. None of that talk between them: "Thank you, Danny." None of that. He's his own man—very cool, very laconic. "All right," he says. "I'm looking down on I-10 West at the Causeway exit. At this time the traffic is moving okay. All westbound lanes are open as far up as Clearview." But there's a freight blocking Airline Highway, he says. He's come in over Airline. "Three of the cars have derailed. One of the tank cars looks like it's leaking gas of some kind. The police and the fire department are on the scene." He picks up the binoculars from the seat next to him.

Officer Scott McLaurin has been with the department six years and he feels like a veteran. A lot of the younger officers have come in since then—department expansion. But not the quality of six years ago, he thinks. They wouldn't have thought of letting some of these in then. Bunch of petty thieves and dopeheads. In another six years, he thinks, they'll be letting in rapists and murderers. Probably have some of those already, they just don't know it.

When he got this job doing traffic there were two of them. He'd pilot the plane, the officer next to him would give the report. First Jimmy Clayton. Then, after Jimmy got it for beating up on his wife, Joe Brocato. Or they'd turn it around. Joe would fly and he'd give the report. Joe would rather just do the flying. Now for the last three months he's been doing it on his own in the mornings and Joe in the afternoons, or the other way around—not exactly the best way, but the station likes it. Saves them money, he thinks. Fuck 'em.

He misses Jimmy Clayton. Joe too, but him and Jimmy got pretty close there. Jimmy Clayton got screwed royal. He should have been suspended with pay, but somebody up the line was gunning for him. Now he's working security at the mall. Bobbie has pulled out on him and taken the kids. Won't let him see the kids but every other weekend. He's one miserable human being.

But what's new about that? Officer Scott McLaurin thinks. He's not exactly happy himself. He still hasn't gotten over Jackie. He still hasn't gotten over what happened to his daddy. His daddy was on the force—had been. He was killed a year and a half ago in a shootout in the Quarter. His daddy was only in his fifties—a lot of years ahead of him. Used to take him and his sister and their mother over to the coast those summers. Being on the force like his daddy was all he ever wanted, even as far back as seventh grade. His daddy liked the idea, but his mother didn't. One policeman was enough, and after what happened she could say I told you so.

He wonders how it's going to come out with Gloria. He hopes not the same as it did with Jackie. God, he was so in love with Jackie, or thought he was. She gave him a hard time, running around with that guy who played for the Saints, then that hippie carpenter from across the river. Screw her, he thinks. Acting like she was doing him a favor. Maybe his luck will change. Maybe things will work out for him and Gloria.

He might even ask Gloria to marry him. She's got her divorce now, so she's free to. She isn't the kind of girl he'd have married if he had married back in high school, or right after high school, but this isn't high school. She's somebody to go with. She lets him decide what movies they see. Hell, she likes them all, he thinks. She's not hard to get along with. That may be the best thing about her—that and the fact that he likes her mother. Mabel could be so funny. You never knew what she was going to say, but it was usually a good one. Mabel thinks he's one of her boys—doesn't treat him a bit different. She'll even take his side against Gloria, which of course pisses Gloria. As much as you can piss Gloria. She's easygoing. She's always there. Well, he thinks, she's the kind you can go over there and get in bed with her at two o'clock in the morning. What am I doing, he thinks, making a list of all the reasons I ought to marry her?

He adjusts his headphones. Danny at Daybreak ought to be giving it back to him. Danny has a caller on the line who wants to talk about Jim Garrison and the Kennedy assassination—there's always one of those. Danny listens for a minute and then zaps him. To the south, toward the bridge, there's a dark cloud of smoke that looks like it might be coming from the river. On the bridge itself there's a line of traffic behind a jackknifed 18-wheeler.

"And now let's go up to Sky Watch and Officer Scott McLaurin," says Danny at the station.

"All right," says Officer Scott McLaurin. He says traffic is building on the Huey P. Long Bridge, there's been a three-car pileup there, but one of the eastbound lanes is open. Also, there's a barge on fire in the river. The Coast Guard is standing by. And oil is spilling out, at least it looks like oil, but he doesn't mention that for the moment. A school bus has sideswiped the bridge railing. He doesn't mention that either. Kids okay. Traffic moving around it. Then back to the station.

There's some guy on the phone who wants to talk about gun control. Says he's opposed to gun control, he believes in Second Amendment rights—they're going to have to take his gun away from him. Danny plays around with him. "Al . . ." —he identified himself as Al— "you sound like you're a member of the NRA. Are you a member of the NRA?"

"Damn right I am," the caller says, "and proud of it."

"Well, wouldn't you agree," says Danny, "that the wording of the Second Amendment refers to an organized militia? It's not the right of just anybody to bear arms, is it? What about antitank guns? What about laser-guided missiles?"

The man has hung up, or Danny has zapped him, but now there's another one on the line. It's a woman and she's mad as hell. She says, "What about Waco?"

Danny at Daybreak is so smooth. He's quick on the draw. He says, "What about Waco?"

"Well," she says, "the government killing all those children. Rushing the compound. Putting tanks in there. Using tear gas. Setting it afire. And that Janet Reno."

"I think," Danny at Daybreak says, "it's pretty well been determined that the fire was set from inside. Don't you think David Koresh had any responsibility? Nut. Child molester. Is that the kind of hero you want?"

And on and on they go, as Officer Scott McLaurin swings low over the Lakefront, over the Causeway, over Carrollton, over the bridge now and the river, over the lines of stalled cars and the patches of brown where the trees have died. The paper says they're magnolias. Says all over the city the magnolias are dying.

Now he's flying over Jackie's apartment complex, studying the parking spots out front through the binoculars—looking for the truck the carpenter drives. He's spotted it there a time or two in the mornings. Once he drove by there on his way to work and let some air out of the tires. But he doesn't see it now, and wonders whose cars those are next to Jackie's red Accord and whether one of them belongs to some new guy who's shacking up with her.

Now he's flying over the mall and the Jayne Mansfield death car and thinking of Gloria and what tonight will bring. He needs her to cheer him up; he needs her to brighten his spirits. Maybe, he thinks, because his thirtieth birthday is coming up a week from Wednesday. Another nine days and he'll be thirty. He doesn't know what he expected by thirty, but it wasn't this. Gloria will fix supper for him, or they'll go out—he'll take her out. They'll probably end up over at his sister's. But Ida has a new boyfriend he doesn't like—can't stand, in fact. He'd bet a dollar to a doughnut the guy was on something. He hoped *she* wasn't on something. His big sister. She used to sit him when he was little, though she wasn't that much older. Well, five years. What a life she'd had. First Tommy. Tommy was a loser. Then the guy from Metairie. Bill. She had to call the cops on him. Now this one. Randy. Unbroken string of deadbeats and dopeheads—shitheads. She'd borrowed two hundred dollars from him. He didn't want to give it to her because he knew where it would go, but he couldn't say no. She'd be hitting him up again, and what would he tell her then?

Oh, Officer Scott McLaurin thinks, it's the ones you love that can hassle you the most, give you the most trouble. Except Gloria. She's never given him any trouble, never asked very much of him, just that he come around, spend some time with her, help her through the divorce, take her to the movies. That shithead she was married to was lucky and didn't know it.

Danny at Daybreak has a lady caller from Chalmette on the line. She wonders why the stores are letting people use food stamps to buy cat food. She was at one of the stores and this young couple bought sixty-two dollars and something worth of cat food and paid for it with food stamps. "It's not I don't like cats," she says.

Danny says, "Maybe . . . do you suppose they ate the cat food?" He wonders aloud how it tastes and how many cats you'd have to have to buy sixty-two dollars worth of cat food.

The next caller is from Gentilly and she begins by asking Danny if he's gotten the birthday card she sent him. They send him birthday cards and try to call him, but he has an unlisted number—in fact, his name isn't Danny. She says she wants to talk about coddling criminals; she wants to know why they sentence somebody to life in prison and then let them out in eight years or less. "*Life* ought to be *life*," she says. "Hard labor. And no TV. And no coming on talk shows. That's why we got all this crime."

Danny asks her what about caning? He asks her if she'd be willing to pay more taxes to build more prisons. Yes, she says to both of his questions, and then she's off on the death penalty. Danny zaps her and goes to an old lady who's looking for her parakeet, and then to the lady just off Claiborne Avenue who says she's got a problem: there's a hole in her front yard, it's big enough to drop a car in. Her husband's tried to fill it with old tires and chunks of concrete, but it keeps getting bigger. Danny wants to know where off Claiborne. Just a second, she says—her husband is telling her something. She comes back to the phone and says she's got to get off now. "My husband says part of the street just fell in."

Officer Scott McLaurin can see the smoke from the plants and the field of junked cars that must run on for a half mile or more, and he passes over the cemeteries—blocks and blocks of them. All those whitewashed tombs, and more people dying all the time. A procession of three cars led by a hearse is turning into the gates of one of the cemeteries.

As he turns the plane toward the business district he sees a man standing on the roof of a building with a gun in his hand. He feels something grab him in the pit of his stomach. But then he sees that the gun is a pair of binoculars. When he looks again the man has them up to his eyes and is following the plane. He swings the Cessna over Claiborne Avenue and tries to spot the hole the woman was talking about. On the second pass he does. There's a crowd gathered around it and the police are blocking off both ends of the street. It really is a big one—something to do with a drop in the water table, he imagines. He's seen other holes like it, maybe not that big, and he's seen the concrete on the parking lots buckling.

But the morning is nothing compared to the late afternoon and early evening in the winter, dark coming, the lights of the city coming on—or not coming on. Lately there have been blackouts, whole sections dark from the lake to the river, transformers going. It's an eerie feeling. He wonders how near they are to the end of it: the city dark, the water gone, fires burning. He's never said anything to Gloria about it because he wouldn't want to worry her. Besides, she'd think this was getting to him, and maybe it was.

Now he's thinking more about Gloria—what to do about her. Whether to go on the way they're going or to take the leap, even if he's not sure he's ready for it. Or when he will be. But how long would Gloria be willing to wait? And who would there be after Gloria?

By the time he has brought the plane down and logged in and gotten into his Toyota, he knows what he wants to do. He's surprised at how sure he is and how good he feels about it. He can't wait to tell Gloria. In fact, he goes to the pay phone in the hangar and calls her. "Hi, it's me," he says.

"Scotty. What are you doing calling me at this time of the morning?" she says. "Something wrong? You didn't lose a wing or something, did you?"

"No," he says, "but I lost the engine over Metairie. The plane crashed and burned." He laughs. If she can do it, so can he.

"Well, why are you calling me?"

He takes a deep breath. The wind is blowing off the lake and it cuts through him. He's shivering. "How would you like to get married today?" he says.

"Oh," she says, "that would be great."

"You mean it?"

"I could ask you the same thing," she says.

"If I mean it? Sure do," he says. "But I'm standing out here in the wind. I'm leaving here now. See you in an hour."

"No, wait," she says. "You don't really mean today, do you?"

"Well, if I don't," he says, "I might change my mind."

"Scotty."

"Just joking," he says. "I'll call in sick. I got plenty of sick leave. But I'll have to be back on traffic report in the morning. That'll leave us a day and night. Where would you like to go on your honeymoon?"

She says, "You've got to be joking."

"What about Biloxi? It's not that long a drive to Biloxi."

"Well," she says, "whatever. What about the license? What about the preacher? What about my mother?"

He says, "I'm not worried about your mother. She'll be glad to get rid of you. Besides, I think Mabel actually likes me. I don't know why, but she does. Got to go now. I'll pick you up in an hour and we'll go down and get the license. You've done this before. What do you have to do? We wouldn't have to wait, would we? If we do, we'll get one in Biloxi."

Officer Scott McLaurin calls headquarters and tells them he's logged in but he won't be in the office the rest of the day, the afternoon traffic report is taken care of. Joe Brocato will be handling it. "Stomach virus," he says. "I'll be back on traffic in the morning."

Then he calls Jimmy Coleman, asks him what he's doing today. Jimmy says he won't be on security until tomorrow. It's his day off. "You lost your fucking mind?" he says. "No, just joking. I'll be there. Just let me know where and when."

He calls his sister. Randy answers and says Ida's asleep. She had trouble sleeping and she's gone back to bed. He tells Randy to have her call him.

He calls Gloria's mother. He says, "Mabel, I got some news for you."

She says, "I already know. Gloria's already called me. And I think it's just wonderful. I'm going to have me some grandchildren." Officer Scott McLaurin is on the phone and she can't see him, but he blushes. She says, "Tell me what I'm supposed to do. Is there anything I can do?"

He asks her if she knows any preachers.

Mabel says she does, she knows one, but she's not sure he's licensed. In fact, she says, she knows he's not. Better get one of the judges. It doesn't have to be a federal judge. "It could even be a JP. There's one on Veterans Boulevard. Of course," she says, "I'd rather it wasn't."

Scotty says he'll call her back, he's headed for his apartment now, going to jump in the shower and then head over to Gloria's and he'll call her back. "Be thinking."

Back at the apartment he checks the clock. He doesn't have much time. Gets in the shower. Goes through his drawer and starts laying things out on the bed: socks, underwear, pajamas. Puts the pajamas back, gets his shirt out of the closet. Two shirts—the one he's going to wear for the wedding and the one to wear back from Biloxi. He won't wear his uniform. He'll go off-duty.

He picks up Gloria and they go for the license. But they forget to bring their birth certificates, and there's a waiting period—seventy-two hours. No blood test though. "Lucky for me," Scotty says, "me with syph and all," and as soon as he's said it, he thinks how nerdy it sounds. There's no one with syph anymore, just AIDS and what have you. But he's not giving up. He says there's got to be a way around the waiting period.

When they're on their way back to her apartment, Gloria says, "You're sweeping me off my feet. You sure you don't want to take this a little slower?" And then she says, "What in the world got into you? What gave you the idea?"

"Oh," he says, "I've had the idea, and today just seemed as good a day as any."

When he gets back to his apartment he keeps the phone busy. Gloria's mother has had an idea. Why don't they call the mayor's office and see if the mayor won't marry them? "After all, you're a police officer and you work for the mayor, in a manner of speaking."

Between the calls he makes he gets a call from his sister Ida. Randy left her a note saying he called. Scotty tells her what he wants. He thought she'd be happy to hear the news. He thought she'd been worried about him, not marrying before now, whether he was queer or something—a queer police officer! —but she doesn't sound especially glad, or for that matter anything. Just takes it in stride, as if he told her he's going to buy a new car, except if he was getting a new car he was sure she'd sound more excited. But she's coming to the wedding—that's the point. They'll be there, she says, which tells him it'll be her and Randy. Well, you can't win 'em all, he thinks. He says he'll call her back and tell her when and where. In the meantime, stay free—if she's out when he calls, he'll leave a message.

Jimmy is the most help of all. Jimmy says he knows a judge in Kenner who'd perform the ceremony. At least he thinks he would. He doesn't know him well. Testified in a case in his court once. So he calls the judge and the judge says yes, he'll be glad to, and the license is his gift to the bride and groom—he'll call the clerk of court's office. If there's any problem about backdating it or anything, getting around the seventy-two hours, he'll arrange to take care of it. "In my district," the judge says with pride, "anything is possible."

As it turns out, they get married at the Kenner post office. The judge is headed out of town for a jambalaya cook-off and he's wearing an apron that says "Ask Me About My Crabs." He tells them he took second place last year. He pronounces them man and wife and kisses the bride and then runs across the parking lot in a shower to get to the cook-off. Refuses the twenty-dollar bill first Jimmy and then Mabel tries to give him.

The judge is nearly to his car before Scotty gives Gloria a little smack on the lips, and he has to do it over. "Go on and kiss her right," says Mabel. "And take off those dark glasses—you look like the Secret Service." So he kisses her right, and the wedding party is off in four cars to the reception. A bystander they picked up is riding with Ida.

Jimmy is there with his present girlfriend. Scotty's sister is there, and her boyfriend. And Mabel, of course. She's wearing a corsage as big as a funeral wreath and she has one for Gloria, a little smaller, thank heavens, and a rose to pin on his lapel, though he'd rather she didn't. But who's to argue with Mabel? She's marrying her only daughter to a man she likes as well as her own sons—better than her sons at the moment, because neither of them can make it. Not enough notice. "Not enough time my foot," says Mabel.

Scotty's mother didn't come, but she wasn't invited. He started to call her, and now he wishes he had, even if she couldn't have made it. She'd have liked being asked. But he didn't want her hassling him. There'd be time for that. Anyway, he thinks, she'll get over it.

There's a brief reception at the Happy Hour Bar and Grill, Scotty's sister and her boyfriend get in a fight, and before it's over Randy walks out on her. "What's he going to do," she says, "call a taxi?" Before Ida leaves she asks Scotty if she can borrow fifty dollars until Friday. He of course lets her have it.

Mabel drinks too much and she wants to go with them. Gloria says, "Mama!" but Scotty says, "Aw, Gloria, it's just for the night. Let her." So they get in Scotty's car— Scotty and Gloria in front, Mabel in back. Ida has brought a bag of Mahatma rice and she's throwing it. Jimmy slips him a box of condoms with a label that says, "One every hour as needed." He wonders what Joe Brocato and the other officers in the department will give him. Probably a rubber dong or a gift certificate to the Magic Fingers Massage Parlor on Veterans, gross bastards.

Mabel is getting her nightgown and toothbrush out of Jimmy's car—he'd brought her. Jimmy's girlfriend is crying. So is the bystander, and they don't even know her. Then they pull out of the Happy Hour and up onto the interstate and head for Biloxi. Scotty feels the same sense of adventure he used to feel when he was a boy and they pulled away from the house bound for the coast, his daddy at the wheel, the saltwater air blowing in the windows. He slips his sunglasses on. He feels for the badge in his pocket. You never know when you might need it. Thinks just for a moment of Jackie. What did a carpenter have that he didn't, besides dirty long hair and nails in his pockets? Gloria is picking the rice out of her hair. She's asking her mother what she thought of the wedding.

"Well, it kind of took my breath away," Mabel says. "Though I do wish the judge had taken off that apron."

The honeymoon in Biloxi is everything Officer Scott McLaurin had expected. The three of them have a nice dinner at one of the gambling casinos. Scotty wins eighty bucks on the slots. Mabel loses the twenty-five she set aside to play, then another ten, but says she had a helluva fun evening.

Scotty and Gloria bed down for their honeymoon night in a room with a view of the back bay. The rooms on the Gulf side are taken. Mabel is in the adjoining room, but she keeps the television as high as she can so she won't hear them. Gloria has set the alarm and they're up at four-thirty and headed back—Scotty has to be in the air by seven. On the way they pass the Jayne Mansfield death car—it's up on a truck being carried to another location. Gloria says, "You know it took the top of her head off."

Scotty steers the car due west into the morning, the casinos and the honeymoon behind him. He's thinking how lucky he is, Gloria there beside him, a married man—he'll have to get used to that—Mabel on the back seat giving him directions. He likes Mabel. He wonders if he married Gloria because of Mabel. If he had had a chance at Mabel when she was younger, he thinks, he'd have jumped at it. Of course, he would have been a boy then. The way life is, he thinks. You get what it hands you. Maybe being thirty wasn't all that bad. Maybe his luck has changed. He won eighty bucks on the slots, didn't he? He's got Gloria here on the seat next to him. He's happy. That's what he hopes for them—not to stay thirty, because they won't, or to never have any troubles, because they will, but just to be happy.

For a moment he remembers what he'd seen from the Cessna, what he'll see again today: the snarl of traffic, the smoke from the plants, the slick of oil on the river, the patches of brown, the hole that swallowed the yard and a chunk of the street off Claiborne. And this evening, though he won't be up there to see it, Joe will: the blackouts, the transformers going, arcing, the lights coming back on in Metairie and the darkness sweeping across Carrollton and the business district.

But maybe it's not as bad as he thinks it is, maybe they'll get the power up, maybe the city really isn't sinking, maybe the trees will be coming out with the first touch of spring. He turns his eyes from the road and looks at Gloria. She's almost asleep, dreaming happily. Maybe, he thinks, they'll give Mabel grandchildren.

On the back seat Mabel puts on her lipstick for the day and says, "I don't believe I've ever seen a sweeter wedding."

DAVID MADDEN

Of the first day of class with David Madden—the auditorium full, the lectern unmanned—LSU students recall their restlessness and speculation about their absent professor; until suddenly a disembodied voice filled the air, and Madden himself intoned over his microphone, "When the student is prepared, your teacher will appear." The academic purpose behind this grand entrance was to give students a dramatic experience of literature, to encourage them to view it as living and breathing from the first day of class.

Madden came to LSU in 1968 partly because of his association with Robert Penn Warren, one of his literary heroes, who had nominated him for a Rockefeller Foundation grant. To the news from Thomas Kirby, then chair of the English department, that Madden had been invited to join the faculty, Warren responded with high praise. Coinciding with that professional move, Madden was chosen for a Rockefeller grant by both Warren and Saul Bellow—a grand entrance to LSU itself. Years later, Madden edited *The Legacy of Robert Penn Warren*, a collection of essays about Warren's influence on literature and culture in America. Apropos of his lifelong interest in Warren, Madden was named Robert Penn Warren Professor at LSU. Madden's positions as professor, literary agent, and lecturer were as significant for LSU before he retired in 2009 as were his roles as fiction writer, literary critic, and playwright. While tirelessly promoting the creative writing program, which he founded, he published two collections of short stories and eight novels, two of which received Pulitzer Prize nominations. Research for the novel, *Sharpshooter: A Novel of the Civil War*, inspired Madden to create and direct the United States Civil War Center at LSU. His most recent novel, *Abducted by Circumstance*, is described by his former LSU student, the fiction writer Allen Wier, as "a thrilling crime story . . . a dark and complex psychological study. . . ."

Madden's experience as an imaginative, unconventional teacher is evident in the story "A Part in Pirandello." The main character, a star college basketball player, plagiarizes an English paper, is caught, and learns a lesson in ethics as well as self-awareness from his professor.

DAVID MADDEN

A Part in Pirandello

"Well, Mr. Cameron, as of now," said Mr. McMillan, letting the research paper slip from his hand, flop on the desk, "you've earned a D-minus in the course."

As Brent stared at "Extinct Volcanoes in the Orient" A-plus, his stomach felt as it did the time he rose against the wobbling of the vaulting pole and crashed his head backward against the cross-bar. Brent saw McMillan flinch at the expression on Brent's face.

"But, sir, that's what I had *before*. I thought this paper . . ."

"I *know* you did." The office was so cramped their knees almost touched. "Compared with your earlier themes, this research paper shows a remarkable improvement in your ability to think, to organize your thoughts, and to express them." Looking narrow-eyed and quizzically into Brent's eyes, McMillan waited for him to respond.

Brent shrugged, closed his eyes. McMillan was a good teacher, a good man, but as he had said the first day of class, "When it comes to cheating, I'm a bastard." Brent *wanted* him to be a bastard, so he could confess, rid himself of the stranger in him who had turned to Kester for help. The doubts about Kester that had worried Brent even back in their early high school days in Ironton made this unconfessed crime twice repugnant. He wished he could vomit.

When he opened his eyes, he would confess and be free of what nagged him about Kester, too. They would kick him out of Melbourne, but kick him out clean, not secretly covered with slime. He never minded fumbling passes, placing third, missing baskets in *public*, because it was in public that he was always striving to make touchdowns, break finish tapes, make baskets, and sometimes did. But private, secret thorns festered.

Licking his lips, Brent opened his eyes. "Sir—"

"Mis—" McMillan stuck up a finger to stop him, "—ter Cameron, I *know* what this means to you. Loss of the sports scholarship, which means, for a young man from a steel town, being dropped from school—and into Vietnam. Going to be a dentist, weren't you?"

"Well, sir," said Brent, untangling his twisted fingers and spreading his hands apart, "the way things look *now* . . ."

"Something just occurred to me. You hear about the play I'm directing?"

"No, sir."

"Oh." A flicker of contempt. "Well, it's by Pirandello, *It Is So (If You Think So)*, sometimes translated *Right You Are, If You Think You Are*. Mysterious. Not a mystery—*psychologically* mysterious. Now, I've got some town ladies coming in to do the older women's parts, but I don't have a tall, beautiful girl to do Signora Ponza, wife of the new secretary of the provincial council. . . . She doesn't appear until the climax of the play, for about three minutes, and she's wearing a black veil over her face until her last line: 'No! I am she whom you believe me to be.' Now, you could memorize a few brief speeches like that, couldn't you?"

"Sir, I don't see . . ."

"Simple. I would feel justified in giving you credit in this course for work done in the play."

"You want me—to—dress up?"

"Crude way to put it, Mr. Cameron. This is not a fraternity romp. This is a serious, witty, play. One of my favorites, in fact. You would impersonate a young woman as convincingly as possible."

"*I* can't act, sir."

McMillan looked into his eyes. Brent tried not to blink. "Mr. Cameron, you are acting right at this moment."

"Sir—"

"Don't push it."

Brent *wanted* to push it—out. Out into the open. Be done with it. I'm guilty—on with the punishment. Though McMillan's reputation as a bastard about cheating had been justified in every instance, he treated each case individually and always put the culprit through the kind of hell he brought on himself. The student who tried to bluff all the way went out on his ear. If he confessed, he failed the course instantly, but was often persuaded to venture upon creative, sometimes profound alternatives for atoning with himself for his crime. Some of these students achieved great things during their chosen method of atonement, and ended up loving McMillan. Brent felt his own spirit go out to such possibilities. But *this* proposal did not at all resemble the kind of intricate moral situations Brent had heard tales of.

"You're worried about the other boys, right? Well, don't. I'll announce that a mystery woman, an old actress friend of mine, is coming to play the part."

"But, sir, the guys'll find out somehow."

Brent saw in his eyes that McMillan was still a step ahead of him. Brent wished he could get on his feet, move around. On a basketball court instead of this tiny closed room where they consciously had to avoid each other's knees, his mind might outmaneuver McMillan's.

"We'll have closed rehearsals, about midnight, just for your part. *I* don't want anybody to know. So together we'll keep this concealed until the moment you step out onto that stage."

"—and fall flat on my face."

"*I'll* be damned. Look, I haven't watched you on the basketball court, but I see you in the halls and on campus, walking. You don't even *sit* like the others. There's a *something* that I *know* I can get in shape, and it'll knock them out of their seats. You know, in the Greek theater, boys always played the female roles. Your great, athletic Greeks. Some young hero at Marathon or Thermopylae could have played Electra the spring before in Athens. Use your imagination, Cameron. Move a while in another dimension of yourself. . . . As you seem to have done in the style of this research paper."

"They'll recognize my face."

"Makeup is a mask. And it won't be *you* behind the mask."

"You make it sound so easy."

"Then you're not listening to what I *don't* say. Learning to walk like a lady will be very difficult. But when you go on that stage, you'll be Signora Ponza."

"And there's no *girl* who's right for the part?"

"I've beaten the bushes from one end of the county to the other. I was just about to switch to another play, when, suddenly, there *you* were, with your extinct volcanoes, your D-minus, and your dilemma."

Coach MacFarland patted his buttocks as he passed, and Brent felt light as a crane, listening to the ball he had hookshot into the basket bounce behind him as he ran out to receive again.

"What are *you* doing here?"

Kester stood between the collapsible bleachers back under the exit sign, holding his books against his chest, watching.

"Just wondering how you made out, Old Sport."

"McMillan gave me A-plus on the damned paper."

"Watch it!"

The blow against the side of his head made Brent go black a moment, then he chased the bouncing ball, blinking into clear vision as it rolled back toward him from the wall by the water fountain.

Brent had never entered Memorial Theatre through the *front* door, much less the back. He had missed, with little regret, two plays, one of them a required Shakespeare. Five minutes early, keeping in the shadows of the shrubs and trees close to the wall, Brent circled the building, unable to discover even a faint night light. No moon, no stars, pitch black, the bite of November in the air.

The stage door slipped open so easily he almost flung it into his own face. A light on an iron stanchion lit the stage. Used to a gleaming court, a well-lighted hive of faces, colorfully clothed bodies suddenly jumping to their feet, Brent stepped into the glare, feeling black-purple velvet hanging around him. He squinted at the darkness beyond the stage, suddenly imagining the audience that, two weeks from Friday, would fill the theater.

"Jesus, Mr. Cameron, you scared the hell out of me!"

"Sorry, sir, I just thought I'd better slip in."

"I'm over *here*. By the exit light."

"What do I do now, sir?"

"Take off your windbreaker."

Though it seemed he had spent most of his life undressing in front of men, Brent felt as if he were stripping nude before the whole school. Affecting nonchalance, he let the jacket dangle by his thumb over his shoulder.

"Now, walk upstage." Brent walked up to the dark footlights. "I'm sorry. *Up*stage means toward the rear." Brent's tennis shoes bumped together, squeaked, as he turned. "And spread the curtains a little to improvise an entrance." Smothery darkness between the velvet curtain and the wall he sensed but could not see. Heavy velvet muffled McMillan's voice: "Now, step out and walk very slowly, but in your natural gait, toward the footlights, *down*stage." Trying to imitate a girl, Brent waddled to the center of the stage before McMillan stopped him. "Mr. Cameron, toss the jacket aside. Now, listen, carefully. Walk *naturally*." Brent remembered that McMillan had said "your natural gait." "We've got plenty of time."

"Sorry, sir." Brent went behind the curtains again.

"I had the boys strip the stage. I want us to start from nothing and gradually work up to Signora Ponza's entrance opening night."

"Mac, does he have to be here?"

"Who?"

"Kester Dunlap."

Coach MacFarland looked around and stopped to get Kester, perched on the top bench of the collapsible bleachers, in focus. "Didn't even *see* him."

"You look around and suddenly he's there. Gives me the creeps."

"Well, you boys could do with an audience, couldn't you? Pre-game cheering section?"

"Practice ought to be closed to outsiders."

"Well, it ain't, Brent, so show him what you can do."

Brent made three baskets in a row, and on his way to the showers, some of the guys gave him a pat and his roommate gave him a quick hug as he passed.

※

"Again."

Anger almost suffocating him, Brent stood behind the dusty velvet curtain, waiting for McMillan to cue him.

"*You must not irritate him. You must leave him alone. Oh, Please!*' . . . We're waiting, Mr. Cameron."

Brent walked out. Even with the rehearsal chairs, the stage felt empty, as though he slogged through a field of sludge.

Out there in the dark, McMillan beat on the back of a seat with a pencil. Brent wished he could see the man. He was never where the sound seemed to come from. Maybe it was part of his directing technique, like some of the tricks MacFarland used. The last tap of the pencil was like a pistol shot at the end of a quarter.

"Mr. Cameron."

"Sir?"

"I can't help but wonder whether you're trying to convince me that you're all wrong for this part."

"I'm trying to do what you tell me to, sir."

"Yes, Mr. Cameron, you *are* doing what I tell you to. But that's *all* you're doing."

"I don't know what else to *do.*"

"Have you read the play yet?"

"No, sir, I had to study for a psych test."

"Read it. This weekend. Think about it. And I'll see you Monday."

Brent slept through most of the weekend. He would master himself enough to open the book, then fall asleep after every five pages. During long lapses into stupor, he stared at the black, purple, green, and white cover: *Naked Masks/ Five Plays/ By Luigi Pirandello.*

Brent wished his roommate had not gone away to visit his girl. With his roommate's Hendrix record going, Brent would have had an excuse for not concentrating. No parties at Melbourne that weekend either. No games. Only Pirandello and assignments in four courses, including McMillan's English class. An interpretation of "The Force That Through the Green Fuse Drives the Flower"—whatever the hell that meant. Dylan Thomas' phrases made Brent's head feel as though his body were adrift in a tiny boat.

He wrote to his mother, but didn't feel at all like writing to his father.

So far Brent had only practiced walking, hardly listening to McMillan reel off the lines. At three AM, Monday morning, he finally read up to the scene he had dreaded: "*Signora Ponza* (turning her veiled head with a certain austere solemnity toward her husband): Don't be afraid!" Suddenly, the fact that he would have to speak like a woman struck him. The sound of his voice as he tried to speak her next speech nauseated him: "*Signora Ponza* (having looked at them through her veil, speaking with dark solemnity): What else do you want of me, after this, ladies and gentlemen? There is a misfortune here, as you see, which must stay hidden; otherwise the remedy which our compassion has found cannot avail." But as he read the rest of her six brief speeches, Brent felt more composed.

"You have to admit," he said, to his face in the mirror over the washroom sink, "it's kinda interesting."

At breakfast, he sat with the boys on the team, laughing so hard at their dirty jokes that he cried, almost hysterically. Seeing the tears, they pointed at him and pretended to jeer as he wiped them away. A hive of nerves, knowing he must sit still and collect himself, he let the boys drift off in groups, until he was alone at the messy table.

"I got an A in Seventeenth Century."

Brent's flesh jumped. He turned toward the table behind, and Kester's face, twisted around on the stalk of his neck, was only a foot away.

"Great." Kester had tested out of freshman English.

"You'd probably get an A, too, if you were in there with *me*."

"I'd regret it, too."

"Don't *be* that way, Brent, hell, we're from the same home town."

"That's an accident."

"True, we didn't choose to be born in Ironton, but that we went to kindergarten, grammar school, junior high, high school, and now to one of the best men's colleges in the country together can't be ruled out as superfluous."

"Stop pretending you like sports so much! And stop coming to rehearsals like that."

"Rehearsals?"

"I mean practice—basketball."

"Moral support, Old Sport. You didn't make those three baskets in a row like that till I waved to you."

McMillan seemed so pleased when he thought up the idea of having Brent wear basketball shorts and go barefoot that Brent hadn't the heart to tell him how *he* felt about it. Walking out onto the stage barefoot, in shorts, was a shock. But McMillan knew what he was doing.

Even "out in life," McMillan had a reputation for doing everything in a slightly theatrical manner, though most of the time you didn't even *know* it until you had *enjoyed* it. But *nobody* could enjoy *this*. Still, Brent had to admit that the idea of starting from nothing, from scratch, made sense.

"'No, no, madam, for yourself you must be either one or the other!'"

"'*No! I am she whom you believe me to be.*'" Through an imaginary thick black veil, Brent looked at all the imaginary people.

"'*Laudisi*: And there, my friends, you have the truth! Are you satisfied?'" McMillan enacted Laudisi's derisive laugh. "Curtain! It's getting better, Mr. Cameron. Once more."

Brent did a smart about-face and started upstage. The door frame made it seem more real. He was eager to do it with walls on each side.

He wouldn't be surprised if McMillan asked him to come out next wearing only his jock.

"I was talking to some townie in this bar—says Stella screws anything that moves. Legend in her own times." Naked, Brent's roommate rattled his locker door.

Brent laughed so hard he cried, and his teammates laughed at him, and the laughter and gentle shoving eased him like watching rainbow trout in a mountain stream.

"How 'bout *you*, Brent? You like to take a turn?"

"Sure. Love to."

"Ever love it *before*?"

"Sure."

"Ah, come on, Brent. Admit it. You're a virgin, right?"

"Well . . ."

"Wasn't you the big football hero at Ironton?"

"Well . . ."

"Sure, he was. My old man used to take the Ironton *Courier*, and we kept track of him."

"Well, there was plenty of girls, you know, but I only had *one*."

"*Had* her?"

"No, I mean *sweet*heart."

"How come she never comes up?"

"She's still in high school."

"Robbin' the cradle, Brent?"

"Well . . ."

"How 'bout Stella? You can *have* some, if you crave it."

"Sure, I'll go along."

"Hell. Even ol' McMillan knocks it off."

"Who says?"

"This townie I was talking to. Stella loves to brag. You know, big English professor."

"Talks like a queer in class." The imitation of a "queer" was perfect.

"He don't talk like a queer, man."

"You're not even in McMillan's class, man!"

"All that poetry!"

"Jesus! The man's a stud. Used to make it with his students at that university. Kicked him out for it."

"Look, don't jump on *me*."

"*Jump* on you? I'll stomp hell out of you. McMillan's cool."

"You ever see him at sports events?"

"I don't *look* for him. I'm playing *ball*, man."

"This guy said Stella told him McMillan begged her to be in this play he's getting up."

"Hey, wouldn't *that* be groovy!" He popped a locker door with his towel. "All us guys out there that's cut her. What an uprising!"

Voices from both sides of the row of lockers volleyed toward Brent.

"Why did she back out?" Brent's face was burning.

"See, this townie's a special friend of hers, don't even make it with her, and she told him she wanted to keep it a secret from *each* of us that she's going with *all* of us. And mainly, she's afraid if we all sit out there and see her, we'll start cheering and stomping, and mainly McMillan'll find out he ain't the only one. Says McMillan's got this purity complex about women, and he's convinced himself Stella's clean."

"What a mind that girl's got. And dropped out in the tenth!"

"Hey, guys, let's make Brent laugh till he cries. I love to watch him."

Brent walked toward the footlights, aware that the stage, midnight, the dark, the presence in the auditorium affected his own walk even before rehearsal began. "Sir?" he said to the dark.

"Good evening, Mr. Cameron." McMillan sounded very tired. "Tonight, I want you to come out nude."

"Sir . . ."

"Yes?" He sounded like a doctor telling Brent to cough. Brent gave up, feeling that to *talk* about it would only make it worse. Because he knew he would *do* it.

Undressing behind the curtain, dropping his clothes over a music stand, it occurred to him that if Stella had not refused the part, he wouldn't *be* here. He had avoided meeting her, going to bed with her, and the boys hadn't pushed it, as though they respected his virginity, realized it was reserved for the "right girl," and he was grateful.

"Mr. Cameron."

"Yes, sir."

"Do you think you can find your way in the dark?"

"I think so."

"Then I'm going to turn out the work light, and I want you, at your *own* speed and in your own mood, while trying to retain the *feeling* of Signora Ponza, to make your entrance, do the movements I've blocked, and deliver your lines in total darkness. Do you know *why* I'm doing this?"

Without stopping to think, Brent said, "Yes, sir, I understand."

After rehearsal, Brent slipped into the dark gym and groped among the basketballs and went out onto the court and dribbled from one end to the other. He aimed at a gleam of light on the rim of a basket. The sound of the ball bouncing off the board sickened him. It rolled under the bleachers, and he had to crawl in the dark.

Gradually he stripped off all his clothes, even his tennis shoes. And after a long while, drenched with sweat in the cold building where the heat had been turned off for the night, he began to make baskets.

The shoosh through the net lifted his pulse and he floated in the dark, imagining himself as Mercury, then feeling like Mercury, and for an instant, as he tossed the last ball, he *was* Mercury.

Late Thursday afternoon, Brent happened to pass through Herald Hall, short-cutting through the quadrangle, late for basketball practice, when he saw Kester sitting in McMillan's office, his books perched on his touching knees, McMillan sitting sideways rared back in his swivel chair, his feet propped up on his desk, an awkward posture of avoidance. Seeing Brent stride past, Kester flicked his hand up, and McMillan turned his head toward the door. But Brent missed his expression.

Brent ran through crisp leaves that lay thick under the close-standing maples, stirring up waves of sound that carried him to the gym door where sunlight glared on the panes.

Kester didn't come to watch practice. When Brent realized that he had made no baskets, he tried harder, then very hard.

Above the roar of the ten showers, somebody down by the door yelled: "What was the matter with you today, Brent?"

"Oh, I was just thinking of Stella."

They all laughed, jumping up and down, feet splashing, bodies glistening.

That night, Brent stripped before he even presented himself on stage. Not until he walked through the wide parlor entrance into the full glare of footlights—turned on for the first time, revealing ornate, heavy Victorian furniture and mock mirrors and Rococo clocks—did he imagine the surprise McMillan would feel at suddenly seeing him there, naked on stage.

"Sir?"

High heeled silver slippers set side by side, glittering in the footlights.

"Sir?"

He had come to feel McMillan's presence out there in the darkness as vividly as when their knees almost touched during conferences in his office. McMillan was not out there. The silence told Brent what was expected of him.

He bent over, picked up the shoes. Then he put them back, stood straight. He knelt, as a young lady would, to pick them up again, then went back through the door, closed it, and stepped into the slippers in the dark, wondering whether McMillan was only pretending not to be out there.

❧

"Wasn't Brent great tonight?" asked Kester, coming up to McMillan and three other students at the Deke victory party. Brent overheard, standing with another group by the window.

"I didn't see the game. I detest sports. Except for the solitary ones—running, pole vaulting, the man against himself, triumphing over himself."

"Well, sir, you don't know what you're missing. Brent finally broke through tonight. Everybody at home always felt he was holding back. Something's brought it out."

"Excuse me," McMillan said to the three students, "I must circulate, like a good chaperon."

"He's a bastard."

"Watch your mouth, Kester," said Brent, coming over to him, as the three students ambled away.

"What cause have *you* to stick up for him, Old Sport?"

"You always drink more than you can hold, Kester."

"Something bothering me, Old Sport."

Brent didn't want to know *what*.

"Don't you walk away from me. We used to play together when we were little."

"Nobody wants to hurt your feelings, Kester." Brent hoped that pacified him.

"Think nothing of it." Kester looked up at the ceiling. "I love it, obviously."

By the phonograph, shuffling through the records, aware that his roommate's girl was staring soulfully at him, Brent glanced over at Kester. He was still staring up at the ceiling. Brent looked up.

Brent swung his body among the desks from the back row toward the classroom door, watching the last student go out.

McMillan, gathering his usual load of books, looked up. "Want to see me?"

"Kester Dunlap . . ."

"Oh, God."

"We better watch out for him."

"We'd better what?"

"He's sneaky."

"Yes, I know he's sneaky."

"He was the one helped me write that—"

"That's past. And your work is improving, by the way."

"I'm failing Psych 7."

"I ought to kick your tail, Mr. Cameron."

"I'm sorry, sir, I try. But I've got basketball and—no, forget that, sir. I don't want to whine."

"Good. Now, what about Kester Dunlap *other*wise?"

"I don't know, sir. I was just saying we got to watch him."
Frowning, McMillan looked so straight into his eyes that Brent blinked.

"Dress rehearsal tomorrow night, Mr. Cameron."
"With the others, sir?"
"No. They won't see you until you make your entrance opening night. I want to give *them* the same impact I give the audience, even at the risk of throwing them."
"Makeup tomorrow night?"
"Yes, and full costume. You're handling the costume very well."
"You going to help me put the makeup on? I don't know the first thing about it."
"Try it yourself first. Then we'll see. Work at it until you make yourself look like what you know the boys will want to see in a beautiful face. Pirandello doesn't let her lift the veil, but just for that last line, '*No! I am she whom you believe me to be,*' I want them to see her face for a moment."
"Will I be able to see them when I lift the veil?"
"Can you see *me*?"
"No, sir."

"Cameron."
"Yes, sir?"
Usually, McMillan gave commands like Major Scott in ROTC, but sometimes he spoke softly, as he did about poetry in class, and Brent had to strain to hear him out there in that theatrical darkness.
"How do you feel?"
"Fine."
"Awkward?"
"No, sir."
"Embarrassed?"
"No, sir."
"Exactly how *did* you feel a moment ago?"
"I can't say."
"Yes, you can."
"Like I was Stella."
"Who?"
"Signora Ponza!" Quickly, to cover, he asked, "Well, sir, how did it look to *you*?"
"Perfect."

MacFarland gave Brent a harder slap than usual. "Murder 'em, kid!"
The curtain was going up. After the game, he would just have time to dash to the theater for the climax.

By half time, Brent had done nothing but stumble.

"Brent?"

"Yes, sir."

"What happened to the grace?"

"The what?"

"The grace you used to have? One thing you always had out there worth watching was grace. Only word for it. Decoration, maybe. Least you could decorate the play with grace, even when you didn't make it on the baskets. Now, I can't even *look* at you."

When Brent went back onto the gleaming court, he tried to move with grace. Bumped off balance once, he landed square. His feet cocked up, he slid four feet and slammed into the wall by the water fountain.

MacFarland didn't put his head in his hands this time. He just stared at Brent, mouth open.

At the end of the game, Brent saw Kester leave with the crowd, and his heart was light, knowing that Kester wouldn't be in the audience when he walked out onto the stage fifteen minutes from now.

The shock of cold water was greater than Brent had ever felt. He worked the water up to as hot as he could stand it, enveloping himself in steam, standing in the middle of the shower room, his eyes closed. He wished the end nozzle in the corner were not in use. The shouts of victorious players in the other dressing room penetrated the cinder block walls. Brent's teammates were silent, each feeling responsible, but he sensed that they blamed him most. Though he was seldom great, he had never been bad. Never, as MacFarland put it, graceless.

With one of the keys McMillan had secured for him, Brent entered the theater through the boiler room door. In a corner, under the air ducts, sat a dressing table, lit up, and from a steam pipe hung the black dress, the hat, the veil. The slippers—black ones, not the silver rehearsal shoes—were on the table beside the makeup.

The secrecy of the setup aggravated his nervousness. But he was not too nervous to observe—as he rose and stepped backward toward the hum of the furnace to look at himself—that the face in the mirror was, indeed, as McMillan had said, "perfect." Perhaps the word was *beautiful*.

He let fall the veil and inserted the brass key. *The door to the regular dressing room also will be locked. Only you can open it.* He opened the door, stepped into the deserted dressing room, and crossed it, shivering. But as he climbed the stairs, he realized that what he was feeling was not nervousness—it was thrill.

People were working backstage. *Don't let them throw you. It will at first, maybe, because you aren't used to seeing them there, but you must stay absolutely in character.* They turned in the faint light to stare, trying to play it cool. But Brent knew that the suspense and mystery made them aware of the beating of their own hearts as he was aware of his own. Will she reveal herself at the curtain call? they are wondering.

When you exit, go straight back the way you came—don't run—stay in character, even in front of the backstage crew, as you leave. Lock the doors behind you. Brent stood behind the masking, waiting for his cue, trying to shut out MacFarland's voice and eyes: *What happened to the grace?*

A voice behind him said, "I'm your husband, Miss."

Brent turned, even more startled to see the face—heavily lined with mascara and rouge, the mouth defined by a false mustache—of the boy who sat next to him in psych class, who passed every test with an A-plus. The boy himself was taking a deep breath, looking at a strange girl—overwhelmed.

"'*You must not irritate him. You must leave him alone. Oh, please!*'" Not McMillan's voice cueing him this time, but the strange voice of a woman.

"Well, you're *on*." When the boy touched his arm, Brent felt and saw a spark.

He stepped out into the entrance of the parlor in Italy.

"Who is it?"

"Kester."

"Go away. I'm asleep."

"You better stop acting so hateful."

"Who *is* that out there?" Brent's roommate looked out from under his pillow.

"Kester Dunlap."

"Hey, boy, you better get away from that door, 'fore I come out there and chew your arm right off your shoulder."

Afraid somebody would recognize him, Brent did not show up at the dining room Saturday morning. For the first time, he missed breakfast with the team. But he couldn't sleep. He lay on his cot and tried to feel real.

The door shot open, straight-armed, and Brent's roommate and three other jocks came in.

"Looks like I'm going to be a playgoer!"

"Hell, me, too!"

"Why didn't somebody *tell* us?"

"Hell, we was bouncing balls all over the place, man, while *she*—"

"Jesus, I never saw guys so excited."

"I was so certain she'd turn out to be Stella after all, I didn't feel too bad about not being there opening night—figured I might go to one of the other performances."

"Hey, Brent, you awake or asleep?"

Brent kept still, made no sound.

༈

At lunch, Brent listened to the talk himself.

He ate a light supper at the Dutchman's, the only other eating place in Melbourne. He walked in the woods until time to perform.

Sunday morning, he went to breakfast. By now, everyone had seen the mysterious lady.

"Hell, I'm going again tonight."

"Most beautiful woman I ever laid eyes on."

"*Girl* is more like it."

"I'd give my left—"

"Ah, watch it, man, she's a damn nice girl."

"How *you* know?"

"Can't you tell by looking at her?"

"Hell, they all the same. They all *like* it."

"All, huh? How *you* know?"

"Ones I ain't had, I ain't met."

"Bull."

"Well, *he'll* bull you, boys, but if you want to know what it's like, *I* can tell you. 'Cause last night after the show, she was hotter'n hell, full of the feeling the guys gave her, sitting out there burning like wicks, so I *got* me some."

"What was it like?"

"Hell, I'm sorry, she swore me to secrecy."

They all laughed until they nearly cried. Brent's laughter, sounding as false as a cracked bell, made them look at him.

In the dressing room, he tried to keep away from the others, but they ambled up to him quite naturally, as though his body, like their own, were a low-powered magnet. Unbuttoning his shirt, he felt the starch brush against his nipples.

"Love to seen her in a tighter dress, wouldn't you?"

"Yeah, it hung too loose."

"I ain't swimming in the same pool with *you* guys. I like my water *cold*."

"Just like to brush with my two thumbs the places where her mourning dress seemed to rise from the dead."

"Man, I'm suffering. Suffering."

"Know how you feel. Sticky dreams."

"McMillan cold-cocked Bronson with the poetry book 'cause he was putting a fourth act on that play, sitting there glassy-eyed. 'It's *your* fault, sir,' he said, and McMillan blushed, and said he was sorry, but we was all laughing. Ol' Bronson, too."

Brent stood with one trouser leg off, balanced on one foot, and slowly pulled the other off, feeling every inch of cloth against his skin.

"Thing about *her* is guys talk dirty 'bout wanting to lay her, you know, but you can tell by their voices they don't think it's right, yet they plow right on. You know?"

"Yeah."

"I'll be honest. I'd just like to *kiss* her one time."

Brent followed them toward the showers.

"Yeah, well, I know what you mean, but when you come right down to it, I'd love to stroke her from ear*lobe* to tip*toe*." The envisioned ecstasy made him let out a raucous scream that roared in the tiled shower room, and as he turned the shower full gush, he looked at Brent through the stream. "Wouldn't you, Brent?"

Awkwardly, standing on the raised sill of the shower room, Brent turned, slipped, staggered, and almost ran back to the locker, reaching for his clothes.

Brent lay on his cot through the supper hour. But avoiding the team only made the things they had said over the past three days come back more lucidly. He saw their faces, and the strange new ways they used their hands.

His flesh burned. When he felt his jock begin to fill and stretch, he jumped up and walked quickly out of the room and down the stairs.

"Yes?"

"You Stella?"

"Yeah."

"I wonder if you'd let me come in."

"What you so nervous about?" She had lowered her voice.

"Stage fright."

"Haven't I seen you some place before?"

"That's a good line," said Brent. "Can I come in?"

"I don't even *know* you." The room behind her was brightly lighted, full of cigar smoke.

"The guys said you were pretty friendly."

"Look, I don't just go out with anybody, anytime."

"Who is it Stella, some salesman?" McMillan's voice, so casual, natural, startled Brent.

"Yeah, honey, I'm trying to get him to take no for an answer."

An indulgent chuckle—McMillan amused at an inept pun.

"We don't want none—*any*."

Brent turned away, nauseated.

"Hey!" she whispered.

"What?"

"*Now*, I remember. When you lifted that veil . . ." At the look in her eyes, Brent shivered. "They sent you to make fun of me, huh? Like the other one—the little one."

"Little one *who*?"

"Called him Keeser or Custer."

"That *you*, Old Sport?"

Up the main street of the toy town of Melbourne, Kester walked toward Brent along an iron fence.

"Keep walking, Kester—the other way."

"You better stop being so hateful to me."

"You needn't worry anymore."

"I've taken enough off you and him."

"You always *did* talk in tongues, Kester, like people in revival tents."

"I won't *tell*, Brent."

"What is there for you not to tell?"

Kester stood on the corner under the streetlight and looked at him. Brent stood in the dark on the sidewalk, afraid to get near Kester. "I saw you that first night, and I went back last night, and I'm going back again tonight. A lot of guys are going their third time. But I knew it was you the *first* night."

"You were at the basketball game the first night."

"I ran over for the ending."

"It's going to end without me tonight."

"Don't let the talk get you down."

"I'm hitting the road."

"You can't do McMillan that way. It's almost curtain time."

"So long, Kester."

"I promise I won't tell."

"Shut up, Kester."

"That's just how McMillan talked. I told him I wouldn't tell about you and him, and first he got mad, and then he laughed like I was an armless freak threatening to slap him, and it was like getting slapped myself, the way he laughed. He's the devil, Brent."

"Shut up, Kester."

"So when he was laughing at me, I decided there wasn't anything going on between you."

"Goddamn you, shut up!"

"Brent, it'll pass over. *I've* heard them talking, too. I walk around and *listen* to them. But they don't know, and I won't tell, and before long, after a few more games, you know, you'll forget it. *You can,* because there's nothing wrong with you, Brent." Brent glanced back. Kester was backing away, out of the streetlight. "Believe me, Brent." Kester backed into the dark under the thick new leaves of trees hanging over the street. "I promise not to come tonight. There's not a *thing* wrong with you!" Then Kester turned and walked through the main gates of the campus.

The leaves loud under his feet, Brent walked into the pool of light, a feeling of grace in his stride.

ALLEN WIER

As a young man in the 1960s, Allen Wier faced an important decision—apply to LSU's brand new graduate program in creative writing, or fight in Vietnam. His student application was accepted, and with the encouragement of Professor David Madden, Wier became the first student to earn an MA in creative writing in the LSU English department. He recalls talking shop in Madden's Allen Hall office "until shadows moved across the floor," and realizing that he wanted to be a writer for the rest of his life. The first story he sold for publication, one that he wrote for a class at LSU, was published in *The Southern Review*. Later, LSU Press simultaneously published his collection of stories, *Things About to Disappear*, and his first novel, *Blanco*, an unsurpassed achievement for any writer at the Press. LSU also provided Wier his first teaching job, a career he has since pursued at various esteemed institutions such as Carnegie-Mellon University, Hollins College, Longwood University, and the University of Texas. Today, he teaches at University of Tennessee in Knoxville.

In 2008, Wier became the 27th writer awarded the John Dos Passos Prize for Literature, an honor established by Longwood University. This is only the most recent of such coveted accolades Wier's work has received, such as his 1997 Robert Penn Warren Award, conferred by the Fellowship of Southern Writers, and his Guggenheim Fellowship.

Wier's knowledge of the Texas landscape was most recently made evident with the publication by SMU Press of his novel, *Tehano*, for which he conducted intensive research of the state's North, South, and Indian cultures. But earlier in his career, too, Texas provided a compelling setting. In the title story of his 1978 collection, "Things About to Disappear," his main character sets out on the open road, observing age-old landmarks and noting the minute detail of the Texas roadside. His interrupted journeys of both body and soul stack up to reveal the wisdom of leaving everything but his memories behind.

ALLEN WIER

Things About to Disappear

After nine months of sickness, slipping away from us a little more every day, my daddy died. Finally the cancer got an artery, it burst, and he went out in a rush. We buried him out on a windy, limestone hill beneath a twisted live oak. It was a time of leaving, the tail end of a sad summer. He was gone, and I was going, leaving Texas again.

Driving east, the air through the car windows felt like the outdoor side of a window air conditioner, and you could smell the wet air, sticky, East Texas hot. I had already left one landscape behind. In the few hours I'd been driving, the white caliche dirt had turned red, rugged hills had smoothed out, gotten more civilized, more used looking, brown grass had gone green, and every mile the trees got straighter and taller.

I had been through Buffalo, Tucker, Palestine, Ironton, Jacksonville. I had crossed the Trinity River way south of Trinidad where I used to cross, used to pass the pink motel all alone at the end of the narrow, old bridge and the fertilizer plant nearly hidden in live oaks on the other side of the river. Once I told a friend the Trinidad fertilizer plant was really a secret laboratory where strange beings from another world were collecting and processing human blood for their dying race. The aliens had taken human form and lived in the pink motel, the tall, futuristic looking water towers were really full of blood, the boxcars on the railroad siding brought bodies in, the brown smoke was from burning flesh. My friend and I made a secret pact, if one of us ever needed the other all we had to do was send a note: Trinidad Aliens, Midnight, December 12. We would never forget. Now I don't even have an address to send the note to. And they've widened the highway at Trinidad, torn down the scary, wonderful, old bridge, and cut out most of the live oaks that used to make the fertilizer plant a secret alien laboratory.

After the Trinity I crossed the Neches, not enough water in the Neches to make one good tear. I left it behind, dry, waiting for water, forever for all I knew. I had two rivers left, two rivers more I knew, the little Angelina, the Sabine.

The sun was in the west, in the mirror. Sundown behind me and darkness coming ahead of me. Lights on in New York, dinner dishes done in Washington, drive-in movies dancing on in small towns all over Virginia, if you could see that far ahead. As the road rose and fell in the piney hills I held and lost this last summer sun.

Leave-taking. I was playing it to the hilt. The tires were whining up and down the hills like a pedal steel guitar and all the old, sad songs about leaving were running like an old, slow record in my head, and I was holding the names of places sweet in my mouth, shaping them with my lips, feeling their flavor like hard candy on my tongue. Melodies of names, names like Dripping Springs, Round Mountain, Marble Falls, Spicewood, Calf Creek, Air. Names that seemed to echo when I thought them, San Saba, Cherry Spring, Mountain Home, Morris Ranch, Stonewall, Blanco. And the name of the man who had left me, the man I was leaving behind, his name I couldn't speak. And the name that rhymed with *breath* and was forever.

Now there were warning signs, and all down one side of the highway were bright orange tags on tall pine trees, tags the color of sunset, and then no trees at all, just a wide, red gash and the dark fingers of stubborn stumps and silent, orange earthmovers parked in the mud.

I topped a hill and a slow, black car appeared in front of me, weaving, back and forth, shoulder to shoulder, covering the whole road. I couldn't see through the glare of the last crack of sun caught on the rear window and flashing as the car careened back and forth in front of me. I honked my horn and flashed my lights, but the car meandered on like the dry riverbed of the Neches. Then, sudden as a dream, the car jerked left, shot off the shoulder and went through a sawhorse barricade where new lanes were being built over a ditch. Broken boards jerked up over me like puppets yanked up off a stage, and the car shot out onto a new, white slab over the ditch and up into the air like one of the spaceships I had imagined the aliens landed at Trinidad. And it stopped there, in the air, nose up. And that second caught and held for me like the car held in air, and I saw all these things: a bird gliding just before it dives; a kite the second its string breaks; a falling leaf; a thrown stick; a fish jumping and caught in the sun; a balsa wood plane at the end of a dip or turn; a man shot out of a circus cannon; a pole vaulter, high jumper, hurdler, lips puckered, muscles tensed, eyes closed, suspended over a bar; wooden rocker runners tipped almost vertical; the crest of a wave curling like a horn back into itself; a last breath held, maybe forever. Then the car rolled slowly over and fell gracelessly across the ditch, hitting the soft mud with an ugly sound, someone breaking wind; a boil lanced; nose blown, phlegm spat. The windshield popped out whole and shot like a clipped fingernail across the ditch. And I seemed caught there, dead still on the road.

Should I go down to the car, upside down in the ditch, surely flattened, surely full of death. Was there anything I could do down there. Should I keep going to the nearest telephone, call help, an ambulance, wrecker, cutting torches. Then, with help on its way, then go back to pull the bodies out. By the time I realized I had made the decision, I was a mile down the road, the black car invisible behind me.

A white frame house sat among pecan trees off to my right. Furiously I skidded up under the trees, nuts popping beneath my tires, emergency brake locking, sticks and nuts and porch boards snapping and cracking and creaking beneath my feet and the noise but not the feeling of the screened door beneath my fist knocking. The screen was hooked, the door behind it open. I smelled the rust of the screen wire as I pressed my face against the door, imagined the red mesh, net, crosses, cross hairs printed on my skin. I looked in and yelled through my cupped hands. Inside a tall, silver, electric fan silently turned back and forth like the face of a robot. On a couch a woman with white hair in a white slip lay. I shouted for her to get up, to open the door. I banged, I pulled at the screen until one screw came out of the handle and it turned sideways in my hand. Inside, in a doorway to another room, I saw two, big, bare feet sticking out into the air. I yelled at them, "Come here, this is an emergency, get up." I drew back my fist, held a second like the car in the air, was going to punch a hole in the screen and unlatch the door, when it swung open against my chest toppling me back a step. An old, old man stood there, dark wool pants, white under-shirt, a long, pink face and empty blue eyes. The face of a rabbit, long, white, rabbit feet on the bare floor. I hurried past him, thinking for a second there would be no phone. Then I saw it, black on a white doiley on the dresser, and started dialing 0 and talking at the same time, to the old, old rabbit man, to the body on the couch in the front room, to the nasal voice in the telephone.

"Who will pay for the call, sir?"

"I'll pay, I'll pay for the call." I yelled my home telephone number, cursed, yelled, "Emergency, emergency."

Again, I was caught, suspended in the moment, feeling the distance, the air in the receiver, in my ear, the feel and sound of a seashell. I saw all these things: A blue and white telephone book for Troup, Price, Laneville, New Summerfield, Gallatin, and Reklaw; the maple headboard and the bed which had a white chenille spread with the long shape of a body on it; a pink and white ceramic cat on the dresser by the telephone; two snapshots in the edge of the dresser mirror, one of a tall man and a tall woman in front of a fig tree, one of a younger tall man holding a string of fish out before his chest, holding the string with both hands so that it curved across his chest imitating the grin held across his face, the fish catching the light in the photo-graph like long, sharp teeth; a calendar stuck with two red thumbtacks into the light blue wall, a bright autumn picture above the days of the week, two brown spotted bird dogs holding a point forever.

The operator wanted to know if I wanted the state police in Jacksonville or Hender-son. For a second I couldn't remember where I was. Had I passed New Summerfield? Had I crossed the Angelina River? No, I hadn't passed the river. Then, the police in Jacksonville wanted to know where I was. I gave them the highway number and started to hang up, when I heard the tiny voice in the telephone, irritated, saying, "Yes, but east or west of Jacksonville?"

"East," I said, I was sure of that.

"How far east?"

"Not far," I said, "not far. Just drive east, we're the only wreck on this stretch of the highway."

The old man was standing in the doorway. He hadn't spoken a word, just stared without comprehension. Skin hung in folds under his arms. I tried to explain again, I left some money to pay for the screen handle, to pay for the call if the phone company charged him. I left, the woman still on the couch unmoving, the fan still moving right to left like a beacon across the room. There were no curtains for it to ripple as it passed back and forth, only the steady turning to prove it was on at all, that and the way you could see blue wall through the spinning blades.

By the time I got back to the accident there were several cars stopped, people standing around. I parked and hurried down the incline, slipping in the mud. One wheel of the wrecked car was still spinning, the exposed underside of the car tilted toward me, a little girl was keeping the wheel going, prodding it with a piece of the broken sawhorse. The windshield was stuck up like a monolith in the mud, still intact. All around sticking up out of the grass or lying in the mud were parts of the wreckage: a headlight, roadmap, thermos, hubcap, pieces of clothing, a suitcase, a woman's purse. A small boy sat on the grass holding his head, blood all down his arm. A man in a brown suit, the cuffs of his pants splashed with mud and a long grass stain down the front of his white shirt like a wide green tie, was walking around and around the overturned car. The car was thrown across the ditch like a bridge, so that the roof stuck down into the ditch instead of being flattened, and every few seconds the man would bend down and look up into the car, making little clucking noises in his throat. One of the rear tires had a big hole in it, the other three tires were bald as the man in overalls who kept sticking his fist into the hole in the rear tire and saying, "They's damn lucky they wadn't killed; they's damn lucky they wadn't killed."

A man in a straw hat was squatted down by the car, and I went down to him. "I saw it happen and went on to call an ambulance," I told him. "Is the little boy hurt bad?"

"There's a woman pinned in there," he said. "I sent a car back to Jacksonville for an ambulance, should've been here by now. Maybe we ought to pull her out?"

"If she's got internal injuries we shouldn't move her, and there's no way of know-ing," I said.

Then a man came down yelling, "What happened here? Let me through, what happened?" The man in the straw hat told him there was a woman pinned inside the car. "I've got the hearse up there," the newcomer said. "I drive for the funeral home in Palestine. We can get her in there and I'll drive her to the hospital." He got down against the front fender and started pushing. The man in the straw hat was pushing by the door and the bald-headed man took his fist out of the blown tire and started helping. I stood back, afraid to get in the way, hoping they didn't do more harm than good. Then the bald-headed man disappeared into the car.

It was dark now. Fireflies blinked farther down the ditch near the woods. Someone had pulled a pickup over and aimed the lights down onto the wreck, and dust danced in the beams of the headlights. They were pulling a woman out of the car, out through the space where the windshield had been. I went over to the man in the brown suit, her husband, I guessed. He was trying to pick up the strewn clothes from the suitcase that had been thrown from the car.

"Can I help you?" I asked.

"I got to get Lizabeth's dress folded up."

I tried to get him to sit down, but he kept talking about Lizabeth's dress. A woman came over and said he was probably in shock, but he'd be okay afterwhile. I asked her about the little boy, and she said he was okay, just a cut on the forehead and scared silly. I told her about seeing the accident happen and that I'd called an ambulance. "They're never there when you need them, are they?" she said.

I felt silly standing there, watching with the circle of onlookers, others who had stopped, boys in levis, men in business suits, overalls, women in dresses, shorts, a girl in a bright pink, two-piece bathing suit that caught the light from the pickup and glowed like teeth and fingernails in a bar with black lights. She was talking to three boys who were sharing their beers with her. I went back up the slope to see if I could help the man from the funeral home who had some people lifting an empty coffin from the hearse. They set it across a couple of remaining sawhorses and he lifted the satin covered foam pad out of the bottom. As they disappeared down the slope carrying the coffin pad like a stretcher, I saw the moon coming up deep red on the far side of the highway, and from an opened car door I heard the tinny sound of an Oklahoma radio station's call letters and then guitar and fiddle as someone sang about love lost for all time.

The woman came, head first, out from inside the wrecked car. Her face was white and puffy, her hair blue-black against the satin pad. She moaned, over and over, a monotone. Moaned and moaned, the whole time they carried her up the hill to the highway, moaned and moaned, as they put her into the hearse, moaned until the heavy rear door of the hearse clunked shut and blocked out the sound. The man in the brown suit wouldn't leave the car and Lizabeth's dress, so the man in the straw hat picked the little boy up and put him in the front of the hearse with the driver. He was crying and screaming, "Mommie," and "Daddy, Daddy," when the big, dark hearse, chrome shining in the headlights of the pickup, swung round and disappeared down the dark highway. The ambulance and the police still had not come.

People began to leave. The moon was higher, turning ivory, moonlight getting brighter as headlights went out and cars drove away. Finally only a couple talking with the man down by his wrecked car remained, and I was alone on the shoulder of the highway. Moonlight had moved onto the trunk of a tall cottonwood tree, the bark soft and lovely, splotches of soft browns and whites like the soft hide of a pinto pony, a delicate birthmark, it reminded me of the old man's rabbit face, and I wondered if the woman had moved from the couch, if the fan still turned regularly back and forth, if the old, old man had lain back down into the shape of himself on the white bedspread beneath the snapshot of his young self grinning down with long, pointed fishteeth.

And I remembered my daddy, in the last week of his last brave month. Remembered the evening I walked into the bedroom where he lay lost in the big double bed, disappearing before our very eyes, his arm going up like a chicken wing plucked and washed for frying, his skinny elbow over his eye, tears running down his sharp, boney cheek, "Don't see me this way, son, please don't," his face gone, only bones left, huge white eyes, nose, teeth, a medieval woodcut of Death. I remembered holding his long, thin fingers, how cool and dry they were, how soft, how much love I felt through those thin pads of his fingers, felt them twitch and tremble with pain and sadness, saw him smile at me, his lips unnaturally wide and pink in his disappearing face. The double windows in which the sickness had made him see men from outer space, aliens from another world who would stand outside his windows or come through the wall and stand around his bed watching him, those same windows growing dark, the soft gray color of slate when he called me in. He would ask me to look and tell him what I saw. Didn't I see that spaceship in the backyard? When I asked him if they were after him he said he didn't know, they just stood, watching. They were all young men with short hair and dark pants and white shirts and dark ties and they stood, arms folded across their chests, around his bed, watching him. He could make them disappear with his flashlight. I remember that last evening we talked, the stone gray squares of the windows, the soft light of an early evening in late summer that smoothed the angles of his protruding bones, softened the ravages of the cancer that was eating him even as we looked at each other, the soft, dim light giving him back, for a moment, his strong arms and full, joyful face, and he said, "You know, son, while I'm lying here the past sort of floats by like a good old movie, and I thought I'd reach out and grab some of it and give it to you." I remember suffering because I couldn't make him whole again, because I didn't have some magic thing to say to him, and he went on, "For instance, when I was a kid," here he stretched out his arm toward the window where I heard for the first time all summer the cicadas in the live oak, "we used to call them—what are those?"

"Cicadas?" I said.

"Yeah, that's right. We used to call them *Crickadees*," and he spelled it for me. And he told me that since I like words he thought I might like a word like *Crickadees*. And I tore off a piece of paper from the telephone pad by his bed and wrote it down and folded it up and put it in my wallet where it still is, *Crickadees*, smelling like leather and sweat.

I walked down to the man in the brown suit and the couple who had stayed to wait with him for the police, feeling my wallet tight against my hip, and asked if he wanted my name and address. "As a witness, or something?" I asked. He said he didn't guess he needed it, and the woman with him thanked me but said they lived nearby and could explain to the police.

So I got back into my car and drove on into the darker east, past the white frame house where perhaps two old people would imagine they dreamed about a frightened young man who came and tried to wake them, past two state police cars, lights flashing, headed west, where I had come from. Wondering about the wreck, about the man and the little boy and whether the woman was badly hurt, I drove on, across the lovely, little Angelina River, through new Summerfield, away from the people who had given me my past and into whatever life I could find in the dark distances ahead, listening for Crickadees and loving so many things that were about to disappear.

REBECCA WELLS

The cult-like following engendered by Rebecca Wells' *New York Times* #1 bestseller, *Divine Secrets of the Ya-Ya Sisterhood*, revealed the need for intimacy among women, particularly within the symbiotic relationships among mothers, daughters, and childhood friends in the South. These avid Wells fans sought to embody her characters by organizing book clubs and social groups with the "Ya-Ya" name. So popular was this novel that it became a smash box-office hit starring Sandra Bullock, Ashley Judd, Ellen Burstyn, and Maggie Smith. Set in Thornton, Louisiana—thought to be a fictionalized version of Wells' hometown, Alexandria—the prequel to *Divine Secrets*, *Little Altars Everywhere*, is a coming-of-age story set in the last half of the 20th century, which reveals with humor the secrets of a dysfunctional family. *Little Altars* won the 1992 Western States Book Award. *Divine Secrets* won the 1999 Adult Trade ABBY Award. Wells' original plays, *Splittin' Hairs* and *Gloria Duplex,* have also drawn national attention. Two novels have followed the huge success of *Divine Secrets*: *Ya-Yas in Bloom* and *The Crowning Glory of Calla Lily Ponder*.

While an undergraduate at LSU, Wells visited Professor David Madden's playwriting classes and performed the roles his students wrote into their scripts. Madden remembers, "She learned about writing from me indirectly, through my students who were her friends; and the ambience of writers working with actors inspired her to write her own one-woman shows and then her first novel." She also studied psychology and became interested in women's politics—fitting preparation for a budding writer.

In Wells' novels, male characters play the secondary roles that complete her Southern matriarchal society. "E-Z Boy War," a chapter of *Little Altars*, shows Big Shep, the main character's father, deep in his memories of Vietnam War-era Louisiana. The only farmer on the draft board, his is a unique experience. While the country club set secures special deferments for their sons, Big Shep is unable to use his position to spare those boys who work their families' farms. While recollecting, Big Shep realizes that his struggles against racism and social hierarchies have led him to a closer relationship with God, or in his words, Old Podnah.

REBECCA WELLS

E-Z Boy War

from *Little Altars Everywhere*

{*Big Shep, 1991*}

I watch all the news from my E-Z Boy lounger. I got the chair by the windows back in my room. Originally put it back there so I could hear the TV over the kids' screaming and carrying on at the other end of the house. Now that they're all gone, I guess I've gotten used to sitting up by myself and watching what's going on in the world.

They started another war. I was down at the grain co-op last week and Charlie Vanderlick told me his grandson was in a Marine assault unit in the Gulf. Not our Gulf of Mexico, the one farther east.

Then, after a Levee Board meeting out at LSU-Thornton, I saw some graffiti on the wall in the men's room that said "18 males per gallon."

Goddamn, I thought, maybe you've lived too long.

Back when they first asked me to be on the Garnet Parish draft board in 1965, I got all puffed up. Figured giving me such a responsibility must of meant they thought something of me.

So I said, Yessir, I'd be proud to.

Our pictures were in the *Thornton Daily Monitor* and I wore a suit like the rest of them. But I was the only one with cowboy boots.

Vivi said, Shep, babe, why don't you wear your wing tips?

But I said, Vivi, let's don't get carried away with this thing.

The rest of the board was your downtown crowd—Neal Chauvin, the lawyer; two businessmen; and that orthodontist who was sending his son to Princeton on my kids' teeth. They needed somebody to represent those of us who farm out here along Bayou Latanier outside the city limits, and I was the one.

The meetings were at the parish courthouse at six in the evening so the rest of them could walk over from their offices after work. I would go home from the fields first, even though once the weather turned good, Chaney and me didn't know the meaning of the words "quitting time." We were making the changeover from cotton to rice

88

back then. Had to get my land leveled perfect and make sure the ridges on the contours held the water like they should. Growing something under standing water was a whole different ballgame from what we'd been used to. We were working with new irrigation pumps and combines—the whole nine yards. Had folks from the Extension Service out there at least once a week to advise me. You got to try and diversify, so the land you inherited doesn't get worn out and useless. Not to mention, you also got to plant you a crop that'll bring in enough cash to keep a roof over your head.

Before the meetings I would shower and shave and put on a suit—foreign to me, but there's such a thing as civic duty. Never saw any battle myself. Had my seventeenth birthday on a train headed for Navy boot camp in Great Lakes, Illinois. I wouldn't wish the kind of homesickness I had on my worst enemy.

Everybody who was anybody was for the Vietnam thing at that point. Get in and get out so the dominoes don't come tumbling down. They weren't even calling it a war then, just a "conflict." Up to that point, I hadn't ever realized that little swamp over there meant so much to democracy, but then I tend to pay attention to things more local.

Vivi would ask me questions about it, and the only thing I could say was, Well, Russell Long and his people seem to think it's important, and they've been in the know since Year One.

Then in September of '65, Hurricane Betsy roared across the Gulf of Mexico and hit the Mississippi Delta like no North Vietnamese mortar ever could. She knocked three-quarters of my rice to the ground and all I could do was stand on the carport with the humidity dripping off me and watch. We harvested the puny portion we could, burned off the rice straw, disked it, then put in wheat. Hurricanes remind you that it's the Old Podnah who's in charge, not you.

By the end of that year, we'd put ten times as many more men in uniform than when I first went on the board. I started reading more news, because I wasn't gonna have the other board members think I was some know-nothing tractor driver when I opened my mouth at the meetings. I read my *Thornton Monitor*, my *New Orleans Times-Picayune*, *Newsweek*, and *U.S. News and World Report*.

One evening I just had to get up and walk down the hall to Vivi's room. I said, Babe, you still awake? Take a look at this, will you? You're a Catholic, explain this to me.

And I handed her a picture in *Newsweek* of this Catholic relief worker burning himself up in front of the United Nations building to protest us being over in Vietnam. The picture showed this young boy going right up in flames. You could still barely make out his eyeglasses and the shape of his sweater-vest and ears.

Vivi said, That's disgusting, Shep. Take it away from me.

I went on back to my room and tried to get some sleep but I couldn't. I sat up half the night with my asthma inhaler and Herman Wouk.

❦

Christmas that year was good enough, for just having come through a hurricane. Vivi charged everything.

I figured, Well, we can't have *two* years of hurricanes, can we?

We had a big Christmas breakfast with all kinds of kinpeople over, the little ones going nuts over their toys the way they do. While we ate our turkey and cornbread dressing, the diplomatic muckety-mucks flew all over the globe pulling out the stops. They had a thirty-hour ceasefire, and man, did they burn some jet fuel hopping from one embassy to another.

I thought, Maybe they can stop this thing after all. I hope so. I'm a farmer, not a military recruiter.

Then '66 rolled in. After the so-called truce, we went all-out to bring the North to its knees. Good, I thought. Bomb the hell out of it and get it over with. I couldn't barbecue a sirloin without thinking about the G.D. war.

I had boys by the dozens coming in front of me, some of them hardly been shaving for a year. I never used to think nineteen-year-olds were so damn young. Well, we got ourselves into this thing; we got to get ourselves out. But I hated the idea of putting anyone through the hell I went through in the Navy. And I didn't even know any combat. Boot camp was bad enough. I had never left Garnet Parish without Mama or Daddy before, and I was sick the whole damn time. Had problems with my bowels and ended up in the infirmary, you can't count the number of times. An obstructed colon, they called it. I called it: Go ahead and shoot me now and get it over with.

Civic duty or not, I could of done without those draft board meetings. I had enough on my hands just trying to run my own farm. I was going all out with the rice. If those Southwest Louisiana farmers could do it, I thought, then so could I. Cotton was a thing of the past by then. It got to where I'd laugh out loud when I'd even hear the phrase "Cotton South." When it comes to cotton, I'll wear it, but I sure as hell won't grow it anymore. It wasn't nothing but a sure way to go bankrupt.

Not that I didn't miss it. Not that I don't still miss it. There is some kind of beauty to growing cotton. First, you got to make sure it survives germinating when the ground is cool. Then summer comes and that plant grows so lightning-fast—it's like watching a kid shoot up from two to twenty in three hot months. You got to really love farming to grow cotton. Because you got to baby it, watch it every day, give it what it needs at every different stage. Keep the weeds out, watch for the boll weevils and bollworms. You can get emotional with that crop, I tell you. Sometimes I wonder if I wasn't better raising cotton than I was with my own children.

And the harvest. The kids used to come out to the fields after school. Vivi would bring a picnic supper and we'd eat under the pecan trees, with the oranges and pinks of the sky. Chaney and Lincoln and the other field hands sitting there with us next to the tin water cooler. Sometimes Willetta would bring out something special for Chaney, those tall, skinny girls of theirs tagging along. I liked showing off what we'd been working, and in those days my family was actually interested. Not like later, when they got ashamed of how I paid for their clothes and food and cars and colleges. Back in those days, the kids would climb up on the high-bed cotton truck and dive down into that freshly picked cotton like they thought they were in the circus or something. I'd watch them come up sneezing, picking fuzz off their eyelashes, then diving down for more.

Those were good times. Hell, we didn't even *drink* on those evenings. Just ice tea. And I'd keep working late into the night, because you didn't want to leave cotton in the field a day longer than you had to. No telling when the rain'd start.

I knew what I was doing then. My father taught me how to grow cotton.

But he didn't teach me how to sit still at no conference table with a bunch of air-conditioned men. At those draft board meetings, you knew you weren't part of their crowd, even though nothing was ever said. They had a club so private it didn't even have a name. Quick sure handshakes. Soft clean hands. Manicured fingernails. When we shook hands, I was always conscious of my calluses and the dirt that wouldn't come out, no matter how hard I scrubbed. I was the only farmer on the draft board and I busted my butt trying to get my fingernails clean as theirs.

There was something in me that would of liked to say: Listen, you SOBs, my Daddy could of sent me to Tulane too, but we had land to farm. While your people sat up at the country club during the Depression whining into their mint juleps, my father was trucking potatoes across the whole goddamn South to hold on to our land.

But I held my tongue. It was all deeper and sadder and more confusing than I had the words for. Sometimes I wondered if this wasn't how the niggers felt.

Oh, I watched that war from my E-Z Boy. We're fighting a jungle war, a ground war, and one in the air. We're kicking ass now, LBJ said. Only no one was telling those VC bastards. They didn't seem to get the message. Maybe it was because they didn't speak English. Hah. They picked our jets off like kites in a storm.

I knew the numbers. We had our draft quotas to meet every month. Quotas everywhere you turned. Started the year with 181,000 and ended up the year with 400,000.

And it wasn't just Vietnam. Meaner mouths than Dr. King were starting to holler. Whatever his dream was, it seemed like it was turning into a nightmare to me. It was war on all fronts. I just wish my own home hadn't been one of them. But don't get me started on that. There weren't any deferments from the battles in my house.

Christmas came again before I'd even paid off last year's charge slips. One night I was at Rotier's Bar having a drink and a bowl of gumbo with the boys. We were always bringing Rotier shrimp or duck, and the man could flat out turn it into something.

BEST OF LSU FICTION

If I'd eaten a bowl of that gumbo every time I ordered a drink from that man, my life might of turned out different. Anyway, the place was all decorated for Christmas, little fake tree up on the bar, the Playmate of the month next to it with her pink tits and wearing a red Santa's hat. And McNamara came on the TV, saying: Progress has exceeded our own expectations. We can now cut our draft in half during '67.

The only problem was, old Westmoreland kept asking for more boys—and what Westmoreland wanted, he sure as hell seemed to get.

Nineteen sixty-seven. Hottest G.D. summer I can remember. Bigger ground battles, more air assaults, same size body bags, only a helluva lot more of them.

That's when the calls started coming regular. Nine o'clock at night, that's when you'd hear the phone ring. I remember the first one. It took me a while to even figure what it was about. It was Mrs. Alma Vanderlick, Charlie Vanderlick's wife.

I said, Hello, this is Shep Walker.

And she said, Mister Walker, I sure hate to be calling you this late at night. I know how early farmers got to get up. Charlie's asleep already.

I said, Don't you worry, Miz Alma. What can I do for you?

Mister Walker, she said, please don't tell Charlie I called. He wouldn't never get over it.

Miz Alma, I told her, you people been farming along this bayou as long as mine have. Now, what can I do for you?

Oh Mister Shep, you got to stop them from taking my son Albert to Vietnam. He's the only one left to farm this place when his daddy's gone. My oldest boy got him a real fine job with Texaco down in Morgan City. He's making good money. He ain't never gonna come back here and farm.

She was crying, and I sat up in bed and tried to unclench my chest.

I'll see what I can do for you, Miz Alma, I told her. Let me see what I can do.

She said, Thank you, Mr. Shep. I'm gonna run yall over a jar of my fig preserves next time I'm up your way.

That call shook me up something awful. Good thing I didn't know it was only the first. Once they started flying those body bags back to Louisiana, there wasn't any medals or patriotic sweet-talking that could hush up the farm mothers who live up and down this bayou. At least not at night, when their husbands were in bed and the supper stuff was put away, and they got to remembering how they'd danced with those baby boys on their hips at Sunday afternoon pig roasts. Or rubbed Vicks VapoRub onto their chests when the bronchitis came around. These ladies didn't burn no flags. They looked up my number from the grain co-op phone list. I was the only country man on the draft board. They called me.

I had a bad taste in my mouth the day Albert Vanderlick stood up in front of us. Boy was asking to be deferred on sole-surviving-son status. He was wearing pressed khakis and a short-sleeve plaid shirt with a necktie. You could smell the homemade starch when he sweated. Healthy-looking boy. Those Dutchmen down the bayou feed their children good, raise them right. I remembered the boy from when he used to tag along with his daddy to the cotton gin. He sat there in front of us with his hands onto his knees, fingers spread out. I could see where he'd scrubbed his hands, could tell by the redness around the cuticles. Shoot, don't I know that look. Don't I scrub my fingernails every evening of the world out in the utility room so Vivi won't have to see the dirt up under my nails? Using the fingernail brush, working it up under the nails, scrubbing my palms with Lava trying to get the earth out from in between the creases in my skin.

I could see Miz Alma, the way she must of called to him through the bathroom door, telling him: Albert, clean up good, you got to make a impression on those gentlemen.

We were scheduled to see thirty-one boys that same evening. We had maybe five minutes to discuss Albert Vanderlick.

Neal Chauvin said, This boy doesn't qualify for sole surviving son. He has a brother.

I said, Well I know that, Neal, but what you got to understand is that his brother has got himself a good job with one of the oil companies down in Morgan City—the fellow's going places. Albert is the one his daddy raised to work that land. A man's gotta have somebody to hand his land over to, or what the hell's it all for?

The orthodontist said, Shep, it sounds like you know these people. Maybe we ought to be a little lenient in a case like this.

Chauvin said, This is all beside the point. There is no legal ground on which to defer him. The boy would make a fine soldier.

I said, Hold on, don't we have any give-and-take in this thing?

And Chauvin said, If we bend the rules for a boy like Vanderlick, we set a dangerous precedent in this parish.

So Albert got put to a vote, and the boy was in uniform before his daddy's cotton had grown another four inches.

We weren't escalating, though. It was just action over and above what had been taking place, is how they put it.

It got to where I had to pour me a quick drink before every meeting, then wash out my mouth with Listerine. Then—I don't know what it was, but I started waking up with the worst nightmares I'd had since daddy died. I'd walk around the house, step out on the carport, try not to think about lighting a cigarette, pour myself a drink, try to read. Then the asthma would start up and I'd spend half the night sitting up in the E-Z Boy trying to keep my chest from closing up. You can breathe a little better if you're leaning back in that chair instead of flat out on the bed.

From where I sat, it seemed like we were talking two different wars. The one we were losing on the TV, and the one the Guv'ment said we were winning. But listen, I'm not a soldier. After that bowel thing, Daddy got me out of the Navy somehow. I didn't even ask what kind of strings he pulled. I was just so glad to be back home. We had a big cook-up in the yard and he never said word one to me about it. The man handed me a lot of shit in my life, but he never said a word to me about leaving the Navy. My people never have been peaceniks or what-have-you. If somebody invaded Garnet Parish, you better believe we'd whip some butt. We just don't like the idea of traveling halfway around the world to fight when we got crops in the ground.

Come to think of it, Daddy never put on a uniform himself. He always said, The fat gonna stay fat. They don't need me to help them do it.

Then don't you know it, Lincoln Lloyd got called up. Chaney's younger brother. Chaney's been my right-hand man since who laid the rail. Damn, Chaney's daddy worked for mine when we wasn't nothing but titty-babies. Lincoln was living down on Lower Levee Road with a sister of his who didn't amount to much. Chaney and Willetta were the ones who got the boy to stay in school as long as he did. When you first met the boy, you thought he was slow because of this stutter he had. I thought it myself till I heard him talking to Chaney in the barn one day. Boy didn't know I was around and there he was, talking clear as any child of mine, not one stutter spitting off that tongue.

Later I asked Chaney about it and he said, I don't know, Mister Big Shep, I think the boy just be scart of white people.

Chaney and Willetta went up to the school one time to talk to an evaluator about Lincoln because of all the notes that teachers kept sending home. And this white evaluator and Chaney and Willetta and Lincoln himself sat up in that office, and the lady said, We have got to try and figure out whether to classify this boy as an idiot or a moron.

Chaney tried to laugh when he told me this but I knew he was mad. I know Chaney. I've spent every one of my working days beside the man and they don't come any better. He's a man who keeps his own counsel, a man you can count on.

Far as I'm concerned, Lincoln wasn't a idiot or a moron neither. He just had trouble getting his words out. He worked for me in the fields since he was ten, and I can't say I knew the boy good, but he rode Shetland ponies with my four kids and I'd recognize that donkey laugh of his anywhere. Yeah, he dropped out of school, but he wasn't as dumb as they thought. Lots of times people make the mistake of underestimating you on account of the way you talk. I've seen this in my own life. That stutter might of made him sound stupid, but it's by a man's eyes that you know his intelligence. And Lincoln Lloyd had some smart eyes. He was as good a worker as you could of asked for. Talked slow and worked fast. Little and wiry, but muscular like Chaney.

I'd never known Chaney to ask a favor before. But one Sunday afternoon he came up to the house and asked for me. I put on my slippers and went out on the carport, and Vivi said, Chaney, let me get you a Coke.

The two of us stood there and stared out at the rice. Chaney drank that whole Coke in silence. Then he said, Boss, I been with you since my daddy worked with Mister Baylor Senior and I ain't never axed you for nothin.

That's right, I told him, you've pulled your load.

Well, I gotta ax you for somethin now, he said.

Chaney wrapped his arms around his chest, the way he does when he's thinking. Rubbed his hand across his face and kept staring out at the fields.

Mister Shep, don't let them take Linc to the army, he said. He done got that stutter and he ain't never been nowhere. Boy ain't never even been as far as Mamou. He ain't gonna make it through no war. I know it up in my joints. See can you do something for my baby brother, could you please sir, Mister Shep?

He didn't beg. Just handed me the Coke bottle and said, Thank you for the cold drink. I gotta get on back, or Willetta'll be wonderin where I run off to.

This is what I got to live with. I didn't do a goddamn thing to keep Lincoln out of the draft. McNamara said the army was the best thing going for your disadvantaged Negro youth. The man stood up there with those glasses on and explained how they were going to give boys like Lincoln special classes to bring them up to par. Teach them skills so they could land jobs they'd never get without the army. Lincoln passed the entrance test, which I guess proved he wasn't no moron. And ain't nobody ever said a thing about the boy's stutter getting in the way of him shooting a gun.

I said to Chaney one day when he was working on the combine, Chaney, the army just might be that boy's ticket out of here. Give him opportunities you ain't never had.

Chaney didn't answer me, just kept on working. I stood there a full minute waiting for him to say something back, but he acted like I wasn't even there.

One day around in that time, I remember I went downtown to Weinstein's Men's Store and bought me a brand-new goddamn suit. The thing was brown with little flecks of green in it. Had the thing tailored and then wore it to the next draft board meeting. I thought: Your uptown crowd are not the only people in the world who can put a decent set of clothes on their backs.

I was walking out the kitchen door and Vivi said, Oooh, Mister Walker, I'd fight a war over you.

I was the first board member to show up at that particular meeting. Me and the draft clerk had to wait fifteen minutes for the others to get there. Well, we all get busy, I thought. But when the bastards waltzed in, they were all wearing madras slacks and topsiders and running on about their golf game. Every goddamn one of them had been out at the country club. You could smell it on them, that sun smell that comes from being outside without breaking a sweat.

The orthodontist looked at me and said, Hey, Shep, sorry we're late. Couldn't take the office one more afternoon. You know how it is.

Neal Chauvin looked at me and smiled. Said, New suit, Walker?

Then Chauvin sat down in his sissy-ass alligator shirt, and we proceeded to see a whole slew of college boys whose student deferments had lapsed.

One of them, the Jarrell boy, was in pre-law. And he actually sat there in front of us and said: If you gentlemen force me to leave school, my father might as well pour $12,000 down the drain. My education is costing him a lot of money. I'm going to be a damn fine district attorney one day.

Later, discussing his case, Chauvin said: You can't send a boy like that to die in the trenches. He's the kind of man Louisiana needs. Then he laughed and said, Besides, I'd never win a case in his father's courtroom again if that young fellow doesn't end up on the Louisiana bar.

And the others laughed along with him, like it was so funny, like it was all so goddamn funny.

Nineteen sixty-eight. Swatting the years away like flies. They kept saying we were winning. Westmoreland and old Ellsworth Bunker—what the hell kind of name is that anyway? —they kept on swearing things were fine. My rice was looking pretty good, but the price of everything you needed was sky-rocketing, and you had to read up every day on all the new pesticides and herbicides. Farming was changing fast, but I was there with it.

I ended up in the hospital for a couple days with the asthma, had to get on the oxygen. Lung guy told me, It's the dust.

I said, Great. I'll just farm without breathing any dust. That oughta be real easy. I'll just sit around and grow rice in a air-conditioned room. Listen, Doc, I got kids to raise. What you want me to do?

He said, Well, have you ever considered a change in professions?

I said, No, buddy, have you?

Chaney and Willetta got them a framed picture of Lincoln in uniform. The boy looked shipshape. They were so proud of him that Chaney gave me a wallet-size picture for myself. That Chaney has always loved his snapshots. Sits out under the mimosa tree on Sunday afternoon and pastes them in his scrapbook.

Sometimes I wonder if any of us are cut out for the lives we lead.

In the middle of the goddamn Tet New Year truce, we had to fight a VC assault against the Saigon embassy. They rained down enemy mortar on all those little towns and dropped napalm on the Mekong delta. We lost over a thousand boys.

Jesus! We are the United States of America, I thought. What the hell are we doing? We're talking a piss-ass little swamp! Can't we get in there and finish this thing off? I found myself getting in arguments with my buddies at Rotier's. Got to where I'd hear the sound of my own voice and think it was somebody else's.

I'd yell, *If we're fighting a war, then let's get it the hell over with!*

What in the world is happening here? I'd think while I watched things from my E-Z Boy. We tore up South Vietnam, the damn peanut-size country we were supposed to be saving. Dropped so many defoliants, that soil will never be the same. Now, I know defoliants. I been around them every day of my life.

I watched it all on the goddamn color TV—little Vietnamese girls running out of burning huts, carrying babies in their arms, squealing high-pitched like rabbits in a trap. They ran across the screen until I thought they were gonna run straight out of the set into my bedroom. I swear to God one evening I thought I saw the Vanderlick boy on the news, thought I recognized his hands.

Man, we beat the whole world and we couldn't even take that little swamp! We trained half those boys down the road at Fort Polk because Louisiana has the same heat and humidity like Vietnam. I know what a swamp is.

LBJ said, Now there will, of course, be nervous Nellies who will buckle under the strain.

I am an American farmer, I thought, I'm not a communist. What do you want from me?

I didn't want to be drinking as much as I was. Then even the bourbon quit working and I was up at 2:07 every goddamn night. I don't know why, but I bolted awake at exactly 2:07 A.M. If I hadn't already had a little problem with the whiskey, I would of gotten me some sleeping pills.

Then we fought back. This time we were really going to do it! Lost 2,000 boys pushing back the Tet offensive. And it took three-and-a-half goddamn weeks to find out here at Pecan Grove that Lincoln Lloyd was one of them. Willetta's the one that told Sidda. And Sidda told Vivi, and Vivi told me.

Four solid days and Chaney didn't come to work, didn't say a word. Willetta took off too, and our house went to pot. All we ate was grilled cheeses. I left for the duck camp and went on a three-day drunk for the first time since Daddy died.

My son, Little Shep, finally drove out there one afternoon and said, Daddy you got to come on home. You're gone, Chaney's not working. I don't know what to tell the rest of the workers to do. We got crops in the field.

I looked at my son, dressed in his jeans and a starched white shirt. Trying so hard to be a man. Freckles, even on his eyelids. I wanted to pull him to me and say, Don't let them take you, Shep. The fat gonna stay fat. They don't need your help.

He dripped us some coffee and I showered and followed him on back home. Vivi thawed out some crayfish *étouffée* and I ate it with some french bread and two glasses of milk. That *étouffée* smelled like the best of everything in this state. The crayfish was from my own bayou. I sat there at the table and ate it, all hot and spicy, and smeared some more butter on the french bread. You can travel to Paris, France, and not do any better eating than we do here in Louisiana.

We were all sitting down together at the table for the first time in I don't know how long.

Sidda had on that goddamn eyeliner she wore back then. And I told her, get up and wipe that shit off your eyes if you want to eat at my table.

She said, This is not just your table. Don't take it out on us because you're upset about Lincoln.

I went to slap her upside the head, but she ducked and ran down the hall. War, it was hanging up in the air, crawling on the ground, swimming in the sea. It was rolling across my supper table.

I screamed: IT'S NOT MY GODDAMN FAULT! YALL HEAR ME? I DIDN'T START THIS. I DIDN'T WANT TO SEE LINCOLN LLOYD GET HIS JAW BLOWN OFF! I'VE KNOWN THAT BOY SINCE HE WAS A BABY.

I had to fight from crying. Couldn't catch my breath. The kids were staring at me, open-mouthed. I could feel the tight fingers squeezing my chest in.

Then Sidda was back in the room, holding something out to me. It was my inhaler. She put it in my hand and I reached out and pulled her to me. My boys looked confused. Lulu stared down at her food.

Vivi folded up her napkin and said, I will shoot my sons' big toes off before I let them go off and fight in a war.

That's the thing about my wife—she is crazy, but sometimes the woman can nail things right on the head.

She was the one who eventually drove me down to the Negro funeral parlor. It was drizzling slightly, and there were little lamps on either side of the entrance to the building that made it look like something from long ago. It's funny—Chaney, Willetta, all of them came to Daddy's funeral, but I don't believe I'd ever set foot in their funeral home before. Going to that section of town at night was like being in a foreign country to me.

I asked her, Please Vivi, would you go in there and tell Chaney I'm out here, that I'd like to talk to him?

Then I waited in the Thunderbird with the window rolled down watching all the Negroes walk in and out. Dressed to the nines, some of them carrying umbrellas. Holding onto each other, handkerchiefs in their hands, hats on.

Everyone used to wear hats, I remember thinking. When did they stop? Are the Negroes the only ones who wear hats anymore?

Vivi stepped out of the funeral parlor and came back to the car. She sat in the driver's seat and stared straight ahead. She wasn't acting like her normal self, but who the hell was? She told me, Chaney says if you want to talk to him, you'll have to go inside.

I took out my pocketknife and started to clean my fingernails. Finally I said, Vivi, what should I do?

Her hands were on the steering wheel, gripping it and letting it go, gripping it and letting it go. Then my wife said, I am dog-tired of all this, Shep. It's got to stop somewhere.

This was the first time I'd ever seen Chaney in a suit. It was tight on him and the pants pulled across the front. He was sitting down holding Willetta's hands, and a little group of women was hovering around them. Their hands together looked so brown and wrinkled. Those hands looked for a minute like the earth itself.

And for the first time, I thought: *Rice. Those people over there grow rice.*

I was frozen. Couldn't take a step. I just stood there, staring at Willetta and Chaney. The man saw me, saw I couldn't move. He whispered something to Willetta and they both looked over at me.

If you've ever done a kind act in your life, Chaney, please get up now and walk over to me and help unglue me from this spot. I am paralyzed. I'm in the middle of battle and I can't move.

Somebody was humming and it was sweet and warm in there. You could smell how dressed up they all were. I felt a dizziness come over me and I thought, Lord, I'm going to faint in this funeral parlor full of grieving colored people.

And then there was Vivi slipping in the door. She had on her chapel veil like the Catholics used to wear back then. She took my arm and we walked across the room to Willetta and Chaney. I was standing right in front of him.

Vivi said, I came to tell you how very sorry I am, Chaney. I'm so sorry, Willetta. I want yall to know you are in my prayers.

Chaney looked at her and said, Thank you, Miz Viviane.

He did not include me in the thanks. I couldn't believe Vivi didn't say: *We* are sorry. She should of said *We* are sorry. For God's sake, I thought, she's my *wife*.

Why was she saying, I'll be waiting in the car?

I looked down at my hands. I was left totally alone in the middle of those people. Tiny flecks of dirt up under my nails. Can't a man ever get his hands clean enough? Chaney's fingers were twined up with Willetta's. His palms had a pinkness to them I never noticed before. I had tears dripping down my face. I don't know where all the tears come from. My sinuses are going to be swole up for hours, I thought.

Chaney, podnah, I finally said. Can you forgive me, buddy?

He lifted his eyes, locked them on me, and left them there. I don't think Chaney had looked at me for that long since I'd known him. And all I could do is stand there and bear it. If he'd stood up and punched me in the stomach, I could not of lifted an arm to defend myself.

He didn't punch me. He reached up and handed me his handkerchief. It smelled like Clorox. I can still see that old white cotton handkerchief passing from his hand to mine. His bloodshot almond eyes, his full face, that big chest of his bulging out of what I realized was one of my old suits. I couldn't use that handkerchief until he spoke.

Until he said, Yeah, bossman, *I* forgive you.

He said it like there was a bunch of others who wouldn't forgive me. I kept on looking at him. Finally he said, Go on now, blow your nose.

I resigned from the draft board a couple of months after that. Figured if I was going to do my civic duty, I'd do it on the Garnet River Levee Board, something that might benefit us farmers. We got flooding and drainage problems throughout all this part of the country. Hell, the Mississippi, Red, and Atchafalaya are powerful big rivers. You got to pay some attention to the land and water in your own state.

Old Lyndon Baines decided not to run again. Said he was going back to Texas. Said his daddy once told him that down home the people know when you're sick and care when you die. I never really thought the man meant to keep us in that war for so long. I feel for him. He ain't never had Chaney forgive him. There's a lot of us on Judgment Day that will be ripped outta our E-Z Boys and thrown into a hell we never dreamed of.

These days, years after my time on the draft board, I'll sit up at night and watch the Gulf War on CNN. And I'll be damned if I can get to sleep, even hours after I turn off the TV. So I'll lay awake and talk to the Old Podnah. I wouldn't exactly call it praying. I just lay there and talk to Him. And sometimes when I listen close enough, I can hear—past the wheezing in my chest—the sound of a heartbeat that isn't coming from my own body at all, but from the fields outside, from the dirt, from the old Louisiana earth.

VALERIE MARTIN

Valerie Martin was already an established novelist and short story writer when her novel, *Mary Reilly*, was made into a major motion picture starring Julia Roberts. Martin's critical and popular appeal was further enhanced when she won Britain's prestigious Orange Prize. Years before, she enrolled in LSU's MA program, studying 18th Century British Literature with John Fischer and creative writing with Warren Eyster. Eyster helped her find her first literary agent and encouraged her to pursue an MFA, which she did at the University of Massachusetts. After moving back to New Orleans and selling her first novel, *Set in Motion*, she studied with Walker Percy and wrote *Alexandra,* which was followed by seven more novels.

In Martin's story, "Spats," her title establishes the controlling metaphor of the story. It is the subject, illustrated by her characters' turbulent marriage; it is the object, personified in the character of a dog by the same name who dominates a relationship with Gretta, the female dog in the story. The obvious parallel between the dysfunctional human and canine relationships adds interest to the already dramatic narrative about love gone bad from the point of view of the suffering wife, who at times wants to kill her husband. In fact, powerful animal symbols and tortured love relationships, at times masochistic, often appear in Martin's fiction. In *A Recent Martyr*, for example, set during a plague in New Orleans, a terrifying scene involving dying rats foreshadows the human deaths to follow. And in the short story, "The Freeze," a young woman finds a dead cat on her front porch the day after her lover rejects her. Always, we see in Martin's work an interest in the extreme psychological states of women, which some readers might find disturbing subject matter; and yet, as Fischer wrote in *The Southern Review*, "Odd as her characters are, they are of us. Through them, we recover ourselves: strange, new, frightening, and at risk."

VALERIE MARTIN

Spats

The dogs are scratching at the kitchen door. How long, Lydia thinks, has she been lost in the thought of her rival dead? She passes her hand over her eyes, an unconscious effort to push the hot red edge off everything she sees, and goes to the door to let them in.

When Ivan confessed that he was in love with another woman, Lydia thought she could ride it out. She told him what she had so often told him in the turbulent course of their marriage, that he was a fool, that he would be sorry. Even as she watched his friends loading his possessions into the truck, even when she stood alone in the silent half-empty house contemplating a pale patch on the wall where one of his pictures had been, even then she didn't believe he was gone. Now she has only one hope to hold on to: he has left the dogs with her and this must mean he will be coming back.

When she opens the door Gretta hangs back, as she always does, but Spats pushes his way in as soon as she has turned the knob, knocking the door back against her shins and barreling past her, his heavy tail slapping the wood repeatedly. No sooner is he inside than he turns to block the door so that Gretta can't get past him. He lowers his big head and nips at her forelegs; it's play, it's all in fun, but Gretta only edges past him, pressing close to Lydia, who pushes at the bigger dog with her foot. "Spats," she says, "leave her alone." Spats backs away, but he is only waiting until she is gone; then he will try again. Lydia is struck with the inevitability of this scene. It happens every day, several times a day, and it is always the same. The dogs gambol into the kitchen, knocking against the table legs, turning about in ever-narrowing circles, until they throw themselves down a few feet apart and settle for their naps. Gretta always sleeps curled tightly in a semicircle, her only defense against attacks from her mate, who sleeps on his side, his long legs extended, his neck stretched out, the open, deep sleep of the innocent or the oppressor.

Lydia stands at the door looking back at the dogs. Sometimes Ivan got right down on the floor with Spats, lay beside him holding his big black head against his chest and talking to him. "Did you have a good time at the park today?" he'd croon. "Did you swim? Are you really tired now? Are you happy?" This memory causes Lydia's upper lip to pull back from her teeth. How often had she wanted to kick him right in his handsome face when he did that, crooning over the dog as if it were his child or his mistress. What about me? she thought. What about my day? But she never said that; instead she turned away, biting back her anger and confusion, for she couldn't admit that she was jealous of a dog.

Spats is asleep immediately, his jaws slack and his tongue lolling out over his black lips. As Lydia looks at him she has an unexpected thought: she could kill him. It is certainly in her power. No one would do anything about it, and it would hurt Ivan as nothing else could. She could poison him, or shoot him, or she could take him to a vet and say he was vicious and have him put away.

She lights a match against the grout in the counter top and turns the stove burner on. It is too cold, and she is so numb with the loss of her husband that she watches the flame wearily, hopelessly; it can do so little for her. She could plunge her hand into it and burn it, or she could stand close to it and still be cold. Then she puts the kettle over the flame and turns away.

She had argued with Ivan about everything for years, so often and so intensely that it seemed natural to her. She held him responsible for the hot flush that rose to her cheeks, the bitter taste that flooded her mouth at the very thought of him. She believed that she was ill; sometimes she believed her life was nearly over and she hated Ivan for this too, that he was killing her with these arguments and that he didn't care.

When the water is boiling she fills a cup with coffee and takes it to the table. She sits quietly in the still house; the only sound is the clink of the cup as she sets it back in the saucer. She goes through a cycle of resolutions. The first is a simple one: she will make her husband come back. It is inconceivable that she will fail. They always had these arguments, they even separated a few times, but he always came back and so he always would. He would tire of this other woman in a few weeks and then he would be back. After all, she asked herself, what did this woman have that she didn't have? An education? And what good was that? If Ivan loved this woman for her education, it wasn't really as if he loved her for herself. He loved her for something she had acquired. And Lydia was certain that Ivan had loved *her*, had married her, and must still love her, only for herself, because she was so apparent, so undisguised; there wasn't anything else to love her for.

So this first resolution is a calm one: she will wait for her husband and he will return and she will take him back.

She sets the cup down roughly on the table, for the inevitable question is upon her: How long can she wait? This has been going on for two months, and she is sick of waiting. There must be something she can do. The thought of action stiffens her spine, and her jaw clenches involuntarily. Now comes the terrible vision of her revenge, which never fails to take her so by surprise that she sighs as she lays herself open to it; revenge is her only lover now. She will see a lawyer, sue Ivan for adultery, and get every cent she can out of him, everything, for the rest of his life. But this is unsatisfactory, promising, as it does, nothing better than a long life without him, a life in which he continues to love someone else. She would do better to buy a gun and shoot him. She could call him late at night, when the other woman is asleep, and beg him to come over. He will come; she can scare him into it. And then when he lets himself in with his key she will shoot him in the living room. He left her, she will tell the court. She bought the gun to protect herself because she was alone. How was she to know he would let himself in so late at night? He told her he was never coming back and she had assumed the footsteps in the living room came from the man every lonely woman lies in bed at night listening for, the man who has found out her secret, who knows she is alone, whose mission, which is sanctioned by the male world, is to break the spirit if not the bones of those rebellious women who have the temerity to sleep at night without a man. So she shot him. She wasn't going to ask any questions and live to see him get off in court. How could she have known it was her husband, who had abandoned her?

Yes, yes, that would work. It would be easily accomplished, but wouldn't she only end up as she was now? Better to murder the other woman, who was, after all, the cause of all this intolerable pain. She knew her name, knew where she lived, where she worked. She had called her several times just to hear her voice, her cheerful hello, in which Lydia always heard Ivan's presence, as if he were standing right next to the woman and she had turned away from kissing him to answer the insistent phone. Lydia had heard of a man who killed people for money. She could pay this man, and then the woman would be gone.

The kettle is screaming; she has forgotten to turn off the flame. So she could drink another cup of coffee, then take a bath. But that would take only an hour or so and she has to get through the whole day. The silence in the house is intense, though she knows it is no more quiet than usual. Ivan was never home much in the daytime. What did she do before? It seems to her that that life was another life, one she will never know again, the life in which each day ended with the appearance of her husband. Sometimes, she admitted, she had not been happy to see him, but her certainty that she would see him made the question of whether she was happy or sad a matter of indifference to her. Often she didn't see him until late at night, when he appeared at one of the clubs where she was singing. He took a place in the audience and when she saw him she always sang for him. Then they were both happy. He knew she was admired, and that pleased him, as if she were his reflection and what others saw when they looked at her was more of him. Sometimes he gave her that same affectionate look he gave himself in mirrors, and when he did it made her lightheaded, and she would sing, holding her hands out a little before her, one index finger stretched out as if she were pointing at something, and she would wait until the inevitable line about how it was "you" she loved, wanted, hated, couldn't get free of, couldn't live without, and at that "you" she would make her moving hands be still and with her eyes as well as her hands she would point to her husband in the crowd. Those were the happiest moments they had, though neither of them was really conscious of them, nor did they ever speak of this happiness. When, during the break, they did speak, it was usually to argue about something.

She thinks of this as she stares dully at the dogs, Ivan's dogs. Later she will drive through the cold afternoon light to Larry's cold garage, where they will rehearse. They will have dinner together; Larry and Simon will try to cheer her up, and Kenneth, the drummer, will sit looking on in his usual daze. They will take drugs if anyone has any, cocaine or marijuana, and Simon will drink a six-pack of beer.

Then they will go to the club and she will sing as best she can. She will sing and sing, into the drunken faces of the audience, over the bobbing heads of the frenzied dancers; she will sing like some blinded bird lost in a dark forest trying to find her way out by listening to the echo of her own voice. The truth is that she sings better than she ever has. Everyone tells her so. Her voice is so full of suffering that hearing it would move a stone, though it will not move her husband, because he won't be there. Yet she can't stop looking for him in the audience, as she always has. And as she sings and looks for him she will remember exactly what it was like to find herself in his eyes. That was how she had first seen him, sitting at a table on the edge of the floor, watching her closely. He was carrying on a conversation with a tired-looking woman across from him but he watched Lydia so closely that she could feel his eyes on her. She smiled. She was aware of herself as the surprising creation she really was, a woman who was beautiful to look at and beautiful to hear. She was, at that moment, so self-conscious and so contented that she didn't notice what an oddity he was, a man who was both beautiful and masculine. Her attachment to his appearance, to his gestures, the suddenness of his smile, the coldness of his eyes, came later. At that moment it was herself in his eyes that she loved; as fatal a love match as she would ever know.

The phone rings. She hesitates, then gets up and crosses to the counter. She picks up the receiver and holds it to her ear.

"Hello," Ivan says. "Lydia?"

She says nothing.

"Talk to me!" he exclaims.

"Why should I?"

"Are you all right?"

"No."

"What are you doing?"

"Why are you calling me?"

"About the dogs."

"What about them?"

"Are they OK?"

She sighs. "Yes." Then, patiently, "When are you coming to get them?"

"I can't," he says. "I can't take them. I can't keep them here."

"Why?"

"There's no fenced yard. Vivian's landlord doesn't allow dogs."

At the mention of her rival's name, Lydia feels a sudden rush of blood to her face. "You bastard," she hisses.

"Baby, please," he says, "try to understand."

She slams the receiver down into the cradle. "Bastard," she says again. Her fingers tighten on the edge of the counter until the knuckles are white. He doesn't want the dogs. He doesn't want her. He isn't coming back. "I really can't stand it," she says into the empty kitchen. "I don't think I will be able to stand it."

She is feeding the dogs. They have to eat at either end of the kitchen because Spats will eat Gretta's dinner if he can. Gretta has to be fed first; then Spats is lured away from her bowl with his own. Gretta eats quickly, swallowing one big bite after another, for she knows she has only the time it takes Spats to finish his meal before he will push her away from hers. Tonight Spats is in a bad humor. He growls at Gretta when Lydia sets her bowl down. Gretta hangs her head and backs away. "Spats!" Lydia says. "Leave her alone." She pushes him away with one hand, holding out his bowl before him with the other.

But he growls again, turning his face toward her, and she sees that his teeth are bared and his threat is serious. "Spats," she says firmly, but she backs away. His eyes glaze over with something deep and vicious, and she knows that he no longer hears her. She drops the bowl. The sound of the bowl hitting the linoleum and the sight of his food scattered before him brings Spats back to himself. He falls to eating off the floor. Gretta lifts her head to watch him, then returns to her hurried eating.

Lydia leans against the stove. Her legs are weak and her heart beats absurdly in her ears. In the midst of all this weakness a habitual ambivalence goes hard as stone. Gretta, she thinks, certainly deserves to eat in peace.

She looks down at Spats. Now he is the big, awkward, playful, good fellow again.

"You just killed yourself," Lydia says. Spats looks back at her, his expression friendly, affable. He no longer remembers his fit of bad temper.

Lydia smiles at him. "You just killed yourself and you don't even have the sense to know it," she says.

It is nearly dawn. Lydia lies in her bed alone. She used to sleep on her back when Ivan was with her. Now she sleeps on her side, her legs drawn up to her chest. Or rather, she reminds herself, she lies awake in this position and waits for the sleep that doesn't come.

As far as she is concerned she is still married. Her husband is gone, but marriage, in her view, is not a condition that can be dissolved by external circumstances. She has always believed this; she told Ivan this when she married him, and he agreed or said he agreed. They were bound together for life. He had said he wanted nothing more.

She still believes it. It is all she understands marriage to be. They must cling to each other and let the great nightmarish flood of time wash over them as it will; at the end they would be found wherever they were left, washed onto whatever alien shore, dead or alive, still together, their lives entwined as surely as their bodies, inseparably, eternally. How many times in that last year, in the midst of the interminable quarrels that constituted their life together, had she seen pass across his face an expression that filled her with rage, for she saw that he knew she was drowning and he feared she would pull him down with her. So even as she raged at him, she clung to him more tightly, and the lovemaking that followed their arguments was so intense, so filled with her need of him that, she told herself, he must know, wherever she was going, he was going with her.

Now, she confesses to herself, she is drowning. Alone, at night, in the moonless sea of her bed, where she is tossed from nightmare to nightmare so that she wakes gasping for air, throwing her arms out before her, she is drowning alone in the dark and there is nothing to hold on to.

Lydia sits on the floor in the veterinarian's office. Spats lies next to her; his head rests in her lap. He is unconscious but his heart is still beating feebly. Lydia can feel it beneath her palm, which she has pressed against his side. His mouth has gone dry and his dry tongue lolls out to one side. His black lips are slack and there is no sign of the sharp canine teeth that he used to bare so viciously at the slightest provocation. Lydia sits watching his closed eyes and she is afflicted with the horror of what she has done.

He is four years old; she has known him all his life. When Ivan brought him home he was barely weaned and he cried all that first night, a helpless baby whimpering for his lost mother. But he was a sturdy, healthy animal, greedy for life, and he transferred his affections to Ivan and to his food bowl in a matter of days. Before he was half her size he had terrorized Gretta into the role he and Ivan had worked out for her: dog-wife, mother to his children. She would never have a moment's freedom as long as he lived, no sleep that could not be destroyed by his sudden desire for play, no meal that he did not oversee and covet. She was more intelligent than he, and his brutishness wore her down. She became a nervous, quiet animal who would rather be patted than fed, who barricaded herself under desks, behind chairs, wherever she could find a space Spats couldn't occupy at the same time.

Spats was well trained; Ivan saw to that. He always came when he was called and he followed just at his master's heel when they went out for their walks every day.

But it ran against his grain; every muscle in his body was tensed for that moment when Ivan would say "Go ahead," and then he would spring forward and run as hard as he could for as long as he was allowed. He was a fine swimmer and loved to fetch sticks thrown into the water.

When he was a year old, his naturally territorial disposition began to show signs of something amiss. He attacked a neighbor who made the mistake of walking into his yard, and bit him twice, on the arm and on the hand. Lydia stood in the doorway screaming at him, and Ivan was there instantly, shouting at Spats and pulling him away from the startled neighbor, who kept muttering that it was his own fault; he shouldn't have come into the yard. Lydia had seen the attack from the start; she had, she realized, seen it coming and not known it. What disturbed her was that Spats had tried to bite the man's face or his throat, and that he had given his victim almost no notice of his intention. One moment he was wagging his tail and barking, she told Ivan; then, with a snarl, he was on the man.

Ivan made excuses for the animal, and Lydia admitted that it was freakish behavior. But in the years that followed, it happened again and again. Lydia had used this evidence against him, had convicted him on the grounds of it; in the last two years he had bitten seven people. Between these attacks he was normal, friendly, playful, and he grew into such a beautiful animal, his big head was so noble, his carriage so powerful and impressive, that people were drawn to him and often stopped to ask about him. He enjoyed everything in his life; he did everything—eating, running, swimming— with such gusto that it was a pleasure to watch him. He was so full of energy, of such inexhaustible force, it was as if he embodied life, and death must stand back a little in awe at the sight of him.

Now Lydia strokes his head, which seems to be getting heavier every moment, and she says his name softly. It's odd, she thinks, that I would like to die but I have to live, and he would like to live but he has to die.

In the last weeks she has wept for herself, for her lost love, for her husband, for her empty life, but the tears that fill her eyes now are for the dying animal she holds in her arms. She is looking straight into the natural beauty that was his life and she sees resting over it, like a relentless cloud of doom, the empty lovelessness that is her own. His big heart has stopped; he is gone.

WALKER PERCY

Long before Walker Percy won the 1962 National Book Award for his first novel, *The Moviegoer*, he wrote a short story called "Young Nuclear Physicist." In it, the hero longs for female companionship, suffers in silent despair from loneliness, and looks to science for a better understanding of his profound alienation. These themes developed into the complex philosophical stance Percy incorporated into the five bestselling novels that followed his 1962 success.

Lewis Simpson, in his zeal to expand and reinvigorate *The Southern Review* as its editor, sought connection with the monumental talent who lived right down the road in Covington, Louisiana. In reply to Simpson's invitation to visit campus for the 1972 Lectures in the Humanities, Percy wrote, "I very much appreciate your invitation, but I do not do this sort of thing—except under duress or in dire need of money." He added, ". . . —one reason I'd *want* to come would be to meet you and David Madden." Simpson persevered, and by 1974, Percy began commuting weekly to LSU to teach The Novel of Alienation. Of the fall semester, he wrote to Simpson that "the students were very rewarding and I found myself thinking a great deal about them and their futures." The same school year, Percy looked forward "like a kid" to seeing his essay, "The Delta Factor" published in *The Southern Review*. Though he left the faculty after one year, he reentered the academic life of LSU through the National Endowment Summer Seminar, which was conducted by Simpson.

Former students report that even though they asked Percy questions about his own work, he would turn the subject away from himself and toward others; that he was, like his character Binx Bolling, modest, ironic, and self-deprecating. But he was also one of the great philosophical minds of the 20th century, a Christian existentialist whose heroes and heroines spend their lives searching for meaning in the face of the crumbling traditions of religious faith and Southern Stoicism.

WALKER PERCY

Young Nuclear Physicist

Ralph moved toward the stern of the ferry. He had seen Miss Terhune, the mesotron technician, and one of his instructors talking together. Perhaps he would join the conversation. They would not know him by name, but as one of the new students, he should be welcome. They were staring at the retreating bank. Ralph looked in the same direction, but there was nothing to see except a large sewer which gaped above the water line.

"It must be very largely digested by bacterial action," the instructor was saying.

"Or perhaps it simply dissolves. Toilet paper is not very substantial," Miss Terhune said.

They continued to stare at the sewer as though the answer were about to emerge any moment. Ralph looked closely at Miss Terhune to see if she were carrying off an elaborate joke. But she was neither amused nor concerned nor revolted. She didn't seem to care whether the East River fairly swam with toilet paper, only interested in the explanation of why it didn't. After all, Ralph admitted to himself, it was an acute observation that one never saw gross pieces of toilet paper floating so close to a Manhattan sewer.

They began talking about the suicides. Sooner or later every conversation on the Island got around to them. It was a bad start for the Institute, especially since the tabloids had made a big thing of it. The front page of one had carried a full-page picture of the men's dormitory with a superimposed trajectory of dashes starting from a window near the top, rising jauntily like a springboard diver, and plunging to a Maltese cross on the gravel path, and a caption below: "Atom Student Takes Dive." That was the Tennessee boy. Ralph had not known him: he jumped the day after school started.

The other was a young Jew from Queens named Tepper, a graduate of Columbia. He had stolen some potassium hydroxide from the chemistry lab and late one night had munched the better part of two sticks, holding them between thumb and forefinger, as the destruction of these tissues clearly showed. The motive in his case was more obscure. An acute attack of homesickness in an unstable person might conceivably induce such an act, but Tepper could hardly have been homesick, since he died within a mile of home.

"It's a psychiatric problem," said the instructor. "There should be an integration of personality studies with matriculation."

"That would do it," agreed Miss Terhune.

"But all in all, it's not too surprising. In any vast new undertaking like the Institute, it's a question of getting the bugs out of it."

Ralph, who was standing next to the rail half-facing them, nodded seriously as the instructor spoke. But by now the ferry had docked at the Island, and they left without noticing him.

He sat at his desk in the dormitory room and made a few calculations on the slide rule. It was the most expensive one that he had been able to find. But how could one waste money on a slide rule? The semester was new enough so that he still felt some of the exuberance of the first day. It had always been the best time of the year for him—ever since the first time with the new satchel, pencils, pencil sharpener, crayons, tin of water colors, compass, ruler, and the books: the stiff primers with the new smell and the limp, slick textbook pages. It was the time for putting on the New Man, for casting off all the old bad habits. Life became simple again. The way was straight then as now. All he had to do, then as now, was to start on page one and keep going, take it all in from the first page of the first primer with the big black A and little a, each covering a whole page.

This fall the renewal was total: a new man, a new school, a new city. The books were bigger than ever, so big that each included a slip of directions on how to open it without damaging the binding. It was easy to fancy that a new textbook was a perfect thing. It was perfectly manufactured, and so its text must be a perfect revelation of the subject. Surely there could be no typographical errors, misspellings, bad sentences, or gross misconceptions.

He swivelled toward the window. Trademark paper and dried putty still stuck to the panes. But he could see almost the whole length of Manhattan. It was hard to understand how anyone could fail to experience the same autumnal joy. Tepper and the Tennessee boy were clearly psychiatric cases before they ever got to the Institute.

Ralph had become adjusted to his surroundings quickly enough, although, unlike other school years, a certain permanent sense of strangeness remained. He was perfectly at home during the lectures and laboratory work. It was all review, covering in a few months all four years of college mathematics and physics. His schedule was regular. After attending lectures all morning and lab all afternoon, he would allow himself a half-hour nap and a bite of supper before getting back to the books. Perhaps the persistent feeling of novelty could be attributed to the Institute buildings. They were certainly unlike any campus he had ever seen before: concrete skyscrapers separated by gravel courts. They completely occupied the north end of the Island almost to the water's edge. Although there were winding paths connecting the buildings, it was more convenient as well as time-saving to use the tunnels. They were well ventilated and lighted by sodium vapor lamps. The tunnel from his dormitory led a few hundred feet to an intersection of several tunnels posted with signs directing one to the classrooms, laboratories, and other dormitories. There was a curious thing about the tunnels. He had to admit to a small sense of embarrassment when approaching somebody. It was the same slight restiveness, multiplied several times, which one feels when approaching a person on the sidewalk. In the tunnel there was no scenery to engage one's eye, only the lines of shining tile converging on the other person. It must have been difficult for women. They solved it in different ways. They would look fixedly at a point in space a few inches from his left ear, or gaze with interest at the sodium lamps in the ceiling. Some few would stare into his eyes boldly, almost accusingly. It was undeniably a minor social crisis, and he always felt positively chivalric when he was able to get past a girl with just the proper mixture of looking at her and looking away. He often wondered what would happen if, as he neared one of the pretty technicians, he should gaze squarely at her, and as the gap between them closed, he should begin to walk at a slight crouch in the middle of the tunnel. She would face a terrible choice: either to keep going and try somehow to pass at close quarters or to cut and run.

To tell the truth, his life in New York had not fulfilled all expectations. Ralph had not thought about it much, but he had expected to divide his evenings between a group of fellow scientists and a second group, a sort of Bohemian coterie of impoverished students, artists, musicians, and chorus girls. He had easily visualized himself as one of an elite few invited to the rooms of the top man in quantum mechanics, a lean boyish sort of fellow, brilliant and erratic, the kind who would pay no attention to the ordinary conventions of lecturing but would wander all over the pit hooking an arm over the railing or sitting on the desk. He would soon recognize Ralph's qualities, and before long Ralph would find himself with a few others in the professor's rooms. There would be much good talk about philosophy, art, mysticism, and a thousand other subjects. He was no longer Mr. Budd, a first-year student who sat near the back of the lecture hall, but Budd: "I say, Budd, you're from the South. What do you think of—," some phase of the Negro problem. All eyes would turn to him, and he would stare thoughtfully into his mug of pilsener before answering.

Ralph only realized how complete a picture he had formed of New York when, as time went by, not a single detail materialized. There was, of course, no such person as Ralph's professor. The instructors were all bored-looking men who lived in Connecticut or Long Island and left as soon as possible after lectures. The only intercourse between student and teacher occurred immediately after the lecture when a few eager students would leap into the pit with well-put questions. Ralph knew their kind of old. He would leave the room alone, full of contempt for student and professor.

Nor was there an elite group of students, or if there was, he didn't know them. After six weeks his only acquaintance was his lab co-worker, a youth named Freddie from Muncie, Indiana.

Nor had he managed yet to fall in with a coterie of Bohemians. In this case, his preformed picture was not quite as clear. He only imagined that he would surround himself with many oddly assorted and carefree companions. They would frequent a regular rendezvous, perhaps a little-known bierstube in Yorkville. There might be on occasions a hoisting of steins, bawdy toasts, and rollicking drinking songs. But above all, there would be the women, the unattached, "unconventional" girls who had come to New York to escape life in small Midwestern towns. He would form a series of attachments with these independent girls. There were other couples who would invade their studio apartment, their arms full of French bread and wine bottles clad in little baskets.

Ralph probably got most of these notions from Dr. Goodbee at the university in Arkansas. Dr. Goodbee had spent a year at a German university at a time when it was good policy for an American professor. He used to tell Ralph about it over bottles of beer in the Campus Corner.

"They had the way of life all right," he would say, picking at the wet label. "The old German university towns before the war. The other war. Bonn, Tübingen, Freiburg, Heidelberg, though of course there were always too many Americans there. The leitmotif was comradeship. I remember the ski trains from München—." Ralph could almost see the young Bavarians sprawled in the aisles and hear the Sigmund Romberg songs, but he could never quite get Dr. Goodbee into the picture.

"But Paris!" With the word alone Dr. Goodbee could conjure up all manner of delights. He was fond of describing a class of women which he said existed in Paris, different from anything in Arkansas or this hemisphere. They were young, clean, attractive, affectionate, even loyal, and desired nothing more than to be mistresses of young American students. Dr. Goodbee would look sorrowfully at the coeds drinking cokes.

"There were no recriminations when time for goodbyes came and never any nonsense about marriage." At these times he wore a troubled expression, for all the world like a man hopelessly entangled with a number of young Arkansas girls who, in spite of his age and family, demanded marriage. All he appeared to want of life during these nostalgic moments was to be allowed to return to Paris for a short time and renew his friendship with another generation of these unusual girls or, even better, to introduce a similar system to Arkansas.

There was no sign of any of these activities in New York. Dr. Goodbee's account of university life was either greatly exaggerated or New York was a hopelessly different sort of place. Ralph knew only two girls and these in the most casual way: Miss Terhune and Miss Cassidy, secretary to the Dean. Miss Cassidy could be eliminated immediately. She lived somewhere in New Jersey and commuted. As for Miss Terhune, it would be unthinkable to ask her for a date. Every other student in the Institute knew her at least as well. He spoke to her once a day and then only to say "good morning" briskly, with the air of a man totally absorbed in his work by day and busy at night with a large and cosmopolitan circle of friends. To approach Miss Terhune, who was, so to speak, part of the mesotron apparatus, would be humiliating. He didn't even know her first name. There seemed to be no way to expand their relationship. It remained static: a series of good mornings. He simply could not bring himself to say to her: "Good morning! I know a little out-of-the way bierstube in Yorkville." It would be an admission of abject loneliness to approach a person who could not even be called an acquaintance, and worse, he would lay himself open to all sorts of devastating rejections.

Something had undoubtedly gone wrong in his calculations. It was a queer thing. For although he did allow himself romantic notions after the fashion of Dr. Goodbee, he had never really taken them seriously, had in fact resolved to tolerate nothing that interfered with his work. He had determined this year to put on the New Man in earnest. Fortunately, his surroundings encouraged him in this respect. The Institute was a house of pure science. There was no sentimental nonsense, no paraphernalia of tradition. He had once visited a medical student in Baltimore. His friend lived with several other students in an old house run by a motherly little woman. She attended to all their needs: nursed their colds, cooked Southern meals for them, arranged for them to meet girls of old Baltimore families. Miss Annie. One hardly knew her last name. Everything in the neighborhood was encrusted with tradition. There was the pub around the corner with the initials of the great carved into the booths and carefully preserved by varnish. Even the Baltimore dirt was hallowed. But the Institute got along without such sentimentalisms. There was very little dirt, only the faint acrid smell of burning garbage from the disposal plant across the river. There was no local movie inevitably nicknamed "The Axilla" or "The Perineum" and frequented by blocs of students who were obliged to hiss and cheer at the proper moments. And thank God there was no Old Pops, the janitor, who has been with us as long as anybody can remember. Since Ralph's class was the first to matriculate, there were not even upperclassmen to send one on fool's errands.

One day as he walked through the dormitory tunnel, Ralph had a strange thought. He was decidedly pleased with himself since a quiz paper had been returned to him with a very high mark. His thoughts flew ahead to the time of the triumph of his career. Although he was not yet a nuclear physicist, or even a student of nuclear physics, since he was still in the review course, he could easily imagine the day when, perhaps still a student, he would make an extraordinarily ingenious discovery (a cut in *Time* magazine of himself in white lab coat adjusting an apparatus). But for once his daydreams carried beyond the day of culmination. Then what? Naturally any job would be his for the asking, and he would accept the plum, a full professorship at the Institute. A lifetime of fifty years or more devoted to pure science. He looked at the gleaming tile of the tunnel. It was durable: no doubt it would be much the same fifty years from now. The yellow sodium lamps swam before his eyes. He was suddenly hot and nauseated. But anyone watching him would have only seen him pause a moment and touch the tile wall.

He took a cold shower and felt much better. Far below his window the ferry was warping in to the Institute landing. It heeled over dangerously as it turned against the current. A weight lifted from his heart. *I have been a fool. My error is simply a failure to apply method. I apply method with competence and success to mathematical and physical problems. Why should I imagine that my personal life is exempt, that it should work itself out with no conscious direction?* He cleared his desk top until nothing remained but a pencil and a sheet of paper. He wrote: *The problem: loneliness.* What a disgusting admission! How humiliating to be subject to such a demand! But already he was consoled by his discovery and by his forthrightness in facing it. How could he have been so stupid as to imagine that upon arrival in New York he would be automatically invested with a complete social life and a fake nineteenth-century one at that? Very well. What was the answer? He wrote: *Possibilities of meeting congenial people.* He realized with some agitation that he was getting unpleasantly close to the Dale Carnegie sort of thing. Nevertheless, he compiled a list:

1. Freddie.
2. Miss Terhune.
3. Prostitutes.
4. Pick-ups in bars, night clubs, dance halls, parks, libraries, zoos, etc.
5. Social Agency which arranges meetings.
6. Call up relatives in Long Island City and meet their friends.
7. Church socials.
8. Arthur Murrays.

He saw immediately that Freddie had no place in the list. He crossed out Miss Terhune next: in addition to the other objections, the truth was that he really didn't like her much. He crossed out prostitutes as inadequate to his needs. He realized that what he was looking for after all was one of Dr. Goodbee's girls, except that she would have qualities that Goodbee would never understand: a sensitivity, an intuitive understanding of him. What a tender relationship they would have! She would be a mild, dreamy girl, a constant and gentle presence in the studio apartment. His life would be a perfect balance of the Tender and the Abstract. He would burst in on her with armloads of foods and wines from exotic delicatessens. Perhaps a third ingredient was needed for the full life, an American equivalent of the drinking fraternity at

Heidelburg. He permitted himself a short fantasy: a duel had been arranged, German style, with sabres. They wore special helmets which allowed only non-fatal cheek wounds. He was wounded repeatedly and honorably. The pain was fierce and exalted; his blood tasted salty and rich. The surgeon, standing by, stanched the hemorrhage, and he and his opponent, similarly wounded, drank a liter of beer through linked arms.

Suddenly, he developed a huge thirst for beer. He dressed and decided to go over to Manhattan.

He saw on the table, where he had emptied his pockets, a folded slip of pink paper. It was in his mail box when he came in. "Call GR 3-4454." He picked up the telephone and gave the number to the man at the switchboard downstairs. Presently a woman's voice said:

"The Betsy Ross Hotel. Good evening."

"Someone left a message for me to call that number."

"Do you know the name or room number?"

"No." He clicked the phone until the man downstairs answered.

"Look. A call came in for me this afternoon."

"Yessir, Mr. Budd. I remember. She left her number."

She!

"The number is that of a hotel. Didn't she leave a name or anything else?"

"No, sir. I don't believe she did."

A woman's voice. He had to concede that it could be his aunt in town for shopping. But it was easier to think of Her as the Stranger, the archetype of all women, One mysteriously sent to him. Perhaps she was a lonely Memphis girl working in New York. She had seen his picture months ago in the *Commercial Appeal*: "Arkansan Wins Atom Post." She had not forgotten, and in a fit of desperate loneliness, she had called out to him as an ally in a hostile city.

It was one of those incidents in all likelihood trivial but which one would prefer to believe fateful and capable, if followed up, of changing one's entire life. Ralph looked up the address of the Betsy Ross and after a quick supper in the cafeteria took the ferry to Manhattan and the subway downtown.

The Betsy Ross was a huge brick affair the like of which he had never seen before. Across the marquee blazed the complete name: The Betsy Ross Hotel for Women. He gazed up at the solid bank of windows. *There must be thousands of them up there!* After some hesitation he entered the lobby. He reasoned that men would surely be permitted there, for how else could they call on their friends? There were, in fact, a few men sitting around the lobby, probably waiting for their dates to come down. A placard over the main desk read: No Gentlemen Guests Allowed Above Mezzanine. Ralph began to realize the hopelessness of his mission. He could not ask for anyone at the desk. He could, of course, sit in plain view until his unknown friend passed through. But that might take days, and even then she mightn't recognize him. Furthermore, the Betsy Ross management had undoubtedly taken stronger precautions than ordinary hotels against men loitering about the lobby with no legitimate business. He sat in a chair facing the elevators in the faint hope that she would emerge as magically as her telephone call. He looked at his watch frequently and assumed an expression of mock annoyance, as much as to say: "Women! They probably don't start dressing until we call for them." The elevators went up and down constantly and dozens of women came out, but no one paid any attention to him. After fifteen minutes he strolled idly across the lobby and mounted the steps to the mezzanine. At one end he found what he was looking for: a deep and poorly lighted recess furnished with writing tables and wicker chairs and sofas. It was a perfect vantage point from which to see the main desk, entrance, and elevator doors without being seen. Most of the women in the lobby were young. Some wore evening dresses. The elevator doors would slide back with their now familiar sound, and they would step out smiling. Their escorts would leap up to meet them. They would stand talking a moment and then walk out together. Some were middle-aged and older. They walked from place to place with the absentmindedness of long habit. Probably, Ralph thought, they were, in their youth, just like the others: out-of-town girls with jobs in New York. The only difference was that nothing had happened to them. They hadn't gotten married, or moved to an apartment, or gone back home. He wondered what happened when one of them died. They had come from the little towns in Tennessee and Iowa and had spent their youth and middle life and old age here in the Betsy Ross. It would certainly not be proper to ship them home to be buried in a place where they were no longer known. No doubt the hotel had foreseen such contingencies and could make appropriate arrangements. There would be services in a nearby place, a decent little chapel, with her friends in attendance: the other old-timers, the desk clerk, the doorman.

After more than two hours Ralph gave up his vigil. But far from being discouraged, he was convinced more than ever that he was on the right track. Logically, this was a lead that should be run down before starting on the list. Since no quiz was scheduled for several weeks, he felt free to spend several evenings at the Betsy Ross.

On Thursday, the night of his fifth visit, there was a dance in the ballroom off the lobby. He could hear the orchestra playing inside. Couples presented invitations at the door. He had not felt well lately, and tonight he was grimy and tired and his forehead throbbed. He held his face in his hands; they came away dripping with cold sweat. He let his head rest against the ridged back of the wicker armchair. After a while a girl came into the recess and, without seeing him, sat at one of the little desks and began writing letters. The yellow light fell on her bare arms. Her hand moved steadily back and forth across the page, the soft muscle rising and falling in her forearm.

"Look, Miss." Ralph stood at her side and gently touched her elbow.

She was startled, but she looked up at him without alarm.

"Yes?"

He must have stood there too long gazing down at her without saying anything, or perhaps she realized that he could only have come from one of the chairs or sofas in the darkness behind her. She screwed the cap on her fountain pen and stacked her stationery quickly, as though this were really all the correspondence she had intended to do for the moment. When she was gone, Ralph moved to the mezzanine railing. The orchestra had stopped playing, and the lobby was filled with the dancers in their tuxedos and evening dresses.

"Hey, Miss." Ralph heard his voice unexpectedly loud, filling the whole room. The girl by now stood waiting for the elevator. At the sound of his voice, she moved closer to the elevator doors. Everyone was looking up at him.

He gripped the rail and leaned over, staring at their upturned faces.

"Hey you girls." He let his voice get louder than ever so that it trembled in the air and echoed from the walls. A girl just below smiled at him expectantly and nudged her escort. She evidently took him to be one of their crowd who was cutting up a bit. He saw her lips frame the question: Who is that?

"This is Ralph Budd in the mezzanine—." Rough hands seized him from behind.

"Hey down there," he cried as they pried his fingers from the rail. "Heyeeeeeee."

The two men hustled him down the steps and through the lobby. They seemed determined to make him look drunk or paralytic, for they propelled him forward with short jerks, lifting him almost clear off the floor so that his feet skipped along, touching only at the toes. His hat fell off somewhere in the lobby. He wondered if they were going to kick him in the buttocks when they got to the door and send him sprawling onto the sidewalk. But they came to a stop under the marquee as if undecided about the next move. The doorman joined them and said to one of the plainclothesmen:

"Is he one of the college boys?"

"Look at him. He ain't wearing a black suit. He was hollering around up in the balcony bothering the girls."

"Okay. I'll take him."

The men were satisfied. They released him and went inside. The doorman didn't touch him.

"Look, Jack. This is not the place for that kind of act. They could've put you in Bellevue with the pansies and the peepers. This place is full of girls, yeah. But you got to meet them right. Now just hold it a minute and I'll fix you up."

He blew his whistle and a cab came around the corner. He had a talk with the driver and held the door for Ralph, stepping back to a smart attention as though Ralph were a frequent and honored visitor at the Betsy Ross.

❦

Ralph did not return to the Betsy Ross. He was too unnerved even to think about his list of "possibilities." As matters turned out, he could have spared himself all the trouble of the past few days. Not more than a week later, he found another folded pink slip in his box. He opened it with misgivings, and when he saw again that dreadful number GR 3-4454, he was seized with panic. *They have tracked me down. Despite the kindness of the doorman I will be exposed.* He was sure at first that the name below must be that of an official of the Betsy Ross, a person who was authorized to take legal steps against him in order to protect the girls from any more antics. "Call Miss Walterene Gross." So Walterene had the job. No no no no no. *She* was the girl who had called him the first time and was calling again because she hadn't heard from him. Walterene Gross. She belonged to his past, a past twice removed, not the past of college years, which he had put behind him to start anew at the Institute, but the past before that, the years of living at home and going to high school. Ralph was still a very young man, yet it seemed to him that he had known her a thousand years ago in a different age, a different world.

They had not known each other well. He had probably not spoken two dozen words to her altogether. But after all these years, it was hard to imagine that they had not been good friends. People spoke of them together because they made the best grades in the class. Walterene Gross and Ralph Budd were the smartest girl and boy in school. It was conceded that Ralph was probably the smarter of the two, even though Walterene nosed him out to be valedictorian. Being a girl, she studied every night and never missed her homework while Ralph relied on heroic cram sessions the night before an exam. They spoke little, but there was (he thought) a silent camaraderie between them, a tacit understanding that they were the elite and nothing more needed to be said about it. They would pass each other in the hall or on the steps with carefully averted glances. She was a thin, dark girl with thick black hair cut in a precise bob which mathematically framed her face in three straight lines. She was forever carrying a tremendous double stack of books and craning her head forward to see the steps below. Incongruously, she had excelled in a minor sport. She was by no means athletic, but she had set a record in rope climbing, which probably still stood. Passing through the gym he would sometimes see her, scrambling agilely up the rope, her thin bloomered legs trailing passively behind.

She had all but died in his memory. When he went away to college he had expected somehow to meet better girls, a superior breed suitable to his higher academic status. He had heard nothing about her. He didn't even know if she had gone on to college.

There was a chance, of course, that she knew about his strange behavior in the Betsy Ross. He had identified himself from the mezzanine. She may even have been in the crowd below. But if she said anything about it, he could make an excuse and hang up and that would be the end of it.

He gave the number in the security of his room and asked for Miss Gross. A voice finally said: "Yes?"

It must have been the wrong Walterene. There were overtones and inflections in the one word, of which the old Walterene had been entirely innocent.

"Is this Walterene Gross?"

"Yes?"

"This is Ralph Budd."

"Ralph Budd! I heard you were in New York. Imagine after all these years."

He heard himself laughing and talking with a ready fund of small talk. In a few seconds they had restored the tenuous bonds of their old relationship and added many more. He kidded her about the rope-climbing act which she denied laughingly altogether. But he still couldn't associate this voice with Walterene Gross. There was no trace of an Arkansas accent. When she said "silly," it was with the heavy lingual L of the North: si-ully.

"I called you," she said, "because I happen to have two tickets to a thing that might be a lot of fun. Have you ever heard of the Arkansas Society? They have dinners and dances and make speeches about the good old days. It's really rare. The only qualification you have to have is that you hail from Arkansas and live in the big city. It might be amusing. Imagine coming all the way to New York to get away from Arkansas and then forming a tight little group of nothing but Arkansans!"

Ralph laughed loudly, hoping it would not occur to her that she was doing just that.

"It sounds wonderful, Walterene. Do we dress?"

"Oh sure. We're uptown hillbillies now."

He was relieved. He would feel much more secure walking into the Betsy Ross dressed in a tuxedo.

Already he was transformed. The Ralph Budd of the past few weeks was a pitiful creature who bore no relation to him. He took out the list from the desk drawer and tore it up, averting his eyes from the shameful words. Yet a sense of misgiving remained. She was so confident and urbane. She had changed enormously, but had he? They would laugh at their fellow Arkansans, but after that, what was left to be said? He smiled: he was inventing trouble. She had just asked him for a date; naturally she had to make use of a special circumstance, take a particular line. What did he expect her to do?

He had a bad moment when he passed the doorman. But the fellow didn't recognize him or was kind enough not to show it. What a difference his new friendship made! He no longer had to devise means of getting to the mezzanine unobserved. He walked straight to the main desk.

"Miss Gross, please. Mr. Budd calling."

He sat in his old chair facing the elevators, holding the corsage box in his lap. He looked with serenity at his fellow men similarly disposed throughout the lobby. Every time the elevator doors opened, he started up anxiously. He tried to picture Walterene's face set above an evening gown. But he couldn't see her without the books. He decided that he could not positively recognize her, that he could only be sure when a girl was *not* Walterene. He sank back and waited for another car.

She stood in front of him, her hands clasped over an evening bag.

"Well, Ralph Budd."

He was caught off guard as she explained about living on the second floor and walking down; and he was further confused when she extended her hand, Northern fashion, to be shaken. He was so occupied with the business of giving her the flowers, getting out of the lobby, past the doorman and into a taxi, that it was actually a minute or two before he could register an impression of her. The doorman gave his arm a friendly squeeze as he helped him into the taxi.

"That's it, Jack. Now you're in."

She was Walterene all right, but in every respect *bigger*. Her thick black hair was still cut in a Dutch bob, but the lower corners curved forward in a bizarre and effective way. She crossed her legs and settled back into her fur coat.

"Say, Walterene—"

"Whup!" She said laughing and grimacing. "About that Walterene. I left that in Arkansas. Up here they call me René."

It seemed that at Wellesley her name had been something of a joke during her freshman year, and a few kind friends began to call her Rene for short. She dropped the Walter and used Rene even to sign her papers. Then one of her teachers in class had addressed her as *René* and it stuck. Ralph reflected that the slight modification of her hair-do was probably designed as a corroborative hint of a French influence somewhere in her past.

They went to the Astor Hotel where the Society had rented a private dining room. Several hundred Arkansans were there, none of whom Ralph knew. At the door they were handed lapel cards on which they printed their names and hometown. Ralph was pleased with Walterene because of her good looks and accent, or rather lack of accent. Some of the girls, it seemed to him, spoke with excessively Southern accents which would have sounded queer even in Arkansas.

After a plate of fried chicken, a man at the end of the horseshoe table rose and tinkled spoon against glass. He made a gracious little speech. He spoke nostalgically of the Southern way of life and told a joke about an Arkansas private and a Yankee general. He concluded ruefully that if "you cain't beat 'em, you have to jine 'em. If any more of us Rebs move up here, we'll make this a good place to live in yet."

René whispered to Ralph:

"If he thinks Arkansas is such a hot place to live in, why doesn't he go back? He came up here forty years ago, and he hasn't even been home for a visit."

"Why don't you?"

René bent over in a spasm; her hair fell forward and hid her face like blinders. Her shoulders heaved. For a second Ralph thought she had gotten sick. But she was laughing silently. He soon learned that this was a mannerism of hers acquired sometime after leaving high school.

He saw her often after that. He sought her company, feeling that he was lucky to know her and that, further, he was bound by his method to do so. But in one way the results were unforeseen. He had expected that Walterene would fill an empty place in his life, that at least she would dispel the loneliness. It wasn't true. His loneliness was only compounded. She shared it but didn't relieve it. Instead of wandering the streets of the city alone, he wandered them with her, and still alone. There was the added burden of forever adjusting himself to Walterene, the tedious chore of dealing with another person on a polite level. For she persisted in trying to extract something comic from every situation. And when he made a reply, however feeble, she would double up in silent laughter. It was hard to account for their unease. They had much in common. They were compatriots in an almost foreign country. They were "intelligent," "liberal" young people. And if they could be certain of anything, it was that both had a sense of humor. They discovered that they agreed enthusiastically on almost every subject. Yet each sally of conversation would leave them straining for the next. He often thought that she was as little to blame as he. It was something apart from them that gave them no peace. They agreed once that silence could be friendly and communicative, but their silences were self-limiting. They were contests, which after a few minutes, became unbearable. After long weary bus rides to obscure places in the Bronx and Washington Heights (they would certainly never go to Rockefeller Center or to the Statue of Liberty), he would feel when he got back to his dormitory room that he had walked the entire distance. *What is wrong?* he thought on the bus top with Walterene. He looked at a street number: ninety more blocks to the Betsy Ross. What he wouldn't give to be rid of her and to be on the uptown bus alone! To be able to close his eyes and rest his head in the corner of the window and seat back. To let his aching abdominal muscles relax. To be surrounded by strangers. It had something to do with the city, he decided finally. There was no place for them to go and be at home and with friends, except the lobby of the Betsy Ross. (And yet, he suspected that if a number of people should suddenly become their friends, it would be no different.) They belonged nowhere now, not even to their own families, except perhaps to the Arkansas Society. It was as if a malevolent force in the city had thrust them into the streets and public places and closed the doors against them.

One night they went to a night club which, as it turned out, made a specialty of making out-of-town people feel at home. A jolly master of ceremonies browbeat perfect strangers into playing parlor games like musical chairs. To break the ice he would go from table to table with his microphone, followed by the spotlight, asking people the name of their home state. Then the orchestra would play an appropriate number such as "Carry Me Back to Old Virginny," or "Alabamy Bound." When Ralph told him they were both from Arkansas, the orchestra was momentarily nonplussed and then for some reason began to play "A Boy from Texas." The spotlight shone full on them while the crooner sang:

> A boy from Texas
> And a girl from Tennessee
> They walked down Broadway
> And were lonesome as can be
> He said Howdy
> And she said Hi you all—

It seemed hours before the spotlight moved on and he could let his face relax from its ghastly fixed grin. They left shortly after and went silently back to the Betsy Ross.

It would not be fair to say that Ralph "dropped" Walterene, for he was careful to maintain their friendship, though in a smaller way. She still figured as a positive, if not very promising, resource in his strategy, certainly not one to be discarded. To tell the truth, Ralph found her company much more tolerable now that his search had moved on. Nor did he despair when it became clear that his association with Walterene was not a success. He compiled another list.

As he studied his new list one winter evening, he conceived another possibility which was so good that it immediately took precedence over all the rest. Its virtue lay in the total absence of risk. Every other instance entailed in some degree the danger of rejection and failure. At some point in every projected campaign, whether it be a straight pick-up or a friendship at a young people's church meeting, he would have to make an overture, ask a question which could only be answered yes or no. His latest notion completely eliminated such perils. He was triumphant. Feeling that the mere conception of such an idea was a satisfactory day's work, he took a light work-out in the gym and went to a movie at Times Square.

Next day he submitted by mail an advertisement to a literary magazine. It read:

YOUNG NUCLEAR PHYSICIST, 22, with a fondness for good books, good music, liberal ideas, and unconventional situations desires acquaintance with young woman of similar tastes. Wishes to supplement the delights of research in pure science with the enjoyment of the good things of New York in congenial company.

It struck the right note. There was the major ingredient proper to such advertisements: a genteel eroticism, plus an interesting fillip, science, that particular science which, next to psychiatry, would be most likely to intrigue the intelligent and liberal readers of the magazine. In addition to the notions of speeding neutrons and incalculable forces which the words *nuclear physics* conjured up, Ralph realized full well that there were also socio-political implications.

"Nuclear physics, eh?" one of his new friends might say. "Fascinating field. Pity you fellows have to be hamstrung by a bunch of politicians and Gestapo agents."

Ralph would shrug philosophically, indicating long experience with these obstructions.

Although he was optimistic about his new venture, he was not prepared for the avalanche which followed. Within a week after the magazine appeared, he received nearly a hundred letters. He sat at his desk, cleared except for the neat stack of the latest batch of replies, and waited for his pounding heart to subside. His achievement was a triumph of method. He had succeeded in reducing a whole field of human relations to the arena of his desktop. He had imprisoned all those forces which had hitherto cast him about at will into a controlled experiment which could be treated as systematically as a textbook assignment.

Ralph reflected that he had discovered a new law in the economy of human relations: that one makes a gain in the social field only with a certain loss of personal dignity. Considered in the clear light of his method, there was, of course, no onus attached to the advertisement. All the same he would hate to admit to Walterene or to his family that he had advertised for love and friendship as others would advertise for a servant or a used car.

The letters showed an astonishing variety. A large number were written by girls who could not possibly have understood anything in the magazine except the advertisements. Their stationery was often tinted and perfumed. Some enclosed photographs showing the writers in bathing suits. Others were from ladies who, though no longer young, offered other compensating inducements. A few had taken Ralph's advertisement as a proposal of marriage.

But many were obviously written by girls of education and breeding. These nearly all began the same way: "Dear Sir," or "Dear Nuclear Physicist," or "Dear N.P.," "I have never done this sort of thing before but—," or "My friend and I would not think of answering this kind of ad ordinarily, but just for fun we were wondering if perhaps you too had a friend of similar tastes." His brain reeled. He was a sultan with a card-index harem.

A difficulty soon presented itself. These discerning girls from whom he would choose (one, or who knows, perhaps two or more) naturally avoided writing the "pen-pal" type of letter. They were not so vulgar as to describe their physical assets like the others ("my friends tell me I have a good figure") or to enclose a snapshot.

This was all very well: beauty was not Ralph's primary objective. But he did not wish to go to the trouble of arranging a meeting only to find himself face-to-face with a monstrous-looking creature. It would necessitate a retreat painful to both. There was only one answer, of course: a reconnoiter before the interview.

After three weeks' accumulation of mail he had selected three letters. One was particularly promising. It was from a girl, twenty-one years old, named Nancy Brough. She wrote with dignity and precision. There were no apologies. She said simply that she had quite a few friends, none of whom interested her especially, and that she could see no harm in meeting the young nuclear physicist. But she wanted it clearly understood that she was not a sex-starved female looking for a man, or worse, one who wanted to exchange prurient letters. And since their meeting, if it occurred at all, would be unconventional, she saw no sense in prolonging it unnecessarily if one didn't happen to like the looks of the other. She was a poet and most of her friends were writers and painters and musicians. He was to reply to her letter, and then, if she still liked the idea, she would consent to a meeting. Her address was intriguing: 16 Coach Row. It didn't sound like Manhattan.

Ralph set out the following Sunday with a large map of the city. He found a bench near the ferry slip on the Manhattan side and spread out the map. Coach Row was a tiny blind alley off Fourth Street. Greenwich Village. He could no longer get excited about the Village. Before he came to New York, the name had always brought to mind narrow cobblestone streets and old gabled houses. But he had seen it. It was, if possible, more dismal than the rest of Manhattan.

Nevertheless, he boarded an open-top bus at Fifth Avenue with a lighthearted air of adventure. There was also the solid satisfaction of conforming to his method. The present action was a systematic elimination of uncontrolled factors. A reconnoiter in force. He couldn't help feeling a bit like Bulldog Drummond in his trench coat and slouch hat.

Coach Row was a surprise. Actually, it was nothing extraordinary: a double row of converted stables, but in contrast with the dreary tenements of the Village it seemed to him charmingly quaint. Number sixteen was nearly at the end of the alley opposite a little tavern. Ralph had formed a plan before he got to the stoop. In the vestibule there were four name cards with bell buttons. Number four was Miss Nancy Brough. No roommate. He pressed the button. Almost immediately there was an answering click in the lock of the front door. It was as if she expected him. He pressed the button again several times and walked quickly across the street to the tavern. He sipped a beer at the end of the bar and waited. Presently the door of number sixteen opened and a girl stepped out onto the stoop. His mission was successful. She was no beauty. Too thin. Her eyes were so dark that the pupil and iris merged into a single disc like a comic-strip character. She hugged her arms and looked up and down the alley. Already he felt a tender solicitude for her. "Get back into the house before you catch cold," he shouted at her silently. Finally, she shrugged and went inside.

Ralph turned back to his beer. The search was ended. All he had to do now was to go home and write a letter, a decent reserved letter with the merest hint of his love for her. He looked at himself between the bottles at the bar mirror and shoved back his hat brim with his thumb.

As he turned to leave, Nancy came in followed by a young man. Ralph was confused and ordered another beer. They chose a booth behind him and to one side. He could see them clearly in the mirror. *What am I worried about? She doesn't know me. If she does recognize me later it will only make a good story. I'll tell her about this anyway.* She drank coffee and smoked. Her movements were quick and nervous. *That's probably her breakfast. She smokes too much.* She held her lips pursed and gazed absently into her coffee cup. Her escort was a damp young man. He talked with great animation. Ralph couldn't hear him, but he shrugged frequently, flipping out a hand palm-up as if he were saying: "And, my dear, what else could I do?"

No wonder Nancy was not especially interested in her friends. He shouldered past them, scowling and exultant, hands thrust deep in his trench-coat pockets.

On the bus top again, he reviewed the situation. The groundwork was well laid. He could think of only one more thing to be done, and although this contingency would not arise for some time, it was well to be prepared. Her friends (and his-to-be) were all artistic. Each had an accomplishment. Perhaps even Nancy read her poetry aloud to a small group. Some had possibly formed a string quartet. Others no doubt were actors at the Village Playhouse. Nancy's friend in the tavern probably told clever risqué stories at the piano. The reality which had to be faced was that Ralph had no such accomplishment. Actually, he had even exaggerated his knowledge of "good music and good books." When Nancy presented him to her friends, he would arouse brief interest. There would be the usual remarks about atomic energy. But he couldn't rest indefinitely on his laurels as a potential nuclear physicist.

Before he reached Seventy-fifth Street he had the solution. It was simple and inevitable. When he examined his resources and his origins, he saw that they could be reduced to two prime elements. He had a good tenor voice, and he came from Arkansas. Folk songs. He would get a collection of Ozark Mountain Ballads from the New York Public Library and go to work. Then, later, when the others had just finished a Haydn quartet, he might say quietly: "Here's one you never heard before," and sitting cross-legged on the floor of the studio apartment and staring into space, he would sing a haunting ballad about the sourwood trees and the stillness of the mountains.

JAMES GORDON BENNETT

 In his discussions with students about the importance of keeping a writer's diary, James Gordon Bennett is fond of telling the story of how he became inspired to write "The Perfect Mousse Ducktail." One day, while retrieving his clothes from Kean's Fine Dry Cleaning, he noticed a teenage boy standing among the hanging garments, trying on a woman's full length mink coat. He recorded the encounter in his own notebook, and, in combination with other observations of his Southdowns neighborhood, created his young male first person narrator—a confused and unhappy teenager who works in a laundry after school and gains momentary solace from trying on women's garments.

Few writers can claim the regularity of publication Bennett achieved from 1974 to 1990, on average one story per year in literary journals such as *The Southern Review*, *The Antioch Review*, and *The Northwest Review*. From these stories came the novel, *My Father's Geisha*, which was followed by *The Moon Stops Here*, his second novel, both works presenting children struggling within their families. A Stanford University-educated Wallace Stegner Fellow, Bennett was hired as an instructor at LSU in the same year as Walker Percy—a coincidence which delayed Bennett's opportunity to teach creative writing courses. Eventually, Bennett became one of the first instructors to be promoted to assistant professor. He quickly became a favorite of students, and the list of young talents who sit in his classes and go on to publish their own work grows longer every year. John Ed Bradley, Laurie Lynn Drummond, and Olympia Vernon are only a few of those who attest to Bennett's generous, subtle guidance in the classroom.

For years, Bennett has been the favorite choice of LSU's English department when a suave and witty master of ceremonies is called for. His dry wit and ironic world view are perfectly suited for departmental award ceremonies, introductions of visiting speakers, and celebratory toasts. Yearly, to an appreciative New Orleans crowd, he serves as emcee for the Words & Music Festival banquet celebrating Faulkner's birthday.

JAMES GORDON BENNETT

The Perfect Mousse Ducktail

I know that as his only son and namesake I'm a keen disappointment to Daddy and the reason why my mother, at forty one, is pregnant. She denies this, of course ("It takes two to lambada, sweetheart."), but then, as the lawyers say, *res ipsa loquitur* (the facts speak for themselves). And lately, with Daddy practically in receivership, there have been a lot of lawyers around.

This afternoon, after closing up shop, I try on the full length faux Russian sable (for appearance sake the owner stores it in our refrigerated vault). Some terrific pieces have come in for our July winterizing special: a velvet bustier, a blue taffeta gown with illusion top (which I can barely squeeze into), a cashmere cowl neck sweater, and a wonderful gunmetal beaded suit (which I *can't* squeeze into). But my favorite, the leather stirrup pants, are badly stained and beyond repair. A pity, too, because even in this humidity they feel as thin and cool as a mud pack.

Afterwards, at the house, I'm out watering the ligustrum when Daddy hot-rods the BMW into the shell driveway. He's just getting home from some construction site and honks the horn until his two Dobermans, Concrete and Truck, are singing in the backyard.

"I'll feed the hounds," he says and tosses me his jacket, his double-starched linen shirt open to his chest. "Go tell Picasso to wriggle into something. We're going out."

I reach into the asphidistra to turn off the hose. The mosquitoes are already swarming and the Bug Wacker's violet coils crackle like static beside the pool.

I have my doubts about dinner. Last Friday at his favorite bar, my father shattered the oval mirror behind the register. He'd waited until the waitress was out of the way and then he looped his chilled beer mug like a grenade. His friend Maggio, the owner, went berserk and was about to call the cops when Daddy persuaded him that he'd have his crew over first thing in the morning to patch things up. And as lagniappe (Daddy claims to have one-eighth Cajun blood), he'd even replace the reproduction with the genuine article: a beveled antebellum piece salvaged from some River Road plantation he'd dismantled.

My mother's in the downstairs bathroom hunched over a machine that steams her pores. She's been working all week on the same portrait of Daddy but is unhappy with the likeness.

"I don't know where your father thinks the money's coming from," she says, flicking the sweat from her slightly double chin.

"Maybe he's running guns to Nicaragua," I say.

She doesn't smile. "You laugh."

After the first court order, we moved back into my mother's childhood home: a three-story Victorian with very little furniture left downstairs (thanks to the IRS). Every so often, just to get on our more prosperous neighbors' nerves, Daddy will throw a crawfish boil in the backyard for his crew, which means ten or fifteen black guys in overalls sucking crawdad heads and slamming back iced Dixie longnecks while the hyper Dobermans pace manically in their chain link kennel.

Later, while my mother dresses, Daddy blasts some Zydeco tune on his stereo upstairs. Because the old house is raised on brick piers, he has the turntable suspended by fishing line from the bedroom ceiling. My mother suddenly appears on the landing, holding one of the dogs back with her foot.

"Don't you look nice, honey," she says to me and then smacks the dog behind the ear. "Truck, sit." I like her dress even though it's a little blousy on me.

My father comes up behind her, his face pink from the shower, his thick black hair slicked over his ears. "Goddamn mutt." And he seizes Truck's collar, dragging him back through the house, the dog's unclipped nails scraping the hardwood floor.

On the freeway, I'm the only one to buckle my seat belt. My mother claims not to be able to take the pressure on her belly anymore. Daddy drives with one lizard skin boot resting on the dashboard, bored with having to stick to fifty-five, the car locked on cruise control for the long stretch across the dark bayou.

My mother accuses me of hero-worshipping my father and believes I'd be better off with a different hero. "How about that kid Canseco, for instance?" she'll say. "Now there's a cutie." But when I ask her how many missions Jose flew in Nam, she'll only roll her eyes. "Honey, he was probably still in pre-k."

The only restaurant that serves Tex-Mex spicy enough for Daddy turns out to have a forty-five minute wait. And by the time we're ushered in to our table, my mother looks a little squirrel-eyed from sitting at the bar.

It's useless to tell her not to try to keep up with you-know-who or even that she's *supposed* to be pregnant. Instead, I just let her lean on my arm as we make our way through the crowded dining room.

As soon as Daddy gives the waiter everyone's order ("Let Pancho Villa handle this."), my mother staggers back to the lady's room.

"Who you supposed to be?" my father says sullenly when I sit back down. I'd helped my mother with her chair. "Robert-fucking-E.-Lee?"

He edges forward, elbows on the table. He can look menacing when he wants to and he's looking menacingly at me now. But this is the risk you take with Daddy: that he'll turn surly with the second pitcher of margaritas.

He reaches into the wicker basket and snaps one of the corn chips as if to start a fire. It's the look he gets whenever he's trying to make up his mind about me.

"About time you met the Amazon," he says at last but then his thick neck seems to retract like a turtle's when he sees my mother heading our way.

Once, when he thought no one was home (in fact, I'd closed the cleaner's up early with a migraine), I gazed down from my bedroom window to see him let a woman out of the BMW who towered over him. A woman who could have played center in the NBA. I'd watched him walk back to the garage and wheel his Harley out. And after she wrapped her long arms around his waist, he twisted the hand grips, shooting puffs of black smoke from the chrome exhaust. All of this in broad daylight. All of it for the benefit of our neighbors.

"Looks like you boys missed me," my mother says. Her face is the color of someone who's just been sick in the lady's room.

My father is squinting at her as if she'd ground his cigar out in his hand. "I was going to ask your boy what his biggest fantasy was," he says. "It's an old business trick. Tells you about people."

But my mother is eyeing me, suspicious that he's said something upsetting to her darling. "I'll tell you why he really asks," she says bitterly and turns the pitcher handle around. "Because he wants you to ask him what *his* fantasy is."

Daddy twists his napkin about her wrist. But not playfully.

"Forget it," he says to me. "I ain't in the mood anymore."

As usual, I'm the only one to eat much of anything. My father picks at his plate until his mood abruptly changes and he attempts to cozy back up to my mother.

"So," he says, his hand moving to her belly to project the shape it will soon take. "What kind of boy we going to have us?"

"Bullheaded," she says. "It's how you'll know he's yours."

But not even my mother can resist Daddy's infectious laugh. And for the first time this evening we all seem at ease together when my father suddenly pitches forward in his chair, his chin coming down hard enough to crack his plate. I jump up, tipping my glass over.

His eyes are closed, the white tablecloth splattered with picante sauce.

My mother waves the waiters back. "Just give him some air," she says. "He'll come out of it."

I stand beside her, studying my father for any sign of life. "You hear of people stopping their hearts," I say under my breath. "It's our fault. We shouldn't have encouraged him."

My mother dampens a napkin and squats down to whisper something into Daddy's red ear.

The maitre d' has turned off the Muzak when a young doctor in Duckheads lopes over with a beeper on his alligator skin belt.

"How we doing?" he says, pinching my father's wrist with his thumb and forefinger.

His curt smile lets us all know that this was supposed to be his night off.

Daddy's eyelids at last flicker and before long he's sitting up grinning.

"Goddamn I love this country," he says, saluting the doctor who returns to his own table. "You ain't going to get that with socialized medicine."

Although I'm embarrassed and want to go, no one, in fact, is really paying any attention to us. Getting drunk in public isn't much of a spectacle anymore in the state's oil-busted economy. Even the few children about have quickly lost interest.

My mother, meanwhile, has wrenched my father's wallet from his tight jeans and charged everything on the one credit card that's still any good.

Outside, she walks ahead of us as Daddy flops his arm over my shoulder and we reel across the parking lot. "'Bout time you got yourself some poontail," he says.

It's his hunting voice. The one he employs when he's drunk and wants to make up for his transgressions.

"Nothing wrong with you, buddy," he says. "You just a momma's boy, is all." Then he stops to poke his finger at my chest. "Your old man's going to build a goddamn skyscraper. And it ain't no shit ass fantasy."

My mother marches back to slap his hand away.

"Some role model," she says. "Some shit ass role model."

My father looks down at his dusty boots as if to catch his balance.

"What's the matter with you, girl?" he says. "I'm talking to my boy here."

At the car, I help him into the back seat.

"He doesn't know his limit," my mother says as I pull the BMW out of the lot. He's already snoring peacefully, his head in her lap.

And so with the cruise control set at the posted speed, I dreamily watch the dark shapes of the drilling rigs loom up out of the abandoned oil fields. He's one of a kind, all right. Who else do I know is bankrupt and wants to build a skyscraper in the middle of bayou country?

Back at the house, as soon as I pull into the driveway, Daddy springs up, eyes darting to take in his surroundings.

"Okay," he says. "Who's up for it?"

My mother smoothes her creased dress. It's damp from his hot head. "I wouldn't mind a nightcap."

"Now we're talking," Daddy says. "You got to be Christian in this life."

My mother comes around the front of the car to steer him up the walkway. "That's straight from the devil's mouth," she says and pats her stomach exaggeratedly. "The man can sell a bill of goods, all right."

But my father's glaring straight ahead now, as if deeply affronted by her banter. It's typical of his mood swings.

"Go on to bed then," he says, dismissing us with the sweep of his arm. "Go to hell for all I care." My mother reaches out to grab him by the collar. "What'd you say, mister?"

His eyes narrow into slits. "You want to take that hand away," he says. "You know what's good for you."

Instead, she yanks down hard, popping one of the buttons.

"Okay," I say, moving between them. "That's enough. No more. Come on."

I can hear my mother trying to catch her breath behind me.

"Get out of my face," my father says, sobered by his own anger.

I turn to see my mother kneeling in the scorched grass. "She's going to faint," I say. My father only hangs back. "She's just screwed up her breathing, is all."

When at last he seems satisfied that she's not hurt, he turns towards the house. But then, like some kind of circus act, my mother uncoils from her crouch and leaps onto his back, digging her heels into his thighs.

"Coonass," she shouts, arms locked about his neck. "Dumb shit coonass."

Daddy teeters with her weight until he careens into the ligustrum, branches cracking like tinder beneath them.

After a frightening silence, only my father manages to extricate himself from the bushes. I reach in and gently pull my mother's arm until I can see her face. Mud is sticking to her chin like a goatee. "It's all right, honey," she says. "Just a little wet."

Across the way I can see our neighbor in his terry cloth bathrobe thinking twice about wheeling his garbage cans down the driveway.

"Let's go," my mother says when Daddy starts taunting him. He's the one who tried to get the civic association to force muzzles on the dogs.

On the back porch my mother takes the key from me when my hand won't stop shaking.

"I'll tell you what my fantasy is," she says. "That this baby's skin winds up as thick as your old man's head."

I turn to see our neighbor scurrying back up his driveway, the aluminum cans rattling behind him.

To try to settle down a little before bed, I stand in front of the bathroom mirror and comb my hair into the perfect mousse ducktail. All the drugstore blood pressure machines agree that I don't have the nerves for this family.

I sit up for an hour flipping through the album with all the pictures of Buddhist temples outside of Saigon. The few shots with Daddy in them (taken, my mother suspects, by "some passing geisha"), he's always tan and smiling and hardly looks much older than me. It's impossible to tell from any of the photographs that there's a war going on. But it's my father's second tour of duty and he's already told my mother that he never wants to come home again.

※

Just before dawn, a sharp cracking sound startles me awake and my mother tip-toes into my room. She peers out my window cautiously as if over the edge of a cliff.

"It wasn't a car," I say.

My mother exhales heavily, shaking her head. "Correct."

I gather the sheet around me and come up behind her. Directly below us, Daddy is standing on the bumper of the BMW wearing only socks and a pair of silk boxer shorts. The headlights are aimed at a pyramid of beer cans.

"Chapter 11," my mother says.

My father is trying to find some more bullets in the glove compartment when the patrol car turns up Hollydale, its lights flashing. There's no siren but Daddy immediately pitches his gun onto the lawn and assumes a comic, spread-eagled pose, fingers splayed out on the hood of the BMW.

Across the street, our neighbor and his wife (she in the leopard trench coat that fits me like a glove) stand beneath their centennial live oak, its sweeping lower limbs held aloft by steel cables. They're careful to keep their distance.

Afterwards, as soon as the patrol car backs out (with my mother following in her Volvo), a small mob of neighbors congregates in the street, the cicadas hissing about them in the faint morning light.

It's useless to try to fall back asleep and so I wander into my mother's room and try on several of her camisoles. I belong to a tanning salon (my skin's too fair to sit long in the sun) and the protective goggles leave a crescent like the natural one under my father's eyes. It's all that we have in common.

Tonight, he'd refused to wear the polo shirt and pants my mother passed to him through the window of the patrol car, choosing instead to sit naked as Buddha in the back seat, his middle finger raised at his gawking neighbors.

Saturday morning I'm out trimming the crepe myrtles when my father walks his Harley from the garage. Typically, he looks as if he's just come back from a health farm instead of having spent six hours downtown being charged with "malicious mischief." When he starts up the cycle it sounds like a helicopter and I cup my hands over my ears.

"Too early," I shout when he pats the back seat of the Harley.

But he continues to hold the other helmet out for me. "What you talking about? It's late."

My mother forbids me to ride with him ("Your Daddy I can replace; I only got one of you."); however, it's the weekend and she's out at some maternity shop.

I reach around his barrel chest just as the cycle lurches forward. But instead of turning onto the street, he bounds over the curb and I'm bucked like a rodeo rider. It isn't until he veers crazily across the driveway that I spot our neighbor. He's polishing his antique Thunderbird in the dark shade of his live oak. When we cut a deep swath through a clump of lariope, he instinctively dives behind his tree, the electric buffer spinning off the hood, sparks spitting from the orange extension cord.

I consider leaping into the soft Bermuda grass when the cycle idles momentarily. Our neighbor has dashed to his gazebo where he's already exclaiming into a phone, his baby face apoplectic. But it's too late to bail out once we accelerate back down the driveway. All I can do is pound on my father's shoulders as we rocket up Perkins Boulevard to the freeway entrance ramp.

There seems no point in protesting once we move beyond the suburbs and out into the country with the magnificent scent of sweet olive in the air and pampas grass swaying in the median. It's almost enough to make me forget that I'm on a motorcycle with a madman.

Still, the more I think about our neighbor, the less inclined I am to be hard on my father. At the cleaners, the man always insists on early pickup and has everything he wears monogrammed in a tacky script.

We take the Denham Springs exit and as my father downshifts, he lifts the face guard on his helmet.

"So how the girls treatin' you?" he says, raising his voice.

"Never mind *them*!" I scream. "What about you!"

But he only mumbles something about "loosening up." Which I take to mean my grip but then he adds, "with Donna."

The reason we're out here, it happens, is for me to see his cabin. It's been built using only non-union carpenters to avoid any of his regular crew knowing more than they (or the reorganization lawyers) need to. This is what makes Daddy an impossible subject for a portrait, my mother will tell you ("He's like a Rubik's Cube, remember them? You can't paint someone who's got a different angle every time he turns around."). She knows he cheats on her. And she puts up with it. We both do.

A dirt road weaves into a stand of loblolly, and at what looks like a cow gate, my father parks the cycle.

"The enchanted cottage," he says, pointing across a field thick with wild flowers.

I squeeze the helmet off and pitch it against the fence.

"You're crazy," I say, my arms flailing. "That guy's a lawyer. He's probably already in court."

My father retrieves the helmet. "You're right," he says. "Might as well just shoot the fucker next time I see him." He unlatches the gate. "What the hell," he says, raising both hands to the cloudless sky. "Ain't life grand?"

There's nothing to do but trot after him as he leads the way down through a canopy of pines that opens onto a small lake. He'd somehow conned Wildlife and Fisheries into stocking it after bartering with a concrete company to dump the several tons of white sand that make up the narrow strip of beach. The cabin's another fifty yards back in the trees, a redwood deck jutting out from its sliding glass doors.

I hadn't noticed the blanket until my father walks over and picks up a paperback from it.

"Peaceful's what it is," he says. Then he points out to what looks like the tip of a cypress knee poking up from the water.

"Donna'll tell you that."

I can see now that it's not a cypress at all. It's a snorkel.

"Speak of the devil," Daddy says, prying his boots off.

Suddenly, as if the lake had magically drained about her, a female colossus rises from the black water that cascades down her broad shoulders. Her flippers smack flatly on the sand, her wet suit glittering like quicksilver in the sun.

"This here's Miss Donna," Daddy says, slogging breathlessly back in ahead of her, his pants soaked.

The woman clamps her palm over her clouded mask and lifts it free.

"How you?" she says.

My father takes the snorkel from her. "Miserable," he says. "A fish out of water."

She steps free of the thick flippers and still stands a head above us both.

"Let me get this stuff off," she says. Her voice is husky, almost guttural. She has the cocoa-colored skin of a mulatto.

"Now we're talking," Daddy says.

She walks on tiptoes back up to the cabin, leaving a trail of black dots in the dimpled sand.

"There ain't a phony bone in her body," my father says with real admiration in his voice. "Not a one."

I've seen how he acts around his secretaries before. This is different.

"Never asks for anything," he says as fiercely as if I'd just contradicted him. "Kind of gal make you want to build a skyscraper."

"Because your Daddy's got some Cajun in him," my mother will say, "he takes that to mean he's more European."

As my heels sink into the sand, my father doesn't even offer to lie to soften the truth. I'm a big boy now and should be able to take his infidelities like a man.

"Hey!"

Confused by the direction of the echo, I glance out at the water. But Daddy turns towards the cabin where Donna has slid open the glass panel to step out onto the redwood deck.

"Hey!" she calls down to us.

Daddy picks up the flippers at his feet. "In all her glory," he says and sounds almost apologetic. "Won't be a minute."

My legs seem to give out and I sit down, on the blanket. She'd been standing in the bright sunlight, the unzipped wet suit hanging like a wilted petal from her naked waist.

I stare at the covers of the other paperbacks: big busted women swooning into the arms of steroid-muscled men.

Pulling the blanket into the shade, I see a tiny flying squirrel soar between the upper branches of the trees, its claws extended, its white underbelly of fur stretched out flat.

There are no barking dogs here. No Bug Wackers. No neighbors. I hadn't slept much after all the commotion last night, and I close my eyes, wondering how many other cabins in the woods there could be in my father's life.

In my most popular dream Daddy leads his squad through a jungle of spiked bamboo and mines, snipers and poisonous snakes. His men, boys really (some looking even younger than me), follow him willingly, knowing they'd be lost without him. "No gook going to blindside the Old Man," they whisper behind his back. "The Man is righteous." It's said that he wears a locket on his dog tags. And inside there is a picture of his new baby boy whom he's never seen. His men's envy of me is palpable. I am his only son.

"Got you some rays, boy." It's Donna. She's standing over me.

I can feel the heat in my face.

"You let that shade move on you," she says, adjusting the strap of her bathing suit.

I follow her up to the cabin where she explains that Daddy has gone for beer.

"Got himself an itch," she says, ducking into the small bathroom. "He likes to keep movin', that's the truth."

I sit down on the wicker couch and watch her twist the top off a tube of suntan lotion. She straddles my legs, squeezing the cream into her palm.

"You want to work that in," she says and presses her cold hand to my neck. "It'll do you."

The cushion she tucks behind my head smells of mildew.

"Here's the deal," she says finally and steps back as if to see me more clearly. "I was somebody's cousin your daddy knows. You understand? Just somebody he knows out golfing."

I don't say anything and after a moment she wipes her hands off on the backs of her legs.

"Okay," she says. "Ready to go on home then?"

She leaves the bedroom door open and changes into jeans and a sweat shirt. "It's fine with me, honey," she says and empties her purse on the mattress, plucking the keys from a tangle of jewelry.

In the car, she reaches across me to fasten my seat belt.

"Everybody's different," she says, resting her large hand on my thigh. "It's the one thing's the same."

When at last we turn off the dirt road onto the macadam the car seems to levitate.

"Your daddy's something else," she says without looking over at me. Her knees almost touch the steering wheel in the small sports car.

I curl my fingers around the door handle.

"He figured you'd be partial to tall," she says, talking to herself now. "Taller the better's what he said."

She knows where I live. Although she promised my father she'd stay clear of the homefront, she can't help being curious. "Not having any blood relations of my own."

Our neighbors are having an outdoor Happy Hour party and she continues halfway up the block before pulling over to the curb. "Nice neighborhood," she says. "Your daddy hates it, am I right?"

I want to turn the mirror. My face feels as if there are already blisters.

"I ought to drop in sometime," she says, tracing her nail down the crack in the windshield. "I mean, it ain't like we don't have names in common."

My mother's Volvo is in the driveway and she's spelled "let them eat cake" across the ice box with the magnetic letters. But she doesn't answer when I call her and it's only when I come up to the first floor landing that I see the smoke out the window. She's standing in the backyard flicking a can of turpentine over the barbecue pit. When she tosses a match in, the fire flares up enough to force her to retreat several paces.

There's a stack of canvases propped against the kennel's chain link fence and after a while she carries one of them back to the brick barbecue pit. The dogs set up a terrible howl as she studies the first painting briefly before pitching it into the fire. She makes several more trips, each time considering the canvas as if judging its individual merits. When only black smoke seems to rise from the brick chimney, she douses the pile with more turpentine until satisfied with the height of the flames.

I can almost feel the fire from here. And half mesmerized by the spectacle, it's a moment before I recognize the dull rumble of Daddy's motorcycle and I take the stairs two at a time up to my room.

From my window facing the street, I can see that it's him all right. He's pulled into the driveway and is watching several of our neighbor's guests milling about on the lawn. He leaves the cycle idling and it's like listening to him think out loud. His damp hair sticks to his forehead from being crammed inside the warm helmet. But his expression, a cocky smirk, makes me believe he's been drinking. At least enough to face my mother after what she's probably already heard from our irate neighbor, if not the police.

In the hall bathroom, I undress and smooth some more baby lotion on my nose. Then I step into a pair of my mother's panties (she claims she can feel them getting snugger even this early in the first trimester). The black leather stirrup pants aren't due back until Tuesday, and I pull them on, pointing my toes like a diver.

Daddy has joined my mother in the backyard and after some discussion he moves over to the kennel and lifts the latch on the door before my mother can stop him. The dogs have been hurling themselves against the fence in anticipation, and once free, streak about the side of the house in the direction of our neighbor's party and his decorative Pomeranians. Meanwhile, smoke rises from the barbecue pit in a long gray tendril that we all stop to look up at as if it were part of a mysterious message. And I suddenly feel like coming out with them. But here's my *other* fantasy: that as my new baby brother grows older, I grow younger until we are exactly the same age, twins actually, dressed identically by our mother, so that not even our proud Daddy can tell us apart.

JOHN ED BRADLEY

In 2007, John Ed Bradley wrote the bestselling memoir, *It Never Rains in Tiger Stadium*, a candid and emotional view of the author's experience as captain of the LSU football team. For those of us who have joined the 90,000 diehard fans in Tiger Stadium, seen the Fighting Tigers blast through the tunnel and onto the field, heard the stirring music of the Tiger Marching Band, and felt the deafening roar in Death Valley, there is no forgetting those electric moments. *It Never Rains* gives us a moving account of how it feels to be a football player running onto the field as part of this pandemonium. What's more, we have a firsthand confession of how that experience affected Bradley forever, how the love of the game and a coach, in this case, legendary Charles McClendon, can enter a man's soul and stay there.

But Bradley's life as a football player is only part of his story. While he attended grueling practice sessions twice a day and played weekly as star center, he was also enrolled in creative writing classes, which continued his high school desire to be a novelist. As he admits in his memoir, LSU was the best time of his life, but he refers not only to the world of football; also he was taken under the wing of one of his writing teachers, Warren Eyster, who encouraged him "to write and be brave." He is remembered by another teacher, James Gordon Bennett, as having "all the makings of a writer in the works: discipline, a thick critical hide, imagination, and above all, desire." Initial success came when the *Delta* literary undergraduate journal published his stories, "Beam," and "Coming Back Down."

Bradley's successful career as sportswriter and novelist challenges the commonly held view that a star athlete's creativity is limited to the playing field. His first job in sports journalism was at *The Washington Post*, followed by *Sports Illustrated* and *Esquire*. He has written six novels—*Tupelo Nights*, *The Best There Ever Was*, *Love and Obits*, *Smoke*, *My Juliet* and *Restoration*—most set in Louisiana where, he claims, "my soul belongs." Bradley skillfully evokes both Tiger Stadium and small-town Louisiana in the opening chapter of his first and favorite novel, *Tupelo Nights*. Its protagonist, with the unlikely name of John Girlie, has given up a pro-football career to return home to care for his mother. Through him, we see the entanglements of love and family that alter a man's destiny forever.

JOHN ED BRADLEY

Famous Days

from *Tupelo Nights*

A few months before he died, my father's father asked me to forgive him for not being able to climb the ramps at Tiger Stadium and watch me play football for Louisiana State University.

"The arthritis is bad," he said on the telephone. "But my heart, the lousy sonofa-bitch, is worse."

Because he was confined to his bed and rarely left the apartment over his clothing store on Union Street, he listened to all the games on KLLO, our hometown station. Hearing my name mentioned, he said, put something like a fat fist in his throat. And once, after learning I'd been named to an all-America team, he'd cried so hard he thought his lungs would burst. He had cried through the first five minutes of our Tulane game and beat his terrible, gnarled hands together and chanted "Girlie, Girlie, Girlie." When I asked him if carrying on that way meant he was proud of me, he started laugh-ing and told me to go to hell. Then he hung up. I figured he was on the bottle again, and hitting it hard. When I called back, he answered the phone during the first ring and said, "Didn't I say it loud enough for you, John? Didn't you hear me? Go to hell."

Again he hung up before I had a chance to talk.

I once told a girl I knew that my grandfather and I had never spoken to each other after that, and she reminded me I hadn't really talked to him during that last call; he was the only one who had said anything. She laughed and tried to make me laugh, but I was hurt and embarrassed. Then she tried to hold and kiss me and love my anger away. "Here, John," she said. "Come here." She whispered a clever, dirty promise in my ear and reached to unfasten my belt buckle. When I pushed her hand away and said what I needed most was to go out into the day and clear my head, she hit me with a large leather-bound textbook on modern dance and said, "Go, and see if I care." Then she shouted, "Go, Johnny. See if I care!"

Her name was Sarah Sanford, but she liked to be called Sissy. I was less than a hundred yards down the street, headed for town, when I heard her calling behind me, "Didn't I say it loud enough for you, Johnny! Didn't you hear me! Go to hell, John Girlie! Go to hell!"

140

As it happened, I had no real place to go. So I walked. I walked through one of those days when the air, heavy and foul with the odor of river sludge and exhaust, felt as if it might explode into a gleaming white blossom of fire right in front of my face. A million other wild voices joined the girl's and screamed through the haze, and for all I knew nothing would ever feel or look or sound or smell right again. I walked aimlessly through downtown Baton Rouge for an hour or more—down Nicholson for about a mile and along the tracks to where they docked the steamboat *Bienville* that made weekend party runs to New Orleans, and then along the levee until I came to the old Southern Pacific warehouse standing hard by the back street. The warehouse was empty except for some torn-open sacks of beans and insulation and what looked like a mound of wet lime. In one dark corner, near a stack of wooden pallets, I saw a man sleeping on a sheet of corrugated tin, his hands shoved into his dirty trousers, clutching at himself. For some reason I thought I recognized this poor fellow, and I nudged him with my foot to wake him up. "Let me look at you," I said. "Look here, friend. Let me look at you."

His face was red and swollen. "Let me look at you," he said drunkenly. "Look here."

"Who do you think you are," I said.

"Who . . . Who do you think you are."

I was headed back to my apartment near campus when I saw a burgundy Olds 98 parked at the Pastime Lounge under the I-10 overpass. This was the same model Jason Girlie used to drive, and it was dressed as his had always been. Standing in the shade of the corner building, the car had tinted windows, spoked hubcaps, thin gold stripes down the sides and political stickers on the back bumper and, it appeared, a new coat of wax. I walked up to the car and rapped on the windshield. "You want to talk to me, Grandfather? What is it you want to tell me?"

There was no one in the car. And I knew there was no one in the car. Still, it wasn't all that difficult, especially with my eyes closed, to picture the old man sitting behind the wheel in one of his seersucker suits and bow ties, heating up the cigarette lighter for the unchewed end of his Macanudo cigar. "Talk to me," I said. "Tell me something." But before he could respond, or the picture I held of him could, I climbed onto the hood and slammed my right forearm into the glass. The pain that ran through my arm and shoulder was not good, but not entirely unpleasant either. The windshield didn't break or shatter as I'd hoped, so I put my best left into it and heard a sound like a pigeon flying blind into a patio door.

I looked through the glass and saw that the only thing behind the wheel was a stack of papers stuffed into manila folders. "You go to hell," I said and forearmed the windshield. Laughing, I said, "I'm not going to hell, old man, you go to hell. You go to hell." I hit the windshield again and again and finally bore a hole through the cracked pane. Blood wet my shirt-sleeves and moved down my arms. I scratched my face and blood streaked it. I slid down from the hood and drove my foot into the door on the driver's side. Unlike the windshield, the door would not give. I dented it with each kick but could not drive my foot through its metal wall and reach the picture of the old man sitting on the other side. "You go to hell!" I shouted. "You go to hell! You go to hell!"

I kicked away at the door until a terrible, hot pain shot up my legs and into my groin. The pain made it hard for me to stand, and I thought I might vomit. I went back to forearming the glass, and by the time the police arrived, their lights flickering a dizzy blue flame over everything, I had punched out all the side windows. I was crying, sitting on the curb with my legs pulled in tight against me, and there was blood everywhere. There was also one very distressed black man in a three-piece suit saying, "My car, what have you done to my car! What have you done to my car!"

One of the patrolmen said, "Hey, Bill, it's Johnny Girlie." And his partner said, "Well, I'll be damned. Johnny Girlie. It is him."

I felt sorry for the old man in the suit, the one who owned the car. When he learned who I was, he said, "Johnny Girlie. Johnny Girlie did this? Why me, John? Why do this to me?"

In those days, when I was just out of the game and it was still good to be bad in Baton Rouge, I was the friend of anyone who knew my name, and a lot of people who knew the game of football knew my name. There was nothing about me and the Olds in the papers the next day. The two policemen let me off after I agreed to pay the man in the three-piece for what damage I had done—about a thousand dollars worth—and after driving me in their screaming cruiser to the emergency room of Our Lady of the Lake Hospital. I needed thirteen or fourteen stitches on the back of my right hand, eight to mend the meaty forearm gash and a shot of Novocain to numb the awful throbbing pain in my feet.

Two or three weeks later, I graduated with a degree in general studies and moved back home to Old Field. I moved back believing I could start all over again now that football and school were out and Jason Girlie was dead and gone and my father was somewhere with him. I went back believing everything would be made right and simple and that I would be the reason for it being made right and simple.

"You always have a place here," my mother said the first night I was home. "I hope Sam always feels the same way, too."

She and the maid, Sylvie Banks, had prepared an enormous meal to celebrate my homecoming. At the center of the red oak table was a huge arrangement of silk and dried flowers surrounded by a dozen burning candles in tall brass holders. "When Sam gets out of college and comes back home to live," my mother said, "he'll get the same royal treatment. He'll get all his favorite food. We'll kill the fatted calf, won't we, Sam?"

Sam, then a graduating high school senior, sat gazing at a bowl of cucumber soup. If he'd heard her, he made no sign of it.

"Sam got drunk last night with his little friends," my mother said. "Tell Johnny you got drunk, Sam."

"I got drunk," Sam said.

"Tell Johnny what else."

"I threw up," he said, still staring at the soup.

"Your grandfather was the last person to throw up in the kitchen sink," my mother said. "That is, until Sam did it last night. Tell Johnny that's right, Sam. Tell him that's right."

"That's right," Sam said.

"And tell him what else."

"I slept on the floor."

"He slept on the kitchen floor, John. I found him at six this morning curled up by the trash can."

"Please pass the sweet potatoes," I said.

It is true that in his last years my grandfather drank too much and often let the bottle fool him into believing he was young and strong and could kick a little ass if asked to. Always when drunk the only ass he kicked was his own, and he kicked it pretty hard. He also let the bottle fool him into believing he was not a bad catch for some of the easy, less discriminating women of Old Field, even some of the young ones. I suppose those football Saturday nights in his apartment over the store, listening in bed to my games on the radio, were not all spent alone, for there were some who still recognized him as Senator Girlie from de Laussat Parish and who were foolish enough to think he had great sums of money safely deposited in the First City Bank of Old Field. Fool women knew that before divorcing my grandmother, Jason Girlie had owned a slaughter house and meat distributing plant, two liquor stores, stock in both the Oldsmobile and Pontiac car dealerships and a small sweet potato farm. Smiling and with one clenched fist raised to the camera, he had managed to appear in the Old Field *Times* about once a week, usually on the front page—at the ribbon-cutting ceremony for a new feed store or attending to the governor on his campaign run through town or looking over flood damage to the bean farms west of Bigger's Swamp.

What fool women did not know was that the parish courts had long ago split up his and my grandmother's estate, and that after serving only one term in the state senate, he lost in a landslide to an attorney thirty years his junior and retired in disgrace from what he liked to call public life. Another thing they didn't know was that Jason Girlie had squandered most of his money trying to make it rich in the oil fields off the Louisiana Gulf Coast. Gone for good was the more than two hundred thousand dollars he had dumped into a project headed by Ben Mawry, his legal counsel at the statehouse. He and Mr. Mawry had hired a petroleum engineer to devise a contraption to filter and cleanse dirty oil on the boats that serviced the offshore rigs, but the engineer turned up missing one day and so did my grandfather's money. His dream of making a quick fortune as an oilman died then, I suppose, and the rest of his savings went into an abandoned building in the middle of Old Field's run-down business district. He became the only man in town who sold Florsheim shoes and Sansabelt slacks. "This is pennies," he used to say. "This ain't money."

He called the place Girlie's Men's-and-Boy's.

When I was still in high school, my mother often took me and Sam shopping for clothes at the store, or we'd stop by just to say hello, but my grandfather was rarely there. I knew he spent much of his time drinking at Trudy's Yam Bar near the fairgrounds because sometimes, when we drove through that part of town, we'd see his Olds parked under the Yam's lighted sign that said RELAX, MAN, RELAX. Sometime after I had moved to Baton Rouge and made it through my first semester, he was thrown out of Trudy's Yam Bar for not paying his tab and stopped going to bars altogether. Sam still shopped with my mother at the store, and he told me they once heard somebody walking up above, on the top floor, and they knew it was him. Sam dialed his phone number and heard it ringing from where he stood at the checkout counter; then he heard it stop. When he put his ear to the receiver, Sam said, he could hear somebody breathing; he knew it was Jason. "This is Sam, Grandfather," he had said. And the old man had hung up. When Sam tried calling again, no one answered.

After that, my mother and my brother decided to let him be. They said he would get in touch if and when he wanted to, and they gave his periods of self-incarceration a name. A few times when I called home from school and asked if they'd seen him, my brother said, "No, the Senator's on another one of his sabbaticals." Other times my mother said, "He called just yesterday. Apparently his sabbatical is over."

The last ten years, arthritis had so twisted and disfigured his back and shoulders that kids in Old Field had taken to calling him the Old Hunchback and not Mr. Jason or Senator Girlie as he often insisted we refer to him. They created wildly imaginative stories about his origins, where he slept at night and why he chose to make periodic visits to our house on Ducharme Road. When the pain was so intense that he could no longer drive, he would call my mother and ask her to send me or my brother over. When he had to go to afternoon mass or to the K.C. Hall or to Bean's grocery, Sam usually took him, but only after a protest.

"Do it for me," my mother would say, "just this once. Do it for your mother."

And Sam would say, "But I did it for you last time, Ma."

"The keys are in the car," she'd say as he headed for the door. "I love you, Sam. I love you for this."

Once Sam had left, she would turn to me and say, "You really ought to be ashamed of yourself, Johnny. Your own grandfather."

A few days after they buried him, a writer with the Old Field paper called to say he was doing a report on Jason Girlie. He asked if I would meet him for breakfast and consent to an interview. I lied and said I knew next to nothing about my grandfather but would be willing to help all I could. We met at Bubba Toussaint's Grill off Beverly Boulevard and sat at the counter. The man put his tape recorder on top of the napkin holder and asked me how I remembered my grandfather, and I said the picture was always the same. I said it was of him and me alone in that fancy Olds he used to drive, and we were making our way through a field of sweet potatoes, out on the eighty acres he owned off the Sunset Highway. In the picture, I said, there were several head of cattle huddled under a run of pecan trees, most of them looking to eat the new green leaves off the lowest branches. We crossed a gully that ran clear to Bayou Claire, fifteen miles away, then up a short climb to the spot where a Houston wildcatter had contracted to set streamers of pipe deep into the belly of the earth. My picture of the old man also had a sound, I said, and it was the sound of a time that was gone and would never come again.

I said if I listened closely enough, I could still hear that seventy-year-old cripple clearing the silt from his pipes and spitting a big gob of phlegm and blood at me for saying, "There ain't a drop of oil in this place, Grandfather. And you know it."

The story ran on the front page of the Sunday paper, and it began with his life as a boy in Thomasburg, led up to what the reporter called "his middle-aged stumbling and bumbling around in the public arena" and ended with his final days of failure, the five years he spent in the apartment over the clothing store that went bankrupt three weeks before he put the busy end of a .16-gauge automatic shotgun into his mouth and pulled the trigger.

"Did he really spit on you," my mother asked the morning the story appeared. By the way her lower lip trembled, I could tell she was about to cry.

"Maybe he didn't mean to," I said.

"You should have told the newspaperman that," she said.

"Maybe. But then maybe I should've told him about the other things me and Jason talked about—like Jason saying he was proud of how he'd been all these years to Sam and me, and Jason saying he was a far better father to us than he'd ever been to your husband."

"Don't call him my husband," she said and pointed at me. "He was your father, too. Why can't you call him your father?"

"The real reason he spit on me was because I said your husband was a coward and an asshole and no different from him."

"Instead of calling him my husband or your father," she said, crying now, "you might consider calling him Jason's son. He was that, too, you know?"

"Husband, father, son," I said. "What's the difference? You married a coward who was also an asshole."

Jason Girlie's suicide came as a surprise to everyone who knew him, including his family, and we buried him in the yard behind Our Lady Queen of Heaven Catholic

Church. It was the winter of my senior year in college, raining and cold, sometime in February. At his wake, the funeral director told my mother it was the largest crowd he had ever handled. This made my mother proud. There was a flower arrangement from the governor and one from U.S. Senator Russell Long, Huey's son. And these were the two she asked people to smell when they approached the open casket.

I told her those flowers were no better than and smelled no different from the ones Old Lady Hazzard and Jippie Babineaux and Joseph Maugham sent, but she pretended not to hear. I told her she was acting as if it was her father who had died, not the father of the man who had left her and me and Sam years ago, and she said, "You're out of order, John. You're way out of order."

When my friend Charley Paul Harwood arrived at the funeral parlor carrying a spray of wild flowers he had picked on his father's soybean farm and arranged in a rusty tin pail full of pond water, she said, "It was a very nice thought. Thank you," and turned away and pressed her nose against one of the blossoms on the governor's fan. She was, I suspected, trying to make me feel guilty for not carrying on as if his death were the absolute worst thing that had ever happened to me. She asked me if I'd heard what Father Ross was telling everybody. "Do you know he prayed for you?" she said.

"Father Ross gets paid to pray for people," I said.

"Not him," she said. "Your grandfather. Jason Girlie prayed for you."

Then she said, "Father Ross was telling Harold LaFleur and Mr. Strother and a few others—they were men who campaigned for him in the old days—he was talking about the time your grandfather sent you a telegram before the Alabama game in Birmingham. I think it was Alabama. The telegram said he was praying that you'd win and make the spread. And you called him from the locker room at halftime—from Legion Field, Father said—and told him not to do that anymore. He asked why not, and you said the players on the other team had grandfathers, too, and they were probably praying just as hard."

My grandparents were divorced when I was still in grade school, but no one mourned the old man's passing more than my grandmother. In the weeks after the funeral, Marie Girlie left her bedroom only to go to the bathroom or to get something to eat. My mother went to see her every afternoon after work, and they huddled together on top of the bedcovers and fingered the beads of their rosaries. There were two full-sized, four-poster beds in the master bedroom. Some nights, after cleaning Marie's kitchen and watching the ten o'clock news, my mother called to report she was staying over and sleeping in the guest bed. She was playing the role of friendly, understanding nurse and having the best time of it.

Once when she came home in the morning, she fixed a pot of coffee and brought it out to me in what we called the outdoor kitchen, though it was really just a large storage room set off from the main house and crowded with broken electrical appliances, sepia-toned photographs in cheap plastic frames, a chewed-up throw rug and a single bed without a headboard. I could see her wet lips. She wore makeup and smelled of baby powder and something else, something like calamine lotion. Her hair was wet and combed straight back from the forehead. You could see the clean lines the comb had made and the hard angles in her face, the way her cheeks seemed to hold the light. You could see the dull heaviness of her body, her wide hips and the way her soft cotton housedress made her breasts look as if they hung down to her waist. "What did you do last night," she asked, putting the pot on the front burner of the stove. "You see Charley?"

"We played some pool at Black Fred's," I said. "I got home after you'd already gone. How's Marie?"

"Marie's fine. She wants to know why you don't come see her."

I didn't say anything because I didn't know what to say. I pointed in the direction of the stove and she understood. She fixed me a cup of coffee and came over and sat on the edge of the bed.

"Every time you try to talk about him, you make me cry."

"You cry because I bring up someone's name you can't talk about."

"Because you bring up your father's name," she said.

"That's right," I said. "I bring up my father's name."

When just out of high school, only seventeen, my mother had entered the Miss Lake Pontchartrain beauty contest in New Orleans and won. I was always much impressed by this and regarded it more highly than I did her brief but prosperous career as a fashion model in Dallas and New York. In the bottom of her antique chifforobe at home, there was a rhinestone-studded crown wrapped in blue velvet and a white sash that said MISS L.P. The velvet and the sash smelled of moth balls. As a girl, my mother had been very thin and big-chested, and she had long brown hair she kept in pigtails. After Sam and I came along, she was always dieting but never very successfully. She wore white nylon girdles and white nylon brassieres that left deep red pinch marks on her back and shoulders. On the phone with friends, she sometimes talked about her figure as if it were something she had misplaced and never recovered. "What happens to people?" she said. "Will you please tell me what happens to people?" At church, or at any closed-in place as quiet as a church, you could hear her thighs rubbing together when she walked. To my ears this was a sexual sound, eliciting thoughts of the bedroom, and when my middle body responded to my lewd thinking, I blushed with embarrassment and my ears burned. I was confused. I invented conversations between my mother and me. "If you're so hot," I imagined myself saying, "then how come your husband left?"

"Your father," I imagined her saying. "Call him your father."

"If you're so hot, then how come he ran off with another girl?"

"You don't think I'm pretty, John? You don't think your mother's pretty? What's wrong with me, John?"

As a boy, I decided they had named her Miss Lake Pontchartrain because of her father-in-law's money. When I confessed this to Marie, she said I was wrong and should apologize to my mother for thinking such a thing. She showed me a picture of my mother in her wedding gown and traced her figure with the tip of her finger. She said Jason Girlie had not begun to get rich selling cars and liquor until after my mother had married and given birth to me. And she reminded me that my mother had come from "a very fine but uncelebrated family," people who lived simply and "without an ounce of fancy to speak of."

"Besides," she said, "my son had good taste. He certainly wouldn't have married Janie Maines unless she was a pretty girl. And what a figure she had, John! It was like an hour glass. You could have turned her upside down and told time by that girl's body."

I could not tell Marie that the real reason I thought Jason had bribed the judges of the Miss Lake Pontchartrain pageant had nothing to do with how shapely my mother was or how she looked in a wedding gown, but why my father had left. The few times I had asked my grandmother about my father's disappearance, she said, "One day you'll understand, Johnny. Give it time. Be patient."

But this was how my grandmother answered all questions that were impossible or too difficult to answer. Why did Jason drink so much? Why did the tomatoes come out so mushy and dull this year? Why do girls have what they have between their legs and boys have what they have? Why, Marie?

"One day you'll understand, Johnny," she said. "Be patient. Give it time."

Now my mother was holding the coffee cup to my lips, letting me sip and inhale the muddy aroma. "You think Jay's no good because he didn't come to his own father's funeral," she said. "Perhaps he had every reason in the world not to come to his father's funeral."

"You'll start crying if I tell you why I think he's no good."

"Tell me anyway," she said. She leaned against me and put her head on my chest. She was still sitting down, holding the cup of coffee in her lap with both hands. She had put her head on me that way because she didn't want me to see her eyes.

"You think I'll ever see him again?" I said.

"I don't want to discuss it, John. Not tonight. Please, baby. The day has been so emotional already. I'm tired of feeling things."

"But, Ma," I said. "You have to tell me."

When she didn't say anything, I said it again. "Tell me now," I said. "Tell me what happened. Tell me why he left."

"You want me to cry," she asked, and started crying. "You want me to cry again?"

"No, I don't," I said. "I just want to know about him. I want to know how he could leave the way he did and still live with himself. What kind of man can walk away from his family and just never come back? His father's dead. Don't you think it's lousy that he wasn't around for the burial? I just don't see how he can stand his own skin."

When she said nothing, I knew better than to push it any further. My mother had a famous way of letting you know when a particular discussion had reached its end. She stood erect and corrected her clothing. She ran her index finger along the space between her neck and her collar or pulled on the bottom of her vest to make sure it covered her beltline or pinched the crease in her trousers. She must've been satisfied that all was well with her housedress because she went about straightening the mess I'd made of the bedcovers. She reached under the top wool blanket and tugged at the sheets, then she worked the blanket until it was as straight as she could get it. She said, "This old musty Army issue thing," and ran her hand over the blanket and across my belly. There was more light in the room, and I could see dusty black smudges under her eyes where her mascara had run.

"That blanket," she said, standing up. "It was his, your father's. I don't know what it's doing here."

"It's only a blanket," I said.

"Yes. But it was your father's blanket."

"That tells me a lot. That really tells me a lot."

"It tells you something," she said.

I waited until we were at the kitchen table, having lunch about three hours later, to ask if my father was in the Army.

"I never said he was in the Army," she replied.

"If the blanket belonged to my father, why didn't you burn it with the rest of his things?"

"I guess I forgot about it," she said.

"Will you burn it now," I asked.

"I might. Or bury it." Then she said, "Oh, baby. You're talking with your mouth full again. Please stop."

TIM PARRISH

To channel his political outrage over 1991 Louisiana politics, Baton Rouge native Tim Parrish wrote "After the River," a story he included in his collection *Red Stick Men*, which was published by University Press of Mississippi. Specifically, he wrote to have his revenge on Louisiana when Edwin Edwards and David Duke were competing in the woeful gubernatorial run-off of that campaign season, Duke having recently recruited outside of Parrish's alma mater, Istrouma High School, after one of several race riots there. Parrish's virtuosity of language keeps the pace of the story quick, and his ironic tone—inspired by Gustave Flaubert's short story, "A Simple Heart"—satirizes the tragic Baton Rouge setting.

At LSU, English department faculty such as James Gordon Bennett, Patricia Geary, Anna Nardo, and Gerald Kennedy opened Parrish's mind to the world of writing and ideas in ways he only barely knew existed. He earned both his bachelor's and master's degrees in education, not yet involving himself in the creative writing world, but teaching developmental reading for three years. He went on to pursue his MFA from University of Alabama. Later, LSU creative writing professor, Moira Crone, heard Parrish read "After the River" in New Orleans, and as fiction editor of University Press of Mississippi solicited his work. He now teaches in the creative writing program at Southern Connecticut State University.

In Parrish's North Baton Rouge experience of growing up near the oil refineries, "an apocalyptic fire always seemed on the horizon." Such a feeling drives "After the River." His irresponsible, law-breaking, fun-loving pleasure seekers are turned on by the possibility that the unlikeliest of unlikely natural disasters will hit the capitol city. When it does, his characters break through the malaise, as Walker Percy would say, staying to witness the destruction of downtown Baton Rouge. He is currently working on a memoir entitled *Southern Man*, excerpts of which appear in *The Cincinnati Review* and *Ninth Letter*.

TIM PARRISH

After the River

A river wants to go straight and that spring the Mississippi wanted to bad, wanted to skip the dogleg that hooked it down past Baton Rouge and New Orleans and go right through the Old River Structure Lock to the Gulf of Mexico. Years, the corps of engineers had been rack-racking about reinforcing the lock, trying to get their hands deeper in our pockets, but Cheryl and me didn't believe the river could really shift, not in our lifetime anyway. The river was something we took for granted, its sludgy back and turd current a kind of comfort that dulled us without us even knowing it. Then record snows covered Minnesota and Wisconsin and all those other states up there and spring brought the heaviest-ass rains you ever saw, pouring like buckets into cups on top of all that winter melt.

At Baton Rouge chunks of ice floated past, telling Cheryl and me something was screwy and then Old Muddy started rising faster than stink on a hot day, on up creeper and creeper so that from downtown ships looked like they were riding the levee. Near the bank where Cheryl worked, water seeped onto River Road, puddling the asphalt rain and shine. Workers sandbagged the leaky levee and set up pumps to spit the water back into the river, a move Cheryl said seemed to her like drinking more to keep from getting drunk. Word went out to stay off the levee to stop it from sogging down and Cheryl actually saw cops nab some kids and tourists who were checking out the swell. That's when we knew it was serious.

South of Baton Rouge, the corps of engineers opened the Bonnet Carré Spillway to take pressure off New Orleans, but the lily-faced engineers who came on TV said that what with the water volume they anticipated, they weren't real sure what was going to happen. Then the youngest-looking one elbowed up to the mike and blurted he wasn't just worried the river would get through the levee, he was worried the whole river was going to try and jump ship. You can believe that kind of talk didn't set well with Governor Fast Eddie and we didn't see that young engineer on the tube again. Eddie said that the corps must have swallowed some bad flood-water, spewing out panic like they were. He crowed it was more likely the moon would singe his hair than it was New Orleans would flood and said that if it did start to flood he'd personally go to the spillway and summon up Jesus himself to keep New Orleans dry. We'd all heard Eddie talk about Jesus before, Satan too, and nobody took that as much of anything.

At work we goofed about it, me and the old-timers with their flood and plant-explosion stories until after a while I thought maybe we were tempting fate and I'm not even superstitious, much. I'd only been at Neptune Polymers a year and I didn't want any stray river screwing my career security, not right after Cheryl and me had bought a new ski boat and laid down a load on a house. Still, Cheryl and me laughed about the whole thing, smoking a doobie during the news and saying, Please, please, Old Man River, don't swamp our dreamboat, laughing like we hadn't a whole lot lately. See, we'd got married straight out of high school thinking two incomes in one house would just double the fun and keep us for good out of the crummy neighborhoods we'd grown up in downwind of Exxon's farts. We wanted to sprout some kids eventually, but first we needed to get all the stuff we'd always wanted and have the freedom to just pick up and party whenever. And I'm telling you those bon temps had roulered for a while until we sunk in a rut, dragging in from work, scarfing something from Taco Hell, arguing over who didn't pay the Titanium SuperCard bill, night after night drifting through another TV evening, Cheryl barely looking at me and our living room feeling about the size of a locker. It was a thrill then come mid-April and the levee was sweating mud onto River Road.

On TV they showed these high bluffs out around St. Francisville and Cheryl stopped mid-chimichanga to look over at me and smile, remembering our early days in heat and out of control when we'd jumped off one of those cliffs into the toxic current only to wash ashore together wet as otters.

"What if it goes?" Cheryl asked, all ashiver.

"We'll be there," I said.

Soon New Orleans started going under for real, their drainage system sputtering down like a roulette wheel, and it didn't take long for serious lawlessness to set in like the best Mardi Gras ever. Fast Eddie called out the National Guard and they showed footage of riflemen in boats like they were patrolling Venice, Italy, or some shit. Cheryl and me had to laugh at that and she stood and pulled me to my feet and waved her arms, leading me through these liquid movements she called the river shifter. Then she said, "Let's party, smarty," even though it was Wednesday night. We plugged some beers in our cooler, rolled a fatty for the ride and threw some clothes in a paper sack just in case we decided to ditch work once we hit the Big Easy. Traffic coming out of the Crescent City was bumper to bumper, but our side flowed fast and free, most of the vehicles filled with people who gave us thumbs up or lifted a drink as they passed. Too bad state troopers had the road over Pontchartrain blocked like some goddamn police state. Still, instead of that sending Cheryl and me into one of our piss-and-moan-and-bite-and-groan arguments over nothing, we just pulled roadside and rehashed the good old days when we used to drink sky labs at Pat O's and stagger down to The Dungeon drunk as legislators. Before we knew it we were shooting beers and hugging tight as a couple of teenagers. When the sun raised his hot round head, he found us flat of our backs, hungover roadkill right there on the shoulder.

Before long we heard about deer herds in the Atchafalaya Swamp climbing onto islands thick as locusts, pawing and biting each other for high ground, and then they started swimming for boats, banging their hooves against the hulls and screaming creepy as hell. Hunters bagged them five at a time with their semi-automatics and Cheryl wondered why Fast Eddie didn't do something to help the poor things. I just shrugged and said, "People gotta eat." At the plant Goudeau told about Hurricane Audrey in '57 washing people out of their beds in the middle of the night. For what reason he told us that I don't know. Then he started in on how this was the start of the last days, Revelations, and the dudes on horses. Old Barefield cracked wasn't there not supposed to be a flood but fire this time after Noah, and Goudeau pointed his finger and said iniquity had to be cleansed before burned. Barefield smirked and said the Mississippi wasn't much good for cleansing what with all the crap we'd dumped into it and besides why didn't God start with New York or Houston if he wanted to do some real good. Goudeau clucked his tongue and said questioning God's plan like we were doing was one reason we'd regret saying and doing what we'd said and done and even though Goudeau had always been full of it, for an hour I felt like I had a gutful of brine.

Way south, Morgan City started freaking cause they were dead on in the path of the new river course. Morgan Cityites wailed how something had to be done to save their great and important town, talking like the place wasn't the cesspool of the universe, home to every driftwood piece of oilfield trash and serial killer on his way to do a Gulf Coast tour. In a minute Fast Eddie showed up with a flotilla of priests, blessing the waters like mad and chanting to God to stop the rage of the river. They dumped in so much holy water they themselves probably raised the level a good six inches.

On CNN they were talking about coffins bobbing down the streets of New Orleans and float-by shootings and showed a fleet of NOPD wielding some gunboat diplomacy on a bunch of looters at the River Front Casino.

Cheryl said she'd heard rumor of rats streaming out of the sewers in New Orleans and stampeding through the French Quarter, spooking the last tourists sticking it out to get rock-bottom beignet prices. Then Cheryl and me took turns baring our teeth and squealing rodent style as one chased the other, a game Cheryl called Last Texan in Jackson Square.

Next day we went to the state capitol building downtown by the river for a twenty-nine-story bird's-eye view and goddamn if the levee on the west side wasn't completely under and our side looking like a sneeze from a sailor would send it splashing into downtown. We highfived, bought little state capitol replicas from the gift shop and drove south on River Road, the ditches brimming and water covering the asphalt some places. We climbed the levee and Cheryl took off her shoes exposing her feet, cute little buns with toes, then told me the junior loan officer at work said he'd been in army intelligence and kept yakking about the Armageddon Detour, a federal plan to explode nuclear bombs in certain underground salt domes to let the overflow run into the earth. We figured the guy was jankin' her but then we thought again because not many years before an oil derrick had poked a salt dome and collapsed it and that salt dome had sucked down a whole lake, a truck, a house, and almost a couple of fishermen. That got Cheryl and me goofing, imagining water sucking into the ground, pouring like snakes through these big bomb tunnels until it hit molten rock and let out with these giant steam hisses and big-ass volcanoes. That hot wet talk got us going and we started swapping spit, water squishing out of the sod right there under us on the levee until a swarm of mosquitoes clouded around us like some Bible plague and we had to run hell to highwater back to the car.

At work, word came out that folks were humping, even couples whose sex lives had gone belly up a quarter century ago. Old Barefield even let on he'd done his wife in a Mexican restaurant bathroom at the mall. All stripe of weirdness began to break. One guy tore his garage down to build an ark, another sealed his house in shrink wrap, still another strapped pontoons to his motorcycle. Squint Millard had heard about creation of the Pointe Coupée Tube Riders, a surf club set on catching the giant wave down the Atchafalaya when the dam lock collapsed. Solemn engineers came into our control room and drank our coffee while they talked about how maybe the river shifting wasn't bullshit. They said a course change wouldn't dry the river bed but would drop the normal level significantly and stop the flow so that everything south of the shift would be perched by the largest, narrowest, most polluted lake ever imagined. The plant couldn't operate more than a week or so without moving water. Then Goudeau started telling how the 1811 New Madrid earthquake in Missouri made the Mississippi flow backward three days and leap out of its bed a mile and never come back because of the sins of the frontier. Old Barefield told him to shut his trap with his friggin 9-1-1-Holy-Christ-with-a-stick stories and before we knew it we were trying to break them up from a brou-haha and then plant security was in breaking us all up from a brawl. Etienne Simac got the worst of it, a pipe across the noggin, but he didn't seem worried, taking as he was a trip down some mental tributary, sitting there muttering about all this being God's judgement on the state for corruption and godlessness while blood poured from his forehead into his eyes.

We all got sent home for the day and I kidnapped Cheryl from the bank, breaking her into a smile big as August sun. We went for oyster po-boys, drive-through daiquiris, and tattoos of Louisiana that when we held our arms together moved the Mississippi to its new course, then Cheryl ruffled my hair and said why didn't we get home and catch the evening news from the couch. We spooned on the sofa like the old days while some Yankees on a talk show slugged each other because somebody'd been screwing somebody who'd been screwing somebody who wanted to be screwing everybody and I was finger-walking along the outside of Cheryl's leg when Fast Eddie came on live at a Biloxi casino placing a million dollar bet that the Old River Structure would hold and was much better than the Bonnet Carré Spillway, which had just washed away, leaving New Orleans looking like water world. The corps was bringing in convoys of huge dumptrucks filled with boulders to shore up the end of the Old River Structure, but traffic jams of people massing to see the big giveway were blocking the road and there were barely enough troopers and guardsmen to even direct traffic since now the rioting and looting was in full revel in Morgan City and some other soon-to-be-Atlantis towns near the coast. Cheryl and me locked eyes in a mind meld like we hadn't had since we'd de-cided to get Miami-sunrise-orange tuxedo jackets for our wedding groomsmen, toasted our sixty-four-ounce Gator-Inflator daiquiris and hurled our shoes into the TV screen, causing a blast that set us to laughing like dental patients forgotten under nitrous masks.

We towed our ski boat out to False River, an elbow lake that used to be part of the Mississippi, and soon we were taking turns nude skiing even though the water was nippy as breams' teeth and a hard rain was falling. Cheryl slalomed like a mad-woman, her bare white self seeming to be midair every time I looked back, and when she climbed back in the boat she dropped her ski jacket and magnetted straight to my lap. "Missed you," she said, and laid a king-size sloppy one right on my lips, then her cool damp body was pressing all against mine and we were twisting and groping to the floor of the boat like teens whose parents have left the house for a half hour. We did the nasty right there in the boat in front of everybody, but everybody was doing it or didn't care. Afterward we sat there in the drench talking about what kind of job opportunities there might be in our backwater town once it really was a backwater town and we both quivered and jiggled a bit considering for real how our comfy lives might really change. Cheryl rubbed her arms worried-like and I remembered how in the old days her and me never worried. Back then we'd just gone with the flow, keeping it spiced however we could, dressing up in animal costumes, ordering anchovy and okra pizzas, skipping work for a day of bat hits and game shows, making love in positions like I was a lawnmower Cheryl was pushing or something. Even so, it'd ended with me up alone, channel surfing and playing spin-the-top with my wedding ring on the arm of my chair while Cheryl dreamed without me.

Where had we gone wrong?

Anyway, I checked Cheryl out there naked in a life jacket and all those other people boating in the buff, wild, and I thought maybe these were the last days. All over the world stuff was going down. People shorting each other cash, fires getting lit nobody knew how, dolphins drowning in nets. Bad business. Like me, what I'd done, fishing here for years, catching more than I needed, letting some die before throwing

them back, throwing bottles in the water. And why? I didn't know. I looked at the
water around us, gray and choppy, and I thought how I loved the lake and catching
fish and taking them home to eat with a whopper plate of hushpuppies and a mound
of cole slaw and why would I ever do something to hurt that? Then I looked around
at how big that lake was and thought how many fish were still in there and no matter what I'd done there would always be fish in that water and I'd love to catch them.
And I thought how when water spilled out everywhere with fish then there would
be fish everywhere and new spots for fishing and Cheryl and me could go there in
our boat and that would be all right. I jumped up and hugged Cheryl and we linked
pinkies and made a pact we weren't going to leave no matter what because we loved
our state and its governor and its food.

Back at the boat dock we found a wild scene like from The Ten Commandments
on the pier, all these people dancing around a bonfire of boat cushions and ice chests.
Cheryl and me grabbed a bottle of Wild Turkey and blitzed out of there. On the
radio we heard there was boat-to-boat fighting between Aryan State storm troopers
and people who got pissed when the Aryans' Grand Duke did an infomercial on how
the flooding was the fault of the underclass conspiracy to subvert Anglo-Euro Christian values. All over the radio, announcers were howling about carnage and Cheryl
lit an A-Pot-Co-Lipt-Us hooter as we sped back towards Red Stick. Out in yards
we saw people in camouflage toting guns and a melee or two at a Piggly Wiggly,
but traffic was surprisingly light and I pushed as fast as I could, both Cheryl and me
knowing we wanted to be up top the capitol when the big shift came.

Parts of downtown were blockaded because of flooding and people were tooling
among the glassy bank buildings in their bateaus and bass boats, but we shoved
on until our car stalled three blocks from the capitol grounds where we unhooked
our own boat and beelined for the observation deck. Atop the levee sat a couple of
runaway barges, and a certifiable train of ships was lined up heading south trying to
escape to the gulf.

The capitol was wide open with nobody in charge and people were tearing chairs
and desks out of the senate chamber while one bald woman in a halter top and
shorts stood at the senate president's podium calling for abolition of Robert's rules of
order. Cheryl and me hopped on the elevator by ourselves and fell quiet as puddles
when we realized we hadn't been anywhere without noise in some time. Cheryl's
hair was tied in a bandanna and she kept pinching her lower lip and for a second I
saw her exactly like I'd seen her the first night we made love right after the Global
Wrestling Confederation's Swamp Spectacular at the Centroplex. I had to lean over
and kiss her on the ear.

At the twenty-fourth floor we changed to the smaller elevator, walking around a
man in a brown suit on his knees praying, stepped past the ransacked gift shop and

stepped out onto the observation deck. People five deep were crammed against the wall looking out at the river, but they weren't struggling and no one was talking loud. About half of them had video cams. We snapped our fingers we didn't have one. The rain had stopped and the sky was a glarey gray and I took Cheryl's hand and eased to a spot where we could see up the river in the direction where the artery was going to be severed.

From way down below us the noise of the city blared, horns blowing and guns shooting and engines revving. On the river, freighters and tankers and barges clogged the water, a convoy twelve ships wide and out-of-sight long, stretching around the bend in both directions, while smoke poured from the plants and refineries all churning at max-plus production. The air burned my eyes and nostrils like skunkweed. We stood for a while, people passing bottles and bags of chips and even joints and nobody being Catholic or Baptist or bastard until a voice said, "It went," and I saw a guy take off his radio headphones. The ships laid on their horns and several tried to make passing maneuvers that rammed them into other ships. Still others tried to veer to the levee and some of the sailors dropped lifeboats, suicide with all those ships in a bottleneck.

Cheryl wrapped her arm around my waist and I put my arm around her shoulders and squeezed and Cheryl's whole body was trembling, I thought, until she pressed a hand against my chest and hugged me with both arms and I found I was the one that was shaking. There was nothing to do for a while except watch the chaos below and think and I thought of worst-case scenarios, a giant wave washing over the banks, toppling the capitol, taking us with it. Then I thought, What if the river did sweep us away, wash the building right from under us, take us into the river and on out to the Gulf? That made my bladder convulse. Then I thought, Wouldn't it be worse not to get to eye this? My legs went jelly and my knees buckled a little, but Cheryl held me steady.

A wave did come, a sizeable one like the river had bucked, one that capsized some ships and sent others over the levee crashing into downtown. But then the wild thing started happening, the river not being the river anymore, its water level dropping like somebody had pulled a plug, the levees on both sides rising up like walls, ships left stranded atop them. I swear even up twenty-nine stories high I could hear guys from the boats yelling, then people on the observation deck began crying and screaming and collapsing. A couple laughed.

Now I know everybody dreams about disaster, imagining nuclear bombs or chemical spills or meteorites hit-ting their house, breaking up the ho-hum with a little gratuitous weak knee, but there we were, Cheryl and me, watching the river we'd watched our whole lives actually leave us. That sucker went down and stayed down, like Huey Long gut shot, and it was the weirdest buzz Cheryl and me ever had, probably ever will have. Cheryl just looked at me, her face gone nine times pale as a death sheet, and said, "Wow." And, you know, I had to say it back.

You can believe things got different fast after that, thousands of people getting the hell out of town and people like me getting laid off work. New Orleans lost its water supply completely and the city went kind of Mad Max until the president of the whole country sent in the serious army and they quieted shit somewhat. All in all, things turned out okay, though, I mean other than a few cities going kaput or being washed away and a few thousand people drowning. Plenty of folks are working on the new levee and ports in the Atchafalaya, and Baton Rouge is one huge gambling town where the river is a putrid lake they run these miniature riverboats up and down piloted by these Mark Twain-looking guys. Soon I got hired back on at Neptune dismantling the unit I'd worked in and for a while after that I ran tour groups describing exactly what it'd been like to be there when the Mississippi changed its mind. Even Goudeau came on my tour once, mostly to show how bitter he was that The End hadn't actually come down on us.

The main thing after the initial excitement, though, was getting through the posthigh depression, like the biggest hangover in history, everybody shuffling around kind of sullen and pissed knowing they'd already seen the wildest thing they were ever going to see. Cheryl and me got real edgy and then real quiet and finally had a huge blowup over whose idea it'd been to bust the TV screen. The bank took our boat and our house and that caused a lot of the old-style grumbling and touchiness we'd had before the river. For kicks we took some trips to where the Old River Structure Lock and the Bonnet Carré Spillway had been. We even took the ferry ride on the New Mississippi all the way south to where Morgan City is now on the bottom, but we might as well have been looking at the spot where a fish jumped as exciting as that was. Finally, to get out of our funk we splurged on a wide-screen TV and subscribed to the Life-Arts channel's World's Greatest Disasters tape series, which we watched every night, ripped, with the lights off and huddled under a tarpaulin. When the latest tape came out, "The Day the Mississippi Missed," we threw a galoshes party, but most of our friends had already split town.

Luckily, Cheryl and me now have jobs working in the old capitol building, a casino since the capital itself moved to Lafayette where Fast Eddie says it should have been all along. We got a better house cheaper because of everybody moving out and then we got jet skis. Yeah, we still get back in that rut we used to get in, but now when every day seems stagnant and every ripple rocks our marital plank, we just look at each other and relive that day up top the capitol. We hold each other and do the screams and the sound of the boats and run through the house hand in hand, whooshing like a wave, the picture of it in our heads, rushing down the river, washing away the old, and leaving us with something special we saw together. After all, we know not many people can say they were there for something.

I mean really something.

MOIRA CRONE

In Moira Crone's short story "Gauguin," from her 1998 collection *Dream State*, a young man "in limbo" from New England plans to leave Louisiana with all its political problems and fly to Boston to begin a romance with an old friend the day before Hurricane Andrew strikes. Baton Rouge readers will feel right at home in this story with its references to the Duke-Edwards race for governor, Perkins Road Hardware, the local weatherman Mike Graham, and other characters behaving exactly as Louisianans do right before a hurricane. The displaced northerner experiences his first hurricane, an event that is perhaps symbolic of other upheavals in his consciousness. In Crone's other major publications—*The Winnebago Mysteries and Other Stories, What Gets Into Us,* and *A Period of Confinement*—she also examines the cultural divide between the South and the North. Her descriptions of Southern people and attitudes are sympathetic, humorous, and intimate. Because she intertwines her own spirituality with her portrayal of the New South, her fiction has been called "Southern Gnostic."

An LSU creative writing faculty member since 1981, Crone served for several years as the MFA program's first woman director. In that role she began to create an online history of all the works produced by the creative writing students. Working with Rosemary James and Joe DeSalvo, pioneers of the Pirate's Alley Faulkner Society Words & Music Festival in New Orleans, Crone arranged for LSU's MFA students to meet with established editors and agents from New York who visit annually to participate in the festival. These meetings allow students to have their work evaluated professionally and make invaluable contacts in the publishing world. Also as director, she worked tirelessly toward securing full financial support for all MFA creative writing students. Among the students Crone knew well and guided are Laurie Lynn Drummond, Matt Clark, Michael Griffith, Connie Porter, and Dinty Moore.

Crone's impact on the world of Southern fiction is made even more significant by her work as fiction series editor of University Press of Mississippi. Additionally, in 2009 she was presented the Robert Penn Warren Award for Fiction by the Fellowship of Southern Writers in recognition of her body of work.

MOIRA CRONE

Gauguin

When people ask him about it, Paul still says it's mysterious to him. He knows he could start back when David Duke was running for Governor of Louisiana. But if someone wants to hear the story, he usually begins with a man in limbo, himself—dusk on a Monday, late in August 1992. He was driving downtown to his office for some files he wanted to look over before he left. He was flying to Wellfleet in forty-odd hours. Meredith would be there. He looked up and saw the overpass: Interstate 10 West a parking lot. He thought, tank-truck turnover, jackknife, petrochemical spill. Bopal. He turned on the local news radio, got the headline, "Coming Up: Mayor Sidney Barthelme on the Evacuation of New Orleans."

He turned around in the road, went back to his little rent house on St. Helena, to wait and see, which would describe his whole life in Baton Rouge at that time—he was waiting and seeing.

The year before when David Duke hit, when he got in the runoff for governor, Meredith called him out of the blue, from Boston. She wanted to know what Paul was going to do. They'd been friends in law school, but involved with other people. Somebody in her new firm told her to call, say, "Stay down there like Nadine Gordimer." But Meredith didn't think so. They went on to other subjects. This developed.

As a matter of fact, that same Duke afternoon, Diana Landry from across the street came over with her son A.J. She was wearing a "Vote for the Crook, It's Important" T-shirt. "Saw your No-Nazis Sticker," she said. Paul assumed he was going to be fired however things turned out. Buddy Roemer, the governor, who hired him through Harvard connections, was out of the mansion in any case. Paul was a lawyer in the Department of Environmental Quality. He'd already made some calls—a friend in Princeton told him about a job in Albany. He was trying.

"Leave, everybody should," she said. "If you aren't from here. I am so ashamed of this place." Then she paused. "But if you want to join the underground I know where to start." Next, she was yelling at her son, who was climbing a delicate crepe myrtle bush. "You can call me. We'll get that sucker." He did join her. There were some crazy weeks that fall.

Now, this limbo Monday, in August, almost a year later, things with Meredith had gotten more interesting. Paul had not been laid off after the new governor was inaugurated. Nobody understood this. Paul just assumed it was a matter of time. Meredith was handing his resume around to institutes on Route 128. It was her cause, others had taken it up as well: getting him back to New England. Although Paul was a stoical young man, rather tall, who could be riled but not easily, he was quietly beginning to panic. He hadn't actually been with Meredith *in person* in all this time. But one thing that kept him going was that he and Meredith were closer and closer, by Internet.

When he got home, his trip to the office denied him, the phone rang. Diana across the street. "We've got some D batteries," she said and he wondered who "we" was, since she told him one morning when he was jogging that she and her husband Virgil (Cajun, ropey arms, a sculptor) split up in the early spring. Otherwise, he hadn't spoken to her for months. "What kind of radio do you have?"

"Huh?" he said. "What's going on in New Orleans?"

"Andrew," she said.

He hadn't been watching TV lately. "Who?"

"After Betsy, we didn't have power for five days."

"I'm going to Wellfleet," he said.

"Where?" Diana said.

"Why are they evacuating New Orleans?"

"Not yet, maybe some early birds," she said. "The hurricane's got them going." He remembered she was a chatterer. To be nice he suppressed his love of the point.

First thing in the morning, Meredith called. He was thrilled. Raised in Newton, she still dropped her r's—he'd almost forgotten. She was at the Cape already, no modem, so they had to use their voices.

"Twenty feet of water in New Orleans," she said.

"There's no water in New Orleans," he said.

"But there will be—"

"No," he said. "This place has a specialty in threatened disasters."

"It's if the locks break, there will be. Do you have them where you are?" she said.

He was interested in her tone. All this time, it had been maybe only chummy. He couldn't tell. The Net is not a hot medium, instead disembodied, like conversations in the afterlife.

"There's a whole Gulf Coast, a thousand-mile stretch where it could hit."

"How do people stand it?" she said. "Waiting, not knowing?"

He didn't have an answer. Call waiting beeped. Because of the time, he decided he'd better take it. It was his boss, Fletcher L'Enfant. Meredith said, "Go ahead, you work for him—I'll call back," before he could tell her L'Enfant could be ignored.

"Son, don't go to work today."

Even if he was waiting for it, it was a creepy feeling, being canned at seven-fifty in the morning. He sat down. L'Enfant called him son. Paul was turning thirty-one. "Nonessential state employees. Just got the call. The hurricane."

He didn't feel relieved. "Will somebody let me in? So I can get that Filtrum Re-processing file?"

"No," he said in that over-slow voice he used when he thought Paul didn't follow, "closed up, zippo."

"But I'm on my way out of town!" He imagined L'Enfant was trying to keep him from recommending fines for that plant, and being exquisitely nice about it.

"Fill your bathtub," L'Enfant said. "You'll be fine. Bye bye."

When he hung up, the phone rang almost immediately. Meredith.

After describing his conversation with L'Enfant, he asked her, to entertain her, "What good does a bath do in a hurricane?"

"That would never happen in Boston. Your boss would never tell you to fill your tub." She was giggling. Phone was so sensual. "Oh, Albertine is desperate to make a call. Ciao."

About nine-thirty that same morning he was in a hardware store on Perkins Road. The atmosphere was snappy. People were out around town, on a mass scavenger hunt. He told himself the best way to make the sun shine in this situation—not that he cared really, since he was on his way out—was to have an ample umbrella. So he was standing in front of a bin full of picked-over supplies—pen lights, busted kerosene lanterns, taped bundles of linty wicks. A woman came up to give him advice—the Radio Shack was having a delivery at 10:30, the D batteries at one chain mart were out of date. And then on to dry ice, how Hurricane Betsy barreled up the Mississippi gaining strength. He couldn't get this woman to stop. He remembered an article he read once, about the southern urge to explain. It didn't explain.

The first day he went out to the market after Duke was in the runoff, a complete stranger, just like this lady, a frank woman in an all-weather coat, the creased upper lip of a smoker, came up to him— "Can you believe it? The Saints are going to pull out. We won't get the Olympic trials . . . Used to tell people he was going to burn his mother's bed. She was an alcoholic."

"Who was an alcoholic?" he asked.

"His mamma. And his daddy—don't believe any of that Laotian stuff."

"Laotian stuff?"

"That he was in Laos with his daddy working for the CIA. S'crazy." She touched his sleeve.

"Who?"

"Who else? The Antichrist. I can't sleep. Can you?" She progressed with him to the cash register. "What can we do?"

He told her about the underground Diana had led him to. A bunch of them, meeting down at an office suite on a boulevard in the deep suburbs. They were using this law firm's seventeen telephones, and a set of disks somebody had stolen from the party headquarters, to reach every Republican in the Parish. Over the first week, all kinds of people showed up: little Jewish ladies, professors from everywhere, kids, old ministers, Italian lawyers, arty friends of Diana's, even her brother Danny, a deputy sheriff. They couldn't park at the complex itself—had to use the back of a Circle K across the street. A secretary let them in, by a side door. There was a password. After this got underway, the hard core of the group—somehow Paul was involved—started pressuring politicians and coaches to speak in public, talking rich people into running ads about Duke's past, haranguing the stations every time a reporter let Duke off the hook. Didn't do anything else for three weeks. Paul got so wrapped up in it he never even called that guy in Albany back. He lost weight. Ran a fever. Meredith's message on the Net: "It's existential. You are a partisan." Smiley.

He wrote back, "Get me out of here."

This Tuesday morning, Andrew still pending, he extricated himself from this lady. His booty: two cheap flashlights, sixteen C batteries, a huge expensive cooler.

As he was driving home past massive oaks, palmettos, big banana trees, it occurred to him all he had to do, of course, was change his ticket. So he went in and dialed, and waited a million years, feeling like a fool, for the Delta operator. He recognized he was losing his edge, down in Louisiana.

While he floated in the crackling phone noise, he saw Cape Cod, the horizon there, so even and free of business, pines, grey and blue. He thought of Thoreau. How Yankee he was. Finally the operator came on: no seats out of New Orleans or Baton Rouge.

In this North he saw, the laws of cause and effect were well established. Meredith and himself because they've always liked each other, it made sense. These rules didn't work in Louisiana. Duke, for example, was not entirely a horrible event in the lives of his many enemies. Even specific irony didn't apply often enough in this place. For example, Paul was prepared, in a matter of speaking, for the hurricane by this time, which should have meant it wouldn't come within a thousand miles. This would work anywhere north of Baltimore.

St. Helena was Mexican slang for blondes, he was thinking as he watched Mrs. Diana Landry crossing the street in front of his house. He cringed a little. Then he remembered he'd tell her that he'd heard that David, politically dead, was taking the insurance exam. Her crinkly light hair in the breeze.

"They have dry ice at Party Time," she said. "You want me to pick you up some?" She was wearing tight floral leggings—wisteria growing on her legs. A.J. was behind her, pulling a red wagon loaded with baseball equipment across the lawn. "Virgil came over and boarded up the house—just left," she said, sounding pissed. From the doorway he could see her place—the old failing oak in the front yard, the mustard-yellow plywood slapped up on all the windows. "I'm sorry to have to ask, but you got a beer?" she said. This was the most personal she'd been in ten months.

He had things called Turbo Dogs, which were beers, in the refrigerator. She had one, he didn't. She went on to say that at Party Time, you had to stand in line. Then she returned to the subject of Virgil. "He wants to see we're okay, okay," she said, biting her lip. "I say like, 'Okay 'til you showed up,'" one side of her mouth drawn up. He wondered if she knew what that did to her face. "Don't look at me like that," she said, her lips going instantly back to a pout. Her manic skittishness should have bothered him more.

Suddenly she announced, "Mike Graham's on." She pulled a big tracking map she got free at a drugstore out of her jeans pocket. They both thought A.J. was in the dark little back room where Paul hid his television, but when they got there, they found he wasn't. Diana picked up Paul's remote.

The weatherman said, "Landfall by late Wednesday. Warnings from Pascagoula to Lake Charles—" They heard glass breaking. Running to the front of the house, they found A.J. putting out the small panes along the side of the front door. With his baseball bat. When he opened the door to ask A.J. what he thought he was doing, Paul noticed the air, still and thick. The entire neighborhood—the little cottages, the huge old live oaks, the lampposts and slate walks—was floating inside a glass of buttermilk. Diana came out and yanked her son inside.

"What's wrong with him?" Paul asked her, sounding more upset than he felt inside—it was this limbo.

She was almost Paul's height, her eyes large. She said, "They don't know. Or won't tell me." He realized this bold, sort of bloated face she had now was the way she looked right before she cried.

She went into his bathroom with A.J., who had nicked his finger on a piece of glass. "I didn't mean—" Paul said. She looked at him as if he knew everything. Then he rushed off to his study for cardboard, filmy brown packing tape. He came back to the front saying, "I can fix it," but when he got there, his broom was leaning against the foyer wall, his front door was closed and locked. Through the broken panes, he could see Diana and A.J. bounding across the street. He felt terrible.

At three, Paul decided to dismiss the thought of Andrew entirely. He was trying to figure out if any dry cleaners would do his things by morning. Then, when he wandered back into the den, the TV was still on, but someone had pressed the mute. There was a computer enhancement of the storm. It covered the gulf, from Florida on the right side of the screen to the tops of the islands south of New Orleans on the left. For a second it came right up off the map, and out of the box. It startled him. He stared. It was like God, or that stuff at the end of *Raiders of the Lost Ark*. The next second, he saw a sign on a boarded-up building in New Orleans, "ANDREW TAKE IT OUT ON FERGIE." He laughed, actually very hard, for someone alone. He watched the Baton Rouge commercials, in despair. Monster truck rallies, half-naked Heather who wants you at the Gun and Knife Show. He wondered what was playing at the American Repertory Theatre. He took a snatch of a nap, woke to banging.

Diana, on his front stoop in a plastic poncho. It was late in the afternoon, getting strange. She was holding a narrow piece of plywood over the place were A.J. put out the window. She had a hammer and nails.

"Hey, I rent, don't worry about it," he said coming out.

"No. I'm so sorry," she said. "I left A.J. on the Nintendo. Maybe I do that too much." She handed him a picnic thermos, huge. "I brought you hurricanes."

He was grateful. Once before he got drunk with her. The night Duke lost. She recited a ditty to him, the Cajun consider-the-lilies-of-the-field, "Look at the birds in the yard/who feeds 'em cher." He remembered this right now. A still drizzle, outside. The buttermilk leaving condensation. That big silent swirling thing he saw on TV, he thought of telling her about it, someone here, who wouldn't think he was crazy, Meredith would, but instead he said, "There's a thousand places it could come in," because he was shy.

"Mike's moved landfall way up," she said. "It's coming in at Vermilion Bay or maybe Morgan City."

In Morgan City the children had some terrible brain cancer. Statistically significant. A lot of people blame the toxic waste processor there. He had been on it for seven months. In fact, in June a guy from Hartford told him about an opening at his firm, but Paul was in Morgan City so much he missed the deadline.

"Winds are still at one-fifty," she said. "The eyewall will be here by midnight."

Eyewall. How fluent she was. He said, "It will fizzle."

"You still going?" she asked.

"Yea."

"Getting outta here, huh?" jutting her lower chin a little bit as if to mimic some matter-of-factness that was generally Paul's and not hers. Suddenly he wondered if she wanted him to go. If she had an opinion about it. This came up, out of nowhere. For a second those big un-dangerous dunes at the Cape spun out into space, and he was just in the present with Diana, in the middle of this late, odd afternoon. He felt a little stunned. Maybe she saw this. "Yea, uh-huh," she said, now nodding to mock him—wasn't he a lucky duck, wasn't he? But he had to do his packing. He had shirts to wash. "Don't you know to fill your tub?" she said—taking off for his bathroom.

"Why's this in here?" she called to him when he got there. "I swear, Paul, you got to get square with your TV, boy." She handed him his remote, which she'd dropped beside the tub herself, some time ago. In several ways, an unstandable woman, he reminded himself.

He stood in the doorway trying to celebrate when she finally left. He noticed breaths, little explosions of rain, under the light on their street, which had come on early. It was an idiosyncratic rain. Usually you could count on rain to be fairly uniform, he was thinking.

He did a damn good job—toothbrush, Mitchum, Vidal Sassoon, the works. All in a little nylon Lands End bag, zipped up, with room to spare. He finished washing and laid out his outfits, even ironed a few shirts—he'd given up on the idea of finding a cleaners. Lined up his socks. He didn't forget the Eternity cologne, the rugged cotton sweaters he never got a chance to wear because Louisiana was too hot. This took time. At ten he watched the local news, which he hadn't done since the Duke campaign. Back then the news made him sick—the reporters milked the story for all it was worth, at the same time they behaved like cowards, he thought. National news was even worse, completely clueless, missed all the ironies. But tonight the local reporters were standing in outrageously windy spots, their cheeks so wet with violent rain, they seemed to be weeping. He suddenly felt he knew them very well, could go into their hearts if necessary. Some had already been told to evacuate, they said, as they wobbled all over the screen. One guy he called a fascist the year before was standing in the middle of tall, violently swaying cane. The scale was off. He was a grasshopper, reporting from a very unruly lawn. "Chances are high it will hit here," he said. A foray into the obvious. Paul felt for this guy, his high eyebrows, syrupy Cajun eyes. He wanted to go into the TV to say, "Pierre, get in the van, it's going to blow."

Thank God he was headed for Wellfleet.

Then there was a live report from the Hurricane Center in Coral Gables. The director had been up for days. The center itself was hit. Some on his crew were electrocuted. He was slovenly, incoherent. Paul was well into Diana's concoction by then. It tasted like Hawaiian punch plus grain alcohol, and he was meditating on the word "here." He called Meredith.

"Oh, Jesus, are you anywhere near La Place?" she asked.

Once again he was thrilled with the sound of her voice. It was throaty. "There was a tornado," she said. "Can you go to a shelter?" just as he saw the red bulletin flash across his screen.

"I'm fine," he said. "That's over near New Orleans."

"I think it's headed right there," she said.

"Hell or high water, really," he said, "the plane's tomorrow, three-thirty."

"We're all worried about you," she said. "Albertine says when she heard you'd gone to Louisiana it was like that painter who went to Tahiti, that's what she thought of."

Albertine was a woman they went to law school with. From Smith. Her eyes were magnified by her glasses. "She and Russell came out, remember Russell?" Meredith said. "We were all so worried. Glued to the Weather Channel," she waited. "Paul? You there?"

"What? Yea," he said. "I'm not there, I'm here."

"Well, yes. I know where you are."

"Here," he said. "It's different."

"I know," she said, "tell me."

"It's insoluble," he said. "Isn't it?"

"I don't think so," she said. "Here is there for you and there for me is here for you," her deep laugh. "For now."

"Yes it is, it is, but not really," he said.

Meredith insisted it was. She repeated herself. She was flirting, he knew, but he was having difficulty responding. He was serious about all this; he wasn't sure at all why.

After they finally said goodnight, he decided to sleep in the back den, which had only one window, and that one shaded by heavy wooden jalousies. He bedded down in front of the TV, under a thin blanket. His flight bag was propped up on his little black couch. He had finished off the jug. And this was all very native, he thought, to be drunk on sweet drinks and be alone, listening to the wind hurling through the banana trees. I really must go, he thought. Really.

At one of the desolate hours, three or four in the morning, he ventured into the kitchen. Cotton mouth. Reaching toward the left, he touched the light switch.

No light. None in the fridge.

In the dark, while he drank all the orange juice from the carton, he thought of the normal-size sky they have up there on the Cape, to try and calm down. He saw himself and Meredith McCartel, a Unitarian, going along the beach, having a thoughtful conversation. He knew peace of mind. He knew exactly what came after that afternoon's walk. He prayed he hadn't upset her.

He staggered back to bed, which was the floor.

When he got up again, the kitchen was filled with a strange pink light. He assumed it was morning. The pecan tree outside his window was waving at the base of its trunk, a big timid hula girl. He put his good French roast beans into the grinder—no whir.

For a long time he sat at his little metal table in an old tubular chair, and watched his tree and the others dance. He listened. Around eight his house started to groan. Then all the trees were swaying back and forth, like backup singers. It was positively choral—the tops in one direction, the bottoms in another. Of course this was terrible, but that didn't keep it from being interesting. Around nine he heard the whistle, like he was on a ship. Andrew going through the lamp that hung from his little porch. His ears were aching by this time. He was surprised when the phone rang.

"I got through!" Meredith said, triumphantly. "How's your airport?" she said. He was thinking about a tree across the street, in Diana's front yard, how heavy it was.

"I don't know," he said. He hadn't called.

"I'll call," she said. "Are you Delta?"

"It's very bad, here," he said. "My ears."

"According to the Weather Channel, it's to your west."

He didn't answer.

"Are you okay?" she said—this irritation, now. "You sounded sort of—"

"I'm fine," he said.

"I don't know, were you drinking last night?"

"Drinking?" This was out of character for him, that he would lie to someone that way.

"I'll call," she said. "Delta." She said it firmly. "How can you stand it. Don't you just wish you knew exactly how this was going to turn out? I'd go crazy."

He agreed he couldn't stand it, of course, but later when he recalled this, he recognized some reservations, which he hadn't uttered. What he said was, "My ears are splitting open." The barometric pressure.

"Last night they said it might fly by and only land in Mobile, how far is that?"

"Mobile?" he asked. "I think it's here."

"I mean your plane," she said.

"I'm too close to the window," he said.

"Oh Paul don't," she said. "How bad can it be?"

"It's a hurricane, Meredith," he said. "It really doesn't matter what they say on cable. I'm so sorry, I really am," and he was, but then he hung up. Next, he was crawling across the floor. As if, if he were to stand up he might be showing the present some disrespect. As if he had seen things, been shown signs. He headed toward the front of the house, though it would have been safer to stop in the little hallway next to the den. He wanted a view of the whole street. When he got there, he saw that the several enormous live oaks on St. Helena looked like giants buried in the sand, their heads poking up, straining to get out. The root systems, their shoulders, pulled up more soil with every heavy gust. The trees were heaving. It was amazing. He gazed over at Diana's house, blank, eyeless, the thick plywood patches.

The night Duke lost the race, he could see the candlelight in her windows from his living room. She used little votives for the party. That way she wouldn't have to really clean, she joked. Her home life was not the best right then. For the three weeks of the runoff, they were arguing—Virgil said she was gone too much, and he wanted to know how she could support Edwards no matter who his opponent was. A lot of couples had split over the election. At the party there was a pool, you could pick the point spread. By that time most people figured Edwards had been bound to win all along—he'd never been in real danger. The underground might have felt used, and bitter. That would have made sense, Paul thought. Instead everybody danced to Neville Brothers, Doctor John, Zydeco, a little Dewey Balfa. There were Creoles there, lawyers and other rich men, with paunches. The journalists who listened to some of them had all kinds of stuff they couldn't print, crimes of Duke, rumors about Edwards. There were professors from Southern University, and a tall woman from Sri Lanka, a physicist, with her husband, Buddhists, a man raised in Hungary, who'd been in the resistance in the war. They had all worked at the phone bank one night or another, but it was sort of amazing to see them there together at once, come from so many different realms, chomping on corn chips. Duke's losing was a certainty, they said they'd never had a question. But at the end of the evening, when it came to how the precincts voted, parish by parish, people from Louisiana went up to the screen, asked for silence. If Duke was defeated in their home precinct, they shouted, "All right!" and held their fists in the air, hugged people. Everybody cried and asked each other personal questions. Where were you from, really, where were you going if Duke had won. When she was in the middle of a long complaint, Paul asked Diana why she ever wanted to marry Virgil. She looked at him—actually very pretty to him just then, another man's wife, and that was okay, that was the mood, no secrets, no status. She said, "Does what you want have much to do with how your life plays out? I think very little." And then she grinned, like it was all right with her, what she'd just said. At the time he thought her remark incredibly strange. He had not forgotten this completely by the day of the hurricane.

Just then the huge oak in her yard succeeded in liberating itself from the soil. A thundering cracking sound. The entire root system toppled out, taking up half the lawn with it. It fell towards her house. In the center of the mass of roots now visible, a black hole ran through. Dead all along. He couldn't see her roofline any more. He crawled to his front door, stood, and opened it up.

Actually, when he unlocked it, it opened itself.

The wind was primary, sovereign. Music, playing at different speeds, different intensities. The rain was being thrown out in gasps, violently, then breathily. As if the wind had to reach inside of itself periodically to find more water to throw forth. Smaller trees, twice as tall as himself, bent down to the ground, then snapped back up, over and over. The street was a river. From his porch he could see that her carport and part of her roof was crushed. He imagined Diana and A.J. trapped inside. Then Paul's nerves were a golden web, lighting him up inside his arms, his thighs, his neck.

He made it across—he was blown, really, that's how it looked, or he was picked up by an invisible hand. He touched down on the little concrete disks that made the path to her front door. He was imagining how he'd break in.

He pounded on the door, stood outside and waited. Never once did he think he was stupid. The door cracked open. There she was. She was fine.

"You crazy? You out of your mind?" She had him in.

It reminded him of a lake at night, inside—so dark with the windows boarded, the light from kerosene lamps. She had shiny oak floors, with puddles here and there. Water was running in underneath the bedroom doors along the hallway on the side of the house where the roof was damaged. There were towels and cotton blankets tossed around, used recently to swab the floors, he supposed, then abandoned. When he looked back to Diana, he saw she was holding a fan of playing cards in her hand, sitting on her skirted, winged old couch in a long cotton nightgown.

She looked flushed, younger. Her calves were very white, and smooth, and in places dappled pink, and she had big work boots on, her husband's old ones, he guessed. A.J., beside her, was also holding some cards, and eating caramel corn from a pottery bowl, dark blue. The boy, who had a ruddy complexion and mousey blond hair, looked strangely cherubic in this light. From a cooler, dry ice mist furled towards them.

"D'you run across in your bare feet like that?" she said. "That's so wild."

"I saw the tree fall."

A.J. was shuffling the cards. He was excellent at this, very smooth, didn't drop one, Paul noticed.

"Did you hear that?" she asked her son, beaming. A.J. was very calm. The hurricane pacified him. "It gave us a scare, but we just sat tight." Paul took a seat on an ottoman, on a damp blanket. They dealt him in. He won a few, but mostly he lost to Diana and A.J. She cheated so her son would win. Generally, he'd say that was a bad idea, but right then he found it endearing. They ate crawfish salad cold from the dry ice, and delicious. Some boudin. He felt as if he'd been there forever, listening to the storm slowly dying down. More than once it occurred to him the house was going to collapse; this made him enjoy the moment more somehow.

A.J. went into the kitchen at one point. When they were alone, Diana looked at Paul with her wide-apart eyes, and reached toward his jaw as if to check his shaving, or to bring his face toward her, or to make sure he was real—the place didn't look real at all, stage smoke creeping along the floor. He leaned forward to hear what she was going to say, or maybe to do, attracted by her lovely attention. It was strange, how calm this all made him. But then she said, "Weren't you the one who was going somewhere?"

And when he tells this story he always jumps a little ahead, at this point, to that walk they took. It was about two-thirty, and the winds had died down and he and Diana and A.J. ventured out into her wrecked yard. Paul was carrying his flight bag. The airport was open. Down St. Helena, almost every tree was down or damaged. Things that were hidden before, he noticed, were exposed now by the winds—the flashy white wood inside old branches, the underside of the leaves, all silver. Immaculate was the word that came to mind. They passed many women, their neighbors, standing on their porches, their front doors flung open, looking out at the damage— smashed cars, lost roofs, twisted bikes, flooded yards—with a grand and easeful awe, the drizzle blowing in their faces. He felt as if he were in that very late painting of Gauguin's—he always mentions this part—the one with the royal pink sky in the background, and the bare-breasted maidens in it, who are gazing up mysteriously at something not pictured on the canvas itself. There are tropical vines in the background—for him these are the power lines, snaking downward. He is supposed to be going to the corner, where Diana's brother Danny the deputy sheriff, out cruising to discourage looters, has agreed to pick him up, take him to the airport. He's planning to dash out onto the runway in the post-hurricane excitement, perhaps holding a sturdy airline umbrella, to board his flight, to escape to New England.

Diana says to him, "Andrew went over Livonia, it missed us by only this much," her papery little fingertips, which he would later learn to care for very much, pinched close together, but not quite touching.

He says, "Did it? Did we miss it?" He finds this hard to believe.

"The eye," she whispers, looking sideways at him, and down, crestfallen when she knows she shouldn't be.

The moment he likes most comes next: he takes her elbow to help her avoid the puddle right beside her—she could be electrocuted. In the same motion, feeling a kind of urgent glory, he picks up A.J. They head back down St. Helena away from where Danny should be waiting, back toward the women on their stoops, Diana's house. What he says to end the story is "And I just knew then." People here are satisfied with that.

It should have been a great disappointment to go back to the fresh chaos blown in on top of the kinds already in his life in Louisiana. He knew this. But he did and he's still there. He was overcome by a sweet homesickness for the very moment he was living in, just then—not the next, not one somewhere else. And the mysteriousness of it, how nothing ever followed. Such a feeling wouldn't travel to New England, much as he might like to take it. It was indigenous he thought; probably rare other places. He wouldn't be able to translate it. At the same time he was ashamed of himself, the delight he felt. Then he knew.

At a distance, the sirens.

ANDREI CODRESCU

From 1984 to 2009, LSU students sought out Andrei Codrescu's particular haunts both on campus and in New Orleans, where he kept a French Quarter apartment. In the French Quarter, he could be found at watering holes like Molly's at the Market, inspiring discussions of his two favorite subjects: love and hypocrisy. Springtime at LSU, students could find him relaxing in the quad, where he claimed to receive inspiration for writing. He says he discovered much of his subject matter there, but that some ideas are happily "buried under the big oaks on campus." At the Chimes Restaurant in Baton Rouge, Codrescu entertained colleagues, friends and students with tales of globe-trotting, his sense of social (in)justice, and his uproarious comic vision of the world. Underground, Codrescu and his literary disciples such as Matt Clark, Rex Rose, and Mark Spitzer worked in the basement of Allen Hall to produce the latest edition of his phantasmagoric online magazine, *Exquisite Corpse*.

Known as a prolific writer of many genres, Codrescu's recent work includes the novels *Wakefield*, *Casanova in Bohemia*, *Messiah*, and *The Blood Countess*; poetry collections *Jealous Witness: New Poems*, *It Was Today: New Poems*, and, with Ruxandra Cesereanu, *The Forgiven Submarine*, a long, collaborative poem; and a book of stories and essays, *New Orleans Mon Amour: Twenty Years of Writing from the City*.

Codrescu often travels back to his homeland, Transylvania, the source of his trademark accent, beloved by NPR listeners and students alike. The three unpublished pieces, "In Praise of Goth Beauticians," "Young Werther at Decadence 2006" and "Dead People in England" are even better when you imagine them read by Codrescu himself, his rolling "r's" echoing in a torch-lit crevice of his newest haunt, his cave in the Ozarks. In any case, they are excellent examples of flash fiction and Codrescu's ironic view of the world.

ANDREI CODRESCU

In Praise of Goth Beauticians

You walk into a hair salon that just opened in the hood. A few ex-goth girls sit on barber chairs having a discussion. All beauticians are now ex-goths who suddenly got to be 28 years old, looked in the mirror and got scared by their own tattoos. Then they went to Beauty School.

"Can I get a haircut?"

The keeper of the Appointment Desk, perched on a high chair framed by hair products and skin creams, opens the Appointments Book and scans it as if my haircut was a matter of grave doubt, maybe possible a month from now. One of the busy beauticians swats a fly. No one is getting a haircut, though from a faroff room come the suspiciously sexual sighs of someone getting shampooed.

"JoJo," the AD lady calls out, "are you busy right now?"

JoJo lifts her black-rimmed eyes from inches away and sighs. "I can take him," she offers.

In the chair, she spends dreamy time running very light fingers through my sparse, almost nonexistent hair. She's thinking. We discuss the future shape of my head, a very simple matter to me but not to JoJo who cuts men only rarely. She must first have a vision. She smells good with her eyes closed and her hand in my hair. But I'm kinda busy.

"How about a buzzcut with a Number Two?" I offer.

We are off. And then I hear her through the buzz: "What is it you do?"

What? Me? Test-drive cars for GM? Smoke opium for a poet with weak lungs? Get paid for sleeping? Body double for Mel Gibson? There is nothing like an innocent question from a beautician to get one going on the path to exoticism. This is an opportunity to reinvent myself.

"I teach the Middle Ages," I say, "when goths roamed the earth."

The Number Two clippers stop buzzing for a second at the top of my skull. The dragon that begins somewhere on her back and snakes down her sleeves ending in short black dots in my hair pulses suddenly with black light. It's a goth dragon from the middle ages when she was young.

She does a masterful job and I get a great shampoo after, as she presses down on my skull with her great sad goth body hoping to absorb all the Middle Ages knowledge in my head.

We are one in a great magical kingdom and it's only twenty bucks.

ANDREI CODRESCU

Young Werther at Decadence 2006

Werther was a man poised between two eras, two centuries, two millennia, dressed in khaki shorts from the Banana Republic, a *Rebuild New Orleans* tee-shirt and orange flip-flops. The Decadence Parade went by—drunk, tired, sweaty, and old— and two brass rings seemed to swing continuously past him: one made of the inflexible dogmatic joy of baby boomers sliding into their graves like chortling Santas, the other a dark-hued object dense with the tears of civil war victims and the braided plaints of organisms suffocating from lack of oxygen. Werther couldn't grab either one: not the first, which appealed to his easy-going nature, nor the second, which would have involved him in instant manual labor. A gaggle of tall, skinny men in gold plastic shorts passed between the brass rings and obscured, momentarily, Werther's vision of the past and the future. He was unsure whether he should laugh or quietly leave the scene and jump into the Mississippi River.

A recent discussion replayed in his mind. Someone had asked of an assembled group: does anyone like any German writer? The members of the group, who were well-read, couldn't come up with many and, at the end, after an hour-long pitching of names, only two Germans remained standing: Bertold Brecht and Hans Magnus Enzensberger. Why? Because, Werther decided, Goethe and the philosophers, Thomas Mann and Günter Grass, cared about the world as if it were theirs, and used its grave substance to fashion brass rings from it. The group was groping for a way out of the increasing heaviness of the world and decided that they preferred French writers who found absurdity and humor a better model for the future. The French were more fun.

Fun was productive. The old men in the parade had worked hard at their costumes of feathers and grass skirts. Sequins cost money. Parades need monitors, music, booze, pain killers, spectators, street food, tourists, cameras, cell phones. The production of hope was socially beneficial, even if it seemed to the untrained eye to be simply a gallows-joke about the passing of the flesh. Sorrow, on the other hand, was a paralyzed beggar who stood in the middle of the intersection with his hand out, waiting for motorists to drop coins into it. In this case, misery stood in front of the parade with his hand out and the revelers ran him over. They rolled right over him.

Werther felt the stirring of optimism.

ৠ

PS: On August 31, 2006, at the Gold Mine Saloon, a big roach-like creature wrapped in trash escaped from a recess of the bar and stepped into the light, horrifying the poets gathered there to celebrate YAWP, a magazine of apocalyptic art. The roach-crit, whose name was Richard Huelsenbeck, turned out to have grown and developed in the unconscious of New Orleans after Katrina. Interviewed, Richard claimed that he was the first of over one million similar creepo-pods ready to invade the city.

PS2: We were visited by Dr. Andy Bichlbaum, the founder of the *Identity Correction Movement* who brought his unique brand of righteousness to a summit meeting on Reconstruction. New Orleans and Louisiana officials, unaware that they were being passed through the meat-grinder of art, allowed themselves the solace of innocence for a minute. The next minute, Dr. Andy dipped them into the acid bath of their own hypocritical brains. We laughed about it over shots of Lithuanian fire-water.

ANDREI CODRESCU

Dead People in England

We ate at a family-style Japanese steakhouse where you sit with strangers around a square communal table with a grill in the middle. Most folks in the room were older, out for the early-bird special, but our table had variety. There was a grumbling silver-haired granma with a middle-aged daughter and an eight-year-old boy. Directly opposite sat a shy young couple who looked distressed by the likelihood that they were eating with their parents and grandparents after having done or were about to do what they were thinking about doing. Granma couldn't figure out the menu and was worried about not getting enough to eat, so I reassured her. The kid had to go potty so his unruffled mother took him to the bathroom. When the kid was reseated, he said, loud enough to be heard by everybody:

"There are dead people in England!"

The grandmother looked pained until she found the proper answer:

"There are dead people everywhere, Tom."

The mother was still unruffled. The couple froze a little more.

Then Chef showed up. He was young and I felt slight terror when he started juggling the prongs and the spatula, which looked too much like a cleaver. His chopping of vegetables wasn't all too steady either, as one end of the broccoli landed in the old lady's iced tea, and one mushroom wedge in my beer. Throwing and catching the egg was positively heart-stopping, and I saw, for a brief second, the egg landing on one of the dating couple, making what was going to happen awkward if not impossible, unless it had already happened, in which case it was going to maybe help. The egg landed with a splat on the grill. Chef built the volcano of onion rings with passing skill and he lit a flame that fascinated Tom, but we knew that it was supposed to be a volcano, and there was no lava. The steak and the shrimp were seared beautifully and the full plates found their intended targets. The table settled into a pleasant buzz as we merged in the act of chewing.

Here is the funny thing: the restaurant was in Springfield, Missouri, and the steak house was styled Japanese but was, like any midwestern steak house, about steak. And the people were just like people, awkward and alive.

To get to Nakato, which bills itself as "the oldest but still the best" Japanese steakhouse in Springfield, you have to drive for a piece on old Route 66, past the Solo

Paper Cup factory, a building that explains why modern art set deep roots in the midwest. American roadside driving culture is all about boxes and advertising, signs and cubes, with one egg rotating in midair.

VANCE BOURJAILY

Vance Bourjaily's tenure as director of LSU's creative writing program, characterized as a time of European-style apprenticeship teaching, is also remembered for its spectacular literary gatherings—parties where wine flowed freely, food was plentiful, and conversation between faculty and students was rich. The atmosphere of these events was fun but hardly frivolous, as they were hosted by one of America's leading novelists, a writer proclaimed by Ernest Hemingway as the most talented of his generation.

Bourjaily brought with him to LSU an intriguing worldliness. He had served in World War II and written novels about that profound experience; taught at the prestigious Iowa Writers Workshop for twenty years; published ten novels, a slew of short stories, an opera libretto, and teleplays; and kept company with movie stars and writers like Vonnegut, Fitzgerald, and Nabokov. He was a powerful influence on many young writers at LSU who found in him a mentor, friend, and educator far beyond the classroom. And so we have reports of the night they learned the proper procedure for Russian toasting, or his weekly scheduled tennis matches, or tall-tale telling of trout fishing exploits, or time spent at his home where the doors were always open—all in the service of creating a writing community that would produce the kind of fiction for which LSU is famous. Among those guided by Bourjaily at LSU were Matt Clark, Michael Griffith, and Connie Porter.

"The Amish Farmer," a compelling story of temptation, obsessive love, and adultery, is set partly in a university community and partly in an Amish village, in the dead of winter, climaxing in the middle of a brutal snowstorm with a daring rescue and fall from grace. In this experimental story-within-a-story, a first-person narrator named Vance, while illustrating point of view to his university class, recognizes his own cynicism and mourns the unattainability of love in the modern age.

VANCE BOURJAILY

The Amish Farmer

A couple of weeks ago in class, I told the Amish farmer story again. I hadn't thought I would and never planned at all to write it down. I guess this was because I used to think it a simple story, which I understood so well that, with any further telling, my own interest in it would be used up. But this particular class had people in it whom I liked, we had an hour of open time, and the Amish farmer story had got people into lively discussions in the past.

The class is a workshop in writing fiction; I got my storytelling energy up for them. Often it helps to pick a particular student, from whom my teaching ego happens to crave a little response, and then to think in terms of summoning energy for him or for her. On this day, the student I held in mind and with whom I had eye contact as I started talking was one we call Katie Jay; she is smart, searching, scathing sometimes, very talented, a leader though not without enemies, cool, almost elegant in her blond slimness. Is Katie Jay. It is because of her that I am writing the story now.

"Listen to this," I said. "What I'm going to try to illustrate is the remarkable power of point of view. I'm going to tell you a story in which I think you'll recognize the kind of material a writer might decide to use. I'll tell it pretty much as it came to me, and then let's talk about how it would change in tone, mood, meaning—in the basic kind of piece it would make—just from changing the point of view from which it's told from that of one character in it to that of another."

Katie Jay smiled and nodded at me slightly; I smiled back and started catching other eyes.

On a spring morning (I said) about ten years ago, I got a call from a friend and student named Noel Butler, asking if he could come to the house. He sounded upset.

"Come along," I said. "You in trouble, Noel?"

"I think somebody just tried to kill me," Noel said.

I stepped outside, onto the lawn, to wait for him. The temperature was up around 60. The dirt glittered and steamed where it showed, wet and black beneath the grass plants. I didn't have much doubt that the situation had to do with Noel's wife.

At that time I had seen Dawn Butler only twice, and four months earlier, but she was vivid to me as she was to all men.

Let me explain that Noel had come to Indiana from Boston to start graduate school the previous September without Dawn and nervous about it. He was someone we'd recruited for the graduate program, an engaging, articulate young writer with a couple of publications, a year of prep school teaching, and a year in publishing. We'd offered him an assistantship, something we rarely do for first-year students; he was going to start right in teaching core lit to sophomores, as well as taking his graduate hours.

It seemed plain from the first look at Noel that we'd made a good move. He was poised, talkative, nice-looking in a horn-rimmed, wavy-haired, Brooks Brothers way. He probably looked archaic to some of his peers, but he looked just right to me; and if his flow of persuasive speech was a little glib at times, he was still a pleasure to have in class. He kept things moving. We heard that his undergraduate students doted on him from the first "Good morning, people."

I was just starting to get to know Noel. It wasn't really quite appropriate yet for intimate matters to come up between us, but he just couldn't keep himself from telling me about Dawn: she was beautiful and wild, and he loved her desperately, and he might even have to leave us if she kept on refusing to join him here in our midwestern city, which she supposed must be pretty dull. He said that at first Dawn had promised to come along as soon as he found them a decent place to live; he had a place located, but she kept delaying. He also told me that she had a child, a boy, born illegitimately when she was seventeen, the son of a celebrated choreographer whose protégée Dawn had been. She'd been scared of the man, who was also a celebrated bisexual and capable of violence, had run away from him, given up dancing, and had the child. But that was only part of it, Noel said. I'd have to see Dawn to believe her.

Midway through October he got himself excused from classes for a week, got friends to cover his core lit meetings, and flew to Boston. He phoned me excitedly from there to ask me to check on his academic arrangements but really to say, triumphantly, that she'd agreed to come. I reminded him that the director of our program was giving a cocktail party Friday for the staff and teaching assistants, and Noel said proudly that he'd be there with Mrs. Butler.

So. It was in the rather formal living room at the director's house that I first saw Dawn. I can almost say, without a sense of exaggeration, that I felt her. She had that kind of insistent sexual presence that men think they perceive as a wave of heat. It makes your cheeks tingle and the hair bristle at the back of your neck. I'd met a few women with that brute magnetism before, but none who had more of it than Dawn Butler and only one, an actress, who combined it, as Dawn did, with more physical beauty than seemed fair.

I remember that I guessed which room she'd be in before I saw her, because every other man at the party was in that room already.

Dawn had dark hair, which she wore brushed back in long, soft waves down to below her shoulder blades. Her face was round and her brown, protruding eyes so large they made the other features seem more delicate than they probably were, and the skin paler. Her mouth, on second look, and one certainly did look twice, was actually quite wide. It was also very mobile, open much of the time, with the small, conspicuously white teeth parted. She had an unsettling way of flicking her tongue forward so that you were aware of the tip of it striking the upper front teeth.

She was not quite tall, but willowy, which gave an impression of height. Her arms were rather short, her shoulders quite square, and she stood dancer-style with her feet spread and toed out, which brought her pelvis forward and her head back and up, there in the director's living room. She had the look of a woman standing her ground and at the same time enticing you to share it with her.

She was wearing black with a silver belt. The dress bared her neck and collar-bones but was not cut low. Instead it was slit, down to the diaphragm, and under it she must have been wearing one of those wire brassieres that create a look of nudity down the center of the chest while providing a slightly unnatural amount of breast separation. It was provocative enough.

She also grabbed my hand with both of hers when we were introduced, not quite pulling me toward her, and exhaled a small sound of some sort. Noel stood beaming at her side.

Say she was overdoing, if you like; that form of greeting wasn't used on me alone, I'd better add. As the evening went on, she was conducting public dalliance simulta-neously with as many of us as could crowd around, four or five at a time.

"I don't know if I can get to like it here," she said. "Noel has us at that Holiday Inn so far, up on the hill. It makes me apprehensive, looking down at your lights, not knowing what to expect." Suddenly she showed us her right palm, ran the fingertips of her left hand over it. "Damp. That's how lie detectors work, isn't it? I couldn't fool a lie detector."

Then she touched the damp palm to her cheek, smiled, flicked her tongue, and wiped the hand on her hip lightly. I remember being both smitten, as were all the other men, and struck by the thought that there was something wrong, something consonant with the overdone greeting. It was what was missing from the voice—a young, light, reasonably well educated, Eastern-city voice. It didn't have, in spite of the smiles and the flicking tongue, much fun in it.

Generally a good coquette, doing her magic publicly, will spurt, shimmer, and sparkle with a kind of laughter, now open, now repressed, a laughter both at the men for being gulled and at herself for spending all that gorgeous candlepower on gulling them. Brilliance, raillery, self-mockery, all of it in fun: Dawn Butler's performance didn't have those qualities. It was as if she had already passed on, with each man who listened to her, beyond flirtation, to some further stage in a relationship already intimate, about to be serious, even dangerous.

The next thing would almost have to be a note, folded very small, pressed into your hand, to be read urgently, secretly, and the note would say, "Where is your car parked?" or even "Save me."

I have splendid resistance to people who dramatize themselves. So when Dawn said, to someone offering her a whiskey, "Oh, but I only drink wine," I collided with the director in the living room doorway, both of us rushing to the kitchen, where I'd left a bottle of wine and he had several on the shelf. Dawn was twenty-two years old.

The other time I saw her that fall was the next evening; she was more relaxed. She and Noel were with some of his student friends, drinking beer at Hickey's Tavern. They asked me to join them, and I did for a few minutes, sitting down by Dawn, asking her about the place Noel had found for them to live in. She replied by taking my wrist between her thumb and forefinger, looking into my eyes, holding on for a couple of beats, and then squeezing quite hard. But her voice, when she let go, was sultry and amused: "Don't you know? Don't you really know? I'm being taken out to a farm, miles away. I'll never see you again."

She came close to being right about that, but before I go on I want to be fair to Dawn. She did display, there with the student group, a little gaiety. It wasn't sparkling, perhaps, but it wasn't stagy, either—a sort of sweet naughtiness that was quite engaging and that had the student males riding around no-hands and standing on their heads, at about the same junior high school level to which she'd reduced the staff the night before.

Then she was gone. Noel did take her far from this city, more than twenty miles, but not just in distance. He came as close as you can to taking her away in time as well, about three centuries.

He took her to an Amish farm, where he had rented the small, spare house intended for the parents when the inheriting son took the place in charge. I will have to tell you a little more about the Amish in a moment. They are, of course, the people who call themselves "plain," the lace-capped women and bearded men who drive buggies and still farm with horses.

"Are you surprised Dawn was willing to go down there?" Noel asked me, visiting one day soon afterward in my office. "I admit I didn't give her much choice."

I said something dumb, like "It should be an interesting experience for both of you."

"We've had enough interesting experiences," Noel said, and then, not very smooth for once: "Dawn agrees. She does now. After Boston—well, look. Otherwise I wouldn't have brought her and Jimmer out here in spite of missing her so much. I told her."

Jimmer, I remembered, was her little boy, but I didn't actually see him until spring. And now you've got to hear about the winter, and more about the Amish, too.

The winter that Dawn and Noel Butler, and Dawn's son—strange changeling child of a passionate adolescent girl and a perverse, creative man, much older—never mind. That winter was a bitch.

It snowed early, got cold, stayed cold. The country roads were often impassable, and it was a struggle for Noel to get back and forth to meet his classes. But he would tell me, from time to time, that it was worth it to him, and I understood him to mean that he and Dawn were happy and cozy and trusting.

About the Amish I'll try not to tell you any more than you need to know. They include several conservative splinter groups from the Mennonite Church, and of them all the most conservative are the Old Order Amish. Like all Mennonites, they are pacifist, believe in nonresistance, refuse to take oaths, and are very strict in matters of recreation and self-indulgence. The Old Order Amish, in addition, try to live just as the first of their faith did in 1650—wearing similar clothing, hairstyles, and face-hair styles, farming by the same methods, without the use of engines or electricity. They are a God-and-family-centered people, and their way of life endures, in its enclaves in Indiana, Pennsylvania, Iowa, and Oregon, because of its tight structure in which the children are brought up believing that they are, like their parents, among the chosen very, very few. They are not quaint; they are proud. They own excellent small farms, farm them well, and pass them along carefully through the generations.

They maintain their own schools, which go only through the eighth grade. They take a distant, not altogether unworldly, interest in us, whom they must meet in bargaining situations, and a very intense interest in one another. Community is hardly less important to them than family.

On the Old Order Amish farm where Dawn, Noel, and Dawn's child spent the winter, there was a patriarch as head of the household, a widower in his late sixties. His older sons were established with families on farms of their own, which he'd helped buy; the youngest son, of whom, Noel said, the old man was particularly proud, was heir designate to the family farm. This heir was called Daniel.

Daniel was thirty-two, with a wife and seven children. Noel found him a scrupulous landlord. Though Daniel worked an extremely long, hard day, he would always take time to make sure Dawn and Noel's cottage was snug and in repair. But though he had provided the cottage with electricity, as well as a telephone, when he and his father had decided to rent it, he would not use power tools nor himself turn off or on a light.

"Strong arms, bright blue eyes, and a reddish-brown beard," Noel said. "With that upper lip shaved clean the way they do. He's always so solemn when we see him, and he won't let his wife or any of the kids come in our door."

That was as much as I knew about the family when Noel arrived at my house, just before noon on a spring day, to say that Daniel, the Amish farmer, had tried to kill him.

❦

Every story has its relatives. This one is some sort of cousin, in my mind, to a play I saw as a boy, called *Rain*. In the play, as I remember it, a missionary and a loose woman are trapped in a hotel in the tropics by incessant rain, which becomes her ally in the temptation and seduction of the man. Dawn's allies were cold, wind, snow, and ice, perhaps, but I don't want to push the comparison with the old play too far: Dawn, after all, was still quite girlish, and Daniel's rectitude was of a personal, not a missionary, kind.

Noel said that as a matter of fact, Dawn first reacted to Daniel with some awe. Noel couldn't say just when Dawn had started regarding Daniel as either an interesting possibility or an actual attraction. Noel admitted quite abjectly his own stupidity. He and the winter had made Dawn and Daniel the only man and woman in the world.

My guess is that she was simply, in the beginning, unable to keep from making just a very slight test of Daniel, a little test of herself as well, with no serious motive except curiosity—I'm willing to see it as innocent curiosity, if it wasn't actually unconscious—just to see if he'd respond to her at all. And once he'd responded just a little—was it with a stammer, or a blush, or a clumsy pressing back against a pressing hand? —then it may suddenly have been too late for both of them.

She had to go on with it. The ice and snow insisted, and her imprisonment. Daniel, I imagine, fought and prayed—and came back for another press of the hand, and one day a hug, and—how much later? —something that was barely the first kiss.

It would all have been very gradual, very difficult, very absorbing to the two imaginations, in a rhythm deliberate as seasons changing. I thought of Dawn, passing her winter days that way, moving toward him, guardedly, the excitement allowed to grow very slowly, having to keep the embraces, as they intensified little by little, out of sight of her child, her husband, the Amish family. The potential lovers were as hemmed in, as hard put to find times of privacy, as any couple could be.

"I know when it finally happened," Noel said. It clearly hurt him to tell me, but he had to. "The first time. Dawn and I drove into Yodertown one afternoon to shop and didn't start back until after dark. It was storming by then, a wet, wild, late-winter storm, with ruts and mud frozen on the surface, soft and treacherous underneath, and the wind howling and freezing and the snow blowing. We got to within about three miles of the place before the windshield wouldn't clear anymore and I ran off the road and got us stuck in the ditch.

"I was wearing boots and outdoor clothing, though not really enough of it. Dawn would never dress for winter when we were going somewhere in a heated car. Her shoes were thin and even had heels on them. She was wearing a kind of high-fashion wool cloak that looked romantic as hell, but nothing to keep the wind out. I'd have given her my hat and jacket, but there was no way to beat the shoe problem.

"We had most of a tank of gas. I might have stayed with her, but Jimmer was home and hungry and the night was scary. The car'd be twice as hard to get out in the morning, when I had to get to school. We decided I'd better go for help. Dawn was to run the motor periodically for heat and to turn on the headlights for half a minute out of every five, to show where she was. So I left.

"God, it was a terrible walk. It kept getting colder. The wind got higher, and the snowfall was the heaviest I've ever been out in. I could hardly see. Luckily, it was coming at my back, but I still stumbled and struggled in the bad footing, and once I got so far off the road I ran into barbed-wire fence. It probably took me an hour to go three miles. I was going to phone..." Noel hesitated. "As a matter of fact, Vance, I was going to phone you, because I knew you had a four-wheel-drive truck. I hoped when the storm let up, you could find the place and wouldn't mind coming after me so we could get Dawn and try to pull the car out."

I nodded.

"When I finally got there, the phone was out. The lights, too. Jimmer was terrified. I didn't know what to do. I lit candles and tried to comfort the boy. The stove worked all right, so I fixed him some soup. I remember standing there, stirring it, with my teeth chattering. I couldn't get warm.

"I thought of putting Jimmer to bed under blankets, taking Dawn's winter boots and jacket, and walking back, but I wasn't too sure I could make it, going against that wind, or that she could, coming back. I decided I was going to have to get Daniel's help and advice. I should be able to say that some damn warning voice told me not to, but it isn't so. Whatever'd been happening, they'd concealed it very well.

"Anyway, I didn't know if his team of horses and the closed carriage—a sort of van they use in the winter—could go through the weather. I was wondering about that when he knocked at the door. He'd seen the candlelight. He knew the car hadn't come in. He came to check up, and I explained.

"When he learned that Dawn was out there alone, Daniel got quite upset. Especially, I suppose, because, not being familiar with cars, he couldn't believe that she was safe and comfortable.

"I asked if his team could go out, and he said no.

"I asked what he thought we should do, and he said, `Likely I'll take tractor to pull out. Sure.' I was almost shocked. There was this monstrous, big old iron-wheeled tractor in the barn. One of Daniel's older brothers had bought it years before, when some of the Old Order people argued that a tractor was permissible on the farm so long as it didn't have rubber tires. Instead, these tractors had lugs, almost spikes, and they tore up the country roads so bad the Secondary Roads Department banned them. Daniel himself didn't use the tractor, but he'd learned to drive it as a boy—an act of rebellion, I suppose, if not real wickedness. A couple of times a year the older brother would come over and start the thing up and do maintenance on it.

"I asked if I should ride along. Daniel didn't even answer. I was in no shape to go out again, anyway. The night was getting worse. Jimmer was there. I gave Daniel Dawn's boots and things to take along, and out he went in his coat and overalls. They're not allowed to use buttons. Their clothes are held together with safety pins. He had a scarf and a black, broadbrimmed hat, knit gloves and galoshes. After a while I heard the big old machine start, and then I heard it lumber past our little house. It didn't have any lights."

Here I paused, as Noel had paused. I looked around the class and seemed to have their attention; but it was hard to tell about Katie Jay, my smart student. Her eyes were down and away, studying her tabletop.

Wouldn't Daniel's father and the Amish family (I asked the class) have heard that tractor moving out? They might have taken it for the county snowplow passing on the road.

The rest is much too easy to imagine: Daniel on his iron tractor seat, laboring against the unfamiliar steering wheel, turning into the wind, chugging through the night. Snow and dark, forces of nature storming in his face, trying to turn him back; the scarf tight, facial skin around his beard getting numb, hands and feet freezing as the slow machine gripped and bumped. But after a time he'd have started to see the faint glimmering of the headlights at long intervals, calling him to her. I don't know whether in his own mind he was damned before he got there; but the great, clanking, spike-wheeled thing he rode was an engine of sin, no question. And it failed him, going into the ditch itself a hundred yards before he reached the car, so that he finished getting there on foot.

Imagine Daniel knocking, then, on the deeply frosted window, and Dawn opening the door to what must have looked like a man of ice.

"Is it Daniel?"

"Are you all right, missus?"

"Daniel, get in. Get in. You'll die out there."

"But it's you worries me."

"Please. Get in."

He does. The door closes. And they are trapped together in the night. There is a nearly frozen man to thaw. She holds him. She croons to him. She wipes his hair and beard with her cloak. I think that an embrace develops out of this, gets almost violent before, perhaps with a sob, he pulls away. And the wind howls, the snow blows and piles. Dawn waits. Perhaps she touches him, and, with another sob, he hurls himself at her again and is, after how many engagements, received into a warmth like no other.

That this happened, Noel was quite sure—whatever guilts and indecisions followed, whatever withdrawals and renewals—because of what took place the next night. It was clear and extremely cold, and in the morning there was a curious frozen smudge in the center of one of the panes of glass in their bedroom window. Jimmer said someone had looked in, very late. Dawn said it was the boy's imagination. But Noel felt sure that the smudge was made, and others like it as other nights came and went, by the Amish farmer pressing his cheek against the cold glass that separated him from the woman he loved.

"God, how we've fought since then," Noel said. "I knew. Dawn has a crazy-lady act that goes with having an affair. I'd seen it before. So I accused her.

"'Oh, what fun, Noel darling, who?'

"'Daniel,' I said, and she almost had hysterics laughing at me. She pulled a handful of her hair around and held it to her chin for a beard, and ran around being Daniel, getting drunk on carrot juice and pinching pumpkins on the fanny. . . . I said to cut it out, that I knew for sure, and she said oh, then she'd run and get Daniel so I could tell him all about it.

"Yesterday I got home an hour before she expected me. I saw Daniel leave the house. I went in, and Jimmer was napping. Dawn said Daniel was getting the sink unclogged. This morning I looked, and then I showed her, there's no way that sink could clog up because the drain's so big. You couldn't stop it up with a sweater.

"So she grabbed a sweater of mine and started stuffing it into the drain, and I told her to go to hell, I was leaving. I got out a suitcase and started to pack it. She grabbed the clothes out of it and ran out the door, screaming and dropping my stuff all over the yard. I was furious. I ran out after her, and there was Daniel, over by the barn, working on that monstrous tractor with a wrench as long as your arm.

"Dawn ran over and got behind him, pointing at me, and right away Daniel started for me with that wrench. First I couldn't believe it. Then I ran. I ran to the car with Daniel after me, and he pounded the car with the wrench as I drove away. You can see the dents, Vance. Look."

Well (I said to the class), Noel needed his clothes and his books. He was afraid to go back. I said I'd go, and my phone rang.

"Is Noel there?" It was Dawn.

"Yes."

"Will he talk to me?"

I asked. Noel shook his head. "I'm sorry," I said.

"Tell him Daniel has to see him."

I did. Noel turned pale and whispered, "Oh, my God."

I covered the mouthpiece and said, "Noel, I don't know the man, but I'll bet you anything he wants to beg your pardon."

"Ask Dawn," Noel said, and I did.

"Daniel's in an agony of shame," Dawn said. "I think he wants to get down on his knees to Noel."

I passed that along. "She's such a liar," Noel said, but he agreed to a meeting with Daniel. I went too. It took place in a local filling station, owned by a backslid uncle of Daniel's. The young farmer was pretty close to tears, if not quite on his knees. He wanted Noel to forgive him and to pray for him, but afterward Noel still felt wary about going for his stuff. I went, after all, and saw Dawn again.

Her appearance was strained—we none of us come out of the winters here looking terrific—but her manner was curiously relaxed. I found her, this time, easy to talk to. She seemed to be waiting, without any great anxiety, to see what would happen. None of the Amish family was in sight when I drove in, nor were they when I drove out again.

Noel graduated and left eight years ago. But Dawn and Jimmer are still in Indiana, as far as I know, living between Gary and Michigan City, by the shore of the big lake. They went there with Daniel. He gave it all up, his God, his inheritance, his family, his community. He's working up there as a truck driver, I understand.

I paused and said, "Okay. True story." Then I looked toward Katie Jay, the bright student I spoke of, who often asserts the privilege of first comment; but her eyes were on her hands and her hands were still on the table in front of her. "Who wants to pick a point-of-view character for it?"

Dave, who is fast and sedulous, said, "Yours. I don't see anything wrong with the way you told it."

"But it stays a raconteur's story," I said. "A pastime. What happens if you use one of the characters?"

"The raconteur could be more involved," Dave said. "Something could happen to him, as a consequence. Or he could be more of a commentator, more cynical or more compassionate or more open about drawing a moral."

"Let's drop him, anyway," I said. "And tell it from Noel's point of view. What happens?"

Ernie's hand went up—but let me summarize rather than try to quote our discussion.

No acceptable serious story could be told from Noel's point of view, the class felt, because he would be weak and a loser, just one more sensitive young man betrayed and asking for our pity. But there were comic possibilities—a mean, ironic one if Noel were the kind of flawed narrator who, thinking he has the reader's sympathy, shows that he really drove Dawn straight into Daniel's arms. Or, said someone, give Noel enough perspective to be aware of that himself now and it could be a farce, about the smart guy who outsmarts himself but comes out a winner anyway because he's free of an impossible situation.

The talk of flawed narrators led to some discussion of having the story seen and heard through the eyes and ears of Jimmer, the child, whose understanding of certain things might be precocious and exceed the reader's, the reader in turn seeing other things of which Jimmer would be unaware. Several in the class saw that solution as being too literary and as taking away a certain harsh dignity the story might have if it were Daniel's.

From Daniel's point of view, we'd have a serious psychological melodrama to write, full of guilt, struggle, and prayer. We would have to decide whether to regard him as a victim or not, and the piece could be pretty heavy going. What about doing it as Dawn would see it?

"A sappy romance," someone said, a male.

"Depends on Dawn," said one of the women. "It could be a sophisticated romance if she's sophisticated. It could even be another kind of comedy, you know, if you make her able to deal with his religion thing."

Again I looked at Katie Jay. I really wanted to hear her get going on Dawn Butler. I expected a strong, funny attack. This was because Katie Jay had once explained to me, when we were speaking about a very cool man-woman piece she'd written, that sex was something she could not take seriously. When she was fifteen, Katie Jay said, and had her first boyfriend, her mother had simply put an extra pillow on the bed. That was all sex meant to slim-necked, caustic Katie Jay, with her shiny blond head and sharp tongue: the essence of no big deal.

When she had nothing to say, I asked my final question: "Is there any way this story could be written as a serious tragedy?" Then I answered myself: Yes, again as a function of choosing a particular point of view. Recently, I explained, I have come to know a very old Amish farmer, a fine, thoughtful man in his seventies. He is, although he interests himself a little in worldly matters, essentially and attractively an innocent man, if not naive. His name is Aaron, and I can admire if not quite envy him. He has lived that life structured for him by fanatical Dutch peasants three centuries ago, and has been fulfilled by it.

"Suppose," I said, "we think of Daniel's father as a man like Aaron, which he must have been. A man who, if only because of his years, is aware before the rest, before Daniel even, of what might happen, yet too appalled to think it really will. He is a man who can truly and simply use a word like *Jezebel* and feel the damnation in it. And he's a patriarch, waiting to be consulted and obeyed, but he will hesitate a long time, too long, to acknowledge so great a sin as actual. Suppose we saw through Aaron's eyes not just the loss, day by day, of his finest son, but the way in which it foretells the whole structure breaking down, the wearing away of order in the world—wouldn't that point of view give you a chance to build some tragic power?"

The class couldn't disagree, because I wouldn't let them. It was one of those days when I felt like having the last word, and it was time to dismiss them anyway. But as they went out, free and clamorous, Katie Jay was still sitting as she had been, not jumping up in her usual way to cry out sharply to her friends, proclaim where they were to go to have a beer. She sat there, uncharacteristically still, but finally she did look up at me.

I went around the table to her and smiled. Katie Jay's hand moved up and took my arm above the elbow, and the grip, between thumb and forefinger, reminded me of another's grip, ten years before, on my wrist.

"Yes, Katie?"

She continued looking at me for a moment. Then her eyes went away, her face turned back toward the table, and she released my arm.

"Katie Jay?"

She shook her head. She gathered up her books and stood. I moved aside, concerned, confused, a little cross, and watched her walk to the door of the classroom where she turned back to look at me again.

"I need him," Katie Jay said, and there was nothing cool, nothing detached, nothing even very smart about her voice. "Oh, I need that Amish farmer. Don't you see?"

LAURIE LYNN DRUMMOND

Katherine Joubert, the title character of Laurie Lynn Drummond's story, "Katherine's Elegy," asks a cadet in the Baton Rouge Police Training Academy why he wants to be a cop. His answer is, "The adrenaline." Drummond admits to having the same reason for working in both the LSU and the Baton Rouge Police departments. When she enrolled in the LSU creative writing program and became a teaching assistant in the English department, she once again saw an opportunity for adrenaline rushes, but in the realm of teaching. The narrative voice of her award-winning stories grows out of her early professional roles—both of them authority figures who must communicate profoundly. The themes of duty, fate, and women's rights find full expression through this energetic yet steady voice.

When she presented to her publisher the manuscript that became *Anything You Say Can and Will Be Used Against You*, it was in the form of a collection of short stories. But because the material was so interwoven, with the same characters appearing in several pieces and most of the settings in Baton Rouge, her editor suggested a hybrid of the novel and short story forms. The result is a remarkable collection of the stories of five women whose lives are inextricably tied to the world of an urban police force.

Anything You Say was published in 2006 after one of its stories, "Something About a Scar," won the prestigious Edgar Award for Best Short Story. The book was a finalist of the PEN/Hemingway Award and won a Jesse Jones Award from the Texas Institute of Letters and the Violet Crown Award from the Writers League of Texas. After this commercial and critical success, Drummond was invited to join the creative writing faculty at University of Oregon, where she is assistant professor.

"Katherine's Elegy," the story of a legendary Baton Rouge policewoman, reveals both the mundane and dramatic events that make up the daily life of a police officer, on and off the streets, in public and in private.

LAURIE LYNN DRUMMOND

Katherine's Elegy

We heard about Katherine long before we ever saw her. Every cadet who attended the Baton Rouge Police Training Academy learned about Johnny Cippoine and his widow, Katherine, sooner or later. Officers who visited our academy class in the former city court building off North Boulevard all mentioned, at some point, the story of how Johnny Cippoine had died, tragically, three years earlier. Although it's been twenty years now since we graduated, they're probably still telling the story.

We heard lots of stories about a lot of cops, but this one was different. Each officer relayed the event in the same manner: briefly and with a clipped, matter-of-fact tone, yet with a touch of lingering regret, the way one might refer to an old lover let slip away. At least that's the way it seemed to us. Such emotion was rare, still is, and this made Johnny and Katherine even more intriguing.

So when Johnny Cippoine's name was evoked, we all paid attention a little closer. It's a simple story, really, told to illustrate how even a good cop can get killed. But Katherine's part in it made the story compelling.

Johnny Cippoine had been a seventeen-year veteran known for his strict adherence to procedure, superb instincts, and passion for bass fishing. His wife, Katherine, was much younger and worked uniform out of what was called Highland Precinct in those days. They'd been married five years, two years after she joined the force. That's a good love story, how Johnny and Katherine met, but we didn't hear about it until much later, when it was unsettling instead of satisfying.

The day Johnny died, he and Katherine were about to meet for lunch. Johnny stopped two teenagers in a neighborhood off Monterrey that had been plagued recently with a rash of daytime break-ins. He did it all by the book, Johnny did; he was never one to take unnecessary risks.

He put those two teenagers on the ground right away, patted the first one down, found a gun, secured it, called for backup, then moved to pat the second teen down.

It was cool that day, early in December, with probably the first hint of winter in the air and the crape myrtles finally dropping their leaves. Katherine had just pulled into the Shoney's parking lot nine blocks away when she heard Johnny go 10-7 with two white males loitering in a driveway. She drove over to back him up, something we had drilled into our heads like a mantra: If you're available, always back up the closest unit out on call, no matter how small or insignificant the call appears to be.

When Katherine and another unit arrived on the scene only seconds after Johnny's call for backup, two white males were running up the street, away from Johnny sprawled out on the ground beside his unit.

"Officer down," Katherine barked into her radio mike. "Ambulance 10-18."

Witnesses said later that when Johnny moved to pat the second kid down, the first one pulled out another gun, one buried deep in his groin that Johnny had missed, and shot him three times, real quick: twice in the chest, neither of which penetrated his bulletproof vest but was enough to put him on the ground; it was the third shot that did it, point-blank in the head.

This all happened in less than a minute.

Many of the officers who told us the tale would snap their fingers at this point in the story. "It can happen like that," they'd say. "Boom, you're dead. Reflexes. You've got to react before the act," and they'd snap their fingers again. "Think like the perps. Suspect everyone."

And we would nod, all of us cadets, visualizing the scene, already thinking that we would never ever let our guard slip the way Johnny had.

According to the story—and everyone told it the same way, memorized as carefully and faithfully as the Miranda warning—Katherine ran to Johnny, checked for a pulse, removed his sunglasses, kissed his face (some said his eyes, some said his cheek, but they all mentioned she had his blood on her when she arrived at the hospital later), then took off running in the direction of the two suspects.

"Don't move him," she yelled.

Even as the ambulance was taking Johnny to the hospital, Katherine was searching the neighborhood alongside fellow officers, looking for the two white males, questioning residents, peering in sheds and under houses, climbing down into the concrete drainage ditch three blocks over.

"They're here," she kept telling the others. "They can't have gone far."

But, as the academy staff continually reminded us, you've got to think like a criminal and remember fear can make feet fly and desperation can create cunning just as easily as stupidity and blunders. The officers were angry, a savage anger provoked by their own sudden awareness of vulnerability and mortality. Units gunned down streets, tires squealed, breaks screeched: by God, they'd flush out the sonsofbitches who'd dared shoot one of their own.

We thrilled to the adrenaline that surged inside us with this story, felt the fury in our blood, our bodies tense and breathless from imagining ourselves there on the streets, looking. And we hated at that moment, more than ever, being confined to the white, overly bright classroom.

And Katherine, we knew, was thinking of Johnny even as she was doing her job; of course she must have been frantic, though she didn't show it. But she was right: those boys hadn't gone far, at least one of them hadn't. She and another officer found him hiding in a drainpipe nearly a half-mile from the scene.

"And let me tell you, she was PROFESSIONAL about it," the academy staff told us. She handcuffed the boy—he was only fifteen—while the other officer read him his rights. She even protected the boy's head, one hand pushing down on his crown, as she put him in the back of a unit.

"She did what had to be done, and she did it right," the training officers said. Of course she did, we thought, it was in her nature. You could tell just from the way she'd reacted when she saw Johnny on the ground.

But the other suspect eluded capture. Finally, after more than an hour, with Johnny's blood turning black on the cement, the Crime Scene officers collecting samples and combing the ground for evidence, the Homicide detectives beginning a house-by-house investigation, and every officer not on the scene calling every CI they had a number on (and those who had neglected the nurturing of confidential informants beginning their own aggressive shakedown on every corner within a five-mile radius), Katherine's captain physically placed her in his unit and drove her to Earl K. Long Charity Hospital.

Yes, we thought. Of course it would be Earl K. We already knew that Earl K, the dilapidated hulk out on Airline Highway that passed for a hospital, was the place to go if you were shot or stabbed. They'd wheel your gurney in right past the fifty or so drunks and drug addicts, scumbags, poor white trash, bafus, prostitutes, and low-down good-for-nothings who'd been waiting, some of them, over five hours to see a nurse, and the best doctors in the business—the ones without name tags or fancy surgical garb who treated more stab and gunshot wounds in a week than the Lake or BRG treated in six months—would save your ass.

Katherine sat beside Johnny for nearly two days, watching his brain swell larger and larger from the bullet lodged inside until two faint pencil lines were all that remained of his eyes, and his nose sank as the flesh around his face bloomed with fluid. She listened to the slow *blip blip* of the heart monitor and watched the downward path of numbers that signified brain activity. When the numbers hit the thirties, she had them disconnect the air tube and the IVs and held his hand until he stopped breathing.

Whoever was telling the story would pause for a moment, and for the first time not make eye contact, but would look out over the class, above our heads, to some spot on the far wall and pronounce softly yet emphatically, the words varying slightly, but the judgment the same:

Strong woman.

Damn fine officer.

One tough lady.

Handled it like a man.

Never broke, not once.

Did the uniform proud.

Oh, we could all see her, tall and straight in her charcoal gray and black uniform at the funeral, brass polished, the black band over the badge perfectly centered, her shoes buffed to such a shine you could see your reflection in them. Hat pulled firmly down on her head, the brim just even with her eyebrows. She would have worn dark glasses, and everything about her would have screamed restraint and professionalism. Perhaps tears fell, but quietly, without any distortion to her features. And she would have saluted her husband at the casket, not kissed him, her wrist snap as sharp and accurate as any honor guard.

And every one of us males in that class, just like the academy classes before and after ours, fell a little in love with Katherine, and every female wanted to be just like her.

We itched, how we itched to hit the streets and show what we were made of.

Richard Marcus was born to be a cop, we could all see that right off, which is why we made him our academy class captain. He wasn't very tall, maybe 5'9" or so; some might even call him stocky, but his build was compact and muscular. He'd grown up in one of the Carolinas and had the drawl particular to that area. His fingernails were always trimmed and clean, his cadet khakis pressed, his strawberry-blond hair razor-shaved. He was top of our class in all areas: academic, out on the pistol range, the physical agility tests—he made it to the top of the rope and touched the gym rafter first, the only one who didn't even grimace initially when Sergeant Jackson walked across our stomachs as we did leg lifts. He had a peculiar combination of relaxation and intensity about him that was engaging yet kept you at a distance. He and his fiancée, Ellen, who was just as clean-cut and sweet as you'd expect, didn't drink at our after-hours parties, kept themselves slightly apart as though theirs was a world no other could truly enter. But no one held this against them; it was just the way they were, and we envied them their calm assuredness, the steady glances they gave us, the way they moved on the dance floor as though they belonged there.

And Richard was a kind man, still is even today from all we can tell, those of us left on the force.

Back then, the academy lasted twenty-three weeks, and just over halfway through, our thirteenth week, we went out on the streets before returning to another ten weeks in the classroom. That's all changed now. No thirteenth week patrol—you get assigned to an FTO, field training officer, when you graduate and spend four months under careful supervision by someone who's learned how to train new officers. But in the early 1980s, they threw us to any cop with at least three years' service who was willing to ride with a raw, eager cadet without a gun—or they'd put you with whomever the Sergeant or Lieutenant was pissed at that week. Some of us ended up with old farts who'd never passed the sergeant's test and were just working out their time in between stops at relatives' houses and coffee shops. But most of us ended up with the hot dogs, the cops who liked to shake things up and believed that the more trouble you were in, the better you were doing your job.

Richard was assigned along with five of us other guys to what cops called the dog shift, 11:00 P.M. to 7:00 A.M., out at the old Winbourne Precinct, the high-crime, high-poverty area of town. We were nervous that first night, coming into roll call, and it's only now, years later, that we know how obvious our nervousness really was. We stood out: shoes too spit-shined, hair too neat and short, faces too blank and smooth, gestures too jerky. Most of us had spent a good two hours getting ready: polishing our name plates, PD pins, and belt buckles with Brasso; rubbing saddlesoap into our shoes; clipping all the loose threads—Sergeant Jackson called them ropes, and if he found one during academy roll call, it was worth at least ten push-ups.

The first few minutes in the precinct are still a blur: crammed with uniforms, sweaty bodies, shotguns being checked out, portable radios being tested and clipped to gun belts, telephones ringing, radios chattering, keys rattling, loud voices and laughter, shoving and jostling, swearing and stories, men and women who knew what they were doing and looked like they belonged in the three small beige tile rooms that made up the bulk of the precinct.

We hung back against a wall, awkward in our uneasiness, wanting to fit in, knowing we didn't, unsure what to do with our hands as roll call started. Only Richard seemed certain of himself, leaning up against the wall, his arms folded, an alert, watchful look on his face.

Roll call hasn't changed much over the years: a short lecture by the Lieutenant about errors in report writing or signing out subpoenas, hot spots of illegal activity, BOLOs—be on the lookout fors—and just basic riding-your-ass reminders like wear your hat, keep incidental chatter on the radio down, stay in your zone. Depending on the lieutenant, roll call is either straightforward boring, or a mixture of joshing, fingerpointing, and veiled threats. Then the squad sergeants throw in their two cents, and units are assigned to their designated zone and told to get out there and go 10-8, in service.

Despite our jitters and the parade of faces and information, we all agreed later that two people stood out from the moment we entered the precinct: a big linebacker of a coonass with a broken front tooth and a kettledrum voice, and a tall slender woman with dark hair done up in a tight French braid, thick eyebrows, and makeup so artfully applied that her uniform was a jarring contrast.

One of us, Mark Denux, was assigned to ride with the linebacker coonass, a Vietnam vet named Joe Boudreaux. And one of us, Richard Marcus, was assigned to ride with the tall woman.

It took a minute for the name to register. "Marcus, you'll ride with Cippoine," the Sergeant said, and both Richard and the woman nodded.

It wasn't until she came toward us, a shotgun propped against one shoulder, and we saw her nameplate—K CIPPOINE—that we truly believed that this was the Katherine, Johnny's Katherine, our Katherine.

Perhaps we imagined the flush on Richard's cheeks, the quick downward glance as Katherine approached. But not the crack in his voice.

"Got a name besides Marcus?" Katherine asked. Her voice was huskier, more coarse than we'd expected.

"Richard, ma'am. Richard Marcus." The words sputtered out soft, his drawl deeper than normal. He no longer leaned against the wall.

Her face twitched, and she smiled, a megawatt smile. "Oh shit, please, no ma'ams. You'll make me feel ancient. Katherine is fine."

Richard nodded.

"Well," she said. "Come along, Richard Marcus."

And then we heard no more between them as we each met our assigned partner and scattered out onto the back lot, listening to the various instructions as to how we were expected to behave ("follow my lead," "let me do the talking on calls," and "don't get in the way," were the most consistent admonitions). But not before one of us overheard Beth Sanderson, an older woman with short bleached hair and sun-blasted skin, mutter, "There goes her latest," as Richard and Katherine passed in the hallway, a comment that carried little weight until much later.

We envied Richard. But we were also relieved. The next week would be a test of our character, a measure of our suitability as police officers. How could you stay inside your own skin if you were assigned to ride with a living legend?

Not well, as it turned out. Not even for someone like Richard Marcus.

These days most of us veteran officers, the ones who've been on the force fifteen years or more, bemoan the lack of camaraderie and closeness on the squads that compose a shift. "Everybody's out for himself," we say with a shrug. "Not like the old days when you could count on cops covering your ass." Some argue that eliminating two-person units contributed to fewer enduring partnerships and shift choir practices, two essential elements for any good squad. Others claim the move to straight shifts from rotating shifts created competition and hierarchy. But the truth is, there have always been close-knit shifts and shifts that never jelled.

The shift the six of us were assigned to was unusually close; most of the officers had worked together for over a year, an anomaly back then as officers seemed to be transferred regularly for no good reason other than the whim of the Uniform Patrol Commander.

So we frequently saw Richard and Katherine those first few nights: on calls as backup, at coffee shops and convenience stores, in deserted parking lots around 4:00 or 5:00 A.M. when officers met to joke, exchange information, stay awake.

It quickly became evident that Joe Boudreaux and Katherine Cippoine were the driving force on the shift. While Joe was loud, blustery, opinionated, and physical, Katherine was steady, contained, mostly quiet except on calls when she seemed to fill up the room. Despite the unexpected obscenities that frequently escaped her lips and the coarseness of her voice, which indicated a childhood lived in some East Coast town, we relished the occasional real smile that transformed her from simply lovely to stunning.

We didn't mingle much with the officers at first, spoke only when spoken to. We listened and we watched. And we talked among ourselves, standing off to one side to compare notes about the calls we'd worked, the partner we'd been assigned.

"What's she like?" Denux asked Richard. Denux was short, skinny, and nearly bald, but he'd flipped all of us with ease during takedown training at the academy. Richard was closer to him than anyone else in our class; they often ran neck and neck on the firing range and during PT, and both seemed to enjoy the good-natured competition.

"Good," Richard said.

"Yeah?"

"Tough. Professional. She pushes hard. Like a drill sergeant."

"She given you any push-ups yet, buddy?" This from Hawkins, a scraggly fellow with a huge Adam's apple who was generally considered the academy washout. We all looked at him, incredulous.

Richard pushed his hands into his pockets and looked down at the ground. "Every moment's a test. 'Where are we now,' she asks me twenty times a night. 'If something happens to me, you need to get backup and you need to know where you are.' Stuff like that."

"Yeah, Boudreaux's doing that to me too. Gets pissed off when I don't get it right," Denux said.

"She doesn't get angry," Richard said. "She doesn't say a word."

"Nothing?"

"Just moves on to something else."

"Like what?"

"How to watch hands and eyes, see in the dark, how to hold a flashlight, how to approach a car, use your hands, the way to talk to people, stand in a room."

Hawkins frowned. "Sanderson's not telling me much of anything, except don't touch the mike and stay in the car. Goddamn dyke, if you ask me."

"That's a bit off base, Hawkins," Richard said.

We all looked over at Beth Sanderson, who was talking to a couple of guys from her squad, and wondered who had the rawer deal: Sanderson for having to ride with such a dipshit or Hawkins for having to ride with a woman who seemed habitually grouchy.

"Hell of a lot more interesting than the academy," Denux said.

Richard nodded. "They both have their place."

We were all silent for a moment.

"She ever mention Johnny?"

"Jesus, Hawkins!"

Richard shook his head, grimaced slightly. "No."

"You gotta admit," Hawkins pressed on, "she is something else."

Richard nodded slowly and changed the subject.

By the third night we felt more relaxed and, through some unspoken invitation, became a part of the semicircle of six or seven units parked in an old run-down high school parking lot off Evangeline Street. It was warm and humid, as most nights are midsummer in Louisiana, and some of the officers had taken off their bulletproof vests, laid them on the hood of their cars beside their portable radios.

It seemed that when cops weren't working calls, they're telling stories. Sanderson was telling about Hawkins leaving his flashlight in the car on a burglary alarm ("You got night vision, boy?" Boudreaux asked.), and pretty soon the officers started telling stories about other officers, mostly the ones who'd done something funny or stupid like Hawkins.

"Remember that rookie Boudreaux had a couple of years back, Jack something or other?"

"Holy shit, that boy was a fuckup from the word go," Joe said. He played a coffee straw around his broken tooth as he talked. "Fresh out of the academy and we're chasing this 42 suspect down Acadian Thruway, and the boy asks me at what point do we load our guns. Shit! When do we load our guns. He's running around with an empty goddamn gun."

We all laughed, shot glances at one another, wondering at poor Jack something or other's stupidity. Hawkins giggled like a girl.

"He didn't last long after that," said a corporal named Akers who looked like an eggplant, both in color and in size, and whose voice faintly resembled Darth Vader's. "What, another couple of months?"

"Didn't make it through probation," Katherine said.

"Should've had you as his training officer," Sanderson said. "You'd have gotten him in line."

"Let it the fuck go, Beth." Boudreaux's tone was cutting, but his body language never changed.

"Fuck you, Joe," Sanderson's fingers curled tightly around the buckle on her gun belt.

"That's a whole lot of goddamn fuckin' going on," Katherine said mildly, looking up at the night sky.

A short burst of air escaped Boudreaux's lips.

"Hawkins." Katherine looked at him, and his whole body lurched forward like a marionette. "Why'd you join?"

"Ma'am?"

"Why did you join the police department?" She spoke slowly, enunciating each syllable.

"Well, ma'am, my granddaddy was a Texas Ranger." He looked everywhere but at Katherine as he spoke.

"Oh sweet Jesus," Akers snorted.

"And he's the one who taught you to call women less than ten years older than you 'ma'am'?"

"Ma'am?" Hawkins squinted at her.

We all laughed, even Katherine. Hawkins smiled hesitantly.

"What about the rest of you boys?" Boudreaux asked. "Why'd you want to become the po-lice?"

Our answers, delivered mostly in a shy, offhanded way, hardly varied: to do some good, to give back to the community, to help people. Richard didn't say a word.

Bemused smiles greeted our answers. The officers cut glances at one another, lifted eyebrows, nudged one another. Only Katherine watched us silently, her fingers playing with a small pearl earring in her left ear.

"Well, that'll get shit out of you within the first couple a months riding the streets," Joe said. He lit a cigarette and pulled hard on it, expelling the smoke in a sharp exhalation. "Doing good and helping people is crap, lemme tell you. All we do out here is answer calls, cover our asses, and try not to get hurt."

"That's about it," Akers said, nodding, the flesh under his chin jiggling slightly.

"And what about you, Richard?" Katherine brushed a stray strand of hair behind her ear, and we caught a faint whiff of perfume, something fragile and sweet.

Richard looked around and smiled. "The adrenaline."

"Now there's an honest answer!" Joe reached over and slapped Richard lightly on the shoulder. "Katie, we've got us a keeper here."

"Could be," Katherine said. "You a fuckin' cowboy, Marcus?" Her enunciation was just as studied as it had been with Hawkins.

"Do I look like a fucking cowboy?" Richard spoke quietly, but his tone was tight. We all gaped.

"She only wishes," Sanderson muttered.

Katherine inspected the toes of her boots, lifting one up slightly to catch the streetlight. "Beth, you want to start exchanging tales, you better ask yourself what I know."

Joe pitched his cigarette. "Whether or not—"

"I killed a man when I was fourteen," Richard said.

"Well hello," Akers muttered.

The 5:00 A.M. train rattled down Choctaw in the distance. We all looked at Richard.

"Man broke into the house. Just my mom, my little brother, and me. My daddy'd disappeared not long before. Another woman, we figured." Richard looked only at Katherine as he spoke. "He had a knife; I had my daddy's shotgun."

"Well didja now." Boudreaux smoothed a thumb across his mustache, looked Richard up and down. "God bless shotguns. They'll trump a knife any day. Sounds like a clean kill to me."

"It was a mess," Richard said flatly.

"They usually are, boy. But it felt good, didn't it?" Boudreaux grinned at him.

"Headquarters, 1D-84." The dispatcher's voice was impersonal and no-nonsense.

Sanderson scowled, creating even more wrinkles than we thought possible, and pulled the portable radio out of its case and up to her mouth. "1D-84, go ahead."

"Got a signal 45, possible shots fired, Starling and 12th. Code 2."

"10-4; enroute." Sanderson moved toward her unit as she spoke, gesturing sharply at Hawkins to join her.

Boudreaux keyed his mike, moving rapidly toward his unit as well. "1D-79 enroute as backup."

Starling and 12th—still a place that gives a cop pause. Back then there were pockets of danger—the Sip and Bite off Acadian that most cops called the Shoot and Stab; a pool hall off Greenwell Springs; Gus Young and 39th; a trailer park off Harding; individual houses and blocks off Plank Road and North Foster—there are even more spots today. But twenty years ago, Starling and 12th was the pucker-up zone: you didn't go in there without backup, even in daylight.

So no one was surprised when Sanderson called for more backup as she and Hawkins arrived. Even with Boudreaux and Denux behind her, realistically she had only one officer as backup. Denux and Hawkins had no guns and little authority. But then Boudreaux's voice came booming through the radio seconds later, calling for more backup *now*, a note of agitation so unusual that Katherine, already in her unit, flicked a look at Richard and told him to buckle up and hold on as she hit the red lights and siren. Four units followed close behind her.

When a second call for backup came from Boudreaux, most of us were only two minutes away. But two minutes can feel like two hours when you hear someone like Boudreaux shouting, "Signal 63, possible CU, Signal 100." And in the background, behind Boudreaux's words, a ragged mass of voices yelling and cursing.

Signal 63—the call that opens the adrenaline flood gates and shakes any officer's gut. Not just that help is needed immediately, but that bodily injury or worse is imminent. Very few officers abuse this call for help—they don't last long on the streets if they do—and someone like Boudreaux probably uses it only three or four times during his career.

The dispatcher's calm voice came right back, clearing the frequency for emergency traffic only. "Headquarters all units, 10-33. Any units available respond Code 3. Starling and 12th. Possible riot situation, possible sniper situation. This frequency is 10-33."

Starling and 12th is one of those strange intersections where five streets converge and create a weird geometric layout that no doubt some traffic engineer way back when thought was classy, brought a little élan to this then blue-collar, white neighborhood of wooden shotgun houses. It hasn't been white in decades. Blue-collar either. The drug dealers like it because they can flee quickly in any number of directions, if they choose to flee rather than dropping their cache in the weed-choked ditches. The cops like it—if any cop can truly claim he or she likes that intersection—because there's a fairly clear view, a quick snapshot of who's where doing what, no matter which street you approach on.

Three blocks away we could see a crowd converged around the two police units and up in the yard of what must have once been a yellow house but now could only be described as dingy. A crowd of thirty-five to forty people, mostly black, of every age, the number growing by the second. It was not a friendly group.

Boudreaux stood on the steps, a shotgun in one hand, his other hand, palm flat, out behind him. Denux was up on the porch beside Sanderson, who was bleeding heavily from a gash in her cheek, her hand firmly gripping the forearm of an emaciated-looking young man the color of café au lait, who looked both frightened and defiant. Hawkins was nowhere to be seen.

Katherine squealed to a halt just on the edge of the crowd, along with the other units. She slid a shotgun out of the dip between door frame and seat, handed it over to Richard.

"Use it if you need to. You'll know. Stick close and do not—DO NOT—get hurt." And she pulled another shotgun, the department-issued shotgun, off the rack on the wire mesh screen behind her.

What we would learn that night, and in the years to come, is that you get thrown into a situation without understanding all the pieces—like entering a movie already in progress—and all you can rely on is your gut, instinct, experience, and, if you're lucky, the officers around you. And only after it was over could you piece together what exactly had happened and why.

At the time, the next eight minutes were mostly a blur, a series of quick snapshots, impressions, and sensations barely coherent for us cadets.

We pushed out into the crowd, Katherine holding her shotgun perpendicular to her body, saying, "Clear the way, move back, back up" as she walked, her voice devoid of emotion but clear and authoritative even over the angry hive of noise. Richard walked sideways behind her, the top of his head just even with the back of her neck, shotgun pointed somewhere between the night sky and the crowd of people folding back around him. Two officers on each side moved forward parallel to them, cutting a small path that additional officers tried to hold open along with a few of us cadets who also held guns, although not shotguns, that our partners had suddenly slapped into our hands as we arrived on the scene, cautioning us to use them only if our lives were in danger.

Up on the porch, Sanderson was swearing profusely. Denux held a small .38 at his side, his mouth a tense line as he sheltered part of her body with his. He looked out at us with a mixture of glee and alarm.

Boudreaux shouted, "One round fired, not sure from where. Chipped out a piece of the railing and hit Beth."

The eight of us moved into a semicircle on the steps. Richard just one step below Katherine as she leaned into Boudreaux. "The neighbors don't look happy, Joe."

"Perp shot up the house," he said. "Didn't hit anyone. Took a swing at Hawkins."

"We got to get off this porch," Akers growled.

The crowd pressed in, shouting, "Let Clay go, man," and "Damn police fuckin' with people."

"Where's Hawkins?" Katherine said.

"Inside," Sanderson yelled. "Gonna whip his pansy ass."

"You, with me," Akers said, pointing a finger at Richard as he moved past him up the steps.

"I'm with her, sir," Richard said.

"Boy, move your goddamn ass."

"Sir, I'm not leaving my partner." Richard never took his eyes off the crowd as he answered Akers.

"It's okay, Marcus," Katherine said.

"I'm not leaving you."

"Denux," Boudreaux shouted. "In the house with Akers."

Within seconds Akers and Denux returned to the porch, each with a hand on Hawkins, pushing him forward. Hawkins squinted, lifted his elbow away from Denux.

"I'm gonna kill you," Sanderson snapped. "If we get out of here."

"We're moving, now," Boudreaux yelled. "Everyone."

Wood spit up from the side of the house as the sound of a shot cut through the crowd. Everyone ducked. Except Katherine. She racked a round into her shotgun, pointed it in the direction from which the shot seemed to come, and yelled, "GO!" For several seconds she stood alone, upright, like a single reed in a field of flattened grass.

Then Richard stood up, pulled Katherine in front of him and pushed her shoulders down as she stepped off the porch. He fired off a round into the air, cracked that night sky wide open with a KA-BOOM, racked another one into his shotgun, and waved it across the crowd. "MOVE BACK NOW."

"Here we go," Boudreaux shouted, grabbing Richard by the arm, nodding down at him for one brief instant.

We pushed forward slowly, steadily, a tight phalanx with guns drawn, pointing outward, as we crab-stepped toward units, shoving back against sweaty bodies, ignoring spit and worse hitting our faces and uniforms.

And then it was over. More officers arrived as we tumbled into our units, but we shook them off with the universal sign for okay and twirling index fingers. Code 4'd the call, pulled away, and headed to the holding cell at the precinct. Two units remained on side streets to make sure that the crowd dispersed, that they didn't take their anger and frustration out on property or people, hoping to find a possible hint of the sniper's identity.

On the sweaty, jittery ride to the precinct, we were counseled not to mention one goddamn thing about having guns or Richard firing off a round, at least not around supervisors, and *never ever* to the academy training staff.

"Didn't happen, understand," we cadets were told. We understood. Cops would lose their jobs, and we'd be out of a career.

Most of the shift arrived back at the precinct, pumped from the aftereffects of adrenaline, high on the sweet rush of being alive.

"This damn sure calls for a choir practice," Boudreaux said to the vigorous nods all around as Sanderson left for downtown booking. Her cheek would require stitches, but only after she'd processed and booked the perp. She left Hawkins behind, and the Lieutenant suggested, none too kindly, that Hawkins go ahead and check out for the night.

And so we attended our first real cop choir practice in a sparsely furnished one-bedroom apartment off Woodward. It's an old practice, still common today. An apartment complex manager makes a deal for extra security and a police presence in exchange for an empty apartment. Usually a cop, and sometimes his family, will live in it, but back then, more often than not, a group of officers, generally on the same squad or shift, used it as a second home—whether during shift as a place to kick back, eat, or use the bathroom, or off shift as a place to sleep during turnarounds or for what's vaguely referred to as "fooling around" and specifically means cheating on one's spouse.

The apartment housed the basic necessities: liquor, sodas, and coffee; a couple of broken-down couches; floor pillows, a boom box, and giant bags of pretzels, chips, and cookies. Toilet paper seemed to be in short supply. Gun belts, shoes and boots, uniform shirts and bulletproof vests were discarded; we walked around in T-shirts, socks, and uniform pants. Beer flowed. The storytelling—and retelling—began. We talked in loud edgy voices, eager to hear what happened to Hawkins (he panicked with the first shot that ricocheted into Sanderson and retreated into the house), to learn more about the perp (he struggled, and his girlfriend ran out into the street screaming that the police were beating him up), to speculate about the sniper (calls would be made to Narcotics to shake down a few confidential informants), to relive Katherine standing on that porch wide open to whoever was taking potshots at the police ("hell of a thing to see") and Richard pulling her down in front of him ("gonna make a hell of a cop").

By the time we popped the tabs on our third or fourth beers, a bunch of us were leaning up against the counters in the alleyway of a kitchen, and the rest crowded around the door.

"You did good, boy," Boudreaux said, slapping Richard on the back hard enough to make beer flip up out of the can he held. Richard grinned, his whole body relaxed in a way we'd never seen. "That was something, you up there waving that damn shotgun around like John fuckin' Wayne."

"Goddamn Rambo, he was," someone said.

"Motherfuckin' Godzilla."

"You're lucky I don't write up your ass for not obeying an order," Akers said in a mock growl. Richard winked, raised his can toward Akers.

"Ah hell, you'd of done the same," Boudreaux said.

"Hell, yes," Akers said.

"You sweet goddamn cowboy," Katherine said, and leaned over and kissed Richard on the cheek.

Richard's face flushed; he tipped an imaginary hat at her without directly meeting her eyes. "Anytime, ma'am."

"Oh freaking Jesus." Katherine laughed, looked at Boudreaux. "They're all out to make me an old woman, Joe."

"Never, Katie," Boudreaux said.

"No ma'am," came from several officers.

We don't know when Richard and Katherine slipped out. One moment they were there with us, sprawled out on the floor, and the next they were gone. No one mentioned it, really, although we cadets talked about it plenty among ourselves in the days to come.

But after they'd gone, on about the eighth rehashing of our adventure earlier that morning, we lingered again over Katherine's moment on the porch.

"That woman," Akers said, a beer balanced on his considerable chest. His tone conveyed both admiration and reservation.

"Wasn't one of her wiser moves," said another officer. "Still, hell of a thing to do."

"That's Katherine," said an older, gray-haired officer.

"No one else like her," Boudreaux said. He sat against a wall, his legs stretched out in front of him.

"Seems she'd know better," Denux muttered, his words slurring slightly.

Boudreaux lifted his index finger and shook it at Denux. "Don't go where you don't understand, boy. She's a damn fine cop."

Separating the truth from myth, the reality from wishful thinking, the facts from the fabricated is a delicate undertaking, sometimes impossible. Over time stories take on their own life as details are discovered and carefully added to the whole or discarded when the evidence doesn't match up; any first year cop can tell you that after working a few crime scenes. But who's to say which details are the truth? Everyone has his own perspective. What's been blurred and forgotten? What is highlighted and exaggerated?

Perhaps it doesn't matter what the exact truth is, if the skeleton is fact, the emotional core is real.

It took us years to piece together what happened between Richard and Katherine before we came up with what we considered the whole story, or as close to the whole story as we were going to get: snippets of information from Richard, seemingly indifferent questioning of cadets who came after us, observation among those of us who worked the same shifts as Katherine and Richard, casual asides from veteran officers, sifting through the rumors about personal lives that inhabit every precinct.

But the story we pieced together, the one we consider true, is one we keep mostly to ourselves. Even now we protect the story of Katherine, as so many officers have before and after us, smiling when we hear the tale of her and Johnny, knowing there is more but reluctant to share it. Protecting Katherine. Protecting Richard. Mostly, though, protecting ourselves, the selves we were so long ago: eager, optimistic, naïve.

There was another empty apartment in the complex to which Katherine, along with some of the other officers, had keys. She took Richard there, his brain softened by more beer than he was accustomed to. A place, she would have told Richard, where just the two of them could talk in peace and quiet. He carried a six-pack of beer in one hand and his cadet uniform shirt crumpled up in the other. Katherine rested her hand on Richard's shoulder as they walked, hips bumping up against each other on the narrow walkway, her gun belt, bulletproof vest, and uniform shirt slung over the other arm.

And they did talk for a while in low, thoughtful voices, mostly about their childhoods, about other cops, about the call at Starling and 12th. And there was silence as well, a comfortable silence, although Richard felt his heart beat more rapidly each time she leaned in close to him, each time she laughed. And he would have still tasted the aftereffects of the adrenaline rush from earlier, that need to feel again how alive he could be.

At some point she would have reached out a hand, slid it along his cheek and up into the hair above his ear, her fingers gently raking his scalp; then she'd have smiled that liquid smile and pulled his face toward hers, told him, "Don't think, cowboy, just kiss me."

And who among us could have said no, her body pressed up against ours, hands traveling down our back pulling us closer, the sweet intoxication of her tongue deep inside our mouth, the feel of her breasts, her hands fumbling with the buckle, then the snap, then the zipper on our pants, that quick shucking of clothing, the headiness of flesh wedded to flesh, slow and fast and again and again.

Who knows how long they stayed there, talking and kissing and touching, Katherine playing with the hair on his chest, her head resting on his shoulder, his hands stroking the skin on her waist and hip, how very white her skin was under that uniform. And no one knows what he said to Ellen, his fiancée, when he returned to their apartment later that day—or even if he did return.

We do know Richard arrived at the precinct that night looking tired, subdued, his eyes tracking every move Katherine made. She sparkled, laughed loudly and frequently, said, "Come on, cowboy" to him when roll call ended.

"Jesus H. Christ, Katherine," Sanderson said as we walked to the back lot, a large bandage covering the hollow of her cheek. "Keep a lid on it."

"Oh, Beth," Katherine said, her voice light and playful, "go home and kiss your kids." And she handed Richard the keys, brushing up against his shoulder as she told him to do the unit check before they left the lot. He smiled at her, a slow smile both tender and defeated.

Later that night, after another impromptu shift gathering in an abandoned gas station parking lot that Katherine and Richard attended only briefly, Katherine seemed so soft and giddy that Boudreaux told Denux after they left, "She's something when she's happy, isn't she?"

"Even when she's not," Denux said. "Seems a little wired at times."

"That's Katie. Comes and it goes." Boudreaux shrugged. "You won't find a better cop, though. She killed a man once, didn't blink an eye about it. Tough gal. Damn good training officer too. She used to train only rookies, but a couple years back, she started working with cadets." He gave a short laugh, shifted in his seat. "That woman was a cop from day one, even as a cadet. Johnny and I knew."

"Her husband Johnny?"

"Yep, he and I were partners out of Broadmoor. Katie road with him during thirteenth week when she was in the academy. You didn't know? That's how they met. She was so sweet and so fierce at the same time. She adored him. He trained her when she came out of the academy too. Hell of a cop, Johnny was. Never should have died." Boudreaux flicked his cigarette out the window. "Let that be a lesson to you, boy. It can happen to any of us, no matter how good you are. And he was one of the best."

Denux was tempted to ask more, but he resisted. As he told us later, "It was just all too frigging weird."

The following week we returned to the academy, feeling even more constrained by the classroom after our time on the streets, bursting with the desire to be done with this. The next ten weeks dragged on in some ways—hour after hour in our seats, taking notes, trying to listen, the sky so blue and promising outside the high, small windows. But it also became more intense and focused as our goal grew closer. Richard mingled with us more frequently, despite seeming distracted. He came alone to some of our parties and drank heavily; we didn't ask about his fiancée, Ellen. His grades dropped some, but he pushed himself hard in the gym and out on the firing range. We never mentioned Katherine, although we saw her on occasion, slipping in during lunch to sit with Richard for a few minutes out in the breezeway. The cadets who hadn't been on our shift tended to find excuses to walk down the breezeway past them for a soda or a cigarette. Richard and Katherine always nodded hello, but that was all.

With only three weeks left until graduation, Hawkins washed out as expected, unable to avoid the reality any longer of less-than-passing grades and poor evaluations from his thirteenth-week ride-along. He'd never been particularly impressive on the firing range either. And he truly was a dipshit. Still, we all patted him on the back, said we were sorry to see him go, suggested he try again.

That was around the time Richard turned morose and short-tempered; circles appeared under his eyes, and he often sat blankly during class, staring at the far wall above the instructor's head. Sergeant Jackson gave him twenty push-ups one day at roll call for an unacceptable uniform. Katherine no longer visited at lunchtime.

Who knows at what point she started to withdraw, or when she actually ended it, but we know it was before graduation. We learned over the years that her pattern was consistent: she selected one male from the academy class and always ended it before graduation. She would have let Richard down calmly, matter-of-factly, just before she'd handed him his graduation present, the graduation present she always gave.

"Early, I know," she might have said. "But this is it, cowboy, between you and me, and I want you to have this before I go."

Did he say anything as she took the tiny St. Michael's medallion out of its box, slipped the silver chain around his neck? Or did he just stare at her, stunned and bewildered, his heart skittering hard against bone?

"There," she said, adjusting the medallion on his chest, her fingers lightly brushing his skin. "You know who St. Michael is, don't you? The patron saint of police officers. You don't have to be Catholic. He'll keep you safe if you do the rest." And she reached down and kissed him, a soft lingering kiss, before she stepped back and began to dress.

"Nice while it lasted, cowboy, but it's over and no harm done. Go back to your fiancée. Go be a good cop."

Did Richard plead, cajole? Or was he more stoic, laying out a rational argument? Did he explode in frustration, tell her he loved her, wanted to be with her? Whatever his approach, he would not have accepted her dismissal. He would not have walked away; he would have laid himself even more bare. Of this we are convinced.

And why would her reply to him be any different than the reply she gave all the cadets who came before and after him?

"So you fucked the legend, Marcus. Congratulations. Now let it go."

And so we graduated and hit the streets. It seems long ago. And it was, nearly twenty years now. Over half our original class has left the force—quit, fired, disabled. Two are dead, but not from the job. The rest of us are sergeants, some even lieutenants, working in departments as varied as Homicide, Auto Theft, Criminal Records, the Chief's Office. Some of us still work uniform patrol, but we're supervisors and rarely go out on the streets. Richard's in Planning and Research, down at Headquarters, after a long stint in Armed Robbery. He's married, but not to Ellen, and has two sons.

Katherine died seven years after we graduated. The last the dispatcher heard from her, she was out with a Signal 34, a prowler, on St. Ferdinand Street. It was a busy night, full moon Friday, and when another unit finally arrived ten minutes later to back her up, it was clear she'd put up a fight: slashes and cuts, some of them deep, covered her arms and face and legs; blood gushed from her femoral artery. The perp lay partway on top of her, the barrel of her gun resting against his cheek; Katherine had managed to blow his head off, even as he stabbed her repeatedly, hepped up on PCP. She was barely conscious when the officers got there, whispering something they couldn't understand. They threw her in the backseat of their unit and hauled ass down North Boulevard to the BRG, but her heart had stopped and she'd lost too much blood.

Her funeral was something to see; the line of police cars stretched over a mile on the way to the cemetery; the department bugler played taps. We all saluted her casket.

Her picture is up on the wall at Headquarters when you first walk in, behind a glass case. The Wall of Honor, we call it: all the Baton Rouge city cops who've died in the line of duty. Far too many of them. After you walk in and out of there day after day, you tend to pass by it without really *seeing* their faces; the wall becomes more of a twitch deep beneath your skin that can't quite be ignored as you turn down the hallway to the evidence room or crime scene division, or wherever your business may take you.

Still, sometimes we do stop and linger, needing to study the too-long parade of faces—good cops we knew like Carl D'Abadie, Chuck Stegall, Warren Broussard, Betty Smothers.

Does Richard occasionally pause here as well, we wonder. Is his eye caught by Katherine's face, more serious and far younger than we ever remember? Does he look at her, and look at Johnny, the two Cippoines up there on the wall? Does he stand here, like we do, and remember when the world seemed good and bright and we were all so alive and full of possibility.

MICHAEL GRIFFITH

His jaw wired shut as a result of a biking accident, South Carolina native Michael Griffith interviewed with James Olney for the position of editorial assistant at *The Southern Review*. Griffith was pursuing his MFA at LSU, having already earned his AB from Princeton in Germanic Languages and Literature. He convinced Olney even through clenched teeth that he loved copyediting and proofreading, and the two formed a working relationship that lasted ten years—Griffith eventually served as associate editor—shepherding *The Southern Review* into the 21st century. Vance Bourjaily, former director of LSU's creative writing program, mentored Griffith during his MFA studies; Moira Crone and James Gordon Bennett were also influential. In 2002, he left Baton Rouge to join the faculty of the University of Cincinnati, where he now serves as associate professor. He also teaches in the Sewanee School of Letters. In 2004, he reconnected to LSU when he became the founding editor of Yellow Shoe Fiction, an original-fiction series from LSU Press. Griffith also serves in the respected role of literary executor for Matt Clark. Along with Josh Russell, he continues to seek posthumous publication for Clark's body of work, much of which Clark wrote when the three friends studied together at LSU.

Bibliophilia, a novella set in LSU's Middleton Library, follows the internal struggles of Seti, an Egyptian graduate student in love with both Lili, his boss' seventeen-year-old daughter, and the lush, bacchanalian environment he discovers in Baton Rouge. Seti's duty is to earn his degree and return to his desert home to share his acquired knowledge of hydrology. But unexpected desires tempt him to stray from his assumed life path. In this excerpt, he recalls his first meeting with Doug the Stoner, the one person who could help him better communicate his feelings to Lili and win her away from Rex, Seti's rival.

Two characteristics of Griffith's work include a writing vocabulary that compels readers to reach for a dictionary, and an underground wit that creates entertainment of the highest order. Readers in Baton Rouge often speculate about the uncanny resemblance of Griffith's fictional characters to members of the LSU community. Even those not connected with LSU will recognize this author's dazzling ability to satirize university types.

MICHAEL GRIFFITH

Flood Festival

from *Bibliophilia*

Fifteen minutes till break, and nothing to occupy Seti except his worries. Almost an hour since Lili borrowed his glasses, and no sign yet of her or Rex. His errand for Mort came to naught. He couldn't find them, though he haunted all their usual places until he feared the woman in reference who was covering for him would think him a malingering dog. Where are they?

Once again Seti anxiously reviews the scene he saw in the lounge. Lili's foot propped between Rex's thighs. Rex's thumbs palpating, his crucifix earring swaying in time with the effort, mouth running as usual. Corrupting her; despoiling her. Grooming her with his forked tongue. Anointing her feet with his snake oil. Just what are these *rock-'n'-reel* and *bumping uglies*? They are the key to understanding Rex's plea, or sermonette, or whatever it was. Immediately afterward Seti had sprinted downstairs, whispering the phrases to fix them in memory, and cracked open the big slang dictionary in the reference room. He saw to his surprise and alarm that "rock and roll" derived from an African-American term for sexual congress, but that was generations ago, keep in mind, before the white people stole it, like everything else, and tamed it down to mean only loud guitar music; and anyway it had nothing to do with "rock and reel," which was distinctly what Rex had said. "Reel" would belong to the idiom of angling, or perhaps the cinema. Yes, sure, Americans and their movies; that made sense. "Bumping uglies" sounded like something from a Mafia film: *Don Corleone, do you want I should bump his uglies*? But Rex was talking about religion, he gathered, about Jesus. Jesus had been a fisherman, right? (Or maybe some of his disciples had been; Christianity was Western through and through, chock full of middle management—priests, vergers, vicars, canons, monsignors, popes. The first thing the Son of Venture Capital did was to tap twelve Executive VPs. daVinci painted *The Last Board Meeting*.)

As Seti stood, puzzled, over the canted wooden lectern that held the dictionary, Myrtle happened by.

"Need help?" she asked. For a moment he didn't respond. "Not that I'll know it if it came into the lexicon since 1970. In America, slang's just another way for the kids to remind elders that our time has passed. Uncool is the first step toward dead. Square, then old, then ashes. Anyway . . . "

Seti brushed a hundred or so pages forward to obscure his tracks, gave a brisk bow. "Thank you for the offer, Ms. Myrtle," he lied with an ease that distressed him. "I was looking for between the rock and the hard place. No problem. And please permit me to say that you are not old, Ms. Myrtle. Your cinders remain hot."

Myrtle glanced away, but too late to conceal the flush in her cheeks. "It's been a long time since anybody told me I had hot cinders, Seti. You're a charmer . . . but your math's not so great. Anyway, I hope you get out from between your rock and your hard place. I've got to chase down some journal orders. Are we still on for coffee?"

"I shall see you at two, Salaam."

"Salaam your ownself," she said over her shoulder.

He couldn't ask her, couldn't. True, she is virtually his only friend here, and kind, and indulgent in her way; she would accompany him to a shabby Lebanese café that serves resiny coffee somewhat like that of home. She has become devoted to phyllo-dough pastries dusted with pistachio, and she'll nibble at them and refill Seti's cup from the earthen urn Mr. Shaheen leaves on the table and listen to him talk about his homeland. But to say to her, "I am lovelorn, Ms. Myrtle, rent in twain by love, and I must know what are uglies and how they bump" —impossible, beyond impossible. She is a priestess, and above such sweaty vanities.

So he lets it go. Rex and Lili were discussing the filmic arts, specifically Christian fishing movies—fine, okay, that must be it. Seti dimly remembers catching a few moments of a New Testament rock musical on late-night TV, and Jesus was wearing a yellow slicker like the old salt on the packages of fish sticks Seti feeds the cats. Yes, and singing a tune called "Fishers of Men" as He walked on water— or, actually, did a splashy disco dance on it. And, too, there is that piscine emblem Christians affix to their cars. Fish and Jesus go together. So it was innocent, after all: Lili's feet had been aching, and Seti would never want her denied any comfort, even from the likes of Rex.

What business is it of his, anyway? He'd listened in like some common, cringing spy. There is no reason to let Lili, her beauty aside—her unpolished big toenail, he'd noticed that day, had at its center a crescent of white like a Moorish moon, and her heel bore a faint amber tinge . . . from the tannins in her shoe leather, most likely, but to Seti it looked like the dust of Cairo streets, and he would have loved to whisk it away with a brush and unguents—there is no reason to let her reduce him to some sort of moony-eyed *majnoon*, a fool, an unman.

But now, today, the worry is reignited—it's been an hour and ten minutes, and Lili can't concentrate for that long, and Rex probably can't *read*, and Seti has to admit, a week late, that there's something maybe not quite totally persuasive about the Jesus-fish link he came up with—and it occurs to him that he could ask his friend

Doug the Stoner to translate. Doug the Stoner does not judge. If only Doug the Stoner were in town.

They met during Seti's first summer in Baton Rouge, three years before. Overnight there'd been a torrential downpour, and Seti woke up to write his parents an ecstatic letter about the thrum of rain on the roof as he slept, the eerie water-shadows projected through his patio door and writhing on the bedroom wall, the flashbulbs of lightning, the grumble and pop of thunder. The trees' dark leafage shuddered and rolled in the wind, and when the thunder got close, his windowsills rattled in sympathy, as though cherishing the memory of being live wood lashed in a storm.

When the letter was finished, Seti tucked it into an envelope and opened his spiral notebook. He reviewed the list, at this point limited—the notebook was near-new—to the wet callings: well dowser; snorkeling guide; professional beachcomber; wave-machine operator at the water park. He tremblingly added "underwater demolitions," then closed the book and flung his pen and prayed for forgiveness, for guidance. He'd justified the purchase of the notebook as a way to burn off his temptations, to set them down on paper and thereby banish them—fleeting silliness—from his head. Thus the Spam logo: what could be more laughable, less alluring, than salted pork shoulder in a sleeve of gelatin? And in a can, and that can opened with a scrolled key that looked like an Egyptian amulet, like the *ankh* that should promote immortality rather than atherosclerosis; and the meat bearing the impress not of an animal's skin and sinew but of the tin tomb (with its thick Frankenstein seam) into which it had been stuffed. But recently a Samoan boy, another Third World lonelyheart whom he encountered at an International Center meet-and-greet, had introduced Seti to something called Hawaiian *musubi*, a sushi made of Spam with pickled plum and seaweed, and it was delicious. Was there no end to the sirens in this place, trying to sing him to watery doom? Even the lowliest things had their hooks into him.

Seti felt filthy, so he kicked the book into a corner and savagely showered and fiercely dressed and stoutheartedly headed to the library for work, never once thinking about wave-making or underwater demolition. Never once, never once, never once.

But when he swung open his door, he discovered that there was water lapping at the threshold. He could see a woman in the middle of the street, and she was in up to her hips, slogging with her head and shoulders pressed forward as if burrowing into high wind. His first response was a flare of jealousy. Wastrel Nature, bestowing its embarrassment of riches. At home, tax rates were once based on the level of the Nile—high in years of exceptional flood, low during drought—and Seti had never seen such munificence; the Nile these days, sapped by dams and diversion canals, had grown sluggish and stingy. The rich richer, the fat fatter, the wet wetter. America, land of absurd overplenty.

But the woman's housedress was floating around her like a floral-print lily pad, and her head was swiveling back and forth, on the lookout. The old Lincolns were in up to their fins. Down the block a shirtless black man was tearing at a roll of tape with his teeth, trying to seal his trunk. Maybe this wasn't munificence after all. Seti could see the Vietnamese women across the way haplessly sweeping brown bilge out of their kitchens and watching it rush back in. One of them was laying down a dike made from burlap sacks of rice. Two husbands sat in a low crook of crape myrtle out front, smoking and chattering and knocking fuchsia blooms into the swill.

In a dim way this made Seti feel better. Americans tended to take abundance in all things as their birthright, and often the costs of wealth were pitifully small. It was right that there be no firm line between plenty and surfeit. It was right that there be some adversity to face, some bill called due. Here was Seti's chance to lead. He built a bank of towels inside his door in case the rain resumed, packed a change of shoes and trousers into his backpack, and waded to the bus stop—he had to get to the library, which would doubtless remain open, a reminder in these troubled times of what was truly important, a beacon of hope. But when he turned onto the main street of his neighborhood, what he saw astonished him.

Bobbing in the wash were two dozen inflatable dinghies, kayaks, kiddie rings bearing the heads of ducks and dragons and superheroes, and Styrofoam pool-recliners with built-in drink holders. A few of the vessels were sloppily tied together with plastic rope. But this was no dismal flotilla of refugees, forsaken by God and ferrying their sodden valuables to high ground and new hope; these were, unmistakably, pleasure craft. Several people had boom boxes on board, with tunes blasting. Students were tossing cigarette lighters and cans of beer back and forth. It was 10:30 A.M.

Seti pushed on to Milo's Kash-and-Karry, which was set on a concrete hummock high enough to keep it dry inside. On the store's door was a notice: NO BEER LEFT. NADA. ZILCH. BUPKUS. DON'T EVEN ASK. NO BATTERIES NO STERNO NO ICE—NO DICE.

At the bus stop just past Milo's, a woman reclined in a tractor-tire inner tube tethered to the smoked-glass shelter. She was wearing a bikini, and her toes were painted with purple polish. Seti averted his eyes. "Pardon me, miss," he said, "but have you seen the campus bus come by?"

"No bus today, guy," she said. "Classes are canceled. You might have noticed, Mother Nature gave us a day off. Want a brew?" She gestured with her thumb to the Styrofoam cooler bobbing beside her.

"No, thank you," said Seti.

A four-wheel-drive pickup with oversized tires rattled over the railroad tracks and splashed heavily into the floodwater— the end of a log-flume ride. The resulting surge soaked Seti's crotch (despite his attempt to time a subtle little tiptoe-jump for when the wave arrived), and the girl's tube nearly capsized. "This is a no-wake zone, motherfucker!" she yelled. Yet the yell was somehow amiable, and the driver flashed her a smile, lifted the bill of his baseball cap. Down the way, rafters made a raucous game of throwing crumpled cans into the truckbed as he crept past.

Seti looked up to see someone pushing across the street toward him and the bikini girl. It was a young man wearing chest waders. There were Rollerblades slung around his neck, and he was attached by a shoulder harness to a small rickshawish thing with overinflated tires; it floated along behind him. The waders were comically large, like the bottom half of a clown costume.

"Hey, Cecilia," he said to the bikini girl. "Bad day to tan, dude. The UV sucks."

"Hey, Doug. I'm laying in a little base. Overcast is good for that. When the sun breaks through I'll be *primed*. You got to take what it gives you, you know?"

"I hear you." Doug readjusted the straps of his rickshaw, which appeared to be filled with a pile of heavy gray tape. He would have been handsome but for a complexion like a baking potato.

Seti could see his friends the cats atop Milo's Dumpster in amazing numbers, almost haunch to haunch, looking out at the water; they looked like mismatched gargoyles riding a parapet.

"You got a long wait for the bus, chief," said Doug, turning to Seti. "I mean 'chief' like, you know, *dude*, not chief like you're an Indian, I mean Native American, in case you are," Doug continued. "In which case I owe you an apology, 'cause we palefaces seriously screwed you over. Hey, I'm Doug the Stoner."

"It is a pleasure to meet you, Doug the Stoner. I am Seti. I am of Egypt." Seti extended his hand politely, and Doug the Stoner lightly slapped it front and back, then extended his thumb and pinkie and oscillated his fist from side to side. He seemed not to notice that Seti's attempt to mimic the gesture looked like a palsy.

Most of Seti's conversations here were brief, superficial, stillborn, like his chat with Cecilia, which had reached its crisis point just as Doug arrived. Seti could only have stood by for a few more seconds waiting for courage, that sad figment, to kick in, then muttered good-bye and waded back home, haunted for weeks by her creamy belly with its winking little sideways omphalos, her plummy toes with their silver rings. It would never have occurred to him to discuss tanning oils and sun-protection factors with her, as Doug was now effortlessly doing, much less to sweep a finger across the shiny bow of Cecilia's collarbone to test her lotion's fastness and then to plant that finger in his mouth and say, "Pure coconut, baby. You be careful now." Seti's only source of social pleasure was eavesdropping. He was awkward, laconic—*foreign*—and Americans tended to leave him alone. But Doug either didn't read the signs or blew blithely through them: "You look like a man with a plan for a tan, Seti," he said. "What do you think? Cecilia here wants to be a Hawaiian Tropic girl. Any advice?"

Seti didn't think anything, didn't say anything either, but he beamed at Doug, glad to have an excuse to keep standing there and taking in the uncanny scene.

These people knew how to wring delight from life, how to make a gray day and ugly water—water full of fast-food flotsam, water that exuded, now that Seti had been in it for a while, a distinct stench of sewage—into a kind of street carnival. He could memorize Cecilia's muscular stomach, the curved staves of her ribs, the three tiny blond wisps below her navel; he could marvel at the boisterousness down the way—canoe races seemed, now, to have broken out—and at Doug, whose pleasant, open, lumpy face wore a ceaseless smile. Why was he lugging a rickshaw full of tape?

"Cat got your tongue, Seti? You think she's got the makings of a Hawaiian Tropic girl or not?"

What was a Hawaiian Tropic girl? "She is beautiful," Seti said. That was bold, frank, a start. But he pressed his luck, or rather his luck pressed itself. "They eat sushi there," he continued, "made of Spam. In Hawaii. All Polynesia, to be the truth. It is savory."

Doug laughed. Cecilia laughed, too, and when there seemed to be no meanness in it, Seti laughed as well. They laughed together. There was a tiny white halo overhead. The sun was trying to burn through a frayed spot in the clouds, and for Cecilia's sake, Seti rooted for it. He even joined in the cheers when the canoes tore past. Everyone seemed to be rooting for the one with a recumbent nude painted on its side, just above the waterline, so Seti too urged the naked woman along. It was strange to hear his voice mingling with others again. Their shouts echoed oddly, exaggeratedly, over the water. It was like being in a funhouse, and for a moment he enjoyed it.

But then he caught the distorted sound of his own laugh, the bray of a donkey, the screak of a crow, arrogant, preposterous—American. His moral compass had gone haywire. This was a disaster, after all. Just around the corner, not two hundred yards away, the Vietnamese women—refugees once already—were fighting a losing battle, trying to beat back the tide with their threadbare brooms. Their husbands roosted in a tree, cursing the slipshod god who let this happen. Those families' few sticks of furniture were going to be waterlogged, and good rice plumped in vain. And still the highboy trucks were prowling the streets, making waves—*wave-making*, came the terrible aperçu, *underwater demolition*. Could all this be punishment from Allah for *his* wickedness, *his* weakness? Was Seti to blame? No, no, best not to think that way. It was the trucks that were churning up higher water yet. Thoughtless; heedless. They couldn't pin this on him. This is a no-wake zone, motherfuckers, thought Seti indignantly. Can you not see we suffer here?

And where were the African-Americans? Half the people in the neighborhood were black, but except for Seti this party seemed lily-white. These were students—kids on the way to snug suburban futures and celebrating the unneed of knowledge, which they'd spend five or six years in college beating back, sleeping through, drowning in skunky beer; impermanent residents who could afford the extra twenty-five a month for upstairs and who, heeding parents' or weathercast's warnings, had moved their cars to higher ground the night before. Or they were tourists, day-trippers from higher ground (and virtually anywhere in town was higher than this). Sure enough, Seti could see several dozen sport-utility vehicles parked around the built-up railbed. They looked like they'd been scattered by a runaway locomotive.

He had sunk to a new low. He was standing in shit-filled water and his moral compass was broken and his privates were wet and he was ogling the comely Cecilia, a *mara*, a loose woman intent on cooking herself, and he had cheered on a bulbous painted nude who cleaved the water with her mount of pubic, and he'd touted the tastiness of Spam, and what under the *shams* was wrong with him? Worse yet, in some sick way he liked it all, reveled in it. The water tugged at his trouser legs, and his nether parts prickled pleasantly, and his feet were slowly sinking. He felt moist and serene, like a crocodile. He had been infected.

Last century, he'd learned recently, people thought disease was caused by the humid air here, which harbored *malades horribles*—and that, the professor said, had been a quaint superstition, like believing in witches or magic beans or Marxism. So much of education consists in learning how foolish people used to be, when they lived in chaos and error. *We are past that now, praise be.*

It was easy enough for people in this country, Seti thought, to cherish the idea of manifest destiny, to believe evolution followed a straightish line from amphibian to ape through Apache to *American*. It's flattering to think oneself the culmination of history. But what about nations that reached their highest flourish three thousand years ago? What about their sons and daughters? Were they merely breathing fossils, holdovers from a dead era when mud people built giant crypts and worshiped the dead and used too much kohl mascara? They'd had the bad taste to endure beyond their allotted time, and America kindly suffered them to keep living, like the elderly in their shuffleboard villages or the coelacanths in their black depths. To live as burdens, oddities . . . and as caretakers of history, which was now just another tourist destination. Were Egyptians supposed to live out their days as pyramid guides and camel keepers and technical advisers to tomb digs or mummy movies? How appalling the United States was, yet how resistless its charms. Seti wondered whether the old fancy had it right after all: maybe Louisiana was full of malign vapors. Maybe he'd been invaded by them. This moral indolence, this lethargy, this growing feeling of giddiness—there was no explanation but that Louisiana had insinuated some poison into his blood.

Two kayakers eggbeatered past, and when Doug the Stoner and Cecilia put in on the side of the red one, Seti found himself whooping, too. What was wrong with him? He should get out of these wet clothes, get home, offer aid to the stricken, pray for pardon. But he was lonely, and in no mood to look askance at a potential friend, even one called Doug the Stoner who was, when Seti looked to see, gulping down the last of a beer and crushing the can against his acne-scarred forehead. He dropped the can, along with the bikini girl's, into his wagon, saying, "Thanks, Cece. That's supplemental income, much appreciated. May you brown evenly and well, my child."

Then he turned back to Seti. "These are lean times, my Egyptian friend. There appears to be a beer famine at Milo's." Doug gestured toward the sign on the door, and it occurred to Seti to wonder why they had no dice left. Were these students setting up casinos in their dinghies, floating craps games? Had the decadence gone so far as that? "But it's nearly eleven, and the bars will be opening. Cecilia's got to turn her mind to serious tanning, so we'll let her be. What say we get some suds?"

Seti was confused. Was Doug suggesting that they bathe together? "I have no need of soap just now," he said, though a shower was his dearest wish.

"No, no, I mean beer." Doug pointed across the street, to the neighborhood tavern.

"I do not drink beer."

"Just come and sit, then. It's dry inside, and they have dollar Pabst, and stale pretzels for free. Come on. Be a pal."

At that moment Seti felt, pathetically, a rush of joy like the one that afflicted him when he met the minister of labor and watched him, across that helipad desk, wipe his lenses. *Mustafa*, chosen.

Be a pal.

The scene in the bar looked like an orgy just getting cranked up, or anyway like Seti's fevered imagining of such. Five minutes past opening, and the place was packed with buzzing college kids in dishabille, many of the boys dressed only in boxer shorts, laughing girls tugging down T-shirts to cover their bottoms. Every ten seconds, somewhere in the room, one could see a young girl reach back to pinch the elastic of her up-riding underwear. There was a horde of ogling bouncers at the door, armed with mops, wringing people out or making them strip. Seti slipped into a bathroom stall and changed into his dry clothes. When he returned, Doug had shed his waders and tossed them atop the giant pile of pants and shoes beside the door. He'd unhooked his rickshaw and persuaded the bouncers to let him display it at the front with a cardboard sign: "Duct-Tape Billfolds and Handbags. Great Gifts. Five Bucks." Scrawled at the bottom in red was an addendum: "They Float." Doug was wearing a surf-shop T-shirt and a shiny green bathing suit. He motioned Seti to the bar.

Seti had never been inside a pub before. It looked like a seraglio gone to seed, with brittle straw blinds instead of muslin curtains, neon beer ads instead of braziers. Women were squeezing water out of their hair, comparing sub-waistline tattoos. There were men wandering about wearing makeshift breechclouts fashioned from T-shirts; they looked like infants, or savages, or infant savages. Rap music was thumping from a corner jukebox, and nearby a few couples were grinding their pelvises together. He and Doug took wobbly stools at the bar, behind which swirled a garish wall of daiquiris in windowed blenders. Seti was given, after a season of whispers and chuckles between Doug and the bartender, a nonalcoholic drink named after a little girl with auburn pincurls whom he'd once seen in a TV matinee. The glass was topped with two soggy, oversweet cherries that were an obscene saturated red, and Seti did not want to know how the concoction earned its name. He took in the blinking bar signs, the nearly nude students, the O's of the girls' mouths when they tipped their bottles up for a sip.

Doug talked. He talked and talked and talked. "I don't want you getting the wrong idea, Seti. I'm not a stoner. Well, I am a stoner, but I wasn't always a stoner. There were two Dougs in my group in high school, about the same build, same bowl cut, same hair color. The real difference between us was that . . . well, it would have been my acne except that he had it as bad as I did. Which is a blessing. It saved both of us, I guess, from being called Zit Doug, or Pizzaface Doug, or Krakatoa Doug. The truth is that he was walleyed as hell. But he was a good guy, and it seemed kind of vicious to call him Walleye Doug, because he was sensitive about it—I mean, hell, how could he not be; it was like he had eyes coming out both sides of his head, like a hammerhead shark—and I had a *Hemp Rules* T-shirt, so I became Doug the Stoner, you know. And when your name is Doug the Stoner, it brings some responsibilities. You may not like it, at first, but eventually you mellow into the role. You step up. Truth in advertising, man. It was my duty. You know about duty, don't you, man?"

The rest of it was a blur to him: stoner walleye hammerhead zit. But did Seti know about duty? Yes, Seti did. He nodded vigorously, then bit a cherry off the plastic sword on which it was impaled.

Doug told him that he traveled by Rollerblade and hitchhiking between Tampa and Houston, staying here a month, there a month, hitting the beach when possible and along the way selling his wallets and bags. The rickshaw marked him as a harmless eccentric (how many homicidal drifters pulled a collapsible homemade cart adapted from an old Radio Flyer red wagon and piled high with tape products?), so folks tended to pick him up to hear his story, and he'd developed a reputation among truckers as decent company, so it wasn't hard to get from town to town. Doug too was a nomad, an outsider, and cut off from these students, too, by his ugliness and his age—only now did it occur to Seti that he was thirty or so, not twenty, that the scars on his face were not ephemeral acne but its permanent tracks. "Yeah," Doug said at one point, "if I were a TV actor they'd only let me play drug dealers. The white suits would be cool, though. Say what you will about dealers, they've got sharp threads."

No one said anything to them, no one looked at them. It was as though they existed inside a bubble of foreignness. The girls cavorted and jiggled, the boys flexed; Doug the Stoner kept talking. The bar grew crowded.

And then they were suddenly surrounded by a coven of beauties shouting out orders for frozen drinks. Seti tried not to notice the freckled shoulders, the crescents of underbuttock, the creamy tops of breasts. He tried not to stare at the fraying peach bra-strap nearest him, at the worn plastic hook and eyelet midway between her shoulder blades. Desperate, he rubbed his fingertips together, let his eyes roam upward, to safety, to the ceiling . . . but it, too, was festooned with bras, dozens of them, limp and smoke-damaged, interspersed with written-on dollar bills.

Precious Allah, forgive me, forgive me.

And then the girls, pursing their lips to suck at straws, sidled away. Doug turned to Seti with a sad smile. His ruined cheeks glowed in the neon. "Water, water everywhere," he said, and slugged down the last of his second can of Pabst. "But not a drop to drink."

Since then Doug and Seti have been friends, of a sort. Doug has introduced him to the other campus legends: Marley-san, the Jamaican jerk barbecue guy from Japan, with his converted ice-cream cart and his Rasta wig-and-hat combination; Lorenzo, the man with the whistle and the tall fur shako who directs traffic from a bus-stop bench; Levi, who sells shrimp and velvet wall hangings from underneath the tin canopy of an abandoned garage; Sybil, the taciturn accordionist; Byron, the elfin dude with the aged green tweed jacket and the thick glasses who carries a sketchbook everywhere; Wino Ike, a former lawyer in a rumpled seersucker suit who earned his name by looking like the swollen-faced alter ego of Eisenhower; the skateboarding skinheads who hang out behind Blockbuster Video, kids whose only politics, for all their warlike piercing and dyeing, turn out to be wanting the world to be a hassleless free-skate.

Seti among the outcasts: cats, crazies, beefeaters, sketch artists, presidents gone bad. And his friend, Doug the Stoner.

But Doug isn't in town now. He's in Florida, enjoying the September lull and living off the proceeds from his new line, with hand-painted "art-deco" curlicues (nail polish, dude, the secret is nail polish) and sterile-gauze dividers. Wino Ike and Sketch Byron aren't fit sources for advice. You don't get your erotic tips from men who cut their stench by carrying urinal mints in their coat pockets. Sure, Seti will ask Doug when he gets a chance. But in the meantime, break is approaching, and he must look for Lili.

MATT CLARK

Matt Clark, rising star in the LSU English Department, respected director of creative writing, inspired teacher, and promising new literary talent, lost his life at age 31 to colon cancer. With publications in *Alaska Quarterly Review* and *Texas Bound*, Clark had established a style, something of a cross between magical realism and West Texas folksiness, well suited for the outlandish, brilliant and very funny stories waiting to be published. His love of tall tales and legends led him to create heroes like Cutter, who, with "the body of Apollo poured into a pair of Levi's," crosses the 321-foot-high Pecos River Bridge blindfolded to win the heart of the redheaded "cactus-flower-smelling" goddess, TexAnn. In his most widely read story, "The West Texas Sprouting of Loman Happenstance," Clark's main character, Cayman Bliss—owner of a boxful of chameleons who regroup, change colors, and transform themselves into works of art such as the Mona Lisa—is a recluse living in West Texas without a car or phone. When Cayman is visited by seed salesman Loman Happenstance, the interaction between the two men introduces one of Clark's major thematic concerns: the transforming, mystical power of art to bring joy into our lives. Referring to the creations of the lizards, Cayman exclaims, "Oh, hell, Happenstance . . . 'Is it art? Is it not art?' . . . I didn't make the lizards, but I gave them the inspiration to paint. If I'm not the artist, then at least I'm the artists' patron. Fact is, it doesn't matter. They're happy. I'm happy. We're both happier for knowing each other."

A native of Texas and graduate of SMU, Clark moved to Baton Rouge to join the creative writing program at LSU. There, Andrei Codrescu was a powerful influence, especially during the time Clark worked at the online literary journal, *Exquisite Corpse*. Vance Bourjaily, Moira Crone, and James Gordon Bennett also guided Clark's development as a writer.

Clark's stories are about magic, that magic is learned, that if you can imagine something, it is as good as real. When reading "The West Texas Sprouting of Loman Happenstance," you will see the many ways that Clark suspends your disbelief and pulls you into a world where lizards paint Van Gogh's Starry Night, where fields of flowers become Edward Hopper's Nighthawks, where people magically change and grow.

MATT CLARK

The West Texas Sprouting of Loman Happenstance

Loman Happenstance's ancient gold Cadillac died finally, sputtering, spasming next to a green road sign which read "Sweetum." Loman climbed out of the car and drank in the surroundings. The skies over the low mountains around him, egg-carton blue purpling up into squid-inky blackness, were nonplussed to witness the steamy demise of a once-regal highway yacht. The short sweet aria of a whippoorwill prodded Loman to begin his eulogy. "You picked a strange graveyard, my love," he said to his failure-belching auto. "Nobody will come to visit you way the hell out here." He stalked to the trunk of the car, gravel crunching underfoot, and removed two suitcases. In one resided his traveling wardrobe. In the other, heavy shifting sighs and whispers, his wares, his life, his trade: seeds. He peddled exotics and domestics of the vegetable and flowering varieties all over the grand expanse of Texas. "Loman Happenstance," he would introduce himself to strangers in cafes and five and dimes from El Paso to Gladewater. "Seed salesman extra-extraordinaire."

I report this to you as if I was there, because, of course, I was. Watching Loman from my front porch.

There was nowhere else for Loman Happenstance to go, really, except toward the dilapidated two-story building in front of him. Everything else was obviously abandoned. The drugstore, the gas station, the old city hall/post office/fire station— all those buildings were shadowy-still and barn mouse quiet. Only the feed store showed signs of life: 1) a light bulb, bare, harvest moon yellow, mermaid-charming moths to its heat; 2) the soft, cricket-purr creak of a rocking chair stroking the time-worn boards of the porch; and 3) a man—me—caught up in that rocking chair's pulse. Loman Happenstance aimed his lily-white bucks toward this new oasis. The two suitcases pack-mule slapped against his seersuckered legs.

"How de do!" the seed peddler announced with zest. "Loman Happenstance: seed salesman extra-extraordinaire."

"Evening," I responded. "Vehicular apocalypse?"

"Yessir," Loman sighed. "The end of a great one, I'm afeared. We've been together for a long while, but I regret to say that our relationship has come to a hot asphalt stop. If I could just borrow your phone, I'll call for a wrecker to come remove Ol' Beulah and myself from your beautiful little town. Do you garden?"

"No phone."

"I beg your pardon?" Loman Happenstance's long-lasting perma-smile faltered for a moment. Lips quivered and met, then reparted to form a disbelieving O. "No phone?"

"Nope. You're in the famed Middle of Nowhere, friend. Communication out here is a thing of terrible uncertainty. My perceptions of time and distance are equally shaky. It's the landscape, you see. Desert meets mountain. Metaphysical borderland."

"Well, how in the name of . . ." Loman paused until he regained his beauty pageant smile. "I suppose if you need something, then you just drive to the nearest town, right?"

"Nearest town is seventy-five miles that way." I pointed my whole hand, empty glass and all, eastward. "And I don't own a car."

Loman Happenstance swooned to a seat on the larger of his two cases.

"Nosiree," I said. "Got shed of it 13 years ago. On the mutual birthday of Shakespeare and Nabokov. Sold it to a football player on his way to college. He gave me a brand new thesaurus inscribed, 'Love, Aunt Enid,' and I tossed him my key ring, feeling a little guilty, knowing full well I'd come out ahead in the deal. Understand the boy has done all right for himself, despite the curse of my Ford. He owns a nightclub in Dallas. Hoss's Beerateria. Sends me a Christmas card each December with a picture of his boy in it. Pup was conceived in the spring-sprung seat of the same truck I drove my daddy's coffin out to the cemetery in. Fathers and sons. Pappies and their midget reflections."

Loman Happenstance did not know how to react to my weird little soliloquy. There was a West Texas pause that a bobwhite rushed to fill with a litany of monotonous, questioning squeaks. Loman rubbed the back of his neck and produced his biggest, bedsheet-whitest grin. "I don't believe I caught your name," he ventured.

(Now, this was a moment of great strife in the roadrunner life of Loman Happenstance. I had thrown him the at-least-partially-true crazy country coot act, and he was at a crossroads. He knew there was no way he could walk seventy-five miles in those dad-blamed shoes. So how would he handle me? He was a salesman, a people person par excellence. Did he have any ready-made plans for being trapped in a ghost town with a lunatic? No. "This will be my greatest performance," he must have thought to himself.)

"Cayman Bliss," I said. "Pleased to meet you."

"Well, Cayman," Loman began. He was back on his feet, ready to try again now that he had a name to play with. "You're a sort of Robinson Crusoe out here it appears. Do you have a Friday-man bring your groceries or how do you get on?"

There was a patronizing tone in Loman's trombonish voice. Like maybe he was humoring a loony woman until her husband wrote out the check for a shipment of squash seeds. I didn't like it one bit. Decided to pull out all the organ stops.

"My childhood was full of balloons and gladiolas," I said. "Daddy was a balloonist, of sorts, and Momma damn near became a gladiola herself. She lived and breathed the blossomy things. Both these hobbies came about in a summer I can remember like my last gulp of wine. The train station over there was constantly getting strange items dropped off with no reason at all. And after letting the mysterious boxes—ill-addressed and full of secrets—sit on the dusty platform a week or so, Daddy would drag home the treasure chests, and we would all hold our breath while his Old Timer cut the cardboard wide open. The lids Jack-in-the-Can popped up, and we leaned forward, then backward while Daddy reached in slow, picked up cautious and raised high and proud a new prize courtesy of God or the Southern Pacific or maybe—as I used to dream—some long lost aunt trying to contact us from elsewhere.

"Daddy, knife bright in his left hand, knelt before a big green box. Momma went and fetched her pinking shears so she could neatly unravel the second package's well-traveled enigma.

"Here's what was inside Momma's package: gladiola bulbs. Twenty-eight thousand eight hundred of them. All colors, we would later find out.

"Here's what was inside the trunk that Daddy sliced into: balloons. Seventy-two thousand. All round. In these colors: blue, orange, green, red, yellow.

"Momma looked at Daddy. Daddy looked at her. I looked at the new treasures and wondered, What on earth will come of this?"

While I spoke, the hours passed, until it was almost midnight and Loman Happenstance sat bolt-upright, half-drunk and wide-eyed in Momma's wicker porch swing. He had taken to the apple wine with some enthusiasm, punctuating my story with gulps, belches and the occasional "Golly." So, I knew I had his fullest attention when I cleared my throat one last time and launched—finally—into the finale.

I said, "The October night we buried Daddy under six feet of soil and a whole layer of gladiola bulbs Momma fell asleep at the kitchen table and refused to wake up. Her poor old heart was broke open like a peacock egg. She'd written 'Fly Me To The Moon,' on the back of *The Farmer's Almanac* in her last lucid moments, and that's exactly what I did. It took 2000 balloons (the orange ones were all there was left) and a whole night of helium pumping, but at dawn—fingernails splintered from tying knots—I was ready to cut the ropes. Momma's old four-poster lifted off like a dream. A princess being carried away off into Mexico by a whole flock of pumpkins. It was a Viking funeral, of sorts, the way Jules Verne might have reported it."

"I'll be damned," Loman said, swaying off into slumber.

The night was velvet-painting smooth and quiet. I could hear Happenstance's breathing, deep and relaxed, an air-conditioner addict coming down off his freon high to find that the natural ether of the night was a trip well worth taking.

"I'll be," Loman mumbled in his sleep.

The next morning, over breakfast, I explained to Loman that he might could catch a ride to town with the postman if he should happen to come by in the next couple of days. "Or sooner or later a train is sure to ratchet by and you could hobo a ride to Dryden. Then again, you are perfectly welcome, sir, to bunk here for as long as you like. I so rarely have the luxury of a visitor. And by the jelly-fish blue bags swimming under your eyes, I can tell you are in most dire need of a week or a month of do nothing vacation time."

"A vacation!" Loman exclaimed. "Never in my life have I been wont to shirk my responsibilities! Do I seem to you, sir, a slacker?" Loman eyed me hurtfully.

"Responsibilities," I mimicked Loman's voice unintentionally, weighed the word on the tip and sides and rear of my tongue. "Who are you responsible to besides yourself? You got any family?"

"No."

"That company you work for gonna holler 'BANKRUPTCY!' if they miss an order or three of pansy flats?"

Loman remained quiet. He listened carefully.

"You'll be a better salesman, boy, if you take a breather and regroup your synapses."

Loman cleared his throat and hummed the first few bars of "Anything Goes."

"A *vacation*. Magic word for most. A mystery to me." Loman wrinkled up his eyebrows. "What in the bejeezus would I do out here to vacation?"

"Wonderful things, amigo," I said. "A sloppy parade of wonderful things."

The chameleons—all 131 of them; I'd tell you their names, but I'm no good with names—the chameleons watched attentively while I thumbed through a stack of postcards. Loman Happenstance's gaze darted ping-pong style between my rustling and the lizards' tongue-flick patience. "*These* were left at the depot?" he asked, pointing at the reptiles underfoot. "*These* came on a train?"

"Indeed. The box in which they arrived," I told Loman, "was addressed to SVEN GARLIC'S VAUDEVILLE HOEDOWN, but it ended up here. Stamped LIVE ANIMALS and poked full of holes. I couldn't endure Pa's traditional week-long 'somebody-might-come-claim-it' wait, you know. I just opened her up and there they were. Four dozen little baby dragons is what they looked like. They've grown quite a bit since then. I reckon this is their full size.

"Now," I continued, "I have always been a lover of art, you see. It has been a hobby of mine to write museums and galleries the world over requesting postcards of their more famous and dramatic pieces. For instance, here's a little 'Guernica.'"

The chameleons, a lime-green, sized-ten tennis shoe army, leaned toward me, their eyes fixed on the postcard I held. I noticed their attention and shielded the card from their hungry stares, slowly put it back—face-down—on the tabletop.

"I didn't realize what they were good for for the longest time. I just let them run around the house like a reptilian Our Gang. Then one day I got a postcard of Van Gogh's 'Starry Night' and just held it up for them look at. As a sort of joke, you know. Bam! As soon as they saw what I was holding they junebug-quick—well, here's that 'Starry Night' now," I said, fishing the battered card out of a pile of Warhol soupcans. "Watch this," I whispered.

I turned the postcard around so that the chameleons could get a good look at it. Without hesitation they began to scurry around the floor, tails sliding and claws scratching maniacally. Then, door-slam resolute, they stopped moving and Loman Happenstance had to suppress the urge to holler.

"It may take them a couple of seconds to get the colors absolutely right," I explained. In a whisper, I added, "Some of them are a little slow."

Gradually the lizards' hides began to change, becoming bumpy brushstrokes of blue and black, sunbursts of yellow. A moment or two later Mr. Van Gogh's far-away suns and swirling cosmic airs sat right before our eyes, a 'Starry Night' more perfect than any your average museum guard has ever frowned upon. "Oh my god," said Loman, dumbfounded.

"This? Oh, this is relatively easy. They do a knockout 'Washington Crossing the Delaware.' And this," I confided, "is my most favorite one."

I held another postcard in my right hand. This time, though, I kept the artwork a secret from Loman. After I flashed the card at the chameleons, I couldn't help but laugh out loud at their jumping-bean deconstruction. Whilst my laughter subsided, so did the lizards' wild contortions.

"The Mona Lisa!" Loman yelled.

"Living and breathing," I pointed out.

The last one to get it right was—as always—the mouth one. He had to readjust his tail several times before the new creation was Xerox-perfect, the tail-turned-mouth blushing, curving ever-so-slightly into . . . what is that? a smirk? a smile? a just-kissed smacker?

After the lizards successfully stacked themselves into a bone-white facsimile of the Venus de Milo, I felt the need to stretch my legs a bit. "Let's give them a rest and take a little stroll," I suggested to Loman.

We meandered out back by the windmill and water tank. It was a hazy, wasp-thirsty mid-morning, and our feet squishing around the wet grass sounded like a bunch of cows molesting a field of bubblegum.

Squish, squish, squish, our shoes went.

For about the millionth time, Loman said, "But—But—"

"Oh, hell, Happenstance," I said. "'Is it art? Is it not art?' Who gives a damn? I didn't make the lizards, but I gave them the inspiration to paint. If I'm not the artist, then at least I'm the artists' patron. Fact is, it doesn't matter. They're happy. I'm happy. We're both happier for knowing each other."

Then it hit me. "Loman Happenstance," I said, "what on earth did you ever make? Did you at any time fingerpaint or mold your Pa an ashtray for Christmas? Build a birdhouse in shop class or spray paint your best girl's name on a train trestle? Have you once cooked a good meal from scratch or sung Puccini in the shower? Surely some summer you lifeguard-tanned at the community pool or beer-dizzy bunny-hopped your way around a Valentine dance? What have you made, Loman Happenstance, with your hands or your mouth or the waggling of your limbs? What's your Momma got magnet-stuck on her Frigidaire that you can call your own?"

Loman, head bowed, admitted, "I don't think I did any of those things." His feet were muddy up to his ankles.

"Well, this is a first for me," I announced to the spiraling buzzards above. "I can't remember ever having had a conversation with a corpse before. And them shoes are ruined."

Loman Happenstance sat at the kitchen table all night long. He had a roll of paper towels, a cigar box full of Crayolas and a bottle of Southern Comfort to keep him company through the night's blackest hours, and the farm report on my radio to occupy his eardrums at dawn.

He spent the whole of the day out by the water tank, measuring with a yardstick and lugging his largest suitcase around.

He spent the next day doing the same.

The postman came by on the third day, and I hollered out the window to Loman that he might be able to catch a ride into town, but he ignored me and went right on crawling around in the short, mushy grass.

That evening he came in for dinner and said, "Voila!"

I rushed to the window and looked out, but the backyard looked the same as ever to me. "Is it something minimalist?" I asked.

"Your perceptions of time and distance are shaky," Loman reminded me. "It's the landscape, remember? Anyhow, the thing to do now is wait." He sat down at the table and began to spoon green beans onto his plate. Shamrock green green beans, Alaska white plate.

For weeks I watched out the kitchen window to see what Loman had wrought. He'd planted a whole bunch of stuff, sure, but it looked kind of haphazard, the sprouts, the sky-pushing green stalks. I never questioned him, though, and he never offered any explanations. In truth, *he* himself never looked out back to see what was growing there. He spent his days like I did. Playing with the lizards. Reading from the family library. Rocking on the front porch with a glass of apple wine and an every-evening earful of coyote choir recital.

Finally, one misty A.M. Loman asked me if I kept a ladder about the place and I showed him out to the chicken shed. We dragged the ladder over to the house and leaned it fully extended up against the rain gutter. It reached the roof and a little bit more.

Without a word Loman began his precarious ascension and—equally silent—I followed.

Ladder tops, as you may well know, are tricky things to handle. The whole of this feat required a slow and muscular patience. At last I stood (warily) on the dewy shingles and looked at where Loman was directing his gaze, to the mysterious back-yard garden of one seed salesman extra-extraordinaire.

"Sweet mother of pearl," I whispered. I was surprised and surprised at myself for being surprised.

"Edward Hopper's 'Nighthawks,'" Loman announced unnecessarily. For this re-production of the lonely night cafe was exquisite beyond belief. A giant, perfect copy of Hopper's famous painting done brilliant in gardenias and mums and lilies and orchids and daisies and enough bluebonnets to make the Daughters of the Alamo Fighters blush in their coon-skinny gift shop. It was a one-better-than the Rose parade would never come close to.

"Loman," I said, "It's beautiful."

Loman took a deep breath and sighed. "It's a picture that has always made me feel like I wanted to be home. I just hate it that they have to be so lonely, those people in that diner. Those poor, lonely souls."

Then Loman, without so much as a sigh, left my side and climbed down the ladder. I heard him go into the house. A few minutes later, he emerged carrying his suitcase and a cardboard sign which read, "MILLER'S POINT." He walked to the side of the road and stood there, not more than ten yards from his dead automobile. I'd never noticed it before, but from up here, I could see that he was a little bald on top.

I started to holler something down to him, but before I could work up the breath, a train came bulleting around the mesa and stopped to drop off my monthly grocery supply. Calmly and deliberately Loman walked to the engine and pulled himself up into the driver's cabin. The train departed with a long, happy whistle.

Every day I climbed roof-top and marveled at Loman's masterpiece, wished that he might have stayed on a while longer. You see, I thought for a time that Loman had left mad at me for my attack on his artless life.

Then, slowly, I began to realize the picture was changing, and it became obvious in leaves and blooms that Loman had left me with a gift of enormous faith and thanks. Maybe even love. Hopper's night diner was magically filling up with customers. They grew into a laughing crowd of nurses and gangsters and symphony conductors and firefighters and astronauts and telephone operators. Eventually, daylight overtook the diner and the people began to leave, going home in pairs and groups of four.

And when it was gone, all of it, the people and the diner, every last hint of the wonderful West Texas Sprouting of Loman Happenstance, I went back to the lizards. They were crawling on the ceiling doing their best to reproduce the Sistine Chapel. But there wasn't enough of them to complete the whole. God reached out to touch Adam, but Adam wasn't there.

As it was, Our Scaly Father Above ended up pointing a wiggling finger at yours truly.

OLYMPIA VERNON

The Manship Theater in Baton Rouge filled to over-flowing when Olympia Vernon received the Ernest J. Gaines Award for Literary Excellence; latecomers had to watch the ceremony on monitors in extra rooms. Vernon and Gaines were seated onstage in comfortable chairs while introductions and speeches were made. Then Vernon herself stood, walked to the podium and began to read from *A Killing in This Town*. Afterwards, a well-known Baton Rouge poet proclaimed that she had never heard anything like it, that it was an out-of-body experience, that Vernon's prose sounded like poetry.

One of seven children, Vernon was born in Bogalusa, Louisiana. "When I was a child," she said, "I slept with pens and pencils in my bed. When I was in the womb, I had words in my head, yet to be sent out into the world." Despite her awareness of these early inclinations to write, she received her BA degree in Criminal Justice, believing she might go into law enforcement "to help people." But even as she studied for that degree, her teachers encouraged her to enroll in the LSU MFA program, where she says she found her voice. In interviews, if asked about her themes of racial injustice, death, violence and cruelty, Vernon replies that she has no thematic intentions; characters come into her head and stay until they're done with her.

And what stories they have to tell. In *Eden,* a young girl, punished for a minor wrongdoing, is sent to her aunt, who is dying a grotesquely painful death from breast cancer; in *Logic,* a young girl, mentally damaged by a fall from a tree, enters adolescence with a skewed view of the world then must deal with her stepfather's sexual advances; and in *A Killing in This Town*, a white boy in Mississippi fights his destiny as the next youth in line to call out a black man so that the whites in town can murder him.

When asked how he taught such a gifted student, James Gordon Bennett, Vernon's professor at LSU, replied with a smile, "I just got out of her way." Olympia herself says that her writing "comes from angels," that she is in another land while telling their stories. In this excerpt from *The Effigy*, Vernon, using her decidedly inventive language, turns her gaze once again to the lives of children confronting the reality of death.

OLYMPIA VERNON

from *The Effigy*

Victory plucked a stain from her white blouse.

She wore trousers of the muslin kind, the fabric blinding.

The sun's impression of her darted ahead with ascension.

A cord of endurance lived in her face: she was an oracle; a wave of heat rose around her; the multiplicity of death and dying, of drownings, of lynchings, of wars layered, equally and without apology, an irrefutable seam upon her flesh.

Unless one were to stand closely, the seam would go unnoticed—it was not so visible—it blended; it shivered in the charcoal-languished river of her pupils and skin; she was the shape and tint of carbon, crushed and excavated from the hand of anthropology; her lips were puckered, as if she were naked, posing with indignation; her hair was white and clamped. A space lingered with a great degree of expansion between her molars. She had not lost her tongue at all. It had not been cut out, as the weak.

It was her property and she spoke of this, as she had spoken of death and dying and those atrocities drawn out before her ineptly.

She lived in Ellis County, Mississippi—she had baptized the two birds in the river, and now they were dead, one dark, one pale, dead—the coroner had come for her, his hair disheveled.

He leaned his ribs over a chair in her kitchen and winced.

The entire happening trembled in her head.

For in this town with its impoverished People, its seasonal pregnancy and warmth, its constant chatter about The Second Coming, there was this, this rising and shifting between the houses, this phenomenal depiction of blood and its speckling of the world's canvas lurking above Them with its urinary-tinted pavilion.

It was this, all of it, lasting and dying throughout the rectangular and squared one-roomed houses of the town, atomizing the honeysuckles and its branches, its dust, so that it seemed to loom covertly in the flesh and stench of the cattle, the sound of the whistling train bellowing and moving on at noon its merciless cadence.

Cubb and Autumn lagged behind her on the road to The Hill.

They, too, were dressed in fabric of the muslin kind: they wore white blouses and trousers, tailored to fit. They endured inexhaustibly. They challenged, lurked in those places of exclusion, and yes, yes, it was Autumn Victory had found spiraling in the river, till she pulled her out of It, and It was always, always there in her mind, having been pulled out of the Mississippi, how Victory put her mouth on hers, until her lungs were emptied so that she lost sight of the world and lay there unconscious.

Autumn was fair-skinned and round. She was twelve. The dirt of the Mississippi was in her hair; it was coarse and parted down the center with a barrette conjoining two braids at the top of her head; she swung her arms when she spoke; she spoke theoretically; there were things she believed not believed previously—in her mind— or told to her and she was not concerned with what *they* felt; she was a liar; she guessed, formed an opinion about the world that cloaked her with illusion; she lied, and pierced her company with her falsities, so that she was comforted.

There was that one about having been born of beasts.

She pointed to a rectangular fold in her sock.

But Cubb could not bear to look at it.

She was of two moons and habits.

A Gemini of ten years who would not purr or express her feelings outwardly.

She only whispered, masking the jury of freckles her face held, into Autumn's ear her words and sentiment, her derision and interrogation, out from the pale and red-haired block of. . . .I don't talk, she whispered, 'cause I don't want to.

With this, she poked Autumn's rib.

She could see them.

Ahead were the mourners.

They fanned and stirred with intensity atop The Hill. Those exposed to the death of the two dead birds stood with their faces veiled and blurred, a cove of children in their presence, as it would not rain.

The urinary-tinted pavilion had vanished.

Cubb and Autumn clung to Victory's waist now.

They had begun to realize they were a part of something new and dirty.

They neared the mouth of The Hill and the crowd dispersed; it was the casket they had noticed suddenly: it lay somberly on the flatbed of a battered automobile.

The men and women further dispersed and the cove of children tilted their faces, the jawline configuring into the brazen heat a soaring blade of pity.

> *The murderer rising with the*
> *Light killeth the poor and needy, and*
> *In the night is a thief.*
>
> Job 24:19.

Victory had spoken.

She lifted her arms and a veiled member of the crowd whispered, *Come, come,* to Cubb and Autumn. They had begun to whimper.

They went with her, their breathing withheld in the pale fabric.

Victory, with her face to the clouds, raised her arms and brought them into her bosom, before releasing them into the crowd. The mourners wept.

For Victory paused and looked upward.

The Spirit had calmed her.

She did not speak for the span of what seemed, to the mourners, an eternity.

The sun interpreted this and moved Its hip over her; a wing emerged in her shadow and she broke through the crowd, the second wing hovering over the width of the coffin on the flatbed—the driver stepped away from the automobile and removed his hat; he was of his late fifties, grey-haired and sodden by the Cloth of living—Victory approached him, while the mourners held their children, and centered the first and second wing of her plumage over the two birds:

Some glad morning when this life is o'er, I'll fly away

One of the mourners crushed her face with a napkin. The first and second wing fluttered over the cave of her mouth and she broke; her husband seemed a pistil amidst the blooming of her sorrow. He held her together.

The others joined Victory.

I'll fly away, O Glory, I'll fly away

The sun's hip bordered the first and second wing with luminosity.

A shrill permeated the lyric.

The mother of the first dead bird stood on the edge of the porch in mourner's white; her head was covered in it; she was barefoot, the destructible age of insomnia in her eyes. For a lighted furnace was inside of her bosom, stirring and fluttering about, burning, burning and death was in the middle of it. The white moon had induced a beam across her round face. She examined her fingers, held her blouse.

She wondered how she could bear this life and sun without Shelby's living under it. Her face was in the clouds. Tears streamed from her breast and heart.

With her husband at her shoulder, the mother of the second dead bird wept into a divided line that sprung forth under the skin—it would forever remain, now that the child of whom she had been a part was dead. Her hair, feverish and wet, was at her shoulders, unbound and clayed like an unclipped ribbon stripped from the poise of a shoulder. She looked at her husband, whose face had been crushed by his mother's pelvis upon his birth, both of them pale and yielding to what had come.

Come, my children, Come, said Victory.

Her wings began to flutter. The mothers of the two dead birds marched, as One, down the steps of the one-roomed house and she drew her wings around them.

Cubb and Autumn looked upon the first and second wing.

The lyric resonated and brewed in their ears, and although Cubb had not spoken, because she had not wanted to, she peered at Autumn from the fabric of a mourner's rib, for both had imagined inwardly, and with mortification, that they were the dead, that this casket bearing the two birds was theirs.

Autumn, with all her embellishments, could not think of a lie in her head of which to seek attention and pity, when the first mother of the dead bird was round like her, with hair like hers, except with a seed that had passed through her stomach that was now dead.

Victory beckoned for the children to come—the mothers of the two dead birds were yet cloaked and sobbing under the first and second wing—and the children, there were eight of them, including Cubb and Autumn, gathered upon the rim of the flatbed, with its petrifaction, its coffin, until sitting sturdily on the shoulder of it.

They could not walk the mile to the river where the two birds would be buried. A fuschia-colored ribbon lulled in the clouded sky.

When I die, Hallelujah, by and by. I'll fly away

Victory led Abby and Tiko Garrett along the journey.

The mourners sang and followed the coffined automobile with their children on it.

The driver waded upon the dirt road and the automobile of death trudged on past the little houses gathered and fixed at the road's edge.

A mother cried out, upon occasion, My Lawd, she whispered. My Lawd.

The second mother comforted her.

Her husband was at her shoulder. The death of the second bird had aged him considerably. He walked as though creeled by a fisherman, thinking of his birth, of having come Here. There was only her now—he knew that—and the paternal elation he had possessed for a short term.

He had not even let his tears flow.

Cubb and Autumn were on either side of the coffined automobile, and Cubb, now that she wanted to speak, could not, with this new and phosphoric energy thrown at her: she gazed at the coffin, her eyes singularly set upon them and Victory. She wished, with her young heart, that she had always spoken and never at all been quiet.

And thus, she hummed:

Like a bird from prison bars has flown, I'll fly away
I'll fly away, O Glory, I'll fly away

Victory and the mourners marched through the womb of Ellis County.

There were children and men and women on the porches of their one-roomed houses, their postures needling through the heat of the breeze the discernible posture of death. They stood with their pale and dark faces, with their poverty, their own phosphoric devastation. They glowed in this heat.

They wept and held their children close.

The dust encapsulated them and their children, once released, ran and followed the Ford down the dirt road and stopped to look at each other, count their fingers.

They were a part of the country, the world, and however unprotected, the vine, webbed with its entangled dust, captured them invisibly.

The bridge approached.

Victory paused atop a little mound of dirt and looked at Cubb and Autumn—a whisper trapped in their throats—where they seemed to ask something of her with their eyes and face that she could not return. Not now.

She raised the first and second wing and brought the lyric to a close.

The mourners quieted and there was only the sound of the coffined automobile upon the earth. It had stopped.

The children were in the green now.

Autumn beckoned with her index finger for Cubb to join her.

An ant had gotten loose in her sock.

She squatted in the distance with her foot angled in front of her.

But Cubb had not come.

For she knew that an ant had not gotten loose, it had not, it simply had not, it was just that, that Autumn had insisted upon bringing that dreadful clipping, that that bloody one of the two birds, murdered, next to, next to that picture of the little, moustached man with the queer tattoo on his shoulder.

Why would she want to look at that?

No wonder, Cubb thought. No wonder it had bitten her.

So she joined the others, the women and children, the mothers of the two dead birds, while the coffin landed near the rectangular hole in the earth.

Let us pray, said Victory.

The blade of the first and second wing hovered over the mothers of the two birds and the remaining mourners took their children's faces in their hands and leaned them forward.

> *So Christ was once offered to*
> *Bear the sins of many; and unto them*
> *That look for Him shall He appear the*
> *Second time without sin unto salvation.*
>
> Hebrews 9:28

A mother cried out, her eyes sheltered from the blinding reign of the sun.

Lawd, have mercy, she yelled. Lawd, have mercy.

The scent of the hammered pelvis rose in the burning heat.

The mourners wept.

This was the lighted furnace, stirring and fluttering about, burning, burning, and it seemed now to belong elsewhere, to be diminishing, and as children come into the

Universe bearing the fossilized orb of the waters . . . it was taking shape, they could not see it, but it was there, drifting down their throats with a current of nostalgia.

Let them sleep, whispered Victory.

Her wings shifted over the northern end of the coffin.

These things do We ask in the presence of the Almighty Father, whispered Victory. Let Us all say, Amen.

The mourners whispered, in unison, Amen.

There she was, lying behind the mourners with the clipping pulled out from under her, as if she were planted; plopped; irredeemable in the center of a vast garden of, of, of poison. Amen, whispered Autumn.

She looked upward.

The urinary-tinted pavilion was returning.

Six men retrieved the coffin from its setting, and lowered it into the ground.

The mother of the second dead bird took up a fistful of mounted dirt and spread it over the coffin. The echo chimed in her bones.

Her husband encased her in his sleeve.

Two women abandoned their children in the nest of mourners and escorted the mother of the first dead bird to the coffin where she partook of the mounted dirt and released it from her fingertips. Someone fanned her with a page.

She could only remember the fall she had not broken when the paper arrived, centered and wedged between her pelvis and spine, how the world would not carry her.

There were those happenings a Mother could not imagine in her mind; but, now, now the rigor mortis, with its phosphoric burning, hung there burning above her, and there was that photograph, the tattoo, all of it, enflamed and bursting.

Her wrist trembled from the cove of children wading past her, peering over the cavity with its edge. They hadn't noticed at all that she'd fainted.

All were there in the cove, but Autumn, who had been lying in the green with her foot jutted out, until the burning reached her eardrum and coughed.

Victory and the mother of the second dead bird heard it.

One could not help but notice.

It was so close.

Come, come, my child, beckoned Victory. Come.

And thus, she went, with her tiny beak opening and closing over the mother of the first dead bird, the dirt of the Mississippi in her hair, until her breath spiraled out of her and she lay there beside the Mother with her young lungs emptied.

She heard voices, of Victory, the children and their cove spinning and darting in and out of the burning, and she imagined that she was dead and this was *her* funeral, and that everyone, all of them had come to see . . . *her*.

The mother of the first dead bird coughed.

Look, Cubb whispered.

The clipping, mired by some sort of weighable deficiency, had begun to toss and flicker under the urinary-tinted pavilion—like a fire dying down in the dust—where an organic trail of blood dotted the contours of Its shoulder and pushed Its jaw forward.

JAMES WILCOX

James Wilcox is widely praised and admired for his diplomacy and professionalism by creative writing students, English department faculty, and, indeed, the university at large. As director of the creative writing program, he has shared the credit with a distinguished faculty for LSU's inclusion on *Poets & Writers Magazine's* list of the top 50 MFA programs in the nation. He has been honored both in and out of the university, with his Guggenheim Fellowship in 1986, repeated listings among the *New York Times* Notable Books, the Robert Penn Warren Professorship from 2004 to 2007, and in 2009 with the title Distinguished Research Master. In spite of these accomplishments, Wilcox remains modest and often self-deprecatory. He would never tell you, nor would he even want you to know, that one of his novels was included in Harold Bloom's *The Western Canon*.

During his time at LSU, Wilcox has produced two novels: *Heavenly Days* and *Hunk City*. But critical acclaim came to him as early as the publication of his first novel. For example, in her *New York Times* review of *Modern Baptists*, Anne Tyler wrote that Wilcox possessed a "comic genius." The story is set in the small southern town of Tula Springs and filled with oddball characters who have become his trademark: Mr. Pickens, whom Tyler described as an "aimless, spineless, weak-kneed, . . . 41-year-old bachelor"; F.X., his handsome, ne'er-do-well brother; Toinette Quaid, Mr. Pickens' love interest and cashier at Sonny Boy Bargain Department Store; and Burma LaSteele, who is 37 years old, yet still lives at home with her mother. These unlikely characters, whose foibles define them, are the staple of the Wilcox novel—we scoff at them and cry for them, but mostly, we laugh at their impossible antics, their unlikely love interests, their beliefs and disbeliefs.

As they search for love and spiritual connection, in almost every way possible, Wilcox's characters, such as Donna Lee Keely in "Camping Out," make their own lives impossible. They are, in other words, much like us when we're at our most vulnerable. And for that reason, Wilcox's avid fans, accustomed to his regularity of publication, eagerly await his newest comedy of manners. Meanwhile, Wilcox persists, quietly adding prestige and dignity to the LSU MFA program, and unobtrusively collecting material.

JAMES WILCOX

Camping Out

Donna Lee and Mrs. Norris went first; behind them in the green, dented eighteen-footer were Donna Lee's father, her brother-in-law, and her nephew, Ralph. Tula Creek was high, and the canoes glided silently, like awkward, heavy-laden clouds, over uprooted trees and clay mounds big as the humped, grey backs of Brahma bulls. Donna Lee was the most experienced canoeist, Mrs. Norris the least, which was the reason they were paired. In the other canoe seven-year-old Ralph was the only one who had mastered the J-stroke, a paddling technique that kept the boat in line from the stern. Donna Lee had tried to teach her father and Henry, her brother-in-law, the J-stroke, but they claimed they already knew.

When they passed the place where the gravel works cut a chunk out of the vine-tangled banks of river birch, Donna Lee looked over her shoulder and shouted back to Ralph that they were out of Mississippi now, in Louisiana. The overloaded green canoe was sliding along sideways, and Ralph's face was red with the effort of trying to get it straightened out. Donna Lee began yelling instructions to her brother-in-law, who was in the stern of the green canoe. Henry was big—six feet eight, a former L.S.U. basketball star—but he didn't know what "draw" meant, which was what Donna Lee was yelling at him. The shouting woke Donna Lee's father, who had been snoozing in the middle of the green canoe with his legs draped over the ice chest, as if the river were his living room. Mr. Keely grabbed a paddle and started churning up the tea-brown water with intense, futile strokes.

Donna Lee couldn't take any more for now. They had been on the river only three hours, including a stop for lunch, but it seemed like days. She was worried about her father—he was overweight and had high blood pressure—and she herself was freezing to death. As she sat in the stern trying to compensate for Mrs. Norris's erratic strokes—they were feathery, artistic, frosting-smoothing strokes—the cold went right through Donna Lee's ancient raccoon coat and lumberjack shirt. The long underwear that she had borrowed from her father hung too loosely on her tall, gangly frame to be any help.

When the bow of the canoe grated on the sandy peninsula where Donna Lee planned to make camp for the night, Mrs. Norris just sat there. Donna Lee politely asked her to try to get out of the canoe. Mrs. Norris, who seemed fairly competent on dry land, had to be told *everything* on the river, as if she had just landed on another planet with a whole new set of physical laws.

Climbing out of the stern, Donna Lee smiled at Mrs. Norris's back. They had met only two weeks ago, in Mr. Herbert's law office in Tula Springs, where Donna Lee, a year out of law school, worked as a junior partner. Mrs. Norris's landlady was trying to evict her. It wasn't a clear-cut case, and Donna Lee had already spent an inordinate amount of time on it, which Mr. Herbert thought unwise. Donna Lee was not concerned; she had decided she wanted to make Mrs. Norris her friend. In her early sixties, Mrs. Norris looked very commonplace, with a bland, weary face and stiff, dyed red hair. But her life had been far from ordinary. Born and raised in South Africa, Mrs. Norris married a French physician who ran a small clinic in Léopoldville specializing in rare tropical diseases. For years she worked alongside him as a nurse, until one day one of the experimental monkeys went berserk— "clear off its rocker," as she had told Donna Lee—and bit the doctor. It was only a minor injury, but he was never the same afterward, and sank into a morose obsession with his stamp collection. They were divorced, and she married her English lover, Mr. Norris, who took her to Bolton, England. Twenty-five years her senior, Mr. Norris died a few weeks later of a heart attack while sparring in an amateur boxing match for a local charity. Next came a Montana ranch, owned by the late Mr. Norris's sister. There, the newly widowed Mrs. Norris was thrown from a snowmobile during a blizzard and nearly froze to death; luckily, all she lost was a big toe. She decided she wanted to live where it was warm, so she moved to New Orleans and had a long, happy affair with a Peruvian who was involved in smuggling something. When New Orleans began to seem too big for her, she moved eighty miles north, to Tula Springs, where she worked as a nurse for a chiropractor and studied acupuncture.

Donna Lee told Mrs. Norris to sit down and rest while she unloaded the canoe. Mrs. Norris found a driftwood log and sat down on it. "Can't I help?" she called out, but the green canoe had just pulled up, and Donna Lee didn't hear her.

Ralph clambered out of the canoe, with tears making his large dark-brown eyes look even larger. He hurried past his aunt and disappeared into the woods at the end of the peninsula.

"He's too sensitive," Mr. Keely said, lugging the ice chest out of the canoe. "Henry didn't even raise his voice to him."

"Dad, be careful," Donna Lee said. She took the ice chest from him. She didn't want to get into a big discussion now about Ralph. Donna Lee thought it was the nuns who made Ralph so sensitive. Henry was Catholic, and Ralph had to go to catechism on Sundays. He had shown her what he was learning about making his first confession, and Donna Lee did not like it one bit.

After they unloaded both canoes, Ralph emerged from the woods with an armload of kindling and set it down in front of Mrs. Norris, who was smiling absently at the river. "That's my man," Donna Lee said, putting a hand on his shoulder. Ralph was big for his age and exceptionally well coordinated. His father had high hopes for him as an athlete. "Now listen, everyone," she said, keeping her hand on the boy, "the first thing we've got to do is get a fire started. Dad, don't try to put up that tent yourself. Help Henry find some wood. And get a whole lot; it's going to get real cold tonight."

The men trudged off through the sand, followed by Ralph. "I'll go, too," Mrs. Norris said, getting off her log.

"That would be nice," Donna Lee said. Although she was only twenty-six years old, Donna Lee was determined not to let age create a barrier between her and Mrs. Norris. She wanted to treat her like any other girl friend.

Donna Lee unpacked the Coleman stove and lit the colorless gas flame, then noticed that Mrs. Norris was still standing right behind her. "I believe Ralph went over there," Donna Lee said, pointing to a thicket of river birch and sycamore. "Honey?"

"Oh, yes," Mrs. Norris said.

"You can stay here, of course. But I think you'd be warmer if you moved around a little."

"I'll help Ralph; lovely idea." She set off rather mechanically for the woods, like one of "Star Wars'" genteel, battered robots. Donna Lee sighed and shook her head.

After unpacking the food from the ice chest, Donna Lee took a swig of Jack Daniel's to warm herself up. She was sure she was going to get a terrible cold from this camp-out and would spend the rest of the Christmas holidays in bed. She was not happy here, but she couldn't have stood another day with the family milling around the house in Tula Springs. She had her own little apartment a mile from the house, but she felt guilty staying there during the holidays, especially after Henry, Ralph, and Sister, Donna Lee's sister, had come all the way from Houston for Christmas. Sister was at home now with Mrs. Keely. They thought Donna Lee was crazy for making everyone go out in freezing weather, and dragging along poor Mrs. Norris to boot. Mr. Keely tried to explain: "How can you appreciate a nice warm home if you don't rough it?" Donna Lee's mother replied, "You birds—you just don't know when you got it good." But that wasn't it; Donna Lee was not trying to help anybody appreciate a nice warm home. She wanted to make her family experience Reality; Reality to Donna Lee was something like going to the dentist—it was difficult and it some-times hurt, but it was necessary if you wanted to stay healthy.

Henry and Mr. Keely broke through the undergrowth at the edge of the woods with an impossibly large water oak. Its branches were tangled in python-thick rattan, which Mr. Keely began hacking at with Ralph's Boy Scout hatchet. Donna Lee went over to take a look; the wood was wet and rotted. "Henry, you think it's worth it?" she asked.

"Watch out," he said. Small brown sticktights clung to his salmon cashmere sweater. He had taken off his down vest and jacket. "Dad," he said to his father-in-law, "go up a little further and get that big branch loose."

"Be careful," Donna Lee said, as Mr. Keely inched himself along the trunk, the hatchet drooping from his back pocket. "I really think—"

"What's for dinner?" Henry asked, giving her a tight smile.

"Mama packed some left-over turkey gumbo, and there's that carrot cake Sister made."

"Is that all?"

Glancing anxiously at her father, Donna Lee said, "Well, Henry, if you ask me, Americans eat too much," and walked into the woods to check on Ralph and Mrs. Norris.

They were sitting around a fire waiting for dinner. The tents were set up, the air mattresses blown up, the sleeping bags unrolled. Donna Lee looked at her watch; it was only three-thirty. She turned down the Coleman stove as low as it would go.

"It's so lovely," Mrs. Norris said. She blew into her hands to warm them.

Donna Lee smiled encouragingly at her.

"The trees, the flowing water," Mrs. Norris went on. "It makes me feel like God is so near."

Henry cleared his throat and hugged Ralph closer to him. Ralph's nose was running, and his eyes were bleary. They had already moved twice to escape the heavy smoke from the water-oak fire, which was not very warm. Mr. Keely was practically sitting in it, trying to keep his teeth from chattering.

"I feel like God is near, too," Donna Lee said from her perch on the water oak. They hadn't bothered to chop the trunk up. They just fed it to the fire little by little, root-end first.

"I thought you didn't believe in God," Henry said through a stuffed-up nose. Smoke rose from the rubber soles of his size-12 shoes.

"I believe, but not in your God." Donna Lee's long, big-knuckled fingers clasped the tin cup from which she sipped bourbon, lemon juice, and hot water. "To me, God is that sumac over there, that piece of driftwood, that Chinese tallow."

"That beer can," Henry continued, pointing toward the water's edge.

"Dad!" Ralph said, twisting his head around so he could see his father's face. Henry winked at him.

Donna Lee stood up and walked over to the beer can, which she hadn't noticed before. As she stuffed it into their garbage bag, another shot rang out in the woods. The shooting had started half an hour ago with muffled blasts from what must be deer hunters' guns. They sounded closer now.

"Well, Mrs. Norris," Mr. Keely said, running a freckled hand through his white hair, "how did you like the canoe?"

"Frightfully nice," she replied, sounding a little more British than usual. She plucked a spring of dewberry from the black leotards she wore under her tweed skirt. "Donna Lee is a smashing conductor. I feel so very safe on the waters."

"Canoeing is really not that hard, is it, Mrs. Norris?" Donna Lee said, sitting down again. "The main thing is, you got to be aware. You can't dream. For instance, remember when we came to that little patch of white water just before lunch?"

"Oh, yes. You told me to stop paddling, didn't you?"

"That's correct. If needs be, only one person should paddle. The bow and stern must be coordinated. You should never fight against each other's efforts." She was looking at Mrs. Norris, but everybody except Mrs. Norris knew she was talking to Henry, who had his eyes closed. "Canoeing should be as effortless as possible. You should always know exactly what you're doing and why."

"Very nice, yes," Mrs. Norris said.

"I think Mrs. Norris is catching on," Mr. Keely said innocently. "A few more times and she'll be—"

"Now, Dad," Donna Lee said, "tell me why you started paddling from the middle of the canoe. You only made things difficult for poor Ralph."

"It wasn't Grandpa's fault," Ralph said, peering out from a moth-eaten army blanket that covered his head like a cowl.

"Maybe not," Donna Lee said.

"Well, it wasn't *my* fault," Henry said, his eyes still closed. "I had a splinter in my hand. And everyone knows that aluminum canoe is harder to steer." His eyes opened. "In any case, I'm sure Mrs. Norris isn't interested in a post mortem. Are you, Mrs. Norris?"

"Oh, don't mind me," she replied. Another shot rang out. It was definitely closer. "But, speaking of post mortems, are we safe here?"

"Of course," Donna Lee said, pulling her raccoon coat tighter about her.

"Well, I must say," Mrs. Norris went on in her mild, singsong voice, "just a few moments ago, when you were down at the river picking up that beer can—why, Donna Lee, with that ridiculous coat of yours on, you looked just like a very tempting big deer."

Ralph laughed, and everybody, including Donna Lee, smiled, because Ralph did not laugh as often as a little boy should. "A beer deer," Mr. Keely said reaching around and tickling Ralph. Ralph squirmed in his father's arms. "More Kool-Aid, please," he said.

Donna Lee poured some into his Daniel Boone canteen as her father gave out some annoyingly fake barks of glee. "I hate to sound preachy, but I do think we should all be more careful tomorrow," she said. "We've got about four hours to go before we get to the cars, and there's some pretty tricky bends up ahead. The main thing is, you've got to be aware."

"You got to be *aware*," Ralph mimicked, astonishingly well. Everyone except Donna Lee laughed.

They held out as long as they could, but it was still light when they ate. Although Donna Lee thought it was silly, her father tied an orange tarpaulin to a pine near the woods, assuring Mrs. Norris that this would tell the hunters that humans were nearby. She thanked him, then gazed up and admired aloud the big birds that were soaring in the thermal drafts.

"Turkey vultures," Donna Lee said.

"How dreadful," Mrs. Norris muttered. She tossed an acorn into the fire and then made a vague gesture toward the white sky. "They don't *eat* turkeys, do they?" she asked.

"They'll eat anything," Donna Lee said. Reality.

"Mrs. Norris, did a monkey really bite off your big toe?" Ralph asked solemnly.

Donna Lee went crimson. She had told Ralph never to mention Africa or monkeys or toes to Mrs. Norris unless Mrs. Norris happened to talk about them herself.

"More Kool-Aid?" Donna Lee said, holding out the plastic pitcher to Ralph.

"No, Ralph dear, I lost my toe in Montana during a blizzard," Mrs. Norris said.

"Ralph is going to be in third grade next year," Donna Lee said.

"How nice," Mrs. Norris said. "And what do you want to be when you grow up, Ralph?"

"A priest," the boy said happily.

"A what?" Henry frowned at his son. "You don't want to be a priest, boy."

"I made up my mind. I'm going to be a priest in Africa, a missionary like Mrs. Norris."

"How lovely," Mrs. Norris said. "Of course, Ralph, I was just a nurse, you know— nothing very religious."

"I'll be a nurse priest, then."

Donna Lee glared across the fire at Henry.

Mr. Keely cleared his throat. "Now, Ralph," he said in a hoarse, raspy voice, "you mean you'd like to be a doctor, don't you? Everyone likes doctors."

"No, Grandpa. I have a vocation."

This was too much for Donna Lee. "Here, drink this Kool-Aid," she said, holding out the plastic pitcher again. "Finish it up for me."

"I don't want any more."

"It's fun, you'll like it," she said sternly, pouring from the pitcher into his canteen.

Ralph took the canteen from her, but when he put it to his mouth his eyes welled up with tears. The next thing Donna Lee knew, he was gone, running across the sand to the tent the men would share that night.

"Here we go again," Henry said, sighing as he stood up. He walked off slowly, a little stiffly, towards the tent.

Mrs. Norris pulled the woolen stocking cap Donna Lee had lent her over her ears and moved closer to the fire. "What happened," she asked. "Is it time for bed?"

"Henry is too soft on him," Donna Lee said, glancing over at their tent. "He's just reinforcing that kind of behavior."

"Donna Lee, let Henry alone," her father said.

"Well, I just can't stand to see poor Ralph get so misguided."

"Misguided?" Mrs. Norris put in. "But he's an angel."

"A little boy should be carefree and obnoxious and dirty and go his own way," Donna Lee said. "There'll be plenty of time to feel guilty when he grows up, don't you think?"

"Ralph can be obnoxious," Mr. Keely said, jiggling a pine branch in the fire. He smiled at Mrs. Norris. "You live way out on Sibley Street, don't you, Mrs. Norris? Those freight trains ever bother you?"

"You have no idea," she replied, shaking her head. "Every night it's the same thing—miles and miles of boxcars. I don't know; somehow it seems so vulgar." She sighed. "Donna Lee tells me you work at the Savings and Loan."

"Yes, Ma'am, I do."

"I hope I'm not being impertinent, but I've always wondered why your office is in a mobile home."

"Oh, the trailer's just a temporary setup, till we get our new office finished. It's that brick building going up by the upholstery shop."

"Of course." She winced as another shot rang out.

Exasperated by this small talk, Donna Lee got up and carried the plates and a few pots to the river. She rinsed them and scrubbed them with sand, the water numbing her fingers and seeping into her jogging shoes. She could hear her father and Mrs. Norris discussing the strawberry wine you could buy at the discount fireworks stand near the Savings and Loan trailer. Donna Lee scoured the plates so hard that a few roses in the dime-store pattern faded away.

"What's become of Ralph and Henry?" Mrs. Norris asked as Donna Lee packed the clean plates into a picnic hamper.

"Want me to go see?" Mr. Keely asked, getting to his feet.

"Oh, I wish you would. Tell Ralph I've got a surprise for him."

"Sure thing." Mr. Keely crunched through the sand to the tent near the woods.

"Margaret—you don't mind if I call you that, do you?" Donna Lee asked. Mrs. Norris smiled. "Margaret, I hope you didn't mind Ralph bringing up your—the blizzard. I must confess, I told him about you. He must have got things a little mixed up —I mean about the monkey and all. But you understand, don't you—you understand why I told him? I thought it was important that Ralph know about these things—

the starvation you saw, the leprosy and all that, what life is really like for most of the people on earth. . . ." She faltered. "I mean, you just can't imagine how parochial some people can be. Henry, for instance. His whole world is the Super Bowl and condominiums—he's in real estate. It's really sad. Anyway, I thought Ralph should know that life can be filled with adventure, that there are people like you who aren't content to just drift along, people who have *seen* things and *done* things. Do you understand?"

Mrs. Norris kept her eyes averted as if Donna Lee were not properly dressed and there was too much showing. "Of course, dear."

Donna Lee was not reassured. "You're not mad at me?" she asked, squeezing her friend's arm.

"Don't be silly."

"You're having a good time, aren't you? I mean, you don't think I've been too bossy, do you? Henry thinks I am; I can tell. I suppose he's right, too." She paused so that Mrs. Norris could contradict her. She didn't. "But I'm working on it, I'm trying to change. And anyway, *someone* has to be responsible, don't you think?"

"You fret so. Really, Donna Lee, stop worrying."

The men were now returning from the tent, with Ralph between them. Frustrated by the remote look in Mrs. Norris's eyes, Donna Lee suddenly reached out and took the older woman's mittened hands. "We will be good friends, won't we?" Donna Lee said as another shot rang out.

"Of course, of course," Mrs. Norris said faintly, freeing her hands. "Oh, I do wish Ralph had something orange to wear."

"Well, here's your surprise, dear." Mrs. Norris handed Ralph a package she had pulled out of her vinyl suitcase. They were all standing around the fire, which had been revived by some fatty pine Donna Lee had found.

Ralph opened the package and took out four long, pointed tubes with strings hanging out one end.

"What in . . . " Henry said, taking the tubes from his son. "Rockets?"

"Fireworks!" Mrs. Norris exclaimed.

Donna Lee began to frown but stopped when she saw Henry's face cloud over. "How wonderful!" she said. "Isn't this exciting, Ralph? Thank Mrs. Norris, Ralph."

"Thank you, Mrs. Norris," Ralph said. He looked over at his father.

"Yes—thank you," Henry said. "Ralph will have a good time with these once we get home."

"Oh, but my dears," Mrs. Norris said, clasping her hands together, "I thought we could celebrate tonight."

"Well, I don't know." Henry scratched his head. "These things can be dangerous. You got to know what you're doing."

"Oh, Henry," Donna Lee said. "There's nothing to it. All you do is light one end and run. Right, Mrs. Norris?"

"Precisely."

Mr. Keely took a rocket from Henry and turned it over in his hands. "Henry is right. This thing looks pretty powerful."

"You babies," Donna Lee said, winking conspiratorially at Mrs. Norris.

"I'm just saying we'll have to be careful," Mr. Keely said. He patted Ralph on the back.

"It's not just that." Henry took the rocket from his father-in-law. "I didn't tell anyone earlier, because I thought it didn't matter so much. But when I was back in the woods getting firewood I saw a no-trespassing sign. We're on private property."

"So?" Donna Lee said.

Henry reached over and took the package of fireworks from Ralph. "So? Well, honey, it just doesn't make sense to attract attention to ourselves. There might be a farmhouse or something on the other side of the woods. And those hunters . . ."

"He's got a point there," Mr. Keely said, rubbing his chin.

"Are we illegal?" Mrs. Norris asked, her smile fading.

Annoyed by the "honey" —after all, Henry was only five years older than she was—Donna Lee knelt beside Ralph and tousled his black hair. "Really, Henry, do you think someone is going to shoot us for camping one night on his beach? What do you say, Ralph?"

Ralph shrugged.

"Oh, please," Mrs. Norris said, "it's too much bother. Take them home with you, Ralph."

"Now, Margaret," Donna Lee said, "it's Ralph's present. We should let him decide. Ralph, look at me." She swivelled him around. "Tell me if you want to have fun tonight or if you'd rather be a stick-in-the-mud like your daddy."

"Donna Lee," her father said.

Donna Lee laughed. "Come on with me, Ralph. You and Mrs. Norris and I will go and have ourselves some fun."

"You're too much," Henry said, trying to sound lighthearted. "First you're lecturing us on water safety, and next, you're trying to blow us all up."

"Please, Donna Lee," Mrs. Norris said, "we'll do it some other time."

"Ralph?" Donna Lee looked him square in the eyes.

"I think if it's all right," the boy replied, turning to Mrs. Norris, "I'd like to do it at home. Thank you very much."

Donna Lee lay wide awake in the greenish dark of the tent. Beside her, Mrs. Norris tossed fitfully, muttering some sort of nonsense about oleomargarine. Squinting at her watch, Donna Lee saw that it was only eight-fifteen. She decided to try to sleep outside the tent. It would be a little colder, but at least she would have some peace.

"No!" Mrs. Norris cried out. She sat up and looked wide-eyed at Donna Lee, who was struggling to get her inflated air mattress through the tent's narrow opening. "Don't, please don't."

"Margaret, it's just me, Donna Lee," she said, a little frightened by Mrs. Norris's own fright. "I'm just moving my stuff outside."

Mrs. Norris rubbed her lumpy face. Her red hair was matted on one side, making her head look lopsided. "Oh dear," she moaned. A wide yawn. "Is it morning already? I haven't slept a wink."

Donna Lee gave the mattress a final shove. "It's still night," she said, rolling up her sleeping bag. "I'm sorry I disturbed you."

"Why are you going outside?"

"It's a little stuffy in here. I can't sleep."

"Let's talk, then. I'm not really tired either." She put her hand on Donna Lee's arm. "You know, dear, you've never told me what my chances are."

"What chances?"

"Of being evicted. All day long it's been preying on my mind. I just don't know what I'll do if I'm tossed out. I love that little apartment so much and it costs hardly anything."

"I thought the trains drove you crazy."

"I'm used to that by now. So tell me, dear, what do you think? I want to know."

Pettiness, Donna Lee thought. No matter where she went she would be surrounded by pettiness. She felt weary and old, old as the cranky old landlady who was squabbling about the eviction. "I'm going outside, Mrs. Norris. We'll talk about it later—at the office."

Lying alone by the river in her sleeping bag, Donna Lee watched the white moon rise over the river birches. She was a little nervous at first. There were strange noises all around her—a splash, a thump, and farther away, the squeal of tires, a horn blaring. But she was determined not to be afraid.

She must have drifted off, for when she opened her eyes all the way she saw that the woods were not on fire. It had only been a dream. But that rustling, that strange stir coming from the edge of the woods—that was definitely real. Her heart pounding, Donna Lee propped herself up on her elbows for a better look. The canoes, the picnic hamper, the canteen by the ashes of the campfire—everything was visible in the brilliant moonlight. And beyond, only a few feet from Ralph's tent, what looked like a single flame danced wildly, convulsively atop a sumac.

"Damn that tarp," Donna Lee said when she finally realized what it was. Getting up she stole across the campsite to the pine from which the orange tarpaulin dangled, brushing the leaves of the sumac. Another strong gust from the river shook the tarpaulin as she untied a half-hearted granny knot; the other knots, which had held the tarpaulin still, had already worked loose in the wind. Then, half frozen but no longer afraid, she went back for her sleeping bag and dragged it, along with the tarpaulin, to the sagging, mildewed tent, where, oleomargarine or no oleomargarine, she would ride out the night with Mrs. Norris—Margaret.

Bibliography

Authors Correspondence, *Southern Review* Records, RG A0040, Louisiana State University Archives, LSU Libraries, Baton Rouge, LA.

Bergen, Teresa. "An Interview with Vance Bourjaily." *New Delta Review*. Spring/Summer 1999. Vol. 16 no. 2.

Blotner, Joseph Leo. *Robert Penn Warren: A Biography*. Random House, 1997.

Cronin, Gloria L. and Ben Siegel. *Conversations with Robert Penn Warren*. University Press of Mississippi. 2005.

Fiedler, Leslie A. *The Fiedler Reader*. Prometheus Books. 1999.

Fischer, John Irwin. "Masochists, Martyrs (and Mermaids) in the Fictions of Valerie Martin." *The Southern Review*. Louisiana State University, Vol. 24, No. 2, Spring 1988.

McAlexander, Hubert H. *Conversations with Peter Taylor*. University Press of Mississippi. 1987.

Stewart, Dee. "Finding Logic: An Interview with Olympia Vernon." Suite 101.com. May 9, 2006. Copyrighted July 21, 2004. http://www.suite101.com/article.cfm/african_american_women_writers/109979/1.

Tyler, Anne. "*Modern Baptists* by James Wilcox." *New York Times*. July 31, 1983.

University of Tennessee Press. http://utpress.org/bookdetail/?jobno=T01374&authorsm=Madden,%20David.

Wilson, Mary Ann. "In Another Country: Jean Stafford's Literary Apprenticeship In Baton Rouge." *The Southern Review*. Winter 1993, Vol. 29 issue 1.

Permissions

"Blackberry Winter" from *The Circus in the Attic*, copyright © 1947 and renewed 1975 by Robert Penn Warren, reprinted by permission of Houghton Mifflin Harcourt Publishing Company. Photo of Warren courtesy of LSU University Relations.

"The Gift of the Prodigal" from *The Old Forest and Other Stories* by Peter Taylor, © 1941, 1945, 1947, 1949, 1951, 1958, 1959, 1979, 1981, 1985 by Peter Taylor. Used by permission of Doubleday, a division of Random House, Inc. Photo of Taylor courtesy of Eleanor Ross Taylor.

"The Interior Castle" by Jean Stafford in *The Collected Stories of Jean Stafford* 1951. Reprinted by permission of Farrar, Straus and Giroux. Photo of Stafford courtesy of Eleanor Ross Taylor.

"Camping Out," by James Wilcox reprinted by permission of International Creative Management, Inc. Copyright © 1982 by James Wilcox for *The New Yorker*. Photo of Wilcox by Dorothy McCaughey.

From *Bibliophilia* by Michael Griffith 2003. Published by Arcade Publishing, New York. Permission granted by the author. Photo of Griffith courtesy of Melanie Cannon, University of Cincinnati.

"Sky Watch," from *Distant Friends and Intimate Strangers: Stories* by Charles East © 1996. Used with permission of the University of Illinois Press. Photo of East: *The Gumbo*. 1947. Courtesy of Special Collections, LSU Libraries, Louisiana State University.

"A Part in Pirandello" by David Madden, copyright © David Madden. Reprinted by permission of the author. Photo of Madden ©2008 Blake Madden.

"Things About to Disappear" by Allen Wier in *Things About to Disappear*. Reprinted by permission of LSU Press. Photo of Wier by Donnie Wier.

"E-Z Boy War" from *Little Altars Everywhere* by Rebecca Wells. Copyright ©1992 by Rebecca Wells. Reprinted by permission of HarperCollins Publishers. Photo of Wells by Susan Rothschild.

Walker Percy to Lewis Simpson, 2 December 1971, in Authors Correspondence, *Southern Review* Records, RG A0040, Louisiana State University Archives, LSU Libraries, Baton Rouge, LA.

Walker Percy to Lewis Simpson, 21 December 1974, in Authors Correspondence, *Southern Review* Records, RG A0040, Louisiana State University Archives, LSU Libraries, Baton Rouge, LA.

"Young Nuclear Physicist" by Walker Percy. Reprinted by permission of *Oxford American*. Photo of Percy courtesy of LeRoy and Ami Percy.

"Spats" by Valerie Martin copyright © Valerie Martin. Reprinted from *The Consolation of Nature and Other Stories*, Houghton-Mifflin Company. Photo of Martin by Jerry Bauer.

"The Perfect Mousse Ducktail" by James Gordon Bennett. Originally published in *The Gettysburg Review*, Fall, 1996. Photo of Bennett courtesy of Carolyn Bennett.

Excerpt from *Tupelo Nights* copyright ©1988 by John Ed Bradley. Used by permission of Grove/Atlantic, Inc. Photo of Bradley courtesy of LSU.

"After the River" by Tim Parrish in *Red Stick Men*. Copyright © by University Press of Mississippi. Reprinted by permission of University Press of Mississippi. Photo of Parrish by Katney Bair.

"In Praise of Goth Beauticians," "Young Werther at Decadence 2006," and "Dead People in England" by Andrei Codrescu 2009. Permission granted by author. Photo of Codrescu by Brian Baiamonte.

"The Amish Farmer" by Vance Bourjaily in *Great Esquire Fiction*. Copyright © 1980 by Vance Bourjaily. Originally published by Viking Press/Viking Penguin. Permission granted by author. Photo of Bourjaily courtesy of Jim Zietz, LSU University Relations.

"Gauguin" by Moira Crone in *Dream State* 1995. Reprinted by permission of University Press of Mississippi. Photo of Crone courtesy of Jim Zietz, LSU University Relations.

"Katherine's Elegy," *Anything You Say Can and Will Be Used Against You* by Laurie Lynn Drummond copyright © 2004 by Laurie Lynn Drummond. Reprinted by permission of HarperCollins Publishers. Photo of Drummond by Bill Kennedy.

"The West Texas Sprouting of Loman Happenstance" in *Texas Bound: 22 Texas Stories, Vol. 2*. Reprinted by permission of Southern Methodist University Press.

The Effigy by Olympia Vernon copyright © 2009 by Olympia Vernon. Permission granted by author. Photo of Vernon by Eddy Perez.